The Rose and The Thorn

MacPherson Brides
Book One

Mischelle Creager

Cover Design and Interior format by The Killion Group
http://thekilliongroupinc.com

DEDICATION

To my wonderful husband, Randy, who has gone through this journey with me. I never could have done it without you.

ACKNOWLEDGMENTS

I wish to thank my husband and children for their love
and patience with me through this process.
Also a special thanks to…
My critique partner and mentor, Lacy Williams.
My editors, Robin Patchen and Lana Wooldridge.
My writers group, OCFW with for all their
encouragement.
And the special ladies at church who read and proofed for
me— Pattie Clements, Kathy Faulkner, Peggy Hudson,
Jean Lowe, and Terri Wooldridge.

CHAPTER ONE

Central City, Colorado Territory, May 1861

"I need a man."

Sarah Hollingsworth Greer's head shot up at the unexpected announcement of her adopted daughter's wet nurse. "What do you mean?"

"I'm sorry, ma'am." Janie twisted her fingers together in front of her middle. "I told you I'd stay with you until Emma didn't need me anymore, but I gotta give you notice. I'm gonna get married, and Bobby's gonna take me and Johnny to his place."

Sarah paced across the room. A shudder ran down her body. She'd never forget Alfred coming to her on their wedding night, drunk and mean. The edges of her lacy deep blue robe flitted back and forth with each step over the wooden floor.

She stopped next to the open window and gripped the curtains, then glanced down to the street below. So many men filled the areas along the street—old ones, young ones, miners in worn denim pants and dirty hats, businessmen in suits. She turned away from the sight, dismissing them.

Unlike Janie, that was something Sarah didn't need to worry about. She would never need a man. Never again would she let another man have that power over her. She swallowed hard, then took a ragged breath. Just because she'd vowed never to enter into marriage again didn't mean that she was against it. With that thought, she straightened her spine.

Sarah turned back to the young woman, who had become more than an employee over the last six months, taking care of the baby Sarah had to keep hidden from her grandfather. "Are you sure? Where did you meet this Bobby?"

Janie's eyes lit up like the sky on a fine summer's day. "When we were in Denver, waiting for you to join us. He's a miner. One day we're gonna be rich. But ma'am, you don't gotta worry none. I won't be leaving right away. Bobby went back to his claim two days ago and won't be back for another month. Says he wants to fix up his cabin for us first." She stifled a giggle. "Actually, I think he wants to make his brothers move out, so it'll be just us. And Johnny, of course. Johnny's so excited about having a pa again."

The knots loosened in Sarah's stomach. There was still time to make some new arrangements. She forced a smile to her lips. At least, she hoped it looked like a smile. "I wish you and Bobby a wonderful life."

"I hate to leave you like this." Tears filled Janie's eyes. "And Emma. It seems like yesterday she was born. And look how big she's grown. It won't be long until she won't need a wet nurse."

"I understand." Sarah nodded.

Janie fidgeted. "Ma'am, I need to be getting back to my room. Johnny and Emma be waking soon, and you know how Emma likes to be fed as soon as she can." With her notice given, Janie eased out the door.

The click of the latch sucked the starch right out of Sarah's spine. Her shoulders slumped. Her chin dropped to her chest. Since becoming a widow, she'd tried so hard to be strong in front of her grandfather, fighting his every effort to control her or her inheritance, but inside she knew she was broken and weak. Drawing in a shuddering breath, she repeated the vow she made the day her housekeeper had poisoned Alfred—*Grandfather will not win again. I will see that my brother and Emma have full, happy lives.*

Her hands trembled, but it was time to move on with the plans she had set in motion. She opened the wardrobe and checked out her new dresses. No widow's weeds here, only dresses in lavender, blue, and green. She took out a new dress of deep blue that matched her eyes. It didn't take her long to finish her toilet. Good thing, since her brother would be coming by in a few minutes.

Pinning up her hair, she glanced at the table that held the remains of her breakfast—tea grown cold and half-eaten poached eggs congealed around the now-limp toast points. Once again she moved to the window. Peace spread through her as she watched the people below. A few women now bustled among the men. Unlike Boston, Central City was nearer to the world she knew, the kind she grew up with in Iowa. This was where she would begin her life again.

Joy filled her as she rubbed her right thumb over her wonderfully bare left ring finger.

She set a bonnet over her black hair.

A shout below drew her attention to some men across the road. A large man in dirty clothes pounded along the boardwalk, yelling for someone to stop. He rushed toward a younger, wirier man in front of the mercantile, spun him around, and raised his fist. The big man let go of the other man and took a couple steps back. They shouted words at each other, words she didn't even try to make out, then the smaller man made some remark and walked away. The bully ripped his hat from his head and ran his large hand through his dark brown hair before smashing the hat on his head. He crossed the street toward the hotel.

Sarah shook her head and wrapped her arms around her middle as her stomach tumbled. Whether in a city as big as Boston or as small as Central City, some men think they can do whatever they want just because of their size and their fists. Thankfully, she didn't have to worry about men controlling her life any more, not with the fortune she had inherited.

Someone knocked on the door. With her fingers moving rapidly, she tied the bonnet strings under her chin.

When she opened the door, her brother Drew stood on the other side, grinning.

"Good to see you're ready. I like the idea of starting the day with you." The grin slid from his face as worry took its place. "Just wish I could figure out what exactly I'm supposed to be doing here for Grandfather."

Sarah stepped into the hallway, closed and locked the door, then put the key in the reticule that hung from her wrist.

When Drew took hold of her elbow to help her down the stairs, she pulled away. His lips tightened as he dropped his arm to his side.

The look on his face cut at her heart. He was trying so hard to help her build a new life. She hated the way she still flinched at a man's touch. Even Drew's, but at least she knew she could trust him. Aside from Drew and her lawyer back in Boston, who had proven his worth in helping her get her affairs in order after Alfred's death, there wasn't a man in the world who would earn her trust again.

When Drew moved over a couple of steps, she slipped her hand over his arm and smiled at him. It didn't bother her so much if she was the one doing the touching. They started down the stairs together.

"As far as what you should do here, we'll just have to wait and see what mysterious instructions are awaiting you." When they reached the first floor, Sarah faced her brother. "But since you're halfway across the country from Boston, you do have a choice. You don't have to work for Grandfather. I have enough money to—"

"Don't." Drew slashed the air with his free hand.

Sarah jerked back from his anger.

Drew tilted his head upward, closed his eyes, and let out a large sigh. His shoulders slumped. He looked down at her. "We've been through this before. I've nothing of my own."

"I have enough for both of us." She hid her smile at the irony of the situation. Alfred had been such a foolish man to think that his grown son, who had rejected his father's greedy ways, would be swayed by a threat of leaving everything to her. She knew Alfred had never intended to make good on that threat, but then Alfred died, leaving her with his entire estate.

"Here in Colorado, I've got a chance here to learn to stand on my own. Then I'll never have to live on somebody's charity. Not even yours." His shoulders drooped even more. "It just takes too much out of a man." They reached the hotel lobby, and Drew waved her toward the dining room.

She wished he'd let her help him.

Drew's lips lifted up in a small grin. "At least, Stanley's not here."

Sarah almost stumbled as memories of that evil man leaped into her mind. She fought a silent, solitary battle against those horrible memories. She feared how Drew would react if he ever learned the full extent Stanley had gone to, in their grandfather's name, but she knew it would only bring harm to her brother. And that was something she would never let happen.

CHAPTER TWO

Mac MacPherson jerked the hat from his head and rammed his fingers through his hair before slapping his hat back on. *Stupid fool.* He needed to get control. He should have been certain that skinny man was his brother-in-law before he attacked him. But if the man had been Hank and gotten away, no telling how long it would be before he came out of hiding again.

Mac stopped in front of the hotel and debated whether or not to enter. He was filthy, smelling a lot like the mules that hauled his wagon, but he was already a couple days late in delivering his freight, thanks to the broken wagon wheel and the flooded creek. Rumbling in his gut settled the matter. He could get two things done at once, fill his belly and find out if the man he needed to contact had arrived yet. If not, there should be instructions on where to deliver his load. He swung the door wide and walked in. The hotel clerk wasn't at the desk, so Mac headed to the dining room.

A tall, good-looking waitress with a big smile headed toward him. When she got within sniffing distance, she stopped and took a step back. "Uh, sir, the desk clerk can get you a room, if you need one. And a bath."

Mac's lips twisted into what he hoped was a smile. "I'm aware of that, ma'am." His slight Scottish burr, tamed more than a mite by his American mother's tongue, differed only slightly from this woman's plain voice, a sound he had heard from Pennsylvania to Illinois to Kansas. His stomach roared to life, sounding like a mountain lion about to attack. "But there's something a wee bit more pressing."

She tried to control her grin, but her pretty blue eyes sparkled. "All right. I have a table over here."

She led him to a table in the corner, far from the other diners. Fine by him. "This is good, ma'am." He removed his hat and set it on the chair to his right.

"Coffee, sir?"

"Yes, ma'am, and a steak about this thick." He raised his hand and separated his thumb and finger about an inch. "A few eggs, biscuits, and gravy."

"Sure you don't want some ham, sausage, bacon, and taters to go with that?" Her cheeks got pinker. "How about a platter of flapjacks?"

His lips twitched a bit. "No, thanks. Just what I asked for will be plenty."

After another smile, the waitress left, her long brown braid swinging across her back.

Mac settled on the wooden chair and checked out the room. Breakfast must be almost over, since there were only a few male customers, all looking, and probably smelling, a heap better than he did right now. Maybe Greer would come in before he finished eating. He'd ask that waitress to point him out, if the man showed up.

As the last of the other customers dropped coins on their tables and left, the girl came back with a heaping plate in one hand and a pot of coffee in the other. After setting the plate in front of him, she filled the cup already on the table. The smell of the food pushed all thoughts out of his mind. With a nod of thanks, Mac grabbed the fork and knife, then started eating. He didn't even taste the first five or six bites. It wasn't until his stomach stopped growling that he slowed down and took a long sip of coffee, followed by a few more bites.

While he'd been shoveling food into his mouth, a pretty black-haired lady in a blue dress and younger man in a suit came in. They looked enough alike, they were probably brother and sister. The woman had a good figure, pretty blue eyes, but she didn't seem happy. In fact, she looked downright sad. Had Lizzie looked like that on that last day? No matter what had happened to his wife, he would've been there for her, loved her. His stomach turned. Why couldn't she have waited a few more hours and talked to him before she went into the barn?

Mac swallowed hard and shoved his plate away. He picked up his coffee and leaned back in his chair. Over the top of his cup, he watched the two choose a table halfway across the room. The woman sat and looked around. When her eyes rested on him, they widened, then narrowed. Her look changed from sadness to utter disgust.

He nodded a greeting.

Her lips tightened as she straightened her back just a mite. She shifted in her chair and looked away while the waitress took her order. Surely the lady couldn't smell him this far away.

He bowed his head and took another sniff. Maybe she could. He shrugged, but nothing could be done about that until he met up with Greer and found out where to unload his freight.

An older, fancy-dressed man walked in the room. The face of the woman in the blue dress turned as white as his granny's hair. And in that pale face, her eyes looked like those of an old owl, large and unblinking. Mac thought she would faint right there. The face of the young man lost his color too, but quickly flushed red.

The fancy-dressed man approached the couple. "Hollingsworth, glad to see you made it." The man smirked. "Why don't you run along to the office I've already set up? Here's the address." He handed over a folded sheet of paper. "You'll find some things to do there." The man didn't even try to keep his voice down. He seemed to revel in the power he had over the younger one.

The color came back to the woman's face. She said something to the young man, but she kept her voice low and patted him on the wrist. The young man looked back and forth between the woman and the older man a couple of times. Without saying anything else, he finally grabbed his hat and left.

Mac swallowed the last of his coffee, then dug in his pocket to pay for breakfast. He stood and dropped some coins on the table.

The older man looked down at the woman. "Ah, Sarah dear, I went to your room. But when you weren't there, I figured you must be here. May I?" Without waiting for an answer, he sat at her table. The woman started to rise, but the man caught her wrist and anchored it to the table with his large hand. The woman struggled for a moment, but the man tightened his grip.

Mac shoved his hat on his head. He hadn't been there to protect Lizzie, but there was no way he would stand by and let another man hurt a woman. Not when he could do something to stop it.

He'd just stood when the waitress brought out a pot of tea and set it in front of the woman. The man let go of the lady's wrist.

Much as he wanted to race over and make sure the woman was not in any danger, Mac took a deep breath. He'd already attacked one man today. This time he needed to take things a bit slower. He drew in another breath and willed his heart to slow down. The woman rubbed her wrist.

Mac decided to wait a moment, just to make sure everything was all right, then he'd go and ask the hotel clerk about Greer. There was a schedule to keep, even if he was already two days late. The miners still needed supplies.

The waitress glanced at the man. "May I get you something, sir?

"I'll have tea, like Mrs. Greer."

Mac looked at the couple. Maybe he didn't have to see the hotel clerk. He stopped a little ways from their table, so as not to offend the lady with his stench. "Mr. Greer, Mr. S. R. Greer?"

The lady covered her mouth with her small gloved hand while the man blustered. "No, no. Snodgrass is my name, Stanley Snodgrass." His eyes narrowed, and his nose twitched.

"Pardon, but when I heard you call the lady 'Mrs. Greer' I thought you were her husband."

"My husband is dead." The lady spoke in a clear voice, a bit hard, not filled with a bit of sorrow. "And I am S. R. Greer. Would you be the freighter?"

"Yes, ma'am. Name's MacPherson. I just need to know where you want me to unload."

"Just a moment. I'll write down the directions to my house." Mrs. Greer opened her small beaded bag and pulled out a paper and pencil.

Snodgrass stared at her for a moment. His face paled, then flushed a bright red like the young man's had a few moments before. "What freight? What house? You just got here yesterday."

The lady ignored the man and tilted her head up. "I should be there within the hour."

The smell of roses drifted toward him when Mac reached for the paper Mrs. Greer held up. He grabbed the directions, stepped away, and left, still smelling the roses. The woman seemed to be holding her own now.

"Sarah, explain." Stanley's hand clenched into a fist on top of the table. "Now."

"I don't need to explain my actions to you or any other man. I've done what Grandfather ordered and left Boston. What I do now is my business." Sarah dabbed her mouth with her napkin, then stood.

"Oh, but you are wrong. Your grandfather sent me out here to watch over your brother. That makes me his boss. Anything that affects him is my business. Just remember that, if you want your brother to stay healthy."

She settled back down.

"Now tell me—"

"Excuse me, sir. Here's your tea." The waitress set a second china teapot, along with a cup and saucer, on the table. Her eyes shifted from Stanley's hand to Sarah's face. Her eyebrows rose just the slightest bit.

Sarah tipped her head. She was fine. Or would be, as soon as Stanley left.

"Girl, leave us be." Stanley flicked his hand as if shooing away a gnat.

The waitress scurried away with several backward glances.

"Now tell me how the freight got here so quickly, and how did you acquire a house when you arrived only yesterday?"

"If you insist." Sarah shrugged as if it were a matter of little consequence. She had to show a strong front no matter how she felt inside. Her plan to get Drew away from her grandfather had worked so far. Stanley had no control over her now, and he never would again. Keeping her back straight, she settled into her chair, at least as far as her hoop skirt would allow and looked, she hoped, more relaxed than she felt. "It's very simple. I figured when Grandfather got angry enough with me because he couldn't control me or my inheritance, he would send Drew somewhere, knowing I would go with him. I sent a few things on ahead and had my lawyer contact a real estate dealer to find me a house."

"But how did you know he would send you here?" He tapped his spoon against his china teacup.

"That part was easy. I knew he'd send me somewhere he felt he could make the most money out of the situation."

"But how did you know where? Who told you about Central City?"

"You did."

"What? Don't take me for a fool." Stanley's eyes narrowed until they were like the slits of a slithering snake. "I never talked to you about this place."

"No, like Grandfather, you thought me of no more value than a piece of furniture. Yet, at dinner each night, the two of you talked of the money that could be made out here with so many men flooding the area, trying to make their fortunes from the gold fields. You even suggested that Drew be sent out here to set up businesses for him. Although, I think you had plans to get him out of Boston so you would be the one Grandfather would count on. As for being a fool, I don't think I need comment on that."

Stanley jumped up, his chest heaving. "You may think you have won, but this was just a little skirmish. The battle is on." He lowered his voice to a near-whisper, his lips twitching in a smile. "You can be sure at the end of it, I will be the victor." He stroked her cheek with his finger.

She pulled back and raised her hand to slap him, but the lessons learned under her husband's fists were too ingrained. She let it fall to the table.

Stanley chuckled and dropped his napkin. "And to the victor go the spoils."

He left the room without a backward glance.

All of Sarah's strength oozed out of her and pooled at her feet. She slumped in her chair.

Something rustled nearby. "Are you all right, ma'am?"

Sarah raised her head and saw the waitress by the table, her brow furrowed. Her hand fluttered close to Sarah's shoulder as if to catch her if she collapsed.

Sarah drew in a trembling breath while a drop of moisture seeped from her eye, followed by another and another. She dabbed them away with the corner of her napkin. "Yes…yes, I'm fine."

"He's a horrid man. Should I send for someone?"

"There's no need of that. I'll be fine in just a moment." She didn't want Drew to know of Stanley's behavior until they were well and settled in the house. Once she was away from the hotel, she'd be safe from Stanley's presence. But for now, she had plenty to do and would need some help. "May I ask your name?"

"It's Helen, ma'am."

"Have you lived here long?"

"Pa brought us up with the first of the gold miners last year."

"So you would know the people around here?"

"Some of them. But there are so many moving in every day, it's hard to know everyone. What do you need? Are you searching for someone?"

Sarah pulled herself up a little straighter. "No, no, nothing like that. My brother and I have just moved here, and I have purchased a house and need a housekeeper and cook. Oh, and a wet nurse for my daughter. Do you know of anyone looking for work?" She rubbed the back of her neck. "Please, sit. Looking up like this will cause a headache."

Helen looked around, then slipped into the chair Stanley had left. "All right, since there aren't any other customers, but for just a moment." She moved her head a tiny bit one way then the other, as if she were going through a list of names in her mind. "Will you be wanting someone to live in or just come in for the day?"

"Well, I thought—"

"Helen Louise, what are you doing? You know you are not to socialize with the customers." A tall, thin woman rushed to the table. "Excuse the waitress, ma'am. She's been taught better than this."

Helen stood. "But, Aunt Carolina—"

"Quiet, girl. Get back to the kitchen. I'll deal with you later." The woman dismissed Helen with a flick of her hand and turned to Sarah. "I'm sorry the girl annoyed you. It won't happen again, I assure you."

The blood pounded in Sarah's head. How many times had she been called "girl" in just that tone, then dismissed like that until her husband wanted her—either in his bed or as a punching bag in his drunken rage?

Sarah stood. "Madam, I wish to set the record straight." Her words came out icy and sharp. "Helen was not bothering me. I had asked her to sit and help me for a moment, which she did most graciously. That is until you so rudely interrupted." She dropped her napkin on the table. "Please charge my bill to my room."

Without another word, she turned and left the restaurant.

A few minutes later, Sarah fumbled in her reticule, found her key, and opened the door to her room. She had to pull herself together. She entered and closed the door behind her, then dropped onto the chair. How had everything changed in the few minutes since she had left this space? Never in her wildest dreams—or nightmares—had she thought Grandfather would send Stanley here to watch over them, over Drew.

Sarah shook her head. Pulling up from the chair, she stood and straightened her spine, then forced her shoulders back. She would be strong. She had to be. There was no way she would allow herself to be drawn back into Grandfather's web of greed and abuse.

She had no illusion about herself where the illustrious Andrew Elijah Hollingsworth, banker, dealmaker, and financial giant, was concerned. After all, she was just a female. Grandfather was nothing like her gentle parents had been. *Oh, Mama, Papa, I still miss you so much. After thirteen years, I still need you.*

Need them? No, she was on her own now. She'd thought that getting Emma and Drew away from Grandfather and Boston would solve everything. *Ah, the best-laid schemes o' mice an' men gang aft agley.*

Well, she would just have to see what else could go awry.

Someone knocked on her door.

Stanley Snodgrass forced a smile to his lips and tipped his hat as he passed two ladies just outside the hotel—one of them was the banker's wife, and he couldn't afford to offend her. After they were long past, he stomped along the dirty boardwalk that connected the hotel with several other businesses, including the office space he'd rented. He hated this filthy place with its stinking miners and even worse freighters. And he hated the way the houses grew on the sides of the mountains that made up this horrible valley.

Old Man Hollingsworth wanted him here to watch over his precious grandson, but Stanley had plans of his own. And those plans all revolved around marrying Sarah, willingly or by force. Then the fortune she inherited and had tied up legally from her grandfather would be his, and he wouldn't have to kowtow to that old man any longer.

He got to his office and shoved the door open. No one was inside. Where was that young pup, Drew? He shouted for him but got no answer, so he pressed on to his office. The door was cracked open. On his desk lay a piece of paper that had not been there when he had left earlier. He grabbed the paper and read.

Stanley, Sarah needs me to accompany her to her new house. I should be back before noon.

Stanley crumpled the note in his fist, then threw it into a small bin he used for trash. So the pup thinks he's grown some teeth, now that he's away from his grandfather. Well, starting tomorrow, he would let the kid know who was in charge. Disobedience would not be tolerated.

CHAPTER THREE

Where was that woman? Mac raised his arm and wiped the sweat from his forehead while he sat on the wagon seat, waiting for Mrs. Greer. Just like he waited in the lobby until Snodgrass left the hotel. He had even peeked back in the dining room to make sure she was all right, then left when he saw her talking to the waitress.

He'd knocked on the front door a half-hour before, then the back door. No one was at the house. He yanked his hat from his head and slammed it against his leg. He wanted to get the freight delivered so he could get back to his room in the boardinghouse, take a hot bath, and get a few hours' sleep. Hopefully without dreams of Lizzie hanging in his barn. Even awake, her haunting shadow traveled with him. He rubbed the pouch he carried around his neck under his shirt. Why, why did she do it? If he didn't find the answer soon, he was going to go mad.

A dog's painful howling sounded down the dusty road in front of the house. Mac looked up as a bloodied hound raced out from between two houses, followed by a small ball of yapping fur. A pack of five or six young boys shouting and swinging sticks chased after the poor creatures.

The hound collapsed about ten feet in front of the wagon. The little dog stood guard over the big one and growled while the jeering boys surrounded them. One of the boys, the biggest of the lot, swung his stick at the little fella, but the dog jumped back quick enough to miss being hit. The little fella turned and bared his teeth at the bully.

"Come on, guys. Let's rush 'em all at once."

Didn't seem like a fair fight. Mac jumped down from the wagon and crossed to the small mob in a few steps. "What's going on?"

"Mind your own business, mister." The leader looked to be about nine or ten years old and better dressed than the rag-tags he was with.

"These your dogs?" Mac stood, feet slightly apart, his thick arms folded across his chest and stared down at the kid, who glared back with a snarl on his lips.

"Naw, they're just old cur dogs. Nobody wants 'em. 'Sides, we was just having some fun."

Mac placed who the boy was. "Your pa, he owns the hotel, doesn't he? What would he say about you going around beating dogs just for the fun it?" Disgust and anger filled his voice. "How would you like to be beaten with sticks?" He took a step closer to the ruffians, knowing full well his size alone would frighten the boys. One of the smaller children dropped his stick. Mac picked it up and slapped it against his other hand. "Just for the fun of it."

A flicker of fear passed through the boy's eyes before he stuck out his chin. "Come on. Let's get out of here. The dogs ain't worth it."

The leader gave a final sneer before he turned his back on Mac and strode away. The other boys separated on either side of him like the water of the Red Sea before Moses and gave him a path to walk through. The boys backed up a bit like the waters receding, throwing out a few jeers and taunts before they followed their leader.

The hound let out a low, pain-filled cry. Mac bent down and rubbed his hand over the dog's head. "There now fella, let's see how you're doing."

The little dog watched with tiny teeth bared as Mac gently rubbed his hands over the bigger dog's sides, legs, and head. Satisfied that there were no broken bones, Mac got his water jug and an old metal bowl he kept under the wagon seat. He poured out some water and sat back on his heels as the dogs drank their fill.

What was he going to do with these two? The woman at the boardinghouse had a rule against dogs and cats. The small fur ball started yapping when a buggy stopped beside Mac's wagon.

The same young man from the hotel restaurant stepped down. "What's going on here?"

Mac shook his head—same question he had asked not five minutes before. After a last pat to the hound's head, he stood and wiped his hand on his pants leg. A glance inside the buggy confirmed the other party. She sat there, regal as any princess in a king's carriage. Well, he was the great-grandson of a mighty clan chieftain in Scotland, even if he was the second son of the first son of the fifth son and therefore would never have the right to the title of clan chieftain.

He extended his hand to the man, who couldn't be more than a year or two past twenty. "MacPherson. While I was waiting for Mrs. Greer, I caught some ruffians beating this poor hound."

The man's handshake was firm. "Andrew Hollingsworth." He nodded to the injured animal. "Do you know whose dog this is?"

"Boys said he was a stray. Thought about keeping him myself." Mac readjusted his hat on his head. He'd have to find a place for the dog to recover, but the hound would make a good traveling companion as he traveled from camp to camp delivering supplies. Maybe he could stay at the livery in between trips. He just wasn't sure what to do with the little one. They seemed to be a pair.

Both he and Hollingsworth turned as excited yips came from the direction of the buggy. Mrs. Greer had climbed down and kneeled, petting the little furry ball, not seeming to care if her dress got dirty from the dusty street and the mutt's filthy paws. The dog kept jumping up and trying to lick her face. Mac's gut tightened. Lucky dog.

No! He wouldn't go there. How could he even think about the possibility of another wife until he knew if he had killed his first?

"Drew," the woman said. "Since Mr. MacPherson isn't planning on taking this little one, I think we should keep her." She faced Mac. "There's supposed be a barn out back of the house, if you would like to put your dog there while you unload the wagon. There should be fresh hay to lay him on."

Her voice pulled at him. He had to get away. "Thanks."

With a nod, he picked up the wounded dog and headed toward the back of the house.

Mr. MacPherson hadn't gone ten feet when the little scamp of a dog deserted Sarah and chased after his wounded friend. She stood still for a moment, then followed them.

"Sis?" Drew called out when she passed him on path, his eyebrows drawn together. "Where are you going?"

"To get my dog, of course, and to make sure the other one's comfortable." Sarah dug in her reticle and pulled out the key the real estate dealer had left in an envelope at the hotel desk.

"Would you please open up the house? I'll be up in a few minutes." She hurried toward the barn again, but looked over her shoulder. "After I check on the dogs."

Sarah reached the barn while Mr. MacPherson, still holding the whining animal, struggled with the latch. She wanted to help, but she couldn't take the final step that would put her so close to him. "I'll get that if you step back."

He looked over his shoulder, shrugged, and moved.

She hurried forward, lifted the latch, and pushed the door open. Dust motes danced in the sunlight, lifted by a breeze that moved through the barn. She covered her nose and mouth with her gloved hand, but she couldn't hold back a tiny sneeze. "Please excuse me."

Mr. MacPherson nodded and headed to one of the stalls and laid his hound down. The little dog raced over, sniffed around, then settled next to her friend.

"They're such a set," she said, "like the salt and pepper shakers in the restaurant. It might be a bit hard to separate them when the time comes."

"Aye, but they'll adapt." Mr. MacPherson gave his hound a last pat on the head and stood. The man seemed to grow bigger and bigger.

Sarah couldn't get her breath. Moisture rolled down her back. The man was so huge, so menacing. She had to get away. Light shone through the door, leading her to safety. She kept her eyes focused on the tree just outside, but it seemed to move farther away by the second.

Some monster reached out and tripped her. With a yelp that almost matched her new dog's sounds, she felt herself falling. She braced for the hard-packed dirt floor that rose to meet her. The monster's arms snatched her and wrenched her upright. She fought it, screaming and crying. She beat it with her closed fists, but it wouldn't let her go.

"Shush, shush, little lassie. You're all right."

A monster with a Scottish burr? No, that can't be right. The arms loosened but still held her. Her hands stilled as she opened her eyes. No monster, just Mr. MacPherson.

Sarah stepped back, out of his arms. "Oh." The whimper escaped her lips when pain shot up her right leg. She shifted her weight off her foot and wobbled. Mr.

MacPherson grabbed her elbow and steadied her. Shaking inside, she batted at the large fingers that held her arm.

He dropped his hand as if he had touched hot coals.

"I think I did something to my ankle." She gritted her teeth to keep from crying out in pain.

"Would you like to return to the house and have your brother help you?"

Her jaws were clenched so tightly together that she couldn't speak. She nodded.

He extended his elbow.

She didn't want to touch him, but she had no choice. She couldn't stand here balancing on one foot until her brother came looking for her. She grasped the freighter's arm. With slow, faltering steps they made it out of the barn and a few feet farther before the pain roared back to life.

She took a step, then covered her mouth to muffle the cry of pain.

Mr. MacPherson let out a huff as he looked down at her. "We can go like we are, causing more pain than is needed and take an hour to get back to the house, in which time your brother'll come looking for us, if for no other reason than to defend your honor." One of his eyebrows rose, causing the skin on his forehead to wrinkle on one side. "Or we can do this."

He lifted her into his arms and started toward the house once more.

"Put me down. Do you hear me? Put me down." She beat at him again with her fists, but she was no more effective against his domination than she had been against Alfred's.

"Hush, lass, or your brother'll be racing 'round the corner any minute and I'll have to thrash him. And I wouldn't like to do that, since I like him well enough."

She quieted down. The bully was right. Drew would try and protect her, but he wasn't a fighter and might get hurt. She tried to relax. The man really wasn't hurting her. He had just startled her. She nodded.

As they came to the front of the house, they met Drew heading toward them.

"Sarah? Are you hurt?" Drew's eyes moved from her to the man holding her, the way his arms were wrapped around her. His eyebrows raised the slightest bit as though he were examining some kind of bug or trying to solve a difficult problem. "Sarah?"

"I twisted my ankle, and Mr. MacPherson's helping me get back to you."

"Let's get you inside out of the sun." Drew rushed up the steps and opened the door. Mr. MacPherson followed him, never letting go of her.

Sarah tried not to let Drew's actions bother her. After all, he was helping, but couldn't he have at least tried to get her out of the big man's arms?

Mac forced his fingers not to grip too tightly while he carried the poor lass into the house. Why was she trembling so? Was she afraid of him? He hadn't done anything to scare her so, had he? He handled her as gently as if she were one of his wee babes, although there was nothing about the woman that reminded him of a child.

Inside, he looked at the first room off the hall to the left, probably the parlor. Good, there was a chair sitting over to the side. Not much else, but at least there was something for her to sit upon. With his long stride, he reached it in a matter of moments, then eased her onto her feet before helping her to the chair.

Once seated, she let out a long sigh. "Thank you for your assistance."

"Think nothing of it. With your brother here to help you, I'll be unloading the wagon." He hurried outside. Once there he took a deep, deep gulp of air. What was it about that woman that caused his gut to tighten? He balled his hand into a fist and smashed the side of the wagon. He wasn't good for any woman, especially not one who shook like the aspen when he touched her.

He rubbed his bruised knuckles then untied the ropes that held down the tarp over his freight. Time to get back to work. If only he could find Hank as easily as he found freight to haul. He grabbed the last box he'd loaded back in Denver several days before and took a deep, cleansing breath before heading for the house. If he could get this finished soon, he would have time for that bath before dinner, then a long sleep before heading back to Denver for another load to take to the mining camps.

"Mr. MacPherson, could you use some help unloading your wagon?" Hollingsworth stood nearby in his shirtsleeves.

"Won't your sister be needing you?" The image of the trembling woman had not left his thoughts or his heart.

"Sarah's fine. She doesn't need anybody. She's about as strong as a person can be." He reached up and took hold of one of the crates. Utter despair mixed with a tinge of anger rested on the young man's face. "Unfortunately, she's had to be."

The young man stomped his way back into the house.

Mac followed a little slower, pain jabbing his middle. No woman should have to be that strong.

CHAPTER FOUR

Two timid knocks on the door. Who wanted into her room at this time of the morning? Sarah grabbed her blue satin wrapper and slipped it over her nightgown, thankful this would be the last day she would have to spend in the hotel. Mr. MacPherson and Drew had unloaded her things, but the place needed to be cleaned before they could relocate there. No matter what, she would get the beds ready today, so tomorrow her little family could move into their new home.

She stepped next to the door. "Yes, who is it?"

"It's Carl, ma'am." A young boy's voice called out from the other side of the door. "I got something for you."

Sarah opened the door but held onto the handle. A boy of about eight stood in the hall, holding a covered dish.

"Miz Thompson said to give this to you with her apole…appall…I think she means she has to say she's sorry about something in the dining room yesterday. That's what she told Uncle Jack, 'cause she's afraid you're going to move out or something." The boy held up the dish and waited.

"And who is Miz Thompson?" Sarah took the dish. The rich smell of cinnamon teased her nose.

"That's what Aunt Caroline says I gotta call her when I talk to customers here at the hotel."

Sarah had to swallow while her mouth watered. She peeked under the cover at the cinnamon roll. "I had one of these yesterday, and it was delicious. Do you know who makes them?"

"Yeah, my sister, Helen. She makes all sorts of stuff in the kitchen." As if he realized he'd stayed too long, Carl edged away from the door. "I gotta go. Aunt Caroline'll get all over me if I'm gone too long."

"Could you do me a favor, please?"

The boy scrunched up his nose. "Will it take long?"

"Not at all. Just ask your sister to come up and see me when she can." Sarah pulled a nickel from her pocket and handed it to the boy. "You've been a big help. Thank you."

Carl's eyes widened so much Sarah thought his eyeballs would pop right out. "Yes ma'am, I'll give her your message."

Sarah couldn't help but smile as he raced down the hall. As the door clicked closed, she took a tiny pinch of the roll. A thought swirled around her head. Helen would make a wonderful cook, and maybe housekeeper. Would the girl be willing to leave the hotel and come to work for her and Drew? Sarah remembered the day before and the way Helen's aunt treated her. If that were indicative of the way she was usually treated, Sarah thought the chances were good.

She pushed aside the rest of the breakfast she had ordered earlier and took some paper from her travel desk. As she nibbled on the cinnamon roll, she started a list. First, she would need to talk to Helen and ask if she would work for her. If not, maybe the young woman could recommend someone else. Next, she needed to check out the different stores in town and see what they had to offer and what she would have to order.

She flexed her foot and then shifted her ankle from side to side. No pain from the accident the day before in the barn. A shiver ran though her as she remembered Mr.

MacPherson holding her in his arms. Once she'd gotten over the shock of him carrying her, it hadn't been too unpleasant. She gave herself a little shake. That was enough of that. She was a matronly widow of twenty-nine with a child and no need of a man.

She returned her attention to the list. Feed would be needed and more hay for the horses she'd bought through her real estate dealer. That man had been such a godsend the way he had chosen the house, found the horse and buggy, and made arrangements for them at the hotel. She needed to thank her lawyer back in Boston for making such a good recommendation. How easily things happen when one has money—the ease, the power.

An icy flush ran through her body. Was this the way Alfred and Grandfather felt when they bought and sold positions of power, hopes and dreams, lives and futures? She trembled. Was she becoming like them? She dropped her pencil. No, no, no. She could never be that manipulating and controlling. Could she?

Someone knocked on the door. Rising on shaky legs, she crossed the room. "Yes?"

"Ma'am, it's Janie. I thought you might be liking to see little Emma. She's awake and just been fed."

Sarah rested her head against the wall next to the door. Time to be a mother at last. She pressed her hand against her middle, the place where her children had lived for only a time. A time cut far too short by angry fists, violent temper tantrums, and drunken rages. She sucked in two or three gulps of air and struggled to push the memories back to the black hole where they belonged.

"Ma'am, are you all right?" The words drifted through the door.

Sarah wiped her eyes, took a deep breath, and opened the door. Time to get to know the daughter she hadn't given birth to, but whom she already loved and would be taking care of when Janie left in a few weeks.

She opened the door. "Yes, I'm fine. Come here, my little darling."

"I've just changed her, and I'll be back in time to feed her." Janie placed Emma into Sarah's waiting arms, then slipped out the door.

Sarah carried her daughter to the chair by the window and sat. She pulled the blanket back and touched the golden curls on Emma's head. The baby—no *her* baby, *her* daughter—looked up at her with her blue eyes. Sarah stroked the soft cheeks. "Mama's little girl. You've been moved from pillar to post since you were born, but that's going to stop. You're safe now. No one can take you from me. Not Grandfather. Not Stanley. My lawyer's seen to that."

Emma's little six-month-old hands batted Sarah's cheeks as she made soft baby sounds. Sarah laughed, which caused the baby to make more cooing sounds.

"Oh, sweetie, I've missed so much of your life so far, but I'll make it up to you." Sarah swallowed hard to keep from crying as she rested Emma against her middle, forever barren from Alfred's last beating. "You're the only child I'll ever have, the child of my heart."

She held Emma in her left arm as she clasped the baby's tiny hand in her right and pressed it against her heart. "I promise you that I'll love you like my mama and papa loved me. I promise you that I'll protect you always, no matter what the cost. You're my daughter, and I'm your momma. No one or nothing will ever, ever change that."

Several minutes passed as she watched her baby being a baby, cooing, gurgling, playing, being fascinated with her hands and feet. Sensations so overwhelming flowed through Sarah. This was love, so pure, so joyful. Growing up and playing house with her best friend Melody had never been like this. Memories flittered through her mind. Memories of rag dolls and mud pies, memories of shared secrets and whispered hopes, memories long gone but not forgotten. Where was Melody now? Did she ever find love and have a home of her own? Babies to cuddle?

Sarah touched Emma's cheek and let peace and love slide around inside her. She hoped Melody had.

While the sun lowered in the western sky, Sarah paced across her room. Fortunately, it was the largest in the hotel, so she had plenty of room to move about. Everything on her list had been handled except the most important. She hadn't been able to see Helen. When Sarah had gone down for tea, the waitress told her the girl wasn't waiting tables that day and had to stay in the kitchen at the owner's directions.

Someone knocked on the door.

Sarah hurried to the door, but didn't open it. "Who is it?"

"Helen, ma'am." The voice on the other side of the door was weak and weary.

Sarah opened the door. Helen stood in the hall, pale with red-rimmed eyes. Short strands of hair fell down the sides of her face. Sarah grabbed the girl's hand and tugged her into the room. "What happened? Why—?"

As Helen passed her, her whole back was visible. That was what it was. Her long braid was missing—cut off in a jagged chunk.

Sarah directed her to one of the two chairs at the small table by the window, then sat on the other one. "Sit and tell me what happened to your hair."

"I couldn't, ma'am. I wouldn't want it to get back to my aunt that I was telling tales." Helen clapped her hand over her mouth.

Sarah felt the warrior coming out in her, the one that had been growing ever since she learned her husband had been killed by the mother of the poor girl he had forced himself on. "Helen, did your aunt cut off your hair?"

Helen wiped another tear from her eyes and shook her head. "Her son, Johnnie, snuck into the kitchen last night, probably to get something to eat. I had fallen asleep—it'd been a long day. One of the kitchen help quit, so after I waited on customers for breakfast and lunch, I had to make bread and rolls for dinner, besides washing dishes. After that, Aunt Carolina told me to make up a triple batch of cinnamon rolls since she wanted to go visiting this morning."

She looked down for a moment, then raised her head. "I was so tired I fell asleep at the table while I waited for the dough to rise. Anyway, that's when Johnnie came in. He grabbed a big butcher knife and cut off my braid. I woke up, and I'm sorry to say I screamed at him. But all he did was laugh at me, then he…he threw my hair into the stove and burnt it up."

"What did your aunt say?"

"She…she said if I hadn't been so lazy and fallen asleep, Johnnie wouldn't have been tempted to do something so silly. She told me to get rid of the stench in the kitchen. Then she sent Johnny to bed, because he was still a growing boy."

"Why do you stay?"

"We've got no other place to go. After Pa died, my aunt and uncle gave room and board to me and my little eight-year-old brother, Carl, even though he's too young to do much work yet. He does dry the dishes and take out the trash."

"What kind of wages do they pay you for your work?"

Helen looked startled. "Like I said, they give us room and board."

"Do you have any dreams for yourself?"

Helen looked at Sarah as if she'd asked one of the mysteries of the universe.

"If you could choose anything in the world to do, what would it be?"

Helen's eyes lit up. "I'd have me a bakery." A moment later, her eyes dimmed. "But that could never be. I don't have the book learning to handle a business like that." Her face flushed a bit. "Oh, I can read some, and I know my numbers." Her shoulder lifted and dropped. "I can make cakes, pies, cinnamon rolls and such. But all that record-keeping and ordering, I don't know nothing about that." Her shoulders slumped even farther. "And I don't have the money to start one anyway."

Sarah smiled. "I've a proposition that I think will solve both our problems. I'd like to hire you as housekeeper and cook. In my house, there are a couple rooms off the kitchen you and your brother could use."

Helen gnawed her bottom lip. "I don't know, ma'am."

Sarah brushed off the reluctant reply. Who could blame the girl for being wary? "I'll pay you a weekly wage, and on your days off, you can bake some of your delicious rolls and sell them to the store, the hotel, or the miners. That way you can save up, so you can eventually have your own bakery."

The girl's eyes lit, then dimmed. "Like I said, I couldn't run a bakery. I don't have the book learning."

"Pash. That is just a matter of training and practice. I can teach you as we work with household accounts." Sarah leaned forward and reached out her hand. "Please say you'll come and work for me."

Helen covered her mouth with her fingers as her eyes widened. "Why are you offering me so much?"

"I know what it's like to feel helpless, having to endure whatever is forced on you, and I want to help." Sarah took a deep breath. "Will you let me do that? Will you come and work for me?

Helen's eyes grew brighter bit by bit. She slowly nodded.

Sarah stood. "Give notice to your aunt now, then get a good night's sleep. We have a lot to do starting tomorrow to set my new house to rights."

Helen could hardly speak, but Sarah didn't need the girl's words to understand how she felt. She'd been trapped, and she'd been given a way out.

As the girl walked to the door and opened it, Sarah spoke again.

"If your aunt threatens to cast you out tonight, come up here." She waved her hand toward the room next door. "You and your brother can share the room next door with my nanny. Tomorrow will start a new life for both of us."

Stanley swallowed a snarl. Sarah was checking out of the hotel. He wouldn't let her get completely away without a new link to him. He held back a chuckle at the plan he had come up with last night.

"You look perfect." He patted the hand of his younger sister, Cynthia. She rested her gloved hand in the crook of his elbow. "You were right. That bit of white powder on your face is just the right touch, and I think that it was a good idea to add that dark area on your cheek. It can only draw Sarah's pity even more."

Stanley loved his half-sister almost as much as he loved money and the power it brought. The fact that both of their fathers had deserted them before birth bound them even closer. At twenty-two, she had grown into a beauty, but somehow had maintained the freshness of a seventeen-year-old. Much as he had tried to shelter her, she had come to the notice of Elijah Hollingsworth, and the man had started seeking her out, trying to get close to her. More and more, a look of lust settled in Hollingsworth's eyes when they rested on Cynthia—a look Stanley had seen many times, just before the rich old man used and discarded a naïve young woman.

Cynthia was the second reason Stanley had agreed to leave his coveted place as the old man's assistant and come to Central City. Once he got Sarah's wealth, he'd have the money and power to get what he wanted and still be able to protect his sister from men like Elijah Hollingsworth.

"Cyn, that's the woman over there, checking out." Stanley nodded toward the counter where the wife of the hotel owner was talking to Sarah. "You understand what you need to do?"

She patted his arm and smiled. "Oh, I know just what to do. Don't worry."

Stanley moved back a few steps. He didn't want Sarah to realize Cyn was with him, not until his little sister had taken in the soft-hearted woman with the tragic story they had concocted together. Once that happened, he would have a wonderful spy to help him conclude his plans.

Sarah stood at the hotel counter while the owner finished figuring her bill. Mrs. Thompson, Helen's aunt, seemed to struggle at keeping a frown off her face. Sarah didn't think it was the numbers that caused the woman the problem, especially when Helen and her young brother met Drew and Janie as they supervised the loading of their luggage onto a cart. If Mrs. Thompson's eyes could shoot daggers, poor Helen would be dead.

The woman handed Sarah the bill. Sarah checked it and realized the woman had overcharged her, and by quite a bit. If that was the petty way the woman was going to try and get back at her for hiring her niece, so be it. She refused to lower herself to the other woman's level, and she wasn't going to stay any longer and argue over a few dollars. Sarah reached into her reticule and pulled out some money. She handed it to Mrs. Thompson and smiled. "Thank you. It has been most...interesting staying here."

Mrs. Thompson flushed red and nodded, then fidgeted with the money box.

Sarah turned to leave. Before she made it across the foyer, a young lady called to her.

"Mrs. Greer. Mrs. Greer. Please wait." The woman wore a hooped skirt with the latest fashions from Paris, but in a dark and dull fabric—not at all complimentary, especially with the paleness of her face. Like Sarah, she was somewhat petite. But unlike Sarah, she had blonde hair done up in a tight bun at the back of her neck. An older woman, dressed in black trailed behind her. When the young woman caught up with Sarah, she waved a white lace-edged hankie in front of her face. "Oh, my. I just had to catch you before you left."

Sarah hoped this wasn't another woman, with her greedy-eyed mama, after Drew. For a town with so many more men than women, the few young single women always seemed to find him and flirt outrageously, often during their mealtimes in the dining room, in the few days they had been here.

"I hope you will forgive my lapse in etiquette." The woman kept her eyes slightly lowered as she stood in front of Sarah, not once looking at Drew, as he took another load of luggage out to the carriage. "But I so wanted to make your acquaintance. I'm from Boston, too, you see, and had to come here with my brother who is determined to make a fortune here among all these miners. I don't know anyone else out here. I am so, oh, so lonesome. I'm hoping we can be friends." She twisted her gloved fingers together. "I had to leave my one friend back in Boston, and now I have no one." She flicked her eyes toward the woman in black and dropped her voice to a whisper. "No one except her, and she is more like a jailer."

The memories of Alfred's imprisoning her in his house flashed into Sarah's mind. Her heart hurt for the girl. Maybe she wasn't after her brother, but something seemed a little off. Sarah chose to smile at the young woman, even though there was something unsettling about her chin and her eyes.

"I have tried several times to meet you, but you were out or it was too early or too late to come calling. Let me introduce myself." She stepped back and almost curtsied. "My name is Cynthia Taylor."

"I'm happy to make your acquaintance." Sarah nodded her head slightly. "Is your brother about?"

"No. He's working, always working. I think he lives to make money." The girl lifted her fingers and almost touched a place on her pale cheek. It looked like a bruise. She dropped her hand and lowered her voice as she moved a step closer. "He's so controlling. He makes me stay upstairs in my room all day long, until he has time for me."

After the years she had dealt with Alfred, Sarah knew first-hand how controlling a man could be. Maybe here was a chance to help this innocent girl. Maybe here was a chance to teach this young woman how to be strong so when that time came, she would be able to conquer the evil that could destroy her.

Sarah took a deep breath as the decision was made. "I would be pleased if you could come and visit me, Miss Taylor." Sarah pulled a pencil and paper from her reticule and wrote her new address on it. "This is where we're moving. You are welcome anytime."

Cynthia took the paper and smiled. "Thank you so much."

Sarah hurried to the hotel door. Everyone was waiting for her. She looked over her shoulder as she went through the open door.

Cynthia rushed across the foyer and linked arms with someone in the shadows.

Uneasiness rode up across Sarah's shoulder. Why had she dropped her guard like that and invited the unknown into her life?

Mac's back ached as his wagon bounced over the ruts in the road. He needed to get one of the boys out here to make some repairs before the ruts got any worse. He snorted. He gave up the right to tell any of the men on the ranch what to do a year ago when he left.

He snapped the reins. The mules picked up the pace. Daylight was burning, and his girls would be waiting for him. Eight weeks. He made this trip every eight weeks. It was hard coming home without having found Hank. It was harder still leaving his girls each time to hunt for his brother-in-law, a man who had been as close as any of Thorn's own brothers.

His heart beat faster when he made the final turn that brought him back to the family homestead and spied the house they'd all built. Of course this was just the main house. All the married couples had their own places scattered nearby, like the one he'd shared with Lizzie, the girls, and Hank. The one he wanted to burn down. He would have if Grandda hadn't stopped him. Who lived there now? It didn't matter. He prayed he'd never enter that house or barn ever again.

Prayed. Right. A snort burst from his lips—harsh even to his own ears. He never prayed any more. Not since the day he found Lizzie's body hanging in the barn. The bucket she'd stood on kicked to the side.

The pouch around his neck rubbed as he shifted on the wooden seat. It always hung there, waiting for the day he would shove it in Hank's face and demand to know why he left his sister to kill herself.

A shout rang out from the yard around the house. His cousin, Daniel, spotted him, and the rest of the family flowed out to greet him. And there they were—his girls. They ran into the yard and jumped up and down, waiting for him to get there and give them hugs.

After the wagon stopped, he set the brake and climbed down. His girls surrounded him, pulling on him and giggling. He dropped to his knees and wrapped his arms around all three. It wasn't hard. At four, six, and eight years old, they weren't all that big.

"Da, you're back."

"Can you stay this time?"

The middle one stuck her finger to her lips and pulled down the bottom one. "I lost a tooth. See?"

Mac's heart tore a little more. Oh, how he wanted to stay with his girls, to see them grow and change every day, to put them to bed every night and watch their sleepy eyes every morning. But he dare not, not until he found out what he'd done to poison Lizzie's trust in him.

Mac gave each one a special hug and kiss, then stood. The young men were unloading the supplies he brought from Denver. Granny stood before him, her eyes shining in her wrinkled face. Grandda waited behind her.

He wrapped his arms around the white-haired woman who had raised him and his brothers and sisters after their parents died of an influenza outbreak. She always smelled like violets and biscuits. She rested her gnarled hand against his heart and wiped away the tears that filled her eyes.

"I'm glad ye're home, boy."

"Just for tonight. I'll leave tomorrow."

"But for tonight, the bairns an' me have ye. For that and much more I thank the good Lord above."

Mac leaned down and kissed her snowy hair, then turned to his grandfather. They clasped forearm to forearm.

"Good to see ye, son. Let's go in. Yer granny's got supper ready."

After supper, Mac played with his girls, then read to them until they fell sleep. He put them to bed and tucked them in, then left the main house where he and the girls now stayed.

In the fading twilight, he stared at the small hill to the north where trees grew and graves lay. Lizzie was buried up there, like all the MacPhersons who had died since they'd come here from the eastern part of the Kansas Territory four years before.

The door opened, and Grandda shuffled out with a cup of tea in each hand. "Thought I heard ye go out." He offered Mac a cup. They sat in the rocking chairs Granny kept on the porch.

Mac leaned back in the chair and savored the warmth of the mug in his hands and the peace of being with his grandfather. They sat that way for a few minutes, rocking and sipping tea in comfortable silence.

When he finished his tea, Grandda turned to him. "How goes yer search?"

His grandfather had aged a great deal in the two years since Lizzie's death.

Guilt weighed heavy on Mac shoulders. It felt like a small calf living on his shoulders, but it was growing to a full-size cow, and he couldn't get the thing off. And questions sat with the guilt. Why hadn't Lizzie waited and talked with him? Why hadn't she trusted him to help her after the attack? That attack didn't wipe out all the love they had shared for ten years.

He hated that men had violated her, but the two of them could have gotten through the aftermath. They'd become one, hadn't they? And she tore them apart. What was it about his love that made her do that? What if his love was not pure enough for his girls? Would they do the same as their mother to get away from him?

He needed to talk to Hank. For a moment, memories of times he and Hank had lived as brothers in the same house flowed through his mind—teaching the girls to ride, fishing with them, quiet evenings with stories and games. Times filled with family and love.

Mac turned to his grandfather. "I think I'm close. The last time someone saw him was two weeks ago."

The old man stood and rested his hand on Mac's shoulder. "Soon ye'll have yer answers. Do what ye have to. The girls are safe with us."

He stopped for a moment and seemed to fidget. "By the by, just wanted ye to know afore ye head up there. The headstone came in for Lizzie's grave. She's a MacPherson bride, and the girls questioned why she didna have one."

Grandda waited for a response, but Mac couldn't say anything. He'd never been able to figure out what he wanted to say on the headstone, so he'd not ordered one. The wooden cross someone had made the day they buried Lizzie bore her name. For now, for him, that had been enough. But Grandda thought differently, and since he was head of the family, he did what he thought needed to be done. So be it.

"See you in the morning afore ye leave." With a last pat on the shoulder, Grandda gathered the cups and went inside to his wife of more than sixty years.

Feeling like an old man himself, Mac pulled up from the chair and headed to the hill like he did every time he came home.

A few minutes later, he entered the family cemetery. There weren't a lot of graves here, but they hadn't lived here long enough to bury many. Nine graves in all, four were cousins who died in accidents or fevers, two stillborn babes, two travelers who arrived sick and never left. And then there was Lizzie's grave. Like Grandda said, there was a headstone marking hers, like the ones marking the other MacPherson graves, even the babes.

Unable to look at the words chiseled in the stone, Mac sat on the ground and leaned against a nearby tree. He always visited the grave when he came home, sometimes to rant, sometimes to ask for answers, knowing he'd get none. Sometimes he came because he didn't know what else to do.

Tonight he felt empty. The chill of the mountain air closed around him as he stared at the headstone. How long he sat there, he didn't know. At last, he stood and left without a word. Maybe, just maybe, tonight he'd get some sleep before he started out in the morning. Once more leaving his girls—and much of his heart—behind.

CHAPTER FIVE

Late in the afternoon, Sarah stood in the hall of her new house and laughed out loud. She couldn't help it. It felt good to be in her own home without Alfred or Stanley or Grandfather watching her. With Helen's help, and that of a daily maid named Judith, it had only taken two weeks to change this shell of a house into a home, even with Miss Taylor—Cynthia as she asked to be called—coming over almost every day for a "friendly chat" as the young woman put it. Even Janie's early marriage and sudden departure didn't upset the rhythm of the house.

She looked down at her dress, the third one she'd worn since morning. Emma didn't like the nursing mixture they'd been forced to use, since they couldn't find a wet nurse who was willing to stay with them or come to the house several times a day. Sarah shook her head. Too many men in the town and too few quality women. It didn't matter. She'd feed her daughter and endure the moments if the contents of the bottle didn't stay down. She'd change clothes a dozen times a day as long as Emma stayed healthy.

The scent of potpourri filled the air, along with Helen's voice singing one of her favorite hymns. Sarah couldn't help but smile. The girl was always singing some hymn or other, unless someone walked across her freshly scrubbed floors with muddy or dusty shoes. Then, she let the offender know that if it happened a second time, that person would never taste another of her cinnamon rolls ever again. So far, the threat never had to be carried out.

Three small wooden crates, lined up like soldiers on the new rug in the front parlor, drew Sarah from the hall. Boxes from a time when her life had been filled with love, boxes that had been hidden from the men who would have destroyed them just to cause pain, boxes kept in safekeeping by Grandfather's housekeeper, who had known her grandmother and father, gentle souls that they were.

With twilight falling, Sarah realized they needed more lamps in the room. She lit a lamp on a small side table by the sofa, then turned to the boxes in the darker corner. Now was as good a time as any to go through those. An iron crowbar lay on top of the first crate.

A shiver ran down her spine. So much time had passed. Would the things inside the box still hold as much meaning as before? Would they give her the comfort of cherished memories, or would they just be cold, empty relics of the past?

"Need some help?"

Sarah swung around, raising the crowbar gripped in her fist. A scream clawed up her throat.

"Whoa there, ma'am. I didn't mean to startle you." Someone bigger and taller stood over her. With the lamplight behind him, she couldn't make out his face. All she saw was a big man, stronger and more powerful than she.

Danger. She was in danger. Memories flooded her mind of all those times before. She wouldn't be used as a punching bag again. Not without a fight.

She swung the crowbar. He grabbed it and ripped from her hand. Sarah lurched backward and moved to the side, out of his reach, or so she hoped.

The lamp cast a dim light on the man. Narrowed eyes glared at her. A scowl settled on his face. The muscles on his arms bulged. His fingers tightened around the metal. His knuckles turned white.

He took a step toward her.

She shifted. Her heel caught in the hem of her skirt. She twisted about trying to save herself, but lost her balance. Her scream shattered the silence. The floor raced up to catch her. She wrapped herself into a ball, closing her eyes and covering her head with her arms. "Don't hurt me. Please, please, don't."

Something thudded nearby.

He was everywhere, above her, all around her. No place to hide.

She tensed for the first blow. Alfred liked...

Something soft touched her hand.

"It's me, Miss Sarah. It's Helen. You're safe. No one's going to hurt you."

Sarah opened her eyes. Helen knelt next to her. No one else was in the room.

Mac breathed hard as he stood in the hall, far enough back so Sarah wouldn't see him, but near enough so he could still see what was happening in the parlor. A door opened somewhere at the back of the house. Probably the same door he had come in. Hollingsworth must be home. Mac headed for the kitchen. He needed to let Sarah's brother know what just happened.

He got to the kitchen. Drew was kneeling on the floor, tickling Emma under the chin while she lay on a quilt. The little girl clapped her hand and laughed, while the little ball of fur— called a dog— jumped around and yapped.

Something deep in Mac's heart twisted. How he wanted to be with his girls.

"Sorry, I'm late. My meeting with Stanley lasted longer than I'd planned." A grin covered the young man's face as the baby laughed again.

"Something happened." Mac wasn't sure what caused it, but suspicions were growing by the moment.

Andrew's face paled to the shade of his white shirt. "Sarah?"

The young man started for the hall, but, but Mac grabbed him. "Stop a minute. Helen's with her."

"Is she hurt?"

"Just scared."

The young man sucked in a deep breath. A little color seeped back into his face. "What happened?"

"I came in the back door there with a few things Helen had ordered and something your sister wanted. Helen said Mrs. Greer was in the parlor and to take it to her." He shrugged. "I startled her when I took the crowbar she was waving around. She screamed, fell, balled up like a baby, begging me not to hurt her."

Sweat popped out on Mac's face and rolled down his face. What had he done to cause the woman's reaction? He wiped his face with the cuff of his shirt. "Helen came in and calmed her down." He shrugged. "Seemed like my presence upset her, so I watched them from the hall."

Hollingsworth slumped against the wall. His head dropped until his chin rested against to his chest.

"I still don't know exactly what I did wrong to set her off that way," Mac continued, "but maybe if you tell me—"

"Nothing." The young man raised his head, his eyes filled with misery. "You did nothing. Sarah has been through…she's been through a lot in the last few years."

The memory of their first meeting in the hotel restaurant flashed in Mac's mind, the woman's icy, hard voice stating her husband was dead. "Bad marriage?"

Hollingsworth nodded, pushed away from the wall, and headed for the hall. "I need to see if I can help."

The babe started crying. Mac bent down and picked her up, then sat on one of the chairs surrounding the kitchen table. He couldn't help but grin when she rubbed her hand across his unshaven face. She twisted up her lips but didn't cry.

His arms ached to hold his own girls, but right now they were better off on the family ranch with his sister and grandparents. He would never have struck his wife, like Mrs. Greer's husband had done to her.

Helen entered the room. "Mrs. Greer's doing better. Her brother's with her now."

Mac kept his face turned from the housekeeper, as much as he could, and handed the baby to her. He grabbed his hat and hurried out the door. With a whistle and call, his dog followed him. Away from the house, he wiped the moisture from his eyes and walked to his room in the boardinghouse.

He trudged down the dark, dusty road and touched the pouch under his shirt. The worn paper barely crackled now. Why, Lizzie? The question kept pounding in his head. When would he find the answer?

Still dressed in her lace-trimmed nightgown and wrapper, Sarah stood by her bedroom window. She pulled back the curtain an inch or two. Her hand trembled as she gripped the fabric. A few choice words rolled around in her mind, but she pressed her lips together so they wouldn't slip out.

Mac, no, Mr. MacPherson, sat in his wagon in front of the house, with his hound perched behind the wagon seat. Good manners dictated that she be dressed and greet him before he and Drew left for the mining camps, but she couldn't face the freighter yet—not after the way she'd acted yesterday. Maybe by the time they returned, her embarrassment would fade enough to speak to him without cringing. But not today.

Someone knocked on her bedroom door. She crossed the room and opened it.

"Mac's here. I'm ready to leave." Drew held his hat in his hands, his fingers playing with the brim. His eyes looked over her face bit by bit, as if he could find answers to the questions he would not ask. "Are you sure you'll be all right while I'm gone?"

Sarah forced a smile. She laid her hand over his to still the movement of his fingers. "I'll be fine. Helen's here. Go ahead and get your business done."

"I'd stay, but Stanley's already threatening to send a letter to Grandfather giving a poor report of my work here. For the life of me, I can't figure out why he wants me to go around to the mining camps and see what kind of businesses the people want set up in gullies and along streams."

"No one knows what goes on in the mind of Snarly the snitch."

Sarah slapped her hand over her mouth. She had to force herself not to look around to see if Stanley were lurking around the corner, trying to find something to use against them.

Drew burst out laughing.

Sarah blinked a couple times, dropped her hand, and giggled. The giggles grew until they became full-blown laughter. She held her sides while tears rolled down her cheeks.

Drew pulled out his handkerchief and handed it to her. "I haven't thought of that name in years. Remember how you used to scrunch up your face and mimic him after he told on us to Grandfather?"

Sarah nodded and wiped her eyes.

The clock on the mantle chimed the hour.

"You'd better go, or that man out there'll be pounding on the front door soon." Sarah stood on her tiptoes and gave her brother a small peck on the cheek. It was the first one she could remember giving him in years. It felt good to reach out and let her sisterly love show. "Please be careful out there."

Drew cleared his throat. "Thanks, sister. I will."

A few moments later, footsteps clattered down the stairs, then the front door opened and closed. Sarah moved to the window and pulled back the curtain as the wagon moved out of sight.

Time to get ready for the day—one that would probably include Cynthia. It had been two days since her last visit.

As the clock in the parlor stuck the ten o'clock hour, a knock rapped on the front door. From the chair where she sat holding Emma, Sarah could see Cynthia on the porch.

Helen set a fresh pot of tea on the table by the sofa and answered the door.

"Miss Taylor to see Mrs. Greer."

Sarah couldn't help but smile. Even out here in a mining town, Cynthia tried to act the part of a member of high society. Sarah knew she was being too hard on the young woman. During their visits, she had learned that Cynthia had grown up with nothing except a drunken mother and overbearing brother. And now the poor girl needed a friend to learn how to stand against the man.

A memory of one of the dinners shortly after she had been brought to Boston flashed through Sarah's mind— Grandfather leering at a young lady. The poor child was hardly older than herself at the time, probably seventeen, maybe eighteen, and kept her head bowed after catching the old man's stare.

Another shudder shook her. What would have happened to Cynthia if she hadn't come to Central City?

Sarah drew in a cleansing breath. Here was something she could do, help that had been unavailable to her during her marriage to Alfred. She could steer Cynthia in the right direction. She just needed to be sure she wouldn't have to deal with the young girl's controlling brother.

Cynthia stepped into the parlor.

Sarah stood. "Good morning. I'm glad you came by this morning." She glanced at Helen, then Cynthia's chaperone, Mrs. Chatterley. As usual, the older woman slipped onto a chair in the corner, took out her tatting shuttle and went to work on some lace. Sarah couldn't remember the woman ever saying anything. "Could you get a cup for Cynthia, please?"

Helen scowled as she stood in the hall. She nodded and slipped away.

Sarah couldn't understand Helen's reaction to Cynthia today.

"I was thinking of going to the mercantile," Sarah said. "Would you care to join me?"

The girl's eyes sparkled. "Oh, yes. I heard they had some new ribbon that is just beautiful, and I wanted to see it, but my brother didn't have time to take me." Her lips puffed out in a pout. "Sometimes I wish I were a man, so I could do the things I really want to do."

Try as she might, Sarah couldn't keep a smile from her lips. She turned and filled the cups Helen brought in to cover it, then handed the tea to the girl. Mrs. Chatterley never took anything.

She picked up her own cup. "What would you do if you were allowed?"

Cynthia set the tea on the table and glanced around the room, as if checking to make sure Mrs. Chatterley wasn't listening. "I want to ride astride on a horse and learn to shoot a gun." She kept her voice low. "Terrible things for a proper young woman to do."

Sarah understood. After all, she had done those things when she was about thirteen or fourteen, although her parents hadn't exactly approved. "Growing up, I used to ride like that with my best friend Melody. Her parents had horses, and we used to race each other and explore the hills around where we lived. Sometimes we even pretended that we were knights of old, rescuing fair damsels. Of course we had to take turns about who got to be the knight. Her brother even taught us how to shoot, so we could protect ourselves when we were out alone. Which was good, because one day we ran across a big old bear."

Cynthia's eyes grew wide. "Really?"

Sarah laughed. "Not really. It was just an old brown quilt that had somehow found its way over a stump. But we pretended it was a bear and practiced our shooting on it." Remembering those fun-filled times, she let out a sigh. "Oh, how I miss Melody."

"What happened to her?"

"I don't know. After I married, I never heard from her again." She patted the pocket in her skirt. "But I think of her every time I slip my derringer into my pocket."

"You carry a gun?" Cynthia's eyes grew even wider.

"Just a small one." Sarah glanced at the chaperone, but the older woman's chin rested on her ample chest. "Don't give up on your dreams. Maybe someday you'll get to ride astride, too."

A little while later, Miss Taylor and her chaperone left.

With a deep frown, Helen returned to the parlor and sat. "There's something I need to tell you."

Sarah smiled at the worried look on her housekeeper's face. "Oh, it can't be as bad as that, can it?"

Helen twisted her fingers together. "I think so. When I was at the mercantile earlier, I saw Miss Taylor. She was with Mr. Snodgrass. When I asked the clerk about them, she told me they lived at the hotel. She is his sister."

Shock ripped through Sarah. *No. No. No.* Sarah kept the words trapped behind her clenched teeth. Sweet little Cynthia, Stanley's sister? Slowly, as she thought about both of their faces, she realized they had the same eyes, the same hair. Why hadn't she noticed that before? What did Stanley hope to gain by using his sister in this way? Was Cynthia aware of what her brother was doing?

She couldn't take the chance of having anything to do with Stanley or his sister. "Thank you, Helen, for letting me know this. I will send a note to Cynthia and explain that we will not be able to continue our visits." She folded her hands in her lap. "If she calls, please let her know that I'm not receiving."

With the reins gripped in his gloved hands, Mac leaned against the wooden back of the seat of his fully loaded wagon in the mid-morning light. The hound behind him let out a mournful howl.

Mac rolled his shoulder backward, nudging the dog. "Tair, quiet."

The dog stopped his howling but continued to whine.

"What's the matter with your dog, Mr. MacPherson?" The young man peeked at Tair.

"Call me Mac."

"Fine, then you must call me Andrew or Drew, if you've a mind."

"Drew it is. Now about the dog. You have to understand just how sensitive he is. He sees you all sad and upset, so he wants to commiserate. His howling is just his way of showing you he feels bad for you."

Drew glanced from Mac to the dog, then back again. "Really?"

Mac loosened his hold on the reins. It was so much fun teasing this young greenhorn, just like fooling around with his younger cousins Daniel and Rob back at the ranch. "Yup, I've been traveling with him ever since he got over that beating those boys gave him, and he's been just like this, sympathizing with anyone he's around who seems sorrowful."

"I've never seen a dog that...that—"

"Or it could be that he's mourning over the fact that you're sitting in his place on the seat." Mac laughed when Drew almost jumped off the seat. "Whoa there, man. Tair's fine where he is."

Drew relaxed on the seat and stayed quiet for a moment, but only a moment. "Mac, can I ask you something?"

Mac tilted his head toward the young man. "What?"

"If I'm to set up the businesses the miners need, I need to understand them more than I do."

Mac nodded. Sounded sensible.

"I've read the stories of men finding fortunes in the gold fields in California, and there's gold here. I guess my question is why aren't you mining for it instead of hauling freight? You're strong and don't seem to have any ties around here. I'd think you could make a great fortune by going into the hills and mining gold. You'll never get rich as a freighter."

Tair whimpered when Mac choked as he tried to swallow a deep chuckle. When he could draw a full breath, he looked at Drew. "First of all, I think you need to put aside those stories you've read. Most men out here barely eke out enough gold to make it worthwhile. Many go back home broken and broke. Some who do strike it rich drink and gamble it away. A few'll save and send it back home. The rest just follow the dream of big riches until they die from the cold, the hunger, or the bullet from a man who thinks he has a better right to whatever gold might be in the land than the man he just killed."

Drew's face turned a shade paler.

Mac snapped the reins as the wagon headed up a slight incline. "Why would I want that kind of life?"

"For the fortune that's out there," Drew said. "So you would be independent. So you didn't have to be at someone's beck and call for your very livelihood. It's what I wish I could be."

Mac shook his head. The boy had some problems to work through. He'd seen it often with his cousins on the farm back East and now on the ranch. Young men who chafe at authority, who buck at having to follow orders. "If it's that all-fired important to you, why don't you go mine for your fortune? You might be one of the lucky ones."

Drew slumped on the seat. His hands clasped as his elbows rested on his legs. "I can't leave my sister. She's been through too much. And besides, there's Stanley. I've got to stay and protect her."

"I've answered your question, now answer mine. What's the situation with your sister and Snodgrass?"

Drew sat rigid for several minutes as his fingers gripped the seat until his knuckles were white as a midwinter's snowdrift. His face hardened like a frozen mountain above the snow. "Stanley's my grandfather's enforcer, the one who does the things that keep my grandfather's hands clean." He lifted his hat and ran a hand through it. "Clean as far as the law's concerned anyway."

He shook his head, then took a deep breath and let it out bit by bit. "I was only ten when all this started, so a lot of it I didn't understand until recently. But Sarah was only sixteen when she was sold off as part of a business deal. That was thirteen years ago."

Mac's head jerked sideways. "He sold his own granddaughter, like a slave?"

"That's what it amounted to, although it was considered legal, because they forced her to marry the old man. She begged them not to."

"This is America. You canna force a woman to marry a man like that."

"You can if you're Andrew Elijah Hollingsworth and think the world exists for your pleasure and profit. Grandfather used me as a pawn and preyed on Sarah's love for me to get her to do what he wanted. The marriage was acceptable to Grandfather, because even though Greer was an abusive drunk, in the man's sober moments, he was good at accumulating wealth. A trait Grandfather prized above all others."

Mac ground his teeth to keep from saying words even his ancient grandda would box his ears for. Scenes of Lizzie's body flashed in his head, the way she swung when the barn door opened, the bruises on her face and body, her ripped dress. His wife's torment, terrible though it had been, had happened only once. How had Drew's sister survived? "What happened to her cur of a husband?"

"While Sarah was healing from one of his beatings, Alfred decided to look elsewhere for his pleasures. When his housekeeper found out he'd forced himself on her daughter, she bided her time. About six months ago, after her daughter died in childbirth and he wouldn't acknowledge the baby, she prepared a special meal for him. His last meal, you might say."

Mac snapped the reins again. "Justice was served."

"You could say that, although the housekeeper died of a weak heart while she was in jail waiting to go to trial."

They traveled on for a bit in silence, but something nagged at Mac's mind. "What happened to the baby?"

"Haven't you guessed by now? Sarah had been left childless and vowed to never marry again. She can't stand a man to touch her. She flinches still when I get too close, though she knows I'd never hurt her." After a moment or two, his lips tipped into a small smile. "She adopted the baby, and Emma couldn't be loved more than if Sarah had given birth to her."

Mac let out a whistle. For thirteen years the woman had lived through torment and made it through. Sarah was a survivor. He didn't think he'd ever met any man with the inner strength it would take to endure that, much less a woman. Somehow he couldn't get her face out of his mind.

CHAPTER SIX

"Can you believe how big she's getting?" Sarah sat on the rug in the parlor and held Emma around the middle, letting her tiny feet tap on the floor. "That's right. Do a little jig for Momma."

Emma lifted her gaze to Sarah. "Mmo, mmo."

Sarah clasped her daughter to her chest and gave her a kiss, then laughed. "Did you hear that, Helen?" Raising her head, she glanced at the woman who was fast becoming her best friend. "Emma called me "Momma."

"Well, wait until Mr. Hollingsworth gets back." Helen let out a tiny sigh. "He's going to be tickled to hear that little one start talking." She blushed. "I mean, well, he does love Emma almost as much as you do."

Sarah turned back to her daughter and tried not to let Helen see her grin. When she had control of her expression, she glanced at Helen. "Yes, Drew loves Emma. He also loves cookies, and I've noticed the cookie jar's never empty."

A deep blush rose up Helen's neck and face. Her eyes opened wide. "Oh, Mrs. Greer." She shook her head back and forth. "I don't—I won't—no, no." She took a step back as she held her hands up.

"Don't leave. Sit and talk to me a moment." Sarah patted the floor near the baby's blanket and waited until Helen joined her. "I don't mind that you like my brother. I think he likes you, too."

"Don't say things like that." Moisture filled Helen's eyes. "I don't fool myself. Nothing can come from it."

"Why not?"

"Oh, ma'am, look at you." Helen twisted her fingers in her hair which had grown some since her cousin chopped it off. "And look at me. I'm just an orphan, a common worker whose dream is to own a bakery where I'll probably work from dawn to dusk. Your brother'll surely want someone who's rich like him, who knows all the right things to say and do, whose family will help him go far."

Sarah cuddled Emma on her lap. "Helen, until I was sixteen, Drew and I lived with our parents. Papa was a preacher in a small town. Mama and I kept our house, grew a garden, and put up vegetables and fruit so we had something to eat during the winter. Drew fished in the nearby creek, so we had some kind of meat. Sometimes, one of the parishioners gave us a ham or a slab of bacon. The only reason I have anything now is that my husband tried to control his only child, a son from his first marriage, by threatening to give everything to me. He died before he could change his will back. And the son refused to accept anything when I offered it to him."

She shrugged. "Drew's not rich. In fact, he has nothing of his own. He works for our grandfather, but he isn't happy. And that's all I want for him—to be happy. With whatever and whomever makes him that way."

Helen couldn't keep a grin from her face. "When do you think Mac and your brother—?"

Pounding at the front door reverberated down the hall. Helen jumped up and hurried to the entry hall. "Good afternoon, sir. Wait, please." Helen's voice went from cordial to concerned and irritated in a breath. "I didn't say Mrs. Greer is receiving." Footsteps neared them, and Helen's voice followed them down the hall. "No, please wait."

Sarah picked up Emma and sat on the end of the horsehair sofa, setting her child next to her. Helen used that tone for only one person—Snarly the Snitch, and there'd be no stopping the man from what he wanted. She rubbed her hand up and down Emma's back. The one thing she didn't want this afternoon was a visit from that man, but for her brother's sake, she would tolerate it.

Stanley, ignoring Helen like he usually did, stopped at the entrance to the parlor, then crossed the room to the sofa. "Ah, Sarah, just the lady I wanted to see." He started to sit without an invitation, until Emma reached out her chubby hands and tried to grab his trousers. He took a quick step back and dropped onto a nearby chair. A look of disgust crossed his face as Emma tried to crawl across the sofa toward him. "Maybe your servant could take the child elsewhere and bring us some refreshments?" Phrased like a question, but it was spoken like a command.

"If you'd like some tea, I'll ask Helen to prepare some for you, but this is the time I always spend with my daughter." Sarah tried to keep a polite smile on her face. "Was there some reason you came by? Drew hasn't returned, as I'm sure you know."

"That's precisely why I hurried over. I needed to let you know what happened within the last half-hour." Stanley's face drew up into a serious expression. He leaned forward in the chair. "An hour ago a man came to my office trying to find out where you live." He shook his head a little bit and tried to look sorrowful. "He said he was the brother of that child's mother, and he wanted her."

Helen took a sharp breath. "No." The whispered word floated around the room.

Sarah grabbed Emma and wrapped both arms around her, pulling the girl onto her lap. "He can't have her. Emma is legally adopted. My lawyer in Boston saw to that."

Stanley slipped over to the sofa where the baby had been moments before. "That was back East. Who knows what the courts will do out here?" He spread his hands in front of him, palms up. "I tried to dissuade him, but unfortunately my secretary told him where you live and I'm afraid he'll be here soon. I came as fast as I could. I wish to offer my help and protection."

Emma patted Sarah's cheeks. "Mmo, mmo."

Sarah gave her daughter a hug, then walked to where Helen stood at the parlor door. She kept her voice low enough, so Stanley wouldn't hear. "Have your brother run over to Mr. Carlyle's office and tell him I need him to come over here right now. Tell him it is of the utmost importance, then take Emma to my room and lock the door. Stay with her. Don't let anyone but me in. Understand?"

"Will you be all right?" Helen took the baby, then glanced from Sarah to Stanley and back to Sarah. "Shouldn't I send for someone else?"

"I can handle this. I just…"

Someone knocked on the door.

Helen slipped down the hall.

Stanley joined Sarah in the entry.

"Please understand. I am here for you." He started to wrap his arm around her, but Sarah stepped to the door and opened it.

A stranger stood on the other side, a man who had the same eyes and hair as Emma. His clothes were dusty and threadbare. His hair needed trimming in the worst way.

As she stood looking at the man, memories and long-forgotten conversations drifted through Sarah's mind—her husband's housekeeper crying over her wastrel son, the woman asking for an advance on her wages to bail her son out of jail, the loud argument between mother and son just before he took all the money she had and left. He had not been home in the last eight years of his mother's life.

Sarah straightened her spine. She had done battle for her daughter once before, and her grandfather hadn't been able to keep the little girl away from her. She would fight for her again. Nobody, especially this excuse for a man, was going to take her daughter from her. "May I help you?"

Stanley moved beside her in the doorway.

The man puffed out his chest. "I'm Petey, uh, Peter Waller, and I'm here about my niece. I know you got her. I want her. She's my only family since my ma and sis died. My sis would've wanted me to have her. Give 'er to me, and I'll leave."

Sarah tightened her hands into fists to keep from slapping the man's face. How dare he come up here like a poor shadow of her grandfather and demand Emma? "I'm sorry. You must have the wrong house. The only children living here are my legally adopted daughter and my housekeeper's brother."

She started to close the door, but the man pushed against it.

"Now you wait just a minute. I know how you Greers are. I saw enough of the illegal ways your husband did things when I was a boy. I'm going to get her away from you before you corrupt her like you did my sweet innocent sister." The man's eyes flickered to Stanley's for an instant.

Stanley moved in front of Sarah. "You get out of here and leave Mrs. Greer alone. The child's hers, and you can't do anything about it."

Mr. Waller glared at them for a moment, then turned on his heel and stomped off, his hands in the pockets of his worn brown trousers.

"It was a good thing I came when I did." Stanley grinned down at Sarah. "I'm not sure what that man would have done to you if I hadn't been here to protect you." He dropped his arm across her shoulders and extended his hand toward her parlor, as if inviting her into his house. "Let's go back and talk about what we need to do next."

What kind of fool did he take her for? Did Stanley think she would fall at his feet in gratitude for helping her save Emma from her uncle? Sarah shifted out from under his arm and faced him. The same spirit of battle filled her as it had when she last faced Grandfather, and the stakes were just as high. She opened her mouth to tell him just what she thought of this manipulation—it had Grandfather's hands all over it.

Something made her close her lips and swallow. Think before speaking. The words rolled round her mind. There was Drew to think about and the power Stanley had over Drew. She couldn't let on that she suspected Stanley had a part in this. And not that she wanted to catch flies, but it didn't hurt being more honey than vinegar.

"Do you think he can take Emma from me?" Sarah didn't have to fake the trembling in her voice or the tear that ran down her cheek. Rage at Stanley and fear of losing Emma, however remote, took care of that. "What should I do?"

Stanley's eyes narrowed a bit.

Had she played it too much the damsel in distress? Her chest tightened. She didn't even try to hold back the next tear. "Please, tell me. I can't lose my daughter."

"She…" He harrumphed. "What I mean is that I'll see what I can do about this man. I will have him watched to see what he does around town. May I call on you tonight, say about six o'clock, to let you know what I have discovered?"

"Drew isn't scheduled to be home before tomorrow." There was no way she would be caught with Stanley at home at night without her brother there, for her reputation if nothing else. "Maybe we could meet at my lawyer's office in a few days, and you can report to him what you've discovered."

Stanley's face tightened, but after several seconds he frowned, nodded, and took his leave. The man sulked— he acted like she'd turned him away instead of agreeing to meet with him. That was just too bad, because she would never invite him into her home.

After the door closed, Sarah hurried to the kitchen and washed her hands. Twice.

That afternoon, Stanley was sitting at his desk when he heard someone tap on the back door to his office, the one that opened to the alley. He unlocked the door and opened it just a bit. Pete Waller stood in the narrow alley. "Get in here before someone sees you."

Waller slunk inside and dropped onto the chair in front of Stanley's desk. "Got any liquor in here?"

Stanley returned to his chair behind his desk. "No, and I don't want you to take a single drink until this is over. Understand?" He stared across at the man he'd had tracked down and brought to Central City. "If I hear that you've had a single drop before then…"

Stanley pulled a pistol from the drawer and rested it on the top of the desk with his finger on the trigger. "Well, let's just say that it'll be your last drink."

Waller swallowed hard a couple of times, his Adam's apple jumping up and down in his throat. "Y-yes, sir. I understand."

"Good. Now this is what I want you to do tonight."

Sarah paced across the parlor. How long did it take to get one man? She turned in the other direction. How long had Helen's little brother been gone? Two hours? Three? She glanced up at the clock on the mantle. A weak giggle burst from her throat. Goodness, it had only been twenty minutes since Stanley had stalked out of the house. How dare he try to come between her and her daughter?

She gasped. Emma and Helen, they were still locked in the bedroom! Sarah lifted her skirt and petticoats and hurried up the stairs.

At her bedroom door, she tapped on the wood. "Helen? It's me. You can unlock the door. Everyone's gone."

The lock clicked. Still holding Emma, Helen opened the door. She stood in the bedroom, shaking, her freckles standing out on her pale cheeks.

Sarah took Emma and hugged her to her chest. "We're safe. Let's go downstairs and wait for my lawyer."

At the bottom of the stairs, Helen took Emma and headed for the kitchen while Sarah returned to the parlor. Carl burst in the front door, followed by Mr. Carlyle. "I brung him just like you said."

Sarah patted the boy on the shoulder. "Thank you. Why don't you go out to the kitchen and tell Helen that I said to give you two cookies."

"Yes, ma'am." His grin spread across his sweat-streaked face. He turned and ran out of the parlor.

"Please, Mr. Carlyle, have a seat." Sarah waved toward one of the chairs near the sofa where she sat. "And thank you for coming so quickly. I didn't know if you would get here before Mr. Snodgrass left or not."

Helen entered with a tray. She set the tea service on the small table next to the sofa, then left.

After serving the tea, Sarah told her lawyer what happened.

He listened, nodding a few times. When she finished, he set his cup down and leaned back in his chair. "I don't think you have much to worry about. As you know, your lawyer in Boston forwarded copies of all your legal matters to my partner in Denver. I've been through them all. You've legally adopted Emma. Added to that, you've good standing here in the community, especially since you have purchased a home here."

Sarah nodded at Mr. Carlyle's words. Peace settled over her. Having a lawyer she could trust helped so much.

"You seem to be well-respected and quite prosperous." He shook his head. "I doubt Waller will take Emma's custody to court. But if he does, we'll win. Don't worry. You have the law on your side. Besides which, you are a true lady, and this town values ladies like you. There are so few women like you here. And I'm sure I don't have to tell you not to do anything that will tarnish your reputation."

He stood and bowed. "I'll check on this man's whereabouts and send a few inquiries into his past. This could be no more than trying to get you to give him money to rid yourself of him. Have a good day, Mrs. Greer."

Sarah saw him to the door, then closed and locked it after he left. She leaned back against the wood surface. A good day indeed. How was she supposed to have a good day when one man wanted her baby, another man wanted her—or at least the money she inherited, and her brother was off somewhere with a man who she wasn't sure she trusted? She'd seen him accost that man on the street long before she met him, and the incident with the crowbar hadn't helped. But then, she didn't trust any man.

She could almost see Mac standing in front of her like he had the day he surprised her when she was opening the boxes. She rubbed her hands up and down her arms. There was something about him that bothered her and she couldn't figure out what it was. She hoped he'd stay away. Then the feelings would disappear. She turned from the door and headed for the kitchen. What Mr. MacPherson did wasn't her concern. She'd ignore him, and that would be the end of that.

Sarah entered the kitchen, and the wonderful scent of fried chicken and yeast rolls made her stomach call out. She rubbed her hand over her middle. Hiring Helen had been one of the best decisions she had ever made. But no matter how good her cooking was tonight, what Sarah really needed was her new friend's peacefulness to surround her.

Helen was standing at the back door, which she held open. After a moment, she closed it and turned around. Tears filled her eyes. "I'll need to be going out. Old Widow Grayson's failing. She might not make it through the night. She's one of the sweetest women I know. Doc just came by and asked me to sit with her."

Carl stood from where he'd been playing with Emma. "Can I go, too? Me 'n' Mike can fetch and carry anything you need. Can I go, please?"

Sarah looked from Carl to Helen.

"Mike is Widow Grayson's grandson and Carl's best friend." Helen ruffled her brother's hair, something Sarah figured the boy tolerated only because he wanted permission to accompany his sister.

Sarah bent and picked up Emma who was fussing. Could a child this small pick up the tension that had come into the house today? "I can finish supper. Why don't you take Carl and hurry over to the woman's house now? If you are as much of a comfort to her as you are to me, she'll surely be blessed by your presence."

"If you're sure." Helen lifted the edge of her white apron and wiped the moisture from her eye. Dropping the fabric, her eyes widened. "But you'll be alone. What if that man comes back?"

"Which one—the slimy one who wants Emma, or the snarly one who wants everything else?" Sarah forced herself to smile as she slid her hand over the small derringer she kept in a pocket of her dress. "Don't worry about Emma and me. We'll be just fine."

CHAPTER SEVEN

Mac checked the harness on the last of the mules, then patted it on the neck. This would be the final rest stop for the day. A day ahead of schedule, they'd be getting back to Central City by late afternoon. He glanced at Drew who was playing with Tair. The young man wasn't a bad sort, reminded him of one of his cousins years ago who stayed in Philadelphia when the rest of the clan moved west.

Aye, Drew and Uncle Finley's boy, Camden, had a lot in common. Both had a lot of book learning and seemed to thrive in the city life back East. Mac shook his head. Too bad. If Drew stayed out here instead of going back to Boston when his grandfather eventually ordered him to, they'd probably become good friends.

With a pat on the mule's neck, Mac headed to the back of the wagon.

"All right, Tair, this is the last time." Drew threw a foot-long stick in the air. The hound chased it, leaped up, and caught it in his mouth. As he landed, the poor mutt's feet got all tangled up.

Mac leaned against the wagon and laughed while Tair got his feet all pointed in the same direction. At last, the dog headed back toward his new friend at full speed, the stick still in his mouth. One of these days that dog was going to grow into those big paws of his. Oh no, there was going to be a collision. Poor thing had better learn to slow down, or someone was going to get hurt.

As Tair ran past him, Mac reached for the dog's neck before he ran into Drew. He missed. "Watch it, Drew! He's gonna run you down."

Tair hit Drew full-force and sent both of them over the edge of the trail. Drew's shout joined Tair's howl.

Mac raced to the place where the two of them disappeared and scrambled down the narrow drop-off. Drew and Tair had landed on a pile of large rocks. Drew lay still, his eyes closed, his leg twisted and bleeding. The dog shuffled off to the side, holding one paw off the ground.

He squatted down by the young man and checked Drew's breathing, then lifted each eyelid. Next he checked out the man's arms and the one straight leg. He would leave the twisted one for last, since it was surely broken.

"I may not be a doctor, but I've plenty of experience taking care of hurt men." Mac hoped his words would soothe the dog as he glanced at Drew's face. He hoped, maybe even prayed, that Drew would rouse, but there was no reaction. "Maybe it's best you're still out. I need to check on this leg."

Mac pulled his knife from the sheath attached to his belt. He slit the pant leg and slid the material apart, then let out the breath he'd been holding. Drew had a bad break in his lower leg, but the bone hadn't cut through the skin. Blood oozed from some shallow cuts.

Mac grabbed a couple of stout branches and laid them on either side of the leg, then took hold of Drew's lower leg. As gently as he could, Mac straightened the leg. With the cord he always kept in his pocket, he wrapped the splint tight.

Drew groaned. His eyelids fluttered. "Hurt…hurt."

"I know. Just try and stay still while I finish checking you out." Mac pulled the dirty shirt up and examined

Drew's chest. Bruises were already forming on the sides—maybe some cracked ribs. "Can you breathe all right?"

Drew tried to take a deep breath, but stopped and shuddered. "Hurts too...much."

"All right. Just try and relax." Mac stood. "I'll be right back."

Within the hour, as the sun touched the tops of the mountains in the west, Mac snapped the reins, and the mules pulled out, moving slowly so as not to jostle Drew too much. Tair lay in the back of the wagon next to the injured man, both of them on a bed of cut tree branches covered with bedrolls to cushion the ride back to town.

Mac rolled his shoulders, trying to ease the muscles cramping with tension. He had done everything he knew for Drew, but it didn't seem like it was enough. The man had seemed clear-headed at first. But in the last few minutes, he'd started rambling.

They weren't far from Central City now. If they hurried, they could be home before it turned dark. But that was the rub. If they hurried, the bouncing around in the back of the wagon could do more harm than good for Drew. But what if something was wrong with him that Mac had not caught, something that could kill the man?

Drew started mumbling again, something about a snarly creature snitching in the grass. Maybe they could move just a tad faster. Mac clicked his tongue, and the mules stepped up their pace just a mite.

Thankful for the full moon that had risen before the twilight passed into the evening dark, Mac reached the edge of town. He pulled up in front of the doc's office as Sheriff Hoover headed toward him on his nightly rounds. Doc was walking alongside the sheriff. The two of them seemed to be having a mighty loud discussion about someone named Sadie Girl.

Well, Sadie Girl was just going to have to wait. Drew needed the doc now. Mac jumped down and opened the back of the wagon.

"Well, Mac, what you got there?" Doc peeked in the wagon. "Who's that?"

"New businessman in town, Andrew Hollingsworth. He's been traveling with me to get to know the miners." Mac shooed Tair to the side, then pulled on the blanket where Drew lay.

Sheriff Hoover and Mac each took hold of the blanket and lifted. Drew started rambling again. Doc opened the door so his patient could be carried inside. Once there, Doc moved into the examining room and lit several lamps. He pointed to a table in the middle of the room, then took off his jacket and hung it on a nail. "Tell me what caused all this."

Mac told them what happened to Drew.

All the time he talked, Doc poked and prodded, cleaned and wrapped. At last, he washed his hands and dried them on a towel. "Need to keep him overnight. You did a purty good job patching him up, Mac, but I want to check on him for the next while 'cause of the head wound." He hung the towel on another nail in the wall. "You gonna tell his sister he's here?"

"Aye, now that I know Drew's going to be all right." Mac slapped his hat back on his head and headed to the door. "When in the morning can she come by?"

"Tell her any time after nine'll be fine." Doc waved him on.

Bone-weary, Mac held onto the side of the wagon for a moment, then heaved himself up to the seat. Tair greeted him with a small *woof*. Much as he wanted to go back to the boardinghouse right now, he had two stops yet to make. First, he left his wagon and mules at the livery. They'd done a good job and earned their rest. Next, he headed over to see Drew's sister with Tair plodding behind him.

With each step Mac took, he tried to figure out what to say to Mrs. Greer so she'd wait 'til the morning before rushing over to Doc's. Somehow he needed to convince her, 'cause Drew really needed his rest, and so did Doc.

As he crossed the road in front of Mrs. Greer's place, a feathery feeling ran down his neck, like someone was watching him. He stretched and shifted. Looking around, he couldn't see anything out of place, but the feeling didn't go away. Maybe he just imagined it. "Come on, Tair. We need to give our news, then go home."

Wood smoke mixed with roses filled the night air around Sarah's house. One thing about this woman's place, it always smelled good here, whether of flowers or cinnamon rolls or beef stew.

He walked up the path to the house and realized that someone was awake. The lamps were lit downstairs, and the shadows showed someone pacing back and forth in the parlor. As he knocked on the wooden door, a baby's screeching filled the quiet night air. Tair whimpered.

"Quiet, boy." Mac rubbed the dog's head.

"Who's there?" The voice on the other side of the door quivered.

"Mac." Something tightened in his chest. "It's me, MacPherson."

The door jerked open. The woman standing in the lamplight looked so unlike the lady he had seen before, Mac blinked a couple times.

Her hair half-hung down around her pale, tear-streaked face. Her shoulders slumped under a dirty dress that smelled of something that tickled his memory— something that had to do with babies. She held her red-faced baby, whose squalls sent Tair howling.

"Quiet." Mac barked out the order as he stared down at his hound, but it seemed as if everyone and everything took it personally. The night went dead still—no crying, no howling, no insects buzzing, at least for a moment or two. Then the baby started up again. Tair lay on the porch and covered his head with his paws.

With memories of his own daughters flashing through his thoughts, Mac took the baby in one arm. With a gentle touch, he guided the woman farther back into the house.

She resisted for a moment. Her eyes widened, and she looked past him to the darkness surrounding the house.

Mac looked over his shoulder to see if he could spot what she was looking for. The baby let out another scream that threatened to deafen him. "Is something out there?"

She shrugged. "For a moment, I thought I saw someone. But I guess it was just my imagination." The baby let out another howl. "I can't get her to quit crying." Mrs. Greer rubbed her hand along the side of her head and more hair tumbled down. "Should I send for the doctor? She might be sick."

With his free hand he directed her to the sofa. She dropped wearily onto it. He wrapped his other arm around Emma and lifted her to his shoulder, then patted her back while he paced back and forth across the room.

He had seen Grandma do this many a night with one babe or another while they screamed and cried. Looking back at Mrs. Greer, he smiled. "There'll be no sending for the doctor tonight. He's needed elsewhere. Besides, as near as I can see, the babe only has a bit of stomach upset. Granny would say, 'The wee bairn is only bein' a bairn. I just have ta walk her through it.' And she's always right."

Sarah tried to relax on the sofa. Mac had returned, so that meant Drew would be home shortly. He probably had to stop at the office and make a report or something. Stanley would demand that. No one would need to know that Helen was gone.

With each step Mac took, Emma quieted a bit more. Sarah could tell this wasn't the first time he'd held a squalling baby. His face eased from stern lines to a gentle smile. Where had he learned to handle a child like this? Was he married? Did he have children of his own? If he did, where were they?

Suspicions crept in, but they were pushed away as he continued to move across the room. Memories floated through her mind, memories of Papa holding Drew as a baby, walking with him like Mac was doing now when Drew had an upset stomach. Memories of Papa holding her and telling her how much he loved her. Memories of Mama watching them as she held Drew, tears flowing down her cheeks. She could hear Mama's voice from years ago as she wiped her face. "These aren't tears. It's my heart's so full of love that it overflows. These are just bits of love."

Sarah rested on the sofa, wrapped in the comfort of her memories. A whisper of sound surrounded her, the soft humming of a male voice. It didn't frighten her. No, it soothed her spirit, unlike anything in many years. A soothing she relished and wanted to hold on to. Not the man, just the soothing peace.

The minutes ticked by on the clock that sat on the mantel. Mac kept pacing. His arms ached, his feet had grown leaden, and the babe's cries had probably damaged his hearing, but his heart lightened as Emma finally nestled closer and quieted her screams. Just whimpers now. And the poor lady relaxed a mite on the sofa.

The house seemed so quiet after the uproar when he had arrived. The hour was drawing late, but thankfully with Helen and her brother in the house, he and Mrs. Greer could claim they were chaperoned, even if the housekeeper's room was at the back of the house.

The babe felt good in his arms, like his own when they were small as this wee one. It had been so long, too long, since this contentment, this peace had filled his heart. Rumbling started deep in his chest. The baby quieted as he started humming.

After several more times back and forth across the room, Emma relaxed and drifted to sleep. Something rustled. He glanced toward the sound. Mrs. Greer rested against the back of the sofa and wiped the tears from her face with a white lace hankie.

"What's that song?" Her voice barely disturbed the stillness of the parlor.

"MacPherson's Lament."

She smiled. "You have your own lament?"

"Nay, t'was Jamie MacPherson's back in 1700. Poor boy."

"It's a beautiful tune. Tell me about him." She reached up her arms.

He knew she wanted the baby, but a shudder rolled through his body. How long had it been since a woman, any woman had raised her arms toward him like that? He needed Emma for a shield, and besides, the little one felt too good in his arms. He was loath to let go of her. He sat on the sofa. "Wait until she sleeps a mite more. We don't want to wake her now."

The lady's eyes, dark and shining in the lamp light, moved from her child to him. She nodded.

Another shudder, smaller this time, but just as deep, caused his hands to tremble. He felt like a callow youth. "The song..." His mind went blank for a moment as he watched her, soft and trusting, and he still hadn't told her about her brother.

For a moment, for just a moment, he wanted to enjoy a bit of peace and sharing. He loved this story and wanted her to know about it. "It's the tune Jamie played on his fiddle as he stood at the gallows tree back in Scotland. A haunting melody, it is. One that drew Bobby Burns to write about."

Her eyes lightened even more. "Robert Burns, the poet?"

"Aye, that's the one. Well, Jamie was a, uh, highwayman of sorts." He always hated telling this part, but one had to know that part to know why poor Jamie swung from the gallows tree. "While in jail, he made up the song and sang it before the people who had gathered there. He challenged any man to play it on his fiddle, and if one could, he would give his fiddle to him. No man took the challenge, so Jamie smashed his fiddle on his knee." Mac shook his head. "A real pity it was no one took up the dare. It might have saved Jamie's life."

Her breath caught. Her eyes grew wider. "How?"

"Well, the men at Banff were determined to do away with Jamie but knew there were those in Aberdeen who had appealed for his life. Those black-hearted men in Banff set the clock in the city tower ahead by a quarter of an hour and executed poor Jamie just before the pardon came."

"Oh, no."

"Ah, but those in Aberdeen got the last laugh, because from there after the town clock had to be a quarter of an hour off."

"You're joking." The lady's full soft lips tilted up in a most tempting fashion.

Her very sweetness was making things happen to him that shouldn't. Tension spread through him. He had to stop his thoughts right now. "No, a MacPherson never jokes about Jamie and his fiddle." He swallowed hard. The time had come to tell her about her brother. "Your brother...I don't want to be the one to tell you, but there isn't anyone else. He—"

"No." Shaking her head, she drew back. Fear seeped into her eyes. "You left him with Stanley Snodgrass, didn't you? You're back a day early and left him there, right? Drew said that he would have to give a report to Stanley as soon as he arrived, or else that dratted man would be upset. Business always comes first to him and Grandfather." Tears rolled up in her eyes as anguish marred her lovely face. Her skin turned pale. She wrapped her arms around herself as if to hold herself together, waiting for a blow, a mighty blow, to strike her.

"Drew's had an accident, but he's not dead. He's over at the doctor, sleeping."

"What—?" She blew out the air that had been trapped inside her. She took in another deep breath, then slowly let it out. "What happened?"

Mac rubbed the back of his neck. The burden of the accident rested heavy on his shoulders. "Twas my fault. Just a few hours ago, we stopped ta rest the mules. Drew threw a stick for Tair ta catch." He could hear his Scottish brogue getting stronger, the way it always did when he was nervous or upset. "You have ta remember Tair's still a growing pup, even if he's big as all get-out. He came running back with the stick and couldn't stop. They both fell down a narrow ravine. Twasn't deep, but Drew landed on a pile of large rocks with Tair landing atop o' him."

"How bad was he hurt?"

"Broke his leg and bruised a few ribs. Bumped his head something fierce, too."

Sarah started trembling, then looked around the room as if to figure out what to do. "I need to go to him." She focused on Emma. "But I can't take her out in the night air, not after she's finally settled. Oh, why did Helen have to go out tonight?"

Mac grabbed the edge of her sleeve as she started to rise. He had to stop her before she took out, running into the night in this wild town. "Sit a minute and think. There's nothing you can do right now. Doc's watching over him tonight. In fact, he told me ta tell you not ta come over 'til after nine in the morning. Doc said he could use your help then, as he would be tired from sitting up all night with your brother."

She dropped back down, rocking back and forth, holding herself together again. "I can't lose him. I can't. He and Emma are all I have. He can't die."

Helplessness stole his strength, as if his heart had been ripped by one of the great war sabers on the walls of MacPherson Hall that Grandda used to tell him about. Drew said this woman couldn't stand to have a man's hands on her, but she needed comfort now. She needed someone to hold her.

He hugged Emma with one arm, thankful the babe had stayed asleep, and wrapped his other arm around Mrs. Greer, pulling her to his chest.

For a moment she sat stiff as the board Granny used to iron her clean washing, then a trickle of tears flowed and became a river, a raging winter-thaw flood. Drew's words about what Mrs. Greer had suffered came back to him. Who had comforted this fine lady through her life? Who had been there for her when her parents died, when her brother was taken from her, when that monster of a husband had beaten and abused her?

He held her as keening cries of utter agony escaped from her heart. Who had held her when she lost those precious babes? He slid his hand back and forth across her shoulders. No words came, but then no words were needed. Like a bad infection, she just needed to let out the poisoning pain that had been held inside for far too long.

The worn-out babe never made a peep.

Slowly, bit by bit, the keening stopped, the rocking stopped, the tears stopped. Exhaustion claimed her.

Mac called her name once, twice, but nothing. What was he going to do with a babe in one arm and an exhausted lady in the other? And his own body crying out for rest. If he could just twist around and lay her down on the sofa, then he could get Helen to look after the baby.

Something tickled the back of his tired mind. Something about Helen.

As he shifted away, Mrs. Greer's arms clung to him, her eyes still closed in sleep. "Help me. Please help me." A cry for help she would never allow to cross her lips if she were awake. With a weary shrug, he leaned back on the sofa, drawing her close. He could let her sleep for a half-hour or so. By then she would be so uncomfortable on the hard sofa, she would surely wake, and he could leave.

Resting the baby against his chest once more, he leaned his head back and closed his eyes.

CHAPTER EIGHT

Sarah tried to sit up, but something held her back—something big and solid. Little puffs of warm air brushed against her cheek. A smell drifted around her, a fragrance dusty, dirty, yet familiar. The something that held her back moved. She forced her eyes open.

Mac slumped next to her on the sofa, sleeping but still holding Emma. Sarah tried to shift away from him, but soreness in her neck and back held her in place. She lifted her hand and rubbed her back, easing the muscles enough so she could sit up straight, then she massaged her neck, tipping her head from side to side.

"Are you all right?"

She tried to bite back the cry of pain as she jumped at the sound of Mac's voice.

He twisted his neck also, grimacing. "Sorry, I didn't mean to fall asleep."

She glanced at the window. The outside had changed from black to gray with tinges of pink just starting in the eastern sky. They had spent the night alone. Heat rose up her neck to the top of her unpinned hair.

Mac handed her the baby and stood. "I best be getting out of here before Helen wakes up and finds me." He kept his voice low as he grabbed his hat and headed for the front door. He stopped and stood still as one of the statues back in Boston, then blinked his eyes as if trying to recall something. "Did you say something last night about Helen not being here?"

Sarah's face felt hotter than a sunburn in the middle of summer.

"I did, but then—oh, it doesn't matter. What's done is done. But you need to leave now before someone sees you."

Mac nodded. "I'll go get cleaned up and be back before nine to take you to Doc's to see your brother."

"Wait." Sarah tried to stand, but her legs felt leaden. She laid Emma on the sofa and tried again. Once she stood steady on her feet, she shuffled toward him. "Thank you for coming to tell me about Drew last night, but I can make it to the doctor's office without you."

Mac smiled down at her. "I know you can, but you can't go out unescorted, and as you said, Helen isn't here for you. Besides, I'm also doing this for Drew. I'd like to think if something happened to me, there would be someone to look after my sisters."

Sarah nodded and reached for the front door handle. For Drew, she could lean on a man. For Drew, she could let him hold her, comfort her. "All right, I'll be ready by nine, but keep out of sight. I don't need any rumors started about me."

"Thank you." He stepped farther back into the darkened entry hall as she opened the door.

"Where's the man you got in there?" Petey Waller stood on the porch, pointing a finger at Sarah. A couple of men stood with him. "I told you she was entertaining men all night. And just look at her, looking like a Jezebel. She ain't fit to raise my niece. I brought me a lawyer and the justice of the peace for witnesses. You can't get out of this now."

Mac took a step forward, but Sarah pushed him back farther into the darkness. "What's all this uproar about? You're going to awaken my household."

"What household?" Mr. Waller snorted. "Your housekeeper left last night with her little brother. And I seen a man come sneaking in late last night. He didn't leave. So you was here alone all night with that rich businessman."

He shook his finger again. "I knew you and that Mr. Snodgrass was sweet on each other the way he skedaddled it over here yesterday when I started asking questions about you." He pushed up his skinny little chin and snorted. "But it don't matter. I'm not letting a hussy like you raise my precious sister's baby."

"Mrs. Greer, what is going on?" Helen pushed her way past the men on the porch. The poor girl looked worn out, red-eyed and tired. Her brother pushed up beside her.

"Who are all these men?" Helen glared at the group of men. "And what are they doing here at this hour in the morning?" She reached the open door. "Are you all right, ma'am? Have these bullies hurt you?"

Helen turned her head a bit to the side and winked at Sarah, then with eyes blazing, turned back and faced the men. "You should be ashamed of yourselves, making trouble for a fine lady like Mrs. Greer. Why, I have a notion to fetch the sheriff!"

Helen sucked in a deep breath and opened her mouth to let loose again when a carriage stopped in front of the house. Stanley stepped down.

Mr. Waller turned pale. "But—but I thought—"

Tair trotted around the side of the house and up on the porch. He barked once, then again. Standing at the doorway, he looked inside and howled.

"Whose dog is that?" The voice came from one of the men on the porch.

Helen looked at Sarah and raised her eyebrows in question.

Sarah gave a slight shake of her head. Hopefully Mac had slipped out the back. Surely she could handle this situation by herself. Maybe she—

"Get that cur out of the way." Stanley raised his booted foot toward the dog. Tair bared his teeth and snarled. Stanley backed off the porch, then lifted his walking cane like a club.

At the moment the dog launched himself at Stanley, Mac rushed out of the hall and pushed Sarah aside, then grabbed the dog's collar. "Down, Tair, down."

For a few seconds the dog strained against the bulging arms that held him, but at last he relaxed and sat. Mac turned to the men who had scattered off the porch. "Mrs. Greer's brother has been gravely injured and is at the doctor's. She needs to be with him if he awakens. You gentlemen will have to excuse her so I can get her to her brother's side before it's too late."

Stanley shoved men aside as he stomped back up to the porch, his eyes narrowing as he glared at Sarah. "Take care, my dear. I wouldn't want anything to happen to you." He shifted his gaze to Mac. "You best be leaving. And keep that dog tied up, or you might find him dead some morning."

A growl started deep in the dog's chest. The sound filled the air as the two men stared at each other. Stanley swung his walking stick wide as he turned to leave.

Tair lunged for the man again. Mac tightened his hold on the dog collar.

Stanley climbed back in his carriage and snapped the whip over the horses' backs.

With his hand still on Tair's collar, Mac glared at the men still standing in front of the house. "You might as well leave now, there's nothing to see."

Pete Waller took a step forward but stopped when Tair growled again. "You ain't heard the last of this. You ain't fit to raise my niece. Just wait till the judge hears about this."

The other men muttered among themselves for a few moments, then left.

Helen pushed Sarah back into the house. Mac slipped in behind them, dragging his hound with him. Once inside, Helen grabbed the dog's collar, and Tair followed her like a little puppy to the back of the house.

Sarah waited until the click of the closed door echoed around them, then rounded on Mac, her heart beating hard and her hands gripped in fists so she wouldn't hit him. "Why did you come out? I had it all handled until you showed yourself. Now they all know who spent the night here."

His lips tightened. His eyes narrowed. "And what would you have had me do? Hide in here like a wee timorous mousie while Tair ripped out the man's throat? Because he would have. Have you forgotten how I came to have that dog? How he'd been beaten by those young boys? And that wasn't the first time someone took a stick ta him. But he's no pup anymore. If you looked at him lately, you'd see he's on his way ta his full growth." His Scottish burr had gotten stronger. "And he'll no take another beating. Someone at one of the mining camps tried that, and the man'll never be taking a stick ta a dog again."

Sarah raised her hand to her throat and tried to swallow. "Did…did he kill the man?"

"Nay, but he'll carry those scars around for the rest of his life." Mac ran his fingers over his hair. "This is getting us nowhere. Your brother's going to be waiting ta see you." He opened the front door, but looked over his shoulder. "I'll be back before nine as I said earlier. Be ready."

"I can go by myself."

Mac turned on his heel and scowled at her. "No."

"No, what? Now I should wait like some timorous mousie until you decide that I can come out of my hole?" Sarah rested her fists on her hips. "Well, thanks to what happened here last night—uh, I mean, what didn't…" She tried to find the words. "The fact that you were in the house most of the night might well cost me my daughter."

"What do you mean?"

Strange how a man so big could stand so still.

"That man on the porch was Emma's uncle, and he wants her. My lawyer said he had no case, but I had to keep myself above reproach." Sarah flung her hands up in the air. "And now I have this mess to deal with."

Mac's face paled as her words struck him.

"You won't lose your daughter over this. You have my word." He opened the front door. "Don't leave until I get back." Without giving her a chance to respond, he left.

Sarah glared at the shut door and huffed. No way was she going to wait for that arrogant man. Lifting the hem of her skirt, she turned to the stairs.

"Mmo-a?"

Sarah's head twisted sideways. Oh no! How could she have forgotten Emma? Racing back into the parlor, she hurried across the carpet and picked up her baby who was about to slide off the sofa. "There, there now. Momma's here. We'll get you cleaned up and see if Helen can tend to you so I can check on Uncle Drew."

With a hug and a kiss on the baby-soft cheek, Sarah laid Emma on her shoulder and raced upstairs. A half-hour later, after a hurried toilet for her and Emma, they came downstairs and entered the kitchen. Helen sat at the table, her back rigid and her head bowed. The stove sat cold, and nothing had been laid out on the table.

Sarah realized the widow Helen tended during the night must have passed. What a mess the poor girl had come home to. "I didn't have a chance to ask about the lady you stayed with last night."

"Widow Grayson passed peacefully. She's free from pain now." Helen lifted her head, her face whiter than her apron, her eyes floating in tears. She gripped her hands so tightly together that her knuckles shone white as her face. "Is it true? Is Mr. Hollingsworth near death?"

Sarah dropped into a nearby chair and sat Emma on her lap. "Drew has been injured—that is why Mr. MacPherson was here last night, to tell me about my brother." Heat burned her neck and cheeks. Maybe that's why he came by, but that's not all that happened. Her muscles all seemed to contract as memories of the way she wept all over the man swept through her mind.

She cleared her throat so she could start again. "Drew was in an accident, but he is going to be all right. He has a broken leg and bruised ribs." She set Emma in her chair and tied the bands that kept her seated. She needed to feed them all before they could go.

Later, after they had harnessed the horse to the buggy she kept in the barn, Sarah snapped the reins. Helen, with Emma on her lap, sat on the seat beside her.

Keeping a tight grip with her gloved hands, Sarah directed the horse through the dusty roads toward the center of the town. She'd seen the doctor's office sign in the weeks since she'd moved into her home.

When they traveled near one of the saloons, a small pack of half-drunk miners stumbled along the side of the road. Sarah jiggled the reins, and the horse picked up his pace. The men stared at them as the buggy went past, then gave chase.

"Hey, hear tell you women opened up a new brothel."

"Be by soon."

"Any more of you gals there?"

Sarah shuddered as she snapped the reins again, leaving the men in the middle of the road. Her jaw ached as she ground her teeth together. She passed the corner of the saloon and saw Pete Waller with a smug look on his face. The hateful, spiteful man was already spreading the word about Mac spending the night at her house.

By the time they pulled up in front of the doctor's office, Emma was screaming and Helen was white as milk fresh from a cow. Sarah gripped the side of the seat and climbed down. Could her life get more complicated?

Mac took the stairs at the boardinghouse two at a time, shrugging out of his jacket and pulling the bandana from his neck. In his room, he splashed water on his face, then grabbed a clean shirt. He had to hurry and get to Drew before his sister did, because he was sure Mrs. Greer was not going to wait until he returned to her home for her.

A few minutes later, Mac stomped down the dirt path leading from the boardinghouse with a couple biscuits stuffed with sausage in his large fists. A third had already been downed, trying to fill the hole in his gut. Bless Mrs. Flanagan's heart. She had seen what must have been a fierce frown on his stubbly face and offered him some of the sandwiches she'd been packing for miners' lunches.

Shoving another one in his mouth, he hurried across the road towards Doc's place. He had to let Drew know about the early morning showdown and what had to happen now for his sister's safety. He swallowed the last sandwich as his throat went dry. The plan had come to him as he dressed, but could he really do it?

Mac pounded on the doc's office door as the sun burst over the horizon.

It was a minute before Doc yanked the door open, a frown beneath his mustache and cup of coffee in his hand. "I told you nine, not seven."

"Sorry, but I need to see Drew before his sister comes. And if my guess is right, she'll be here well before the time you set."

Doc waved him in, then pointed to the room where he'd left Drew. "He's awake. Just don't excite him too much."

Mac opened the door to the sickroom while Doc went back to his breakfast.

In the dim room, Drew lay in the bed. The covers lifted above his splinted leg. He turned his bandaged head toward the door. "Have you told Sarah? Did you tell her not to worry?" His voice was low but clear.

"Aye, I told her and I'm sure she'll be here soon to see for herself how you are." Mac pulled a chair closer to the bed and sat. "But before she gets here, I've got to tell you something."

"Is she all right? Did someone try to hurt her?" Drew lifted his hands and tried to push off the bed coverings.

"Nothing like that." Mac told Drew what happened the night before and earlier that morning as quickly as he could.

Drew relaxed back against the bed. "As long as Sarah wasn't hurt."

"You miss the point, man. Your sister isn't safe now. Her reputation's in tatters." Mac stood and paced the too-small room. He had to do this, but would Mrs. Greer consent? If she didn't, she'd have to leave town. There would be no way she would be held in respect now. Word spreads in this town faster than fire in a sawmill. "I dare say Waller and those men with him have already spread the word that your sister had a man stay with her last night. That means that the drunken miners will think of her like those in the saloon or worse. They'd probably pound on the door of that large house and figure it was just another brothel." He sucked in a deep breath and took the step he vowed he never would until he solved the mystery of his wife's death. "And since I'm the one responsible, I'll have to marry her."

"How very gracious of you to offer yourself for such a sacrifice." Sarah stood at the door of the small whitewashed room where her brother lay in a narrow bed. She shook as the blood pounded in her head. How dare this man make such an assumption? As if she would marry him because he was seen at her house in the early morning. She had survived much worse than her reputation being besmirched. Her husband had seen to that.

She no longer cared what society said about her. And there was no way she was going to tie herself to another man. No way would she willingly put herself under a man's thumb or in the way of his fists. Once was more than enough, much more.

"So you plan to leave town, then do you?" The big, brawny man looked at her, one of his eyebrows lifting in question.

"I'll not be leaving my home, scurrying away like a frightened bunny before a pack of howling dogs." She straightened her spine and stood a bit taller, but nowhere near as tall as the man before her.

He rubbed his hand over the stubble on his face. "Mrs. Greer, you don't understand."

"Oh, I understand perfectly. Helen and I were verbally accosted by some drunkards on our way here."

"Sit down, both of you, and let's talk this matter out." Drew held onto his head with one hand and pushed up in bed with the other.

Helen handed Emma to Sarah, then rushed to his side. "Please, Mr. Hollingsworth. You need to lie back." She helped him adjust his pillows and lay back against them.

When he settled down, Sarah smiled at her brother. "All right, Drew, we'll do as you say as long as you rest. You have to get better."

She sat in the only chair in the room with Emma on her lap. Taking a deep breath, Sarah raised her head and stared directly at the big man standing at the foot of her brother's bed. "Go ahead, Mr. MacPherson. Explain to me just why I must marry you."

CHAPTER NINE

Mac rolled his shoulders as the mid-afternoon sun beat down on him. He sighed deeply, then stepped up on Mrs. Greer's front porch. Mrs. Greer. The day before he would marry the woman, and he was still calling her that. He pulled his hat from his head and ran his fingers through his hair.

He had to do this. He caused the problem, and he would fix it. But first, he needed to tell her about Lizzie and the girls. She had a right to know just what she was getting into. And even though he had not thought of marrying again, he knew that once he took those vows, once he gave his word to this woman, he would be bound in marriage for as long as they both lived.

He rammed his hat back on his head, then knocked on the front door. A few moments later Helen opened the door.

Mac shifted from one boot to the other like a schoolboy. "I came to see Mrs. Greer. Is she in?"

"Come on in, Mac." Helen opened the door wider. "She's in the parlor with Drew... I mean, Mr. Hollingsworth."

Mac lowered his voice. "He's a good man, Helen."

She blushed. "I know." Motioning for him to follow her, she raised her voice to normal. "This way, please." They stopped at the parlor entrance. "Mac's here to see you, ma'am."

Mac entered the parlor but stopped in his tracks when he saw Mr. Carlyle sitting on the sofa with Mrs. Greer. They were both holding some kind of legal documents. Drew sat nearby with his leg on a stool.

"Mac, I'd like you to meet my lawyer, Mr. Carlyle." Mrs. Greer met Mac's eyes straight and bold. "Mr. Carlyle, Mr. MacPherson."

Mac offered a wry smile while he shook hands with the lawyer. "We've met before."

"Good, that will make things easier." She laid the papers on the table. "Please have a seat while Mr. Carlyle explains the agreement."

Something twisted in Mac's gut. Whatever this *agreement* was, he wasn't going to like it. "What kind of agreement?"

Mrs. Greer sat up a tad straighter and gripped her hands together in front of her. "It only makes sense. It's like what I did before I moved back into Grandfather's house so I could be closer to Drew. It is just for protection for Emma and me."

Mac's heart pounded hard and fast. His whole body tightened. What was it about him that caused women to fear him so much they would kill themselves or need legal agreements to protect themselves from him? "You think you need protection from me? Then why would you marry me in the first place?"

"I understand the need to marry, so I'm willing to go through with it. But you have to understand, I'm a wealthy woman. I respect you and what you're doing for me. But the fact is that I know nothing about you except you have a wagon and haul freight. Drew says I...I can trust you."

Mac closed his eyes and leaned his head back. Memories of what Drew told him about what she'd gone through stabbed in his mind. She was afraid, and she had a right to be. It didn't change what he had to do. He blew out his breath, then glanced at Drew and nodded. He would keep his word and marry his sister. "Since you know nothing about me, I came over to discuss a few things. Let you know more about myself."

"That doesn't matter now. What's done is done. As long as you don't have a wife somewhere waiting for you to come home, nothing else matters. We can marry tomorrow."

Her words sent a knife right to his heart. If he had a wife waiting at home right now instead of buried in a pine box six feet under, he wouldn't be standing here making an agreement that went against everything he believed in. Fury at the whole situation exploded inside him. "All right. Write up your papers. I'll sign them, but I want two things included."

"What are they?" Her voice wasn't too steady.

Mac looked her in the eye. "First, I get nothing, absolutely nothing if anything happens to you. Everything you own goes to your brother and child. Second, this marriage will end only if you end it. When I give my word, it is binding. Agreed?"

"Before I agree, there is one more point I want to include." Fire flashed in her eyes as she stared back at him. "This will be a marriage in name only. You may live here to keep up appearances, but you'll have a separate bedroom, across the hall. And at no time will you enter my bedroom."

"You need not worry about that, ma'am." Mac turned to the lawyer. "You got all of that?"

Mr. Carlyle nodded.

Mac nodded back. "Good. Have the papers ready to sign first thing in the morning. I'll be by your office. Have two, no, three people there to witness it." He picked up his hat. "I'll be back here tomorrow in time for the ceremony. Good day."

He slammed the door behind him, fearing a new nightmare had just begun.

Late the next afternoon, sitting on the side of her bed, Sarah fingered the heavy gray silk of the dress she wore. Her wedding dress. She swallowed back a sob. How had this come to be? Oh, she knew the facts. She understood the reasons Mac gave for the need of this wedding were true and sound. She would give him that, but that was all she would give.

She was the one responsible for Drew being in this place and under Stanley's thumb. Grandfather wanted her out of Boston, and the best way to do that was to send Drew away, knowing that she would go with him. There was no way she would leave Central City, leave her brother here on his own. She loved her brother, but she had no illusions about him. The boy she had raised until he was ten had been taken over by a monster who tried to bully and squash everything good and strong out of him. Then tried to make Drew a version of the most feared and hated businessman of Boston.

Others saw him as weak, and he was. But she hoped that given time away from their grandfather, he would find the path that would make him into the man their father would want him to be. But if she stayed, she would put his reputation in ruin, too, and Grandfather might recall Drew to Boston, since no one would want to do business with him, other than the foul business of men wanting to spend the night with his unmarried sister.

No, she had to go through with the wedding. The one saving grace in the whole matter was that Mac agreed it would be a marriage in name only. The papers had been signed that morning in Mr. Carlyle's office.

She opened the box beside her on the bed and picked up one of the items she had bought the day before. A small but deadly pistol, bigger than the derringer she always carried in her pocket. This one she would keep under her pillow or carry in her reticule when she went out. Never again would a man beat her. Never again would a man use her against her will. No, never again because he would die, or she would. And she planned to live to a very old age and bounce her great-grandchildren on her knee.

Someone knocked on her door. She slid the gun under the skirt of her dress. "Yes."

"Ma'am, your brother said to tell you the parson's arrived." Sally, the new maid who also helped with Emma, spoke through the wooden door.

Sarah shuddered as she slipped the gun into the drawer of the table beside her bed. Her feet dragged across the woven rug as she moved to the door. A prisoner preparing for the last long walk to the gallows. A morbid chuckle threatened to escape her dry lips. Taking a deep breath, she opened the door. "I'm ready."

A few moments later, Sarah entered the front parlor. Helen had worked hard to give it a festive air. Bowls of potpourri and vases of flowers graced the small tables that sat around the room. She would thank Helen later, but none of it really mattered. The legal act would be done, her protection and her brother's reputation ensured, giving her, Emma, and Drew what they needed. That was all—nothing more.

Mac paced the floor in the parlor. What kind of fool was he? How could he marry another woman when he didn't know what he'd done to make Lizzie do what she did? And what about his girls? He should leave this woman, this house, and this town and go home to his girls. But how could he do that before he found out what caused his wife to put that rope around her neck?

His gut twisted. None of this made sense. He shouldn't be here. He should be out looking for his brother-in-law. His girls needed their father home and soon.

The rustling of Mrs. Greer's dress reached Mac's ears before the woman entered the room. His heart pounded. Something slammed into his gut.

Mrs. Greer came toward him as a woman, not a shy girl like his Lizzie had been on their wedding day. No, the woman before him was a woman who had faced some of life's harshest realities and survived them. A woman who had the same queenly bearing as his grandmother, although Granny came from long lines of Scottish nobility.

His hands shook so he shoved them in his trousers' pockets, then turned and stepped to the preacher.

Sarah nodded just the tiniest bit, took a deep breath, and walked toward him. Alone. She had refused her brother's offer of giving her away. Not that he'd have been able to walk with her on that injured leg.

Mac bit the inside of his lip to keep from grinning as he recalled the words from the day before when she told her brother she wasn't something to be bartered, sold, or given away. She was doing this of her own free will, and as such she would walk alone.

He didn't love the woman. He wasn't even sure he liked her, but he did admire her. Not many women could survive what she had and face life with the bravery and strength she did. She would have made a fine MacPherson.

As she joined him, they turned and faced the preacher together.

Mac let the words about the wonders and blessings of marriage flow past him. He had heard the words before. They had no meaning now. They were only meant to secure protection for this woman. Somehow that thought seemed a bit hollow as he struggled to keep his eyes on the preacher and not on the woman beside him.

Sarah pressed the forefinger and the thumb of her left hand tightly together as she and Mac were asked to join hands. She could do this. A few words more and it would be over.

"Do you, Thornton MacPherson, take this woman, Sarah Rose Hollingsworth Greer, as your lawfully wedded wife?" The white-haired minister's voice rang out like a teacher asking a class to recite their lessons.

Thorn? His name was Thorn? She quickly raised her head and stared at the man she was marrying.

His eyes held a humorous glint in their depths. "Aye, I'll take Miss Rose for my wife."

The preacher harrumphed at the answer before he turned to Sarah. "Do you, Sarah Rose Hollingsworth Greer, take Thornton MacPherson as your lawfully wedded husband?

Sarah couldn't help it when her response slipped out of her lips. "Yes, Miss Rose takes Mr. Thorn as her husband."

The old man made that sound again.

Sarah felt her muscles relax. The vows were exchanged. It was done.

Then the preacher told Mac he could kiss her. Her finger and thumb tightened against each other again. She had forgotten the kiss. With a slight turn of her head, she glanced at the people watching them. She had gotten through the ceremony. Surely she could get through a peck on the cheek.

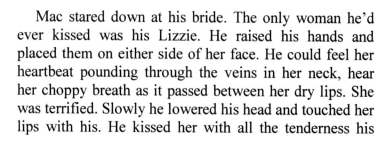

Mac stared down at his bride. The only woman he'd ever kissed was his Lizzie. He raised his hands and placed them on either side of her face. He could feel her heartbeat pounding through the veins in her neck, hear her choppy breath as it passed between her dry lips. She was terrified. Slowly he lowered his head and touched her lips with his. He kissed her with all the tenderness his granny had instilled in him, all the honor a man can give a woman who has just put her life into his hands. The moment was brief. The moment lasted a second less than eternity. And he pulled back.

Sarah touched her lips, her eyes shining in wonder.

"What's the matter?" Mac kept his voice low as he stared down at his new bride.

"I've been kissed in violence and drunkenness and lust." Her lips tipped up into the first smile he had seen since he had told her they had to get married. Her voice came out soft as a sigh on a summer's eve. "But I've never been kissed with gentleness. Thank you."

Her silky pale throat moved with a rolling motion as she swallowed. She ducked her head and turned to those watching them.

At that moment, against all he had planned for the rest of his life, Mac vowed to do everything in his power to ensure that no one ever hurt this lady again. But then the angry voice that had haunted him since he found his wife's body echoed in his mind. *Aye, but can you keep her from the harm you will do to her?*

"Thank you for doing this today." Sarah led the preacher to the front door and opened it.

"Happy to do it. I hope to see you and your family in services. Miss Helen has said such kind things about you and your brother."

Uneasiness rolled around Sarah's middle at his words, both from the idea of attending a church service again and the idea of Helen talking about her. "Thank you. We're still a little unsettled right now, with my brother's accident and all."

"Of course, I understand, but you always have an invitation to join us." The preacher stepped onto the porch, then set his hat on his head. "May God bless your marriage and your family."

After he left, Sarah closed the door and leaned back against it. Her marriage. She hadn't wanted it, and now she had to figure out how to live in it. Bands of nervousness—no, fear— around her chest tightened. She eased away from the door and rubbed her fingers over the derringer resting in the pocket of her wedding dress. As long as Thorn kept his distance from this Rose, everything would be all right.

Helen came down the hall from the kitchen where she was cleaning up after the cake and punch she had insisted on making then serving. She carried a droopy-eyed Emma in her arms. "I think this little miss will be wanting her momma before she falls asleep for the night."

Sarah reached for her daughter but couldn't help but notice the look of sadness in Helen's face as she looked into the parlor.

"I think your brother needs you." Helen set Emma in Sarah's arms, then rushed back down the hall.

Sarah looked over her shoulder.

Drew sat there, alone, with his broken leg propped up on a chair. His head was bowed and his shoulders slumped. His hands were balled up on his legs.

"Drew?" She slipped in and sat on a nearby chair. "What's wrong?"

He lifted his head and looked at her.

She shuddered at the look of despair that filled his face.

His eyes flickered to the hall, then down again. His voice dropped low. "I love Helen, but I'm not good enough for her, not after dealing with Grandfather and Stanley all these years. I've got to get away from them. Make my own way. Try to be the man Helen could love." He thudded his fist against his good leg. "But how? I'm just some silly, pampered, brok...broken creature."

Sarah's heart ached. She was thankful Drew wanted to break with Grandfather at last, but she hated to see the pain he was going through. She wasn't sure what to say to ease that pain. "Drew—"

She stopped when a hand came to rest on her shoulder. Her head jerked sideways. Thorn stood next to her chair. She hadn't heard him come into the room. How much of her brother's shattering confession had he heard?

He bent down close to her ear. "Let me talk to him."

Thorn's words were softer than a whisper, but she shook her head hard.

With his head still close, he added, "Please. He doesn't need sympathy."

Anger raged in her heart at his words, then her mind took over. He was right. She would try to ease his pain, and maybe that wasn't what her brother needed right now. If he left Grandfather, Drew would need a strong man to help him, to guide him. As much as she didn't want to be Thorn's wife, the man was strong and willing to help her brother.

She nodded, stood, and walked out of the room with Emma in her arms. In the hall, she looked over her shoulder. Her new husband took her seat and leaned toward her brother. She watched as they talked, but they kept their voices low, and she couldn't hear what they were saying.

Sarah nibbled on her lips on her way upstairs, hoping, maybe even praying just a tiny bit, that she had made the right decision to trust Thorn with Drew.

Stanley smashed his fist against the top of his desk. "What do you mean, Sarah Greer married that freighter?" He paced his office, then stopped and stared at Waller as the witless man cringed. If only Waller had followed instructions and waited to make sure who had entered Sarah's house that night. If only Cyn hadn't gotten sick from that food at the hotel. If only…

"What do you want me to do?" Waller kept rolling the brim of his dirty hat with his dirty fingers.

"Get out and stay out of my sight until I send for you. Are you still at Grayson's place?"

"Yup. With the Widder Grayson dead, Jim's letting me stay with him and his kid."

Stupid thugs, worthless creatures. Stanley swiped at the air, trying to blow away all that useless information. "Fine, just leave and don't come around unless I send for you. I don't want anyone to connect us." Stanley sent the man another hard stare. "Understand?"

"Yes, sir. I'll get out now."

Stanley dropped back into his chair behind his desk. Now he needed to figure out how to make Sarah a widow again, so he could marry her and get all that money she was hoarding.

The morning light hadn't begun to seep through the curtains when Sarah struggled to get out of the tangled bed linens. Memories of her first wedding night had haunted her dreams during the long night.

She untied the ribbon that held her braid together and let her hair fall around her shoulders and down her back. This wedding night she had been alone, and that was the way she wanted it. Her fingers dropped to her lips as the memory of Thorn's kiss made them tingle.

She slapped her hand down on the bed. No. She wouldn't even think about that. Still, she felt ready to see what the day had to offer. She lit two of the lamps in her room and laid out one of the new dresses she had recently bought from a dressmaker on Main Street. It was a lovely shade of rose. Maybe she would be like the other women around here and not wear her corset and crinoline. A shiver ran through her as she wrapped her arms across the top of her thin white nightgown. A small giggle slipped past her lips. No, she wasn't quite that brave yet.

While she gathered her underthings from the chest of drawers, she heard a strange sound coming from the nursery.

She dropped her things on the bed, then hurried across the room and opened the connecting door to the nursery. A low humming filled the darkened room.

Mac had planned to be out of the house before Sarah Rose got up, but now he was comforting the babe whose tiny whimpers had called to him as he left his room. He paced the nursery trying to soothe the wee one while thoughts of his own girls, laughing and teasing each other, hopped around in his head. How many times had he sat with one of his own, while Lizzie got some much needed rest after tending to one of their bairns, dealing with a fever or teething?

He kept pacing, but his mind was tearing apart. He needed to keep up the search for his brother-in-law, but his girls needed him to be home with them and stay there. But if he got the girls from his sister and grandparents, would he do to them what he did to Lizzie—whatever that was? And then there was Sarah Rose. She'd be safer at the ranch, but he knew she wouldn't leave her brother. He hoped the talk he'd had with Drew the night before helped the young man.

Still, Sarah Rose stayed in his thoughts. Would his name be enough to protect her? From some, maybe. He was respected and liked by both the miners and the townspeople. But a good reputation wouldn't be enough to put off Snodgrass.

The best part of this whole mess was that Sarah Rose's reputation was restored so that uncle wouldn't get his hands on Emma. He was thankful that he'd thought to ride over to Mountain City to talk to the judge and be sure of that before the wedding. He had also talked to a friend about watching the house until he came back and could make other arrangements to keep Sarah Rose and Emma safe.

The door that connected this room to the next opened. He couldn't take his eyes off the woman in the open doorway. The lamplight glowed behind her like sunshine. Her dark hair hung down to her waist. The sweet rose fragrance she wore floated on the early morning air from her room. His jaw tightened as he struggled to keep his hand from tightening on the child.

Two thoughts battled in his mind. What had he gotten himself into? But that thought was pushed aside by the second. Sarah had no idea she looked like every man's dream in her white nightgown.

Taking a deep breath, he turned and laid Emma back in her crib. He had to get out of this room. Now.

He made it to the door before he felt her hand on his shoulder.

"Wait."

He stopped, but didn't dare look at her. "What?"

"How is Drew?"

Mac gripped the doorknob until his fingers ached. "He's trying to find his way. Don't coddle him. He's struggling to see where his path leads, and only he can determine that."

"But—"

He had to leave now or he was going to take her in his arms. "The wee bairn was whimpering a mite. She's cutting a tooth." He couldn't help that his voice came out harsh, but he couldn't stay in the room another moment. "I have to check on my wagon and mules. I'll be pulling out early tomorrow morning."

Boots thumping, he raced across the hall to his room. At least he had his job, which would take him out of town. There wouldn't be many mornings like this. He hoped.

Sarah dressed for the day and went downstairs. She stood at the entrance of the kitchen, holding Emma on her hip. Thorn sat at the kitchen table, a cup in his hand. A wide smile spread across his face as he listened to Helen and Carl prattle on about something. Why didn't he smile like that at her?

She closed her eyes and touched her lips with her free hand. It was the kiss, that silly kiss yesterday. A long-forgotten memory floated back to her mind, watching her mother touching her lips after her father kissed her before he left to minister to one of his flock. Now she knew how her mother felt.

Emma whimpered. Sarah opened her eyes. Heat stung her cheeks. Thorn and Helen were staring at her. Helen's eyes sparkled. She grinned and gave a slight nod, as if she knew what had been going through Sarah's mind.

Thorn frowned at her. But when she said nothing, he raised his cup and took a long drink.

So be it. Sarah entered the kitchen. "Morning, Helen, Carl. Morning again, Thorn."

He sputtered.

Good. At least he didn't have the upper hand.

Helen took Emma from Sarah's arms, then looked from Thorn to Sarah and back again. Shaking her head, she mumbled to the baby, grabbed the bottle, and fed her.

"And a good morning to you, Rose MacPherson." Mac stared at her, one eyebrow raised as if daring her to say something. He picked up the coffee pot from the table and poured some into a cup, then nudged it toward her. "For you, Sarah Rose."

She grabbed the cup. "The name's Sarah, or Mrs. Gr— uh, Mrs. Mac—" Even to her own ears that sounded silly. She didn't expect her husband, even if it was in name only, to call her Mrs. MacPherson, especially if she called him by his first name.

"Nay." His head shook. "I can't be calling you Mrs. Mac, and since yesterday, I've been thinking of you as a sweet Scottish rose."

He grabbed his hat and walked out the door.

Sarah dropped into one of the chairs by the table, her hands trembling. The coffee sloshed and dribbled over the side of the cup. She set it down, then rubbed her temples with her fingertips. Why did this man disturb her so? Why had she let him have that power? It had to stop. No man would ever have any power over her again.

"Give it time. Everything will work out as it should be." Helen's voice drifted across the table, comforting and soothing. "Just wait and see."

Sarah hadn't felt that comfort since her mother died. Her heart craved it. Her spirit drank from it. She wanted more.

Dropping her hands onto her lap, Sarah looked at Helen. "No matter what else has happened since I've come here, I'm so happy you're here with us now."

Helen blushed. "I was thinking that same thing this morning and thanking God that He brought me to this time and place." She handed Emma back to Sarah. Her cheeks grew pinker. "I think your brother will be about ready for his breakfast. Carl, please come with me."

She loaded a tray and left the kitchen with her young brother following.

Sarah's stomach soured. Breakfast no longer held any appeal. Just the mention of God's care had brought back memories she didn't want to face. Memories of her first husband's ridicule of her faith, then the beatings when she dared to read her Bible or refused to join him in vulgar acts, and finally being ignored by God when she cried out and begged for the lives of her unborn children. No, she didn't want to think about such a God.

Dragging herself up from the table, she took her precious daughter and left the kitchen. It was time to take back some of the power that had been taken from her.

With the new nanny, Sally, tending to Emma and the daily maid, Judith, there to check on Drew, Sarah and Helen headed to the mercantile. Carl tagged along, carrying the shopping basket. It was the first time Sarah had gone out since the morning after Mac...when all this started. But she wasn't afraid. She was tired of staying in the house and tired of people telling her what to do. She was even beginning to wonder if what Thorn had said was true.

Aside from those drunken fools who'd accosted her on the way to the doctor's office that morning, no one had treated her any differently than before the night Thorn had stayed in her house. Had she really needed to get married? What if Mac only wanted her body or her money? But that couldn't be true, since he'd signed that agreement and had no rights to either.

Helen approached the counter and placed the order for the groceries they needed while Sarah wandered around the store looking for something for Drew. The poor boy was trying to make the best of being confined to the parlor sofa. Maybe he would enjoy a new book.

Don't coddle him. That's what Thorn had said. Still, it wouldn't be coddling if she bought a book. They both liked to read.

She hadn't taken three steps when Stanley and his sister entered the mercantile. Sarah stepped back so the bookshelf partially hid her.

Cynthia held onto Stanley's arm. "When we finish here, can we go to the milliner's shop? They have the most beautiful hat there. I need it so much."

"Of course." Stanley chuckled. "Anything you need so much, sis, we will have to get for you."

"Thank you." Cynthia grinned. "And maybe we could stop at that new seamstress in town. I heard she makes the newest fashions from *Godey's.*"

He patted her hand. "Whatever you want."

Sarah stood as still as she could until the two moved further into the store, then she caught Helen's attention and motioned toward Stanley and his sister, then the front door. Helen nodded her understanding.

Sarah slipped out the door, intending to stay close. As she closed the door, she saw four or five miners in front of her. Covered in dirt and smelling like they hadn't bathed in weeks, they shuffled a bit. All at once bumping into Stanley in the store didn't seem so bad.

She tried to slip back into the mercantile, but found herself surrounded by a circle of stinking, hungry wolves, only she didn't think they were after food. The look in their eyes and the licking of their lips between their droopy, dirty mustaches and their ragged, nasty beards shouted what they wanted.

"Well, if it ain't the uppity girl. The one with the new place in town."

"Heard she only likes to entertain after dark."

"Maybe she'll give us a taste of what she serves up at night."

They shifted, moving closer, forcing her to move several feet down the sidewalk to keep from being pressed against them. They made vulgar comments as they rubbed their hands along their filthy trousers. How many more steps before she passed the corner of the store and into the alley beside it? She had to get away.

A scream born of fear, fed by past pain and bruising fists, clawed up her throat. Her lips opened. Before her throat gave birth to the blood-curdling cry that was begging for life, a hand clamped on her shoulder.

"You're safe, Rose." Thorn held a pistol, cocked and ready to fire.

The men stopped and stared.

"One warning. That's all you men get. This is my wife, and if I see any of you so much as looking at her again, much less saying what you just did, you won't live to see the sun go down." Eyes narrowed, Thorn pointed his gun and glared at each man.

The men backed up, dropping their eyes and muttering.

"Didn't know she was yours."

"Word around town is she's just 'nother soiled dove."

"Didn't mean no offense."

As the miners scattered, Mac grabbed her and urged her to the side of the mercantile. He pulled her to his heaving chest.

She went willingly since her legs wouldn't hold her. The shaking wouldn't stop, nor would the tears. What those men had planned to do…No, it was too horrible to think about.

Thorn slid his gun in his holster. His narrowed eyes glared at her. His jaw tightened. "How could you even think to come shopping by yourself?"

Sarah felt each word as if it were the jab of a knife, but she stiffened her spine and stared right back at him. "I'm not that foolish. Helen and Carl are inside the mercantile." She took a small breath. "Besides, I thought our marriage would protect me from…from that."

"In Boston, it might have. From what I gathered from Drew, your grandfather's name protected you from everyone but your husband." Thorn pulled his hat from his head with one hand and ran the other through his hair. "But Rose, things are different out here. You've got to remember there's over five hundred men living in this town and more than six hundred in Mountain City. Who knows how many hundreds of miners, gamblers, and no-accounts living up in these hills and come into town all the time. There's less than two hundred women between the two towns, and not all of those are the decent type."

Thorn's face tightened as pain filled his eyes. He slapped his hand against his denim-clad thigh. "You've got a little girl who's counting on you to care for her.

You've got to be careful when you go out, very careful. It's more than your reputation you've got to protect."

Sarah nodded. She couldn't take her eyes off his face. What caused such pain? What had he lost? Who had he lost?

She was raising her hand to touch his cheek when a young man raced up to them. "Mrs. Greer, Mrs. Greer, I got a letter for you. It's marked 'urgent'."

Thorn shifted and put himself between her and the young man. "It's Mrs. MacPherson now."

The young man nodded and swallowed a couple of times as he stared at Thorn's hand resting on his gun. "Sorry, sir, ma'am, uh, Mrs. MacPherson, but Pa said to get this to you right quick."

"Thanks." Thorn flipped him a coin, and the young man backed away, then turned and ran across the dusty street.

Sarah glanced at the cursive writing on the envelope before she slid her finger under the flap and opened the letter. What would be so important that her lawyer in Denver had sent her a letter with *urgent* spread across the front of the envelope with such a bold hand? Why hadn't he just contacted his partner, Mr. Carlyle, here in Central City and let him handle it?

The letter gave no answers, just an imperative request that she come to Denver, as there was a crucial matter that he needed to discuss with her in person, as soon as possible. She crushed the letter in her fist. Whatever it was, it had to have something to do with Grandfather or Stanley. Their power, their greed reached far. What were the two of them up to now, and how would it affect Drew?

CHAPTER TEN

Mac watched Rose crush the envelope in her gloved fist. Who had sent the letter, and what did they want? Whatever it was, he needed to find out quickly. The other teamsters were planning to pull out in the morning for Denver, and he needed a new load if he was going to continue to search for his brother-in-law.

"Thorn, I need a ticket for tomorrow's stagecoach to Denver." Rose tapped the crumbled envelope against her open palm.

"You can't get one. The—"

"Don't start telling me what I can do." She dropped her voice. "Remember, this is a marriage in name only."

He tightened his fists and rested them on his hips. *Give me patience.* "What I was going to say was you can't get one for tomorrow because the coach's been damaged. Some drunken traveling salesman left a lit cigar on the floor when he got out. It'll be two or three days before it's ready to use."

Rose's cheeks took on the color of a pink rose. "Oh, I'm sorry. I just thought—I mean I didn't –I—" She sighed. "I need to see my lawyer as soon as possible."

Mac's chest tightened. "You don't mean to try and undo the marriage right away. That doesn't make sense."

She swiped her hand in the air in front of her. "This has nothing to do with that. My lawyer needs to see me." A breeze swept past them and made the loose hair around her face dance a little. She held up the letter. "It has to be something important for him to send a letter like this."

Even as the words formed in his head, Mac knew it wasn't a good idea, but it was all he could come up with as the lines of pain and fear gathered on her face. "Early tomorrow morning, several of us teamsters are heading to Denver for supplies. I have a standing order from the mercantile to haul freight for them. I can take you, if you want to come with me. But let me warn you, it'll be a hard trip." He was a fool to invite her. "Still, it'll get you to Denver quicker than waiting for the stagecoach to get fixed."

Emotions raced across her face almost too fast for Mac to keep up with them—denial, fear, hope, and finally, acceptance. "That sounds good. Thank you. I'll need to return home and get ready."

Just then, Helen and Carl stepped out of the mercantile. Mac helped them into the buggy.

As they left, Mac wanted to find a tree and pound his head against it until he beat some good sense into it. How was he going to get through this trip with her by his side? Why had he thought giving her his name would protect her? Waller was still spreading rumors about her, and Snodgrass, too, if his guess was right.

The pouch with Lizzie's note rubbed against his chest. He shook his head. The past pulled him back. The future jerked him forward. And his little girls needed their da right now. But he needed to protect Sarah Rose and Emma.

His feet pounded along the dusty road as he left to prepare his wagon and check on his mules for the trip. This was going to be one long trip with Sarah Rose sitting by his side for four days.

Sarah sat at the kitchen table the next morning, her body already tired and the day hardly begun. All night long she had tossed in bed, tangling herself in the sheets. And that was after she'd spent the evening arguing with her brother about the trip. At last, everything was set. During the day, Sally would take care of Emma while Helen took care of the house and kept an eye on Drew. At night, when Sally went to her own home, Emma would stay with Helen in her room near the kitchen.

Sarah didn't plan to be gone but a few days, but oh, how she was going to miss her little girl. Her arms already felt strange not to be holding her child. She couldn't help but smile as she thought of Emma. She was the only good thing that came out of her first marriage, disastrous as it was. For she knew with all certainty that if Alfred had lived, he would never have let her adopt the baby.

"More?" Helen held out the coffeepot.

Sarah shook her head. "I'd better not. I've had two cups already."

Helen nodded. "I'm glad you took my advice and aren't wearing that corset and crinoline. You'll be so much more comfortable, even if you are sitting on a piece of wood."

"I know you're right, but I feel so—so undressed." Sarah crossed her arms over her chest.

"Don't worry about that. Your modesty's fully intact." Helen continued to fill the large basket at the far end of the table. "I've packed biscuits and ham for later this morning. There's sandwiches, pickles, and an apple pie for lunch. Mac said you'd be staying at a place along the way that serves meals, so I didn't make anything for supper or breakfast tomorrow. I did pack three pans of cinnamon rolls and some cookies along with some cheese and bread for the second day, to get you through until you hit Denver."

"Three pans of rolls?" Sarah could feel her waist growing just thinking of all that food.

Helen giggled. "You don't know the reputation of my cinnamon rolls. The other teamsters always ask for a couple of pans before they leave."

Memories of when she first came to Central City flooded Sarah's mind—something about Helen making cinnamon rolls for her aunt at the restaurant and her wanting to have a bakery. In the weeks that had passed, Sarah had forgotten her promise to help her friend learn what she needed to set up her own business. "I'm sorry I haven't helped you like I said I would—with your business—I mean."

Helen waved her hand in front of her. "But you have. You've taught me how to keep the housekeeping books, and from that I've learned how to keep records for my baking business."

The woman blushed. "Sometimes when I've had a problem or question, Drew—I mean Mr. Hollingsworth—helped me out."

Helen brought a small plate with a cinnamon roll on it and set it in front of Sarah. "And because I don't have to work from early morning to late at night like I did for my aunt, I've had more time to bake." She glowed with pride. "I already have a long list of miners that I bake for each week, and I've been saving for the time I can have a place of my own and bake all day."

Before Sarah could respond, boot thumping and childish giggles filled the back stairs. Moments later, Thorn entered the room, Emma in his arms.

With all the looks of a proud father, he presented the child to them. "Emma has her first tooth. And the second isn't far behind."

Happy as she was that her daughter was no longer in pain from the tooth trying to emerge, Sarah couldn't understand why a man without a family would know so much about babies and take such pride in the little things they did. Where had this man come from, and what was his past like? She tapped her finger against her chin.

Maybe this trip would be a good time to start learning some of those things. After all, she was legally tied to him, and these were things that might affect her daughter.

As the hot sun climbed higher in the sky, Mac's neck and back ached, but not from the pull of the mules' reins against his arms. He was used to that. No, it was trying to balance what he was saying to Rose against what he wasn't saying. Guilt and uncertainty ate at his insides.

He hadn't thought through this marriage. True, his name had given her what she needed to save her and her brother's reputations and insure there was no problem with Emma. Or he had thought so until those miners the day before.

But what about the future? What about Emma? That baby was weaving her way into his heart, just like his girls had. And what about his girls? He couldn't ask his sister and grandparents to care for them forever.

After he got his answers, he'd go home. But what about Rose and Emma? Would they come with him? Could they be a family? Did he want them to be part of his family? Stupid question. They were part of his family. When a MacPherson makes a vow, he keeps it. So unless, Rose annulled the marriage, it was forever. Where would that lead?

Sarah gripped the wooden seat on the wagon as they bumped along the dusty trail. The other freighters allowed them to go first so they weren't getting as dirty as the ones behind. She was thankful for that small favor. Throughout the morning, she had tried to be friendly with Thorn, who was truly living up to his name—sharp and prickly. Every time she tried to pull him into conversation, he gave short, pointed answers.

Well, she would try one more time. "You have never said, but where does your family live?"

"I thought you didn't want to know anything about my past." Thorn kept his eyes forward.

A wave of guilt ran through her as she remembered Thorn offering to tell her about his past the day before they married. Heat, which wasn't from the sun shining down on them, flooded her face. "I'm sorry. Can we start over?"

Thorn stared at her for a moment or two, then gave a sharp nod. "They've moved around a bit—New York, Pennsylvania, eastern Kansas Territory, then south of here before the gold rush began. It was much calmer in those days. Not anywhere near as many people. You could ride your horse for days at a time and not see another white man."

His family lived nearby? "Your family, where do they live exactly?"

"We're spread across the country from New York to, well since I'm here, I guess to here. Speaking of family, your brother did mighty fine dealing with the miners when he was with me."

Sarah was glad to hear that about Drew, but she wanted to know more about Thorn. "I'm happy to hear that, but what about your family, your parents, brothers, sisters?"

"Parents died from fever before we moved west."

"Oh, I'm sorry. I know what it feels like to lose your parents. I wish they could have known Emma. They would have loved her so much."

Thorn nodded. "Yeah, mine never got to see my gi—" Some kind of furry animal raced across the road and startled the mules. He gripped the reins tighter and called out to the mules. They settled. He snapped the reins again, they continued on as if nothing happened.

Sarah stared at Thorn. His face had tightened and his jaw clenched. She didn't think it was from something running across the road. It was what he was saying. Did he have a family, another family? "Were you married before?"

His hands tightened on the reins, but he gave a brief nod.

"What happened to her?"

Thorn's lips formed a thin, straight line, at least the part she could see, since he kept his eyes on the backs of the mules. After several seconds, his lips moved, but the answer was no more than a whisper in the air. "She's gone."

Silence mixed with the dust the mules' hooves kicked into the air.

The question pounded in Sarah's head and slipped between her lips. "Do you have any children?"

Thorn gave a sharp nod. "Three girls."

"Where are they?"

"With their great-grandparents."

Before she could ask another question, something pushed against her arm. She shifted to let the dog stick his head between them. Thorn took a deep breath.

"Feeling a bit lonely back there, Tair boy?" Thorn, his face relaxing a bit, shifted the reins and held them all in one hand. With his now free hand, he ruffled the fur on the dog's neck.

Sarah couldn't hold back a giggle when the dog let out a long sigh.

Thorn chuckled. "Tair's used to sitting up here with me. I think he's feeling a little out of place."

"Why do you call him that?"

"Actually, his name's Bhatair, Warrior, which is what I thought of the way he fought until he ran out of strength when those boys were beating him. A Scottish warrior, still valiant in defeat." Thorn gave the dog a last pat, then shifted the reins and held them in both hands again.

"I knew that was a bit of a brogue I heard when you get worked up about something." Sarah patted the dog's head.

He gave her a look that seemed to ask, *When was he ever worked up?*

Memories of Alfred getting upset with her popped into her thoughts. Time to back away and distract Mac. It had worked sometimes with Alfred.

"Oh, never mind. I love to hear how families got their start in America. Tell me about yours."

He seemed to relax a bit against the back of the wagon seat like someone settling down for a cozy after-dinner chat. "Angus MacPherson was the fifth son of a mighty Scottish laird, and as such never had hopes of ruling the clan, especially since his older brothers all had sons of their own. He had another problem. Young Angus was in love with a pretty lass by the name of Mary Campbell, the daughter of a wealthy and powerful man who had already arranged a marriage for the lass, as he had for her older sister."

"Did Mary love the other man?" Sarah's stomach tightened.

"Nay, he was older, and the agreement had been made when she was just a wee thing."

Sarah drew her hand back from the dog's head and clenched her fists in her lap. She knew where this story was going, what would happen to the poor, helpless girl, what she would have faced in a loveless marriage. "Was she happy with him—the older man, I mean?"

"They would have been, if they married. He was a kindly man, well-respected and greatly loved by the people in the town." Thorn smiled as he glanced at her. "The thing about the whole matter was that Mary Campbell loved Angus. Even as a young girl, she was headstrong and determined to have her way."

A seed of hope, maybe happiness, sprouted in Sarah. Her fists unclenched. Her stomach eased. "What happened?"

"Angus decided that his future lay far from Scotland, so the laird gave his son his inheritance in gold and the young man set out for the coast to catch a ship to America, where he planned to make his fortune. When Mary heard about that, she took her jewels, her father's best steed, and her mother's wedding veil, then set out after him, dressed as a boy." His grin grew wider. "When she presented herself to his cabin, he did what any good MacPherson would do. He married the girl with the ship's captain's approval and a traveling minister's blessing."

The seed had sprouted leaves, and joy of a once-trapped girl finding happiness danced along her veins. "Were they happy together?"

"Aye, they were, with twelve children, eighty-nine grandchildren, and who knows after that."

Sarah couldn't help herself. She turned half-way around and stared at Thorn. "You mean to tell me you have twelve aunts and uncles and eighty-eight cousins?"

He laughed. "No, you have to take my da into account. I've got twenty-two aunts and uncles when you consider the ones that married in, and I've got seven brothers and sisters, so there's only eighty-one cousins."

"Where are they all? I haven't heard of any other MacPhersons around here."

Thorn chuckled. "Well, by the fact that some of my grandparents' children were girls—three to be exact—not all of the cousins are MacPhersons by name. Add to that, with the moving the clan's done over the years, along with some of the aunts and uncles staying when others left, it's not surprising you haven't met any of the cousins. Especially since none of them live in Central City. Well, at least not until recently."

She faced forward again, the number of his family beyond imagination. "My parents were only children, as were my grandparents. I've never had aunts and uncles. Now there's only Drew, Emma, and me."

"Aye, but maybe you will start your own dynasty out here in the west."

"Maybe Drew will, but not me. After we have this marriage annulled, I'll never marry again." Sarah swallowed down a sour feeling. She wasn't sure if the feeling was caused by the idea of an annulment or the knowledge that her body had been so damaged she could never have another child.

Mac felt the punch right to his gut. Annulled. Well, he'd given her that choice when he signed those papers before the wedding. Still. *Annulment.* The word left a bitter taste in his mouth. When he had spoken the vows, he had meant them. And yet they had agreed to a marriage in name only.

He shook his head. Even though he might have been foolish to rush her into marriage without thinking about the future, he could not lie. He did want her. When he let himself, he could still feel the sweetness of her lips on his at the wedding. But her words after were the needle that kept pricking his heart. Memory of her astonishment that a kiss could be neither unkind nor hurtful nearly undid him. He repeated the vow to himself that he made following that kiss. He would never hurt her or stand by and let any other man hurt her.

Mac felt her snatching little glances at him. Was she trying to see how her words had affected him, if he agreed or not? For right now, the best thing he could do was say nothing.

Thankfully, a few minutes later, he got to the place they always stopped for the midday meal. Beside a small stream, he pulled the mules to a halt just as the sun had started its downhill journey. Time to rest the animals and eat some of what Helen packed for them. All morning long, he'd smelled the sweet rose scent the woman beside him wore, even over the smell of the ham and bacon in the basket.

Tair leaped from the wagon and headed to the water. Mac helped Rose down, then pointed to the slight shade cast by the side of the wagon. "If you set out the meal there, we'll have a little shade from the sun."

He noticed her nose had sunburned, even with the sunbonnet Helen had lent her. While she spread out a quilt, he joined the other teamsters as they released the mules from the wagons and led them to the stream.

As the other men sat on the edge of the quilt, they glanced over at him. He knew what they were asking, but he couldn't do it. More often than not, one of the teamsters would ask the blessing on the meal. But on this trip none of them volunteered, and there was no way he could pray, not now. Not until he found out what happened that day at the ranch. Not while his heart was still full of anger, questions, and hatred both for himself and whoever did those horrible things to Lizzie.

He grabbed a sandwich. "Just eat."

The men shrugged and grabbed their food. Without saying anything, Rose joined them.

He had never thought about it before, but Helen always said grace before meals back in Central City. Neither Drew nor Rose took that lead. Even though he wasn't ready to share his past with Rose, he did wonder about hers. He knew about her grandfather, but what about before? Drew had said they'd come to live with their grandfather when she was sixteen, but had they grown up in Boston? She seemed like such a city kind of woman.

When they'd polished off the meal, Rose pulled out the pans of cinnamon rolls and handed them to the men. Their faces lit up like full moons at midnight.

"Thank ye, ma'am. Dearly love Miss Helen's cin'mon rolls."

"Best I ever had. Cain't wait 'til she opens up a bakery of her own."

"Forget the stew and steaks. Just give me them rolls for the rest of my life, and I'll die a happy man."

"Think she's looking to marry up any time soon?"

"Might be, she shore does take a shine to that fancy young man she works for."

Rose giggled at first, but the last remark made her smile. Maybe there was hope if she could see marriage in a good way through Drew and Helen. Maybe there was hope for the future. Maybe.

CHAPTER ELEVEN

Sarah could barely move her aching body when they turned off the main road to Denver and onto another, less traveled one. A rocky mound caught her eye. Behind it stood two trees that had grown entangled and now grew tall and straight together. They traveled a half-hour or so more, then pulled into a small homestead.

Thorn had said they would spend the night there. She tried to swallow her groan as the wagon jerked to a halt. A man in worn clothing came over and welcomed them like old friends, which they probably were, since Thorn said he and some of the freighters made this trip quite often.

After Thorn jumped down from the wagon, he helped Sarah to the ground, then turned and shook hands with the homesteader. "Sarah Rose, this is a good friend, Jason Dunn. He raises some of the finest horses in the territory. Jase, I'd like you to meet my wife."

"My honor to meet you, ma'am. My wife's in there." He pointed toward the wooden house. "Glad to see Mac finally got hitched."

She pulled out the satchel that contained her nightclothes and headed to the main house.

"Just go on in, ma'am. My wife's fixin' supper for you all. She'll be happy to see another woman." With that said, he joined the men to care for the stock.

With the satchel bumping against her leg, Sarah made it to the cabin. She knocked on the door.

"Come on in." A woman's voice rang out.

The door screeched when Sarah opened it. The noise was loud enough to wake the scarecrows in the cornfield, as her mother used to say. Why didn't the owner oil the hinges? As soon as that thought popped into Sarah's head, she realized the value of the alarm. No one was going to sneak in through that door without the woman hearing him. And in the isolation of this homestead, that could be a blessing.

A blonde woman whose swollen middle was the biggest part of her pushed out of a large rocking chair and shuffled from the back of the room. Three young boys trailed behind her. The boys looked to be from two to five years old.

"We're always glad to have Mac and his teamsters stop over, but it's a rare and true blessing when they bring a woman with them." She shooed the boys back to the rocking chair. "There's water and a towel over in that room, if you want to freshen up a bit. Supper'll be ready in just..." The woman stopped and stared. Her mouth dropped open for a moment before she snapped it closed. "Sarah?" She blinked and took a step closer. "Sarah Hollingsworth?"

Something floated around in Sarah's memory. The voice. The sparkling green eyes. Then she saw the necklace hanging around the woman's neck—silver with a small cross. Sarah had had a matching one years ago. Her pa had given her and her best friend each one on the day they were baptized when they were about thirteen. He'd said since they were best friends and now shared the same birthday, they should have something to remind them they were sisters in Christ, especially when they got upset with one another.

Sarah lifted her hand and touched her throat. She had worn her necklace from that day until the time her grandfather had ripped it off her neck, the day she'd told him she wouldn't marry Alfred. Not that her defiance had done her any good. She had never seen the necklace since.

"Melody Hawkins?" After all this time and halfway across the country, Sara couldn't believe it. She'd found her best friend. With arms uplifted and boots thumping the wooden floor, Sarah hurried across the cabin. She was met partway and wrapped in a warm hug that seemed to bridge the years.

"Sarah, I can't believe it's you. Where—how—who— oh, never mind." Melody giggled and started over. "I'm just so happy you're here right this moment." Tears ran down Melody's plump cheeks.

All at once there was the pattering of small feet on the floor. The boys surrounded them.

"Don't cry, Ma."

"Get Pa?"

Someone hit and pushed Sarah's leg. "Don't hurt Mama."

Melody shushed the boys. "It's all right, boys. This is my friend. I haven't seen her for a long, long time. I'm fine, just very, very happy." She gave each of the boys a hug and sent them back to where they had been playing.

"I want to sit and catch up on all the years right now, but the men'll be here in a few minutes, and they'll want something to eat." Melody dried her cheeks with the corner of her apron, straightened, and rubbed the small of her back. "We can visit after I get supper on the table for you and the teamsters. We've already eaten, so why don't you go freshen up?"

Sarah pushed her satchel out of the way. "I'll help. That way we can start visiting right away."

Melody smiled and nodded.

After washing her hands at the pump, Sarah grabbed the knife and the warm bread. She glanced over at Melody, who was stirring the stew.

Sarah turned her attention to the bread. "With three boys already, are you hoping for a girl this time?"

The smile on Melody's face brightened as she rested her hand on her middle. "Well, this one'll be the ninth."

Sarah dropped the knife. "Nine? But I only saw those three little darlings over there. Where are you keeping the rest?"

"The two oldest are out in the barn helping their pa take care of the animals." Her smile dimmed a bit. "Eliza, Katy, and Prudence are all resting up on the hill under a beautiful elm tree surrounded by sweet-smelling wildflowers. Their bodies are, anyway." Her smile grew brighter again. "Their spirits are with Jesus, waiting for the time we'll all be together again."

Sarah stepped over to the stove and wrapped her arms around her friend. "I'm so sorry. I…I know that pain. I lost three precious babes, too. But I never knew if they were boys or girls."

"I'm sorry you had to bear that pain." Melody gave her a hug. Turning back to the stove, she started stirring again. "Do you have any other children?"

Sarah set the sliced bread in a napkin-lined basket. "Oh, yes. I adopted a little girl. She's less than a year old. Her name's Emma."

"That's wonderful. If this one's a girl, maybe they'll grow up to be best friends." Melody ladled the stew into a large serving bowl. "And if it's a boy, maybe they'll have an even closer relationship. Then we would all be one big family."

Sarah enjoyed her friend's giggles, but there was one thing she knew. She would never, ever force her daughter into a marriage just to make others happy.

By the time the men entered the room, food was on the table and the young children had been put to bed in one of the two small rooms off the main room.

While Sarah and the men ate, Melody and her husband sipped coffee and shared the news that had come from

Denver. All through the meal, Sarah snuck peeks at the way Melody and her husband held hands. She wondered what it must be like to live in a marriage like that, where love and friendship was so deep and strong that it was visible to those around them. Her parents had had a relationship like that, and a part of her mourned the fact that she hadn't and never would.

As she swallowed the last bite of buttermilk pie, Sarah caught Thorn staring at her with a questioning look in his eyes.

She ducked her head. Grabbing her plate, she hurried over to the dry sink. She planned to wash the dishes and give Melody a break. As she reached out to lift the bucket of hot water off the stove where it had been heating, rough hands shooed her away.

"Now, Mrs. Mac, I know how my missus has been yearnin' to be jawin' with you. Why don't you ladies go out and sit in the cool night breeze and let me and your big ol' husband tend to this clean-up?" He looked over his shoulder. "O'course, any of you other men who want to help are welcome to stay."

Thorn shrugged and stood. "Won't be the first time I've helped in the kitchen."

The rest of the other teamsters hurried out the door while Thorn stacked the dirty dishes.

Sarah wondered if he'd helped his wife, his first wife, with the dishes. But then she caught something in the corner of her eye that made her yearn for something she never had.

Melody kissed her husband as he rubbed her back, then she whispered something in his ear that made him turn red up to the tips of his ears. He hugged her and whispered something back in her ear. She giggled and swatted his arm before turning back around. She grabbed Sarah's arm. "Let's go while we can."

The two of them hurried outside and settled in a couple of wooden chairs near the front door. Melody was the first to speak. "Mrs. Mac? The last I'd heard you were going to marry that horrible Mr. Greer. After that, I never got another letter, even though I sent you several more. Tell me everything that's happened since the last time we saw each other in Iowa."

Sarah gave a very brief account of her life while she was married to Alfred and how she and Drew came to be in Central City. When she finished, she noticed Melody wiping her eyes with the corner of her apron.

"Oh, Sarah, even with those few words, I could feel the pain you went through. I'm just thankful you had your faith to carry you through that terrible time. And now God has brought you out here, and we'll be able to see each other again." She rubbed her swollen middle. "I'm not sure how often I'll be able to come to Central City to see you, but maybe you'll be able to stay overnight sometimes when Mac goes to Denver to get supplies. Then he could pick you up on the way back."

Sarah held back a sigh. Melody would never be able to understand the extent of the anguish and loss those years of marriage to Alfred Greer had brought her, and she hoped she never would. Some things were just too horrible to share. Best to get the conversation onto another track.

"I'm curious about something, if you don't mind me asking. Eliza was your mother's name, and I'm guessing Katy was your mother-in-law's name, but who did you name your other little girl after?"

Melody giggled. "I wondered if you saw anything special about that name. Actually her name is Prudence Hill Dunn. Jase couldn't understand why I insisted on it until I told him why that name meant so much to me. Remember?"

Memories marched through Sarah's mind—the two of them getting into scrape after scrape and using the name as a code word for help. Knowing if that name was used either verbally or in a note, the other would come and be there for support.

"Of course, I remember. How many times did the teachers get confused when they snatched up a note from one of us signed with Prudence Hill, since there never was anyone in the school with that name?"

"When I saw the face of my third daughter at birth, that name came to me. I felt that she wouldn't be with us long. I prayed and prayed to God." Melody's hands rested over her unborn child. "And God answered my prayer, just not the way I wanted. But He did bless me in letting me see the beauty of that child and the joy she brought to our family. I keep that in my heart." She wiped another tear from her cheek. "And now He has blessed me with another life."

Sarah swallowed back her angry reply. Would she ever be as accepting of what happened to her as her friend?

Melody yawned. "I still haven't heard how you became married to Mac. As far as I've ever heard, he's never been sweet on any woman in the time we've known him."

Sarah decided to leave Melody to her imagination and stood. "I think it is time for you and that little one you're carrying to get some sleep. We can talk some more in the morning."

Melody nodded, and they entered the cabin. "You can have the boys' room. The two oldest are already out in the barn, and the younger ones are asleep in our room." She pointed to the door that was closed as she headed for the open one, where a man's snores could be heard over childish giggles. "I hope you have a good night's sleep."

Sarah smiled at her childhood friend. Nothing had felt as good in a long time as the precious moments they'd shared. The door to Melody's room closed. Sarah turned the door handle and entered the room where she would sleep.

She felt the smile drop from her face. If she looked down, she was sure she would see the broken pieces of it lying on the hard-packed dirt floor. Thorn stood by the bed, his bag sitting by the washstand, his hat on a hook near the window.

She opened her mouth to demand to know why he was in her bedroom.

He pressed his finger against his lips.

"Quiet." He stepped around her and closed the door, his voice lower than a whisper. "I don't mind sleeping in the barn with the boys, but I figured you might not want to explain to your friend about our marriage."

Sarah couldn't move. He was right, but where did that leave them?

"I'll sleep on the floor." Thorn remained by her side, his voice still low.

She couldn't look at him but bowed her head. The dirt floor stared back at her. Her bones ached. If she spent the night on that hard floor, she wouldn't be able to move in the morning. But to share a bed with a man, her legal husband...a shudder ripped through her. She clasped her hand over her mouth.

Thorn moved across the small room and pulled his slicker from his bag. With a flip of the wrist, he spread it out.

Her shoulders relaxed. Thorn wouldn't hurt her or take advantage. "Stop."

The word was a mere wisp of sound, but it rang out in the room and jerked Thorn's head around. His eyebrows raised in question.

"You can't sleep there. It's too hard. We—we'll share the bed."

He left the slicker on the floor and stepped close to her. "I don't mind the floor. I've slept under the stars lots of times. This is no different, except I don't have to worry about rain falling on my head tonight." He touched her cheek. "I'll be fine."

He moved to the door and rested his hand on the doorknob. "Think I'll get a drink of water. Give you a chance to change and get into bed."

He left the room.

Sarah grabbed the slicker and shoved it into his bag. All right, so he was being considerate, and she could be, too. She rushed to change into her nightgown and crawled onto the hay-stuffed cotton tick mattress, then pressed her body against the wall. That way Thorn could get in without having to crawl over her. She left his covers laid back.

Seconds passed as fast as a race between two old— two very old—snails bent on seeing who could come in last.

Sarah's grip on the bedcovers grew tighter and tighter.

She gulped down a cry when the door opened at last. Thorn stepped into the room, then closed the door.

The lamp threw light on his face. His eyebrows pulled together. His eyes moved from the now-bare floor to the empty half of the bed to Sarah.

"I said we could share." She turned and tucked her nose against the wall. "Good night."

Thorn blew out the lamp and sat on the mattress. The rope-hung bed swayed a bit. One boot thudded on the floor.

Sarah's stomach clenched.

The other boot thudded.

She covered her mouth with her hand. Not a word, not a sound would pass. She could do this. They both needed sleep in order to finish the trip tomorrow.

The bed shifted.

She peeked over her shoulder.

He stood and pulled the covers back over the mattress. When he lay back on the mattress it shifted again. He was going to sleep on top of the covers.

She let out the breath she had been holding.

"Sarah Rose, go to sleep. Have sweet dreams. No one's going to bother you tonight."

After shifting a couple times, she finally drifted off to sleep, only to fight an evil king who looked like her grandfather and his cruel knight who had the same face as Alfred. They threw her, the fair damsel, in the cold, dark dungeon with rats and bats and other horrible creatures. She fought them. She tried to outrun them, but they sunk their claws into her and pulled her back. A shining white knight appeared and slew the creatures. He set her on his trusty steed and took her off into the sunshine as he sang a song with a Scottish burr.

CHAPTER TWELVE

Sleep fled when something moved up and down Sarah's arm.

"You need to wake up and get dressed. The men'll be ready to leave in a few minutes."

Sarah opened her eyes.

Melody stood by the bed. "Mac said to let you sleep as long as you could. He said you weren't used to traveling on a hard wagon seat all day." She rested her fist on her hip. "I know what he means. On the few times we've gotten to go to Denver, I couldn't wait to get there. All that bouncing." She walked back to the door. "I'll have breakfast ready when you get dressed, but you need to hurry."

By the time the freighters pulled out thirty minutes later, Sarah felt she had been through a whirlwind. Hurrying to get dressed, rushing through breakfast, hugs and kisses and promises to come visiting again. Yet all the time, something kept nagging at the back of her mind, something just out of reach.

The mules plodded along the dirt road. The sun blazed down on them. She snuck peeks at Thorn, but he didn't notice. If the look on his face were any indication, he was caught in some dark thoughts. Fortunately, Tair kept sticking his big head with those sorrowful eyes between her and Thorn, begging for attention.

So she talked to Tair, teased him, and ruffled the fur between his floppy ears, all the time keeping an eye on Thorn. He spoke once when he pointed out the stage stop a few miles from Melody's place. Sarah still had vague memories of stopping there on the way to Central City several months before. After that, he lapsed back into silence. But bit by bit, the man seemed to work through whatever was bothering him, and by noontime he was in a more talkative mood.

After they ate and let the mules rest a while, they started out again.

"We should get into Denver close to suppertime. Maybe have time for a bath and clean clothes. I've got a place I'd like to take you to eat. Think you'll like it. I always eat there." Thorn snapped the reins.

"Oh, Thorn, I just had an idea. If we have time, I'd like to stop by a bakery or two, maybe a small café, and talk to the owners. See what it costs to get a place up and running."

"You thinking of Helen?"

Excitement bubbled up in Sarah's heart. For a few weeks, she had forgotten her promise to help Helen get a business of her own. But after watching the freighters devour those cinnamon rolls and praise the cook, she knew she needed to do something to help make that dream come true.

While they traveled, Sarah thought about the questions she wanted to ask, then pulled out her pencil and paper to write them down. When the sun drew closer to the tops of the mountains in the west, she realized Thorn hadn't said anything in a long time. She put her pencil and paper back in her reticule and chanced a glance at him.

He wore the same quiet, almost troubled look he'd had when they had started out. Even Tair seemed to sense his distress and rested his head against Thorn's shoulder.

He had helped her out so many times when she was worried or upset. Could she help him now? "Thorn, is something the matter? You look…I don't know exactly what…upset, worried, something."

His grip on the reins tightened, then he let out a deep breath. "I wasn't sure if I should bring it up." He glanced sideways at her. "I was just wondering if you have those nightmares real often. It's been a while since your husband died and all." He turned his head back so he could watch the road.

Where there had been excitement filling her moments before, the bristles came out. How dare he think that what she had endured could be glossed over in a few months? He had no idea what she had gone through. She gripped the wooden seat, ready to tell him to mind his own business.

"The reason I ask is that I knew a woman who'd been hurt really bad." The muscles of Thorn's throat shifted as if he had trouble swallowing. "She was a strong woman. But she didn't want to live after that. There were people who loved her, but that didn't matter." He shrugged as if it didn't matter, but judging from the waves of agony flowing from him, it mattered a great deal. "I'm just trying to understand why she did what she did. We—we found her hanging in the barn."

The bristles melted into a puddle of mush. Tears Sarah wouldn't let fall rolled down inside her. Her lips moved but no words came out. She clenched and unclenched her fists, then wiped her hands on her skirt. This was hard, so hard, to talk to someone about, but for the other woman, for the brutality she had to endure, Sarah had to speak.

"I was only sixteen when I was sold into marriage. I had only seen the stranger once before the day my grandfather told me I had to marry the man." The memory of her fear, her pain, rolled over her. "If I didn't, Grandfather said he would send Drew out on a merchant ship as a crew member, a cabin boy. Drew was only ten, a boy, still reeling from the sudden loss of our parents and being ripped from the only home he had ever known.

Grandfather told me not all the crew survived, and those who did survive always joined their crew members at brothels and bars when they got shore leave."

She struck her right fist against her left palm. "Silly, naïve fool that I was then, I believed him. After all, he was my grandfather, even if he treated me horribly. Also, I didn't know that he wanted someone to carry on his name and the banking empire he'd built. All as a monument to the great man that he thought he was. I know now he would never, ever have carried out that threat, but at the time I didn't..." She shrugged. "All I knew was that I couldn't let my little brother face that kind of life."

Even to her own ears, her voice had grown harsh and hate-filled. She pulled away when Thorn's hand rested on hers.

"Rose, ye needn't go on if it's too painful."

She stared at the only man other than Drew who had shown her any kindness in more years than she could remember. For that, for him, she would do what she could to help. And in some way, it was helping her. Some of the stone around her heart chipped away with the words. The tomb where her heart lay, shriveled and cold—at least as far as men were concerned—didn't seem so black anymore.

With a twist of her hand, her palm nestled against his. She gave his hand a short squeeze, then withdrew it and shifted on the seat.

He nodded and gripped the reins with both hands.

"What I was trying to say is that I was young, ignorant of the world, and had been protected by my parents until their deaths. Suddenly I found myself married to a rich man who wanted a young woman, a brood mare, to give him a son to replace the rebellious one he had."

A bitter laugh burst from her lips. "The irony was that my husband also was a drunkard and abusive when he drank. And in those drunken rages, he killed my three unborn children."

She realized she'd leaned forward and wrapped her arms around her middle, as if she were trying to roll up into a ball. Pulling her shoulders back, she sat straighter. "What I am trying to tell you is that I wasn't strong like the woman you knew. I—I lost all hope. I didn't die, even after his beatings. I didn't die, so I survived. I just survived for years and years until the day an angry woman fed poisoned eggs to my husband for forcing himself on her innocent daughter, then denouncing her and their child."

A single tear rolled down her cheek, but she blinked time and again to keep the rest at bay. "So you see, I don't know if I can help you understand how a strong woman couldn't deal with a brutal attack. I wasn't strong. I just survived. For thirteen years, I barely survived."

Thorn sat silent for long minutes. His jaw grew tighter and tighter. At last, he took a deep, deep breath and let it out in a gust. "Sarah Rose, you are the strongest woman I've ever met. And for as long as we're married, I'm proud to call you my wife. I'm proud of the woman you are."

Now she couldn't stop the tears. She shifted so Thorn couldn't see her wipe them from her eyes. Since she was sixteen, the men in her life had called her vile and demeaning names, had used and abused her, had counted her as having less worth than the cur dogs that nobody wanted.

Nobody had ever said they were proud of her. The tomb where her heart lay opened to the light of his words.

Mac couldn't think of anything else to say to his Rose. He hadn't realized her torment had gone on for so long. How had she survived it and come out as loving as she was? He had seen her with Emma, how protective she was of Drew, how kindly she dealt with Helen.

He didn't know where his search for his brother-in-law would lead him, but he would always be thankful he had met Rose.

Sarah Rose fell asleep against his shoulder like she had the day before, and the rest of the trip passed in relative silence. And for that he was thankful. His mind was full of things he couldn't talk about to her.

Two years ago, he thought he had everything a man could want. A loving wife, three beautiful daughters, family nearby, the ranch they all worked, a faith in God. And now he had nothing but a scrap of paper hanging around his neck and a hunt for a man he might never find.

Was it all worth it? Couldn't he go back home and take care of his girls, work the ranch? He could watch everything that he did so he wouldn't cause the problems, whatever they were between him and Lizzie. Maybe that way, they wouldn't come between him and his daughters?

He shook his head. A disgusted sigh burst from his lips. That wouldn't work. He had tried that for the first six months after they buried Lizzie. The girls grew scared of the way he acted when the anger over Lizzie's choice got the better of him. They started asking if they could stay with Grandda and Granny. That's when he knew he had to find Hank.

The weight of Rose's head against his shoulder felt good. What was the difference between Lizzie and Rose that one would live and one chose to die?

The only thing he was sure of was that he would protect this woman beside him from all dangers, Waller, Snodgrass, or himself. No matter what else happened, he would protect her.

When they entered the outskirts of Denver, Mac wiggled his arm to wake her. She sat up and yawned, then worked the wrinkles out of her dress.

"We haven't talked about where we're staying tonight." Mac glanced down at her. "I usually stay with my cousins. Is that all right with you?"

Sarah Rose stopped straightening her clothes. "I thought we'd be spending the night at a hotel. There was a very nice one Drew and I stayed at when we came from Boston."

"In the last few months since you've been in Central City, Denver has grown. Hundreds of settlers and men who've left their families behind have moved in. The place where my cousin lives is on the edge of town." He smiled at her. "I always stay in the barn. You'll be able to share a room with Duncan's two daughters. That's what my sister does when she comes. They're used to family coming all the time. Remember the eighty-one cousins."

Sarah Rose relaxed. "Thank you. That'll be fine."

The next morning, Mac turned in the order to his supplier so that it would be ready early the next day, then left his wagon and rented a buggy. He'd been surprised that Sarah Rose agreed with his suggestion that he go with her to the lawyer's office.

While they rode through the streets of Denver, Mac couldn't help but notice how straight and stiff Sarah sat, like someone had slipped his granny's wooden ironing board down her dress. Or how she kept twisting her gloved fingers together in her lap. Was she ashamed of the way they looked, a lady and a freighter?

He couldn't help but notice how the businessmen were dressed. He didn't have to look down at himself to know what he looked like in his work clothes instead of a suit. There wasn't time to get one before they got to the law office, even though he had the money for it, thanks more to the ranch than the freighting business. But none of that mattered now. They didn't have time to go shopping before the appointment.

When they pulled up in front of the law office, Mac glanced at his dusty pants, then turned to her. "If you would rather have me stay out here with the buggy, I understand."

Her hands stopped fidgeting. "Don't you want to go with me?"

"If that's what you want, but I didn't come dressed for a business appointment." He pointed to his clothes.

"Oh, pash. That doesn't matter."

"You seem unsettled. I thought maybe…my clothes—"

"I'm just nervous about what could be so important that he would need to see me here."

Mac covered her fists with his hand. "Relax. What's the worst your lawyer could tell you?"

Sarah Rose's face grew tighter and paler. "I fear it's something concerning my grandfather. And if it is, it could be worse than anything you could imagine in five lifetimes. That man is pure evil. All he lives for is money and his legacy. People don't matter. They are to be used and thrown away."

When they entered Mr. Williams' law office, Sarah introduced Thorn as her husband.

Mr. William, elderly and portly, shook hands with Thorn, then smiled, at least as much as the lawyer ever did. "Good. Mrs. Greer…Excuse me, Mrs. MacPherson will need someone strong by her side, especially now."

Sarah tightened her grip on her reticule. Her spine snapped a little straighter. "Mr. Williams, I don't need—"

The lawyer held up his hand. "I'm sorry. I didn't mean any disrespect. Please have a seat. Let me explain what happened."

Sarah wanted to stay strong, but a horrible dread settled on her. Something bad was coming, and she wouldn't be able to stop it. She needed to hold onto something, something that would help her stay grounded against the bad news.

THE ROSE AND THE THORN

Thorn folded his arms, and she twisted her own fingers together to keep from grabbing his hand and clinging like some weak female.

And then her hands were covered by rough warmth as Thorn's hand slid over hers. She couldn't look at him, but she gave a tiny nod of thanks. His fingers tightened for a moment, then loosened and remained resting on hers.

"Mrs. MacPherson, I have sources in your grandfather's household and also around Central City, like you requested."

Sarah sensed rather than saw Thorn glance at her. Would he understand just how much she still needed to protect herself?

Mr. Williams must have seen Thorn's reaction for he paused and looked from her to Thorn and back. Seeming satisfied with what he saw, he started again. "Mr. Carlyle reports there is nothing new in Central City now that Pete Waller seems to have left town."

He cleared his throat. "But things have changed in Boston, according to this report from your lawyer there. It seems your grandfather invested heavily in some schemes that didn't work out. He lost a great deal of money. In order to pay off those debts, he had to borrow some funds. Word got out, and rumors, mostly exaggerated, spread like chaff in the wind. Soon there were runs on the banks he owned."

Mr. Williams mopped his brow with a handkerchief. He gave her a steady gaze. "He probably could have survived all that on the strength and fear of his reputation alone, if not for the stroke."

Sarah gripped Thorn's hand and held tight. "Is he dead?"

The lawyer shook his head. "The doctor said he'll survive, although he seems paralyzed on one side and is bedridden, at least for now. Also, your Boston lawyer informs me that they are about to foreclose on his house."

Sarah stood and paced the floor. Thoughts and memories flooded her mind. She tried to sort them out, the good from the bad. Although she had not lived in that house very long, she associated her grandmother and father with it. And even with her house in Central City, the place she thought of as home was that large house in Boston. She knew she would never set foot in it again, but it was the family home, and it held some of the family treasures she would love to have—her grandmother's portrait and personal possessions, the family Bible that listed all the generations before her, and several portraits of her father. If the price of getting those things meant helping Grandfather, so be it.

She stopped in front of Mr. Williams' desk. "Please send word by Pony Express to my lawyer in Boston and have him purchase the house with all its contents. In years to come, I may want to sell it, but for now I'll keep it in the family. Grandfather may continue to live there. I'll pay for the upkeep and three servants. I'll send you a list of family things, like my grandmother's portrait and the family Bible, that are in the house. I'd like to have those things shipped to Central City. Good day."

She needed to get out of the office. Too many thoughts buzzed through her head. Emotions she didn't want to feel tugged at her head, her heart, her stomach. A crack started somewhere deep inside of her, and she didn't like it. It wasn't that she wanted her grandfather dead. She just wanted him out of her and her brother's lives. She wanted to be free of his control. She wanted Drew free of him. But she never wanted him dead.

Thorn stood as she turned to leave.

"Wait a moment, Mrs. MacPherson." The lawyer hurried across the room. "There is another matter I need to discuss with you. This one concerns your life in Central City."

Sarah paused and looked over her shoulder. "What else?"

"Please, have a seat. It won't take long." Mr. Williams gestured toward the chair.

She took her seat once more. This time Thorn stood behind her, his hand on her shoulder.

Mr. Williams looked a bit uncomfortable as he fiddled with the collar of his jacket. "Ah, that is, Mr. Carlyle's sources report to him that it seems Mr. Snodgrass has been heard to say he plans to force you to"—He glanced at Thorn, then returned his attention to her—"marry him one day soon."

Sarah couldn't hold back a small, unladylike snort. "I'm already married. And even if I weren't, I'd never marry that man. Next to Grandfather, he is the most evil man I've ever known."

"Be that as it may, remember your grandfather is now penniless, his fortune gone." Mr. Williams tapped the papers in front of him on the desk. "I doubt anyone has had time to express the news concerning your grandfather's reverse in fortune to Mr. Snodgrass. When he does learn of it, please, be careful around him." He lifted his gaze to her husband. "As should you."

He held Thorn's gaze a moment longer, then looked at her. "Snodgrass may be more determined than ever to get his hands on your fortune, through fair means or foul." He cleared his throat. "I'm just trying to prepare you."

"Do you have any idea how quickly he might be notified?" Sarah slipped the straps of her reticle over her wrist. When the lawyer shook his head, she stood. "Will that be all?"

Mr. Williams rose and came around the desk. "I wish I had better news for you, Mrs. MacPherson, but I'm glad to know that you have Thorn by your side. He's a good man with a fine reputation."

Sarah wasn't sure which shocked her more, that Mr. Williams already knew her husband or that he called him by his given name as if they'd known each other for years. She glanced from one man to the other. "I didn't know you knew each other."

"Yes, ma'am. I've known Thorn and his family since they moved to the area several years ago. Haven't done business with him though, since one of his cousins, Duncan MacPherson, is a lawyer here in town and he handles all their legal matters."

"Oh!" She looked at Thorn, who stood still as a statue, expressionless. She turned back to Mr. Williams. "I've met Duncan and his family. As a matter of fact, we are staying with them."

"Good, good. Well, if you need anything of me, just send word. As always, I am at your service." Mr. Williams tipped his head and shook hands with Thorn.

With this talk of protection, an idea popped into Sarah's thoughts. "Oh, wait, one more thing. The business situation in Central City will affect my brother's reputation. Using my funds, could you do whatever is needed to protect the people Stanley might try and swindle in my grandfather's name, without using my name, of course?"

A rare grin slid across Mr. Williams' face. "I'll handle it right away, very discreetly."

Sarah smiled in return. The lawyer understood her need for protection through control. Would that be enough protection against Stanley? If not, the weight of the gun in her reticule reassured her that she had other protection, if she needed it.

CHAPTER THIRTEEN

Sarah, in her white nightgown, clutched the curtains while she stared out the window of the bedroom where she was spending the night. After leaving Mr. Williams' office, the rest of the day had passed in a hazy blur.

Thorn double-checked with his suppliers to make sure everything would be ready the following morning, then took her to a couple of bakeries, as well as the shops she needed to visit. Those purchases lay strewn on her bed. He took her to a restaurant for lunch, but she couldn't remember what she'd eaten or what they'd talked about.

Supper was the same. Sleep eluded her as she lay in a darkened room at Duncan's house. Ah yes. Duncan the lawyer, Thorn's cousin, a friend of Mr. Williams, who also knew Thorn. Circles within circles. Was she caught in some kind of scheme? Who could she trust? Was Grandfather really ill?

The room seemed to close in on her. She pulled on her robe and slipped out as quietly as she could, hoping not to wake Duncan's two daughters who lay sleeping in the second bed.

She left the questions in the room and stepped lightly as she hurried down the back staircase, then out the kitchen door to the porch. Childhood memories of times spent with her father watching the stars drew her gaze to the sky. She drew in a deep breath, and another. Like a gentle wave sliding across the sand at the seashore back

East, the tension eased. Even her fingers lost their grip on the ties of her robe as peace settled over her.

The late night breeze carried the mingled fragrances of lilac and roses, then danced with the dangling leaves of the overhead trees. The full moon slipped in and out of the wispy clouds high in the dark sky. It was like a fairy land out here, where all the pressures, demands, and fears disappeared. Sarah let out a soul-easing sigh.

This was what she needed—peace, just for a few moments. Peace from all the problems that tried to cling to her. Peace from the fear that ever traveled with her. Peace from…from what? Need? Desire?

She brushed against a rose bush that grew up the side of the porch and along the railing. One of the thorns snagged the sleeve of her robe while the rose's fragrance surrounded her. She grinned and slid the fabric from the barb. Rose and Thorn. The rose on the bush needed the thorn to protect it, but what about her. Did she need Thorn?

Sarah's fingers pressed against her lips. Thorn's face filled her mind. She was torn about him. She liked him, was drawn to him. But she feared him, feared what he could do to her life. Never again would she let another man have the control over her that Grandfather and Alfred had. Never again would she submit to that cruel authority.

But that was the problem. Mac filled her thoughts too often. Her thoughts of him had changed so much from the time she had seen him from her hotel window her first morning in Central City. He had been kind and helpful to Drew and Helen. Even with her, he had been gentle, never cruel. Rough maybe. Definitely not like the gentlemen back in Boston.

Boston. She chuckled. She had come outside because she couldn't sleep with all that had happened in Boston, and now, Thorn filled her thoughts.

She touched her lips as the memory of their wedding kiss flooded back. "Thorn."

Unable to sleep, Thorn had been sitting on the moon-lit porch for an hour when Sarah Rose stepped out of the house. She was so beautiful. And strong. And brave. Only she didn't see all those things about herself. She wasn't truly his wife, and yet she was. What if she decided to return to Boston now that her grandfather had lost his control? Could she be happy to stay in Colorado? Would she be willing to live on the ranch with him?

If Sarah Rose left him, he'd also lose Emma. The baby had wormed her way into his heart. He loved her as much as he loved his first three. His gut clenched, and he rubbed his fist over his chest. He needed to find Hank and get that matter settled so he could go back home to his family, his girls, and hopefully with Rose and Emma.

At the sound of his name whispered in the darkness, he couldn't keep his boot from scraping against the wood porch or stop the chain on the swing from creaking.

She turned toward him. "Thorn?"

He stood and walked across the porch. "I didn't want to bother you."

Laughter burst from her lips. "I think it's too late for that. You have bothered me ever since we met."

Thorn stopped. What did she mean? He would never force himself on her, like her husband had, or those miners back in Central City. He took a step back, then another.

Sarah Rose moved forward and touched his arm. "I didn't mean it to sound like that. You do bother, disturb, annoy me, but that's because I've never met a man like you. I don't understand you." She shrugged the tiniest bit. "I don't know how to deal with you."

She ducked her head and turned away, but Mac tugged her back toward him again. His heart pounded in his chest. "I don't know how to deal with you either."

Mac sucked in a deep breath. Her eyes grew wider. His arms tightened around her. He waited for her to pull away. Looked for the fear he'd seen so often in her eyes. Instead her lips parted. He drew her closer, paused again.

She didn't pull back.

He lowered his head as the words whispered after the kiss following their wedding vows pounded through his head. He had to be gentle with this woman. He needed to kiss her, but he had to give her what no other man had.

Their lips touched. She tensed. He kept his hold on her loose. He brushed his lips against hers.

She pressed closer to him and returned his kiss.

His blood pounded. His chest threatened to explode. He couldn't get enough of this sweet woman.

Little girls' giggling joined with the closing of the back door.

His head shot up but he kept his arms around Sarah Rose as she trembled.

"'Scuse us." Duncan's older daughter tugged on her sister's hand. "I gotta take Betsy to the outhouse." The two scurried down the steps.

"They was kissing. That mean they're gonna have a baby now?" Betsy's loud whisper rang out through the moonlit night.

"Shush. Let's just get your business done."

Sarah Rose pulled out of his arms and stepped away.

"Rose?"

"No...no more. Nothing more." She sucked in a shuddery breath. "I'll be ready to leave in the morning when you are." She slipped into the house.

Thorn slammed his fist against his thigh. Had he pushed too far? The more he saw of Rose the more he liked. And still, he'd frightened her, sent her scurrying away.

Would he ever understand women?

Sarah bounced on the wagon seat on the road to Central City. Her arms ached as she pulled the floppy sunbonnet Helen had loaned her a little farther forward, trying to keep the sun off her face. Every part of her ached.

Sleep hadn't come easily the night before, and what sleep she'd had was filled with dreams of Thorn and babies and snarly Stanley. Well, after this trip, Stanley was out of the way. She wasn't sure yet how Grandfather's loss of wealth would affect his businesses in Central City, but at least Drew would be out from under Grandfather's thumb.

Her foot bumped the jar of water Duncan's wife brought out as they left. She had filled it with ice from their small icehouse and wrapped it in rags. Just what they would need for the hot trip.

She pulled it up and glanced at Thorn. "Want a drink?"

At last, he turned his head and spoke to her. "Sounds good."

While he shifted the reins from his left hand to his right, she twisted the lid off the jar. They bounced over a rut in the dirt road and the water splashed up on her shirtwaist. The chill of the cold water across her chest battled the heat in her cheeks. She stared at the wet area that caused the fabric to become stuck to her chest like a second skin.

Without a word, he grabbed the jar and took a long, thirsty drink.

Sarah couldn't take her eyes off the muscles in his neck as the water slid down his throat. When he finished, she took the jar, screwed on the lid, and set it back at her feet. Staring ahead but not seeing anything of the land, her mind fought her heart. Even though she sensed small changes in her when she thought about Thorn, she knew nothing lasting could come from the situation between them. He was a healthy man, and one day, he would want sons to carry on his name.

Hadn't that been what her own father wanted? When Drew was born, he was named after his father, just like her father had been named after Grandfather. But that was something she could never give him or any other man. Alfred had seen to that. She slid her hand under her crossed arms and touched her middle. Barren. That's what the doctor had told Alfred the last time he had pushed her down the stairs in one of his drunken rages. She had lost yet another baby, but that time she had lost so much more.

And through all that, Stanley stood by her bedroom door. He told her once that Grandfather sent him to make sure she survived her injuries, because she was needed to control Drew. The hated man smiled at her in her loss, smiled while he stood next to the doctor as Alfred was told the damage was too great this time, and that she would never bear another child. Stanley smiled when Alfred cursed her yet again for being useless.

She snuck a peek at Thorn when he snapped the reins, urging the mules up a small incline. He hadn't said much since she saw him that morning, He'd worn the same frown all day. Was he as troubled as she was about the kisses last night?

A tickling thrill raced around her insides at the memories. But she pushed them away. Hopes and dreams would have to stay locked away where she'd had to put everything special since her parents died. Those things had to stay there so they couldn't be used against her.

But then, that was also the place where she couldn't visit. The day might come when no one could use hopes and dreams against her. Then she might chance a visit to that locked-away place. For now, she would just enjoy the gentleness he showed her.

Mac jiggled his arm when they drew near to Central City. He couldn't help but grin as Rose woke. His wife rubbed the tip of her nose with her gloved hand. He returned his gaze to the road, both to give her a moment to straighten herself after her nap and to think about that thought—his wife.

Things had changed on this trip. He understood her a mite better. His Rose had survived more than most women ever had to face, at least the women he knew. The women in his clan faced hard lives, but those lives were shared with their men and the other women of the clan. Sarah had been alone, at the mercy of the grandfather who should have loved her and a husband who should have treasured the precious woman she was.

The knot that had been twisted tight in his gut loosened a bit. The knot that had tied itself up when he found Lizzie in the barn.

Lizzie had been a strong woman. As strong as Rose. Surely she knew he would love her no matter what happened. There had to be more to what happened with her that day. He had to learn the truth. Only then could he know if he had a hand in Lizzie's death.

He glanced down at Sarah, then back at the road. When he knew the truth, would he be able to drop the shackles that held him to the past?

Sarah peered through the darkening twilight when they reached the edge of Central City. Soon she would be home with Emma. Her arms felt empty without her baby girl. Had Emma said any new words while she'd been gone? Gotten any more teeth? She wanted to jump out of the heavily laden wagon and run home, but instead she gripped the wooden seat.

"We'll be home in a few minutes." Thorn snapped the reins, and the mules stepped up their pace a tiny bit. "You should be in time to feed Emma her supper. Unless you want to clean up first."

"I can't wait to hold her. If I get her dirty, we'll just clean up together." Sarah took a deep breath while Thorn directed the mules to the barn at the back of the house. Feathery tingles crept up her back and around her neck. Something was wrong. Drew and Helen knew they were coming home tonight, but no light shone in the windows. The house sat as a dark shadow against the mountains behind it and the darkening sky above.

Thorn didn't say a word as he pulled into the path that led to the back of the house. She could feel the tension rolling off him. The mules stopped. He tied the reins around the brake and grabbed his rifle. "Stay here."

No way would she stay behind. When he climbed down, Sarah jumped off the other side. Let Thorn say what he wanted. This was still her house, her home, her family. She slipped her pistol from her reticule and followed him.

Tair growled low in his throat, jumped down, and followed them.

Thorn let out a hiss when he realized she was by his side, but he seemed to know better than to say anything. "Please stay behind me until we see what's going on in there."

"All right." Her voice wasn't as strong as she would have liked. But then her mouth was so dry, she was surprised anything came out at all.

The swing on the back porch creaked in the evening breeze as they moved up the steps.

They stepped through the door into the kitchen. The cocking of a rifle deeper in the room shattered the silence around them.

"Stop right there. I've got you in my sights. If you come any further, I'll shoot." Though laced with fatigue and anger, Drew's voice rang out clear and loud.

"Ease up, man. 'Tis me, Mac, and your sister." Thorn stood solidly between Drew and Sarah, even though she tried to push him aside to get to her brother. Thorn lowered his gun, but held her back with his other hand. "Stay still until your brother can make us out."

Drew struck a match and lit the oil lamp. Light skittered to the doorway. Her brother sat on one of the worn wooden chairs, his splinted leg resting on another one, his face pale with dark shadows beneath his eyes. His hair stood on end as if he'd been running his fingers through it. He dropped his head to his chest. "I'm glad you both got back."

Sarah pushed Thorn aside and hurried over to her brother. She dropped her gun and reticule on the table, then grabbed his shirt sleeve. "What's happened? Where's Emma? Where're Helen and Carl?"

Drew tipped his head toward the small rooms off the kitchen, Helen and Carl's bedrooms. "They're all right. I put Emma in with Carl. They're sleeping. Helen…Helen…someone attacked Helen." His voice cracked. "She's hurt real bad. Doc's in with her."

Sarah started shaking. Memories flooded her mind again. Beaten. Angry fists pounding. "Is she…will she—?"

Thorn wrapped his arm around her shoulders and steadied her. "What's the doc said?"

Sarah hadn't known how supportive a man could be. She wanted to lean back into the warmth, the protection. With great reluctance she straightened up and stood solidly on the kitchen floor.

Thorn released her and checked the coffee pot on the stove.

"Doc hasn't said anything yet." Drew's fists rested on the table. He kept his eyes on the rifle he had set nearby. "I thought whoever did it might come back and try again." He slapped his injured leg. "I couldn't guard both doors. I locked the front so I could watch this one in case he came back." He glanced out the door. "Hadn't realized how dark it'd gotten."

Sarah pulled a chair closer to her brother, sat, and took hold of one of his hands. "Back here? Was she attacked in the house?"

"Not in the house. She and Carl were coming back from doing something at church. She sent Carl on ahead while she gathered some clothes hanging on the clothesline."

Drew shook his head. "I was coming from the parlor to eat the supper she'd left for me. Carl told me what she was doing, and I decided to go help her. Before I made it out the door, I heard her scream. I hobbled as fast as I could, but the attacker was gone. She lay on the ground bleeding." Her brother slammed his fist on the table. "He used a knife on her."

Drew stopped talking. He dropped his head into his shaking hands.

Sarah wanted to wrap him in her arms as she had when he was a little boy. But he wasn't a little boy any longer. He was a man, and someone hurt the woman he cared about, maybe even loved. She rested her hand on his shoulder and gave a small squeeze.

Thorn set three cups of steaming coffee on the table, then sat. His body tensed as he stared at her gun. He glanced at her.

She stared back at him. Let him say anything about protecting herself.

He gave her a small nod, then turned to his brother-in-law. "Do they know who did it?"

Drew shook his head. "No one saw anything, and Helen hasn't been able to tell us."

"Coffee smells good. I could sure use a cup." Doc stood at the doorway to Helen's bedroom. Bloody streaks covered his white shirt. He wiped his hands on a once-clean towel.

Thorn grabbed a mug and set it on the table. Doc dropped onto the last empty chair.

"She's sleeping. Best thing for her." Doc blew across the coffee, making little ripples move across the surface. He took a sip. "Ahh. Don't know what people would do if they didn't have this."

Sarah glanced between the bedroom door and the doctor. "How is she?"

Doc set his cup on the table, then pulled out his crumpled handkerchief and wiped his eyes. "I've known that girl since I moved here last year, and she still surprises me." He tucked the crumpled mass back into his pocket. "I know she had to be in pain as I sewed her up, but she kept on praying and thanking God for bringing her through." He tugged out his hanky again and wiped his nose. "Makes a man want to go to church just to get some of what she's got."

Drew gripped his hands together. "How bad is she hurt?"

Sarah leaned in closer to hear the answer.

"Well, son, it could have been a lot worse. Apparently he tried to kidnap her, but she fought back." Doc took another sip of coffee. "She lost a lot of blood. He cut her in several places, none of which are life-threatening in themselves. I don't think he meant to kill her, just take her. But she fought him off."

Sarah trembled and wrapped her arms around her middle. A hand lay on her shoulder. She didn't have to look up to see who stood next to her. Only Thorn comforted her with just his touch. Only Thorn seemed to know when she needed that comfort. She tilted her head and rested against his hand. Somehow they both knew the worst was still to come.

"She has a bad cut on her forearm that took ten stitches to close, one on her opposite shoulder that took seven. No broken bones." He glanced at Drew, then back at the coffee. "The cut on her face. Not that it's life-threatening. Just…life-changing for a woman." Doc shook his head. "She has a deep gash from here to here." He traced down the left side of his face with his index finger from his temple to his chin. "I don't know how bad a scar it'll leave, but I did my best with it."

Sarah couldn't hold in the gasp that burst through her lips. Thorn's fingers tightened.

Drew pulled his hurt leg from the chair and pushed himself up. "I don't care about the scar. I just want her to be all right." His eyes narrowed as he stared at the doc. "Did she say who did it?"

Doc stood and nodded, then turned and shuffled toward Helen's room.

"Who, Doc? Who did this to her?" Drew's voice rumbled low. He grabbed the rifle off the table.

The old man looked over his shoulder. "She swore me to secrecy. Told the sheriff when he came by, though."

"Who's she protecting? Why's she letting him get away?" Drew grabbed his crutches and hobbled toward Helen's room.

Sarah grabbed his arm, but he shook her off.

"Well, it's obvious as the nose on your face, young man." Doc glanced at the gun and back. "She's protecting you. Doesn't want you to do anything in anger and vengeance you'll regret." He looked at Sarah. "I'll stay with her a while. You keep an eye on him."

The doctor returned to Helen's bedroom.

Drew struggled toward the back door. Once outside, he slammed it shut. Sarah stood to go after him.

"Let him be." Thorn stood very still as if waiting to see if she would defy him. "He's hurting and needs to be alone for a little while."

"If he's hurting, I need to be with him."

"In a while, he'll need you. But now he needs to get a handle on how he feels." Thorn ran his thumb down her cheek. "As a child he turned to you for comfort, but he's a man now. Let him have this time."

Sarah let out a deep sigh. She knew he was right, but she felt so helpless.

"Why don't we check on the children? Emma might need to be changed. And when we tell Carl about his sister, he's the one who'll need someone to hold him." Thorn dropped his hand to her back and gave a small nudge.

She glanced at Thorn for a moment. He wasn't young and weak like Drew or hard and self-centered like Grandfather and Alfred. And he wasn't cruel like Stanley. Still, she wasn't sure she wanted to find out what made him different. Did she?

"Did you kill her?" Stanley sat behind his desk and tried to figure out how much trouble the fool had gotten himself into. They had been seen together a few times, and he didn't want to take a chance on the law trying to connect him to anything right now, not until he got hold of Sarah's fortune and the power it would bring.

"Just cut her when she fought me." Jim Grayson shuffled from side to side. "I didn't mean to hurt her, especially after the way she stayed with my ma when she died. It's just, she's the woman I want."

Stanley drummed his fingers on his desk. He hated to be reminded of the fiasco that led to Sarah marrying the freighter. Still, Grayson had proved loyal in the past and might be needed in the future. It might be a good thing to get him out of town for a while. He took a small bag of coins from his desk drawer. "Waller is in an old miner's shack three miles north of Nevadaville. Know the place I'm talking about?"

Grayson nodded.

Stanley tossed the bag to the man. "Take this and stay at that shack until I send word."

"Yes, sir." Grayson shoved the bag into his pocket, then slapped his hat on. He had almost reached the back door when Stanley stopped him.

"One thing." Stanley waited until the man looked over his shoulder. "If you get in any more trouble, you're on your own. I'll denounce you for the thug you are. And if you try to implicate me in anything, you won't live to see the next dawn, no matter where you are. Understand?"

Grayson swallowed hard and nodded.

The door slammed shut. Footsteps sounded down the alley.

Stanley chuckled. These moments of power were what he lived for. He could hardly wait until he had more. And that would come in time. He just needed to figure out how to get rid of one unneeded husband. And without suspicion being directed towards himself.

CHAPTER FOURTEEN

Sarah peeked in Carl's room. The boy's eyes were huge. His freckles stood out against his pale, tear-stained face. He seemed to be holding onto the baby for dear life, even though she had leaked through to his blood-streaked clothes.

"Miss Sarah, is my s—sister gonna die?"

Sarah's heart hurt for the little boy. Someone should have been comforting him, but he had guarded Emma by himself. She scooped him into her arms and sat on the bed with both of the children in her lap. She hugged him, and between kisses on his head, she murmured reassurances that all would be well.

After a few moments, she pulled back. "Carl, I'm so proud of the way you took care of Emma. Let's get you both cleaned up." She glanced up at Thorn who stood in the doorway. "Would you please get me a pitcher of warm water?"

He nodded and disappeared, returning a few minutes later with the water. "While you take care of the children, I'll take care of the mules."

"And see about Drew?"

Thorn nodded and left.

"All right, Carl. Let's get you and Emma cleaned up, then maybe the doctor will let you see your sister. And I'll fix us something to eat."

After lighting a couple of lanterns, Thorn wheeled the wagon into the barn and removed the harness from the first set of mules.

Drew stepped up beside him. "Need some help? I used to be good at this kind of thing."

"Help's always appreciated." Thorn watched the younger man struggle with his crutches as he removed the harnesses from the mules. "You know what you're doing. Fair bet you didn't learn that from your grandfather."

Drew made a sound, probably meant to be a chuckle, but the unexpected sob muffled it. "I used to help my pa with the animals, hitching up the buggy for Ma and Sarah." Drew stood on the far side of the light. The sliding of leather across the mules' backs, the chinking of metal bits, and the night owl's hoots filled the air. "I'd give anything if they hadn't died and left us at Grandfather's mercy. Mercy, ha. That man had no mercy for anyone." The pounding of his fist against the barn wall battled the other night sounds. "Why does God let there be wicked men like Grandfather, Stanley, and the man who hurt Helen?"

Mac wanted to add the names of the men who hurt Lizzie. But like Drew, he didn't know them. And he couldn't answer Drew's question, a question he'd asked in his own mind more than once over the last two years.

When the last of the harness was cleaned and put away, Thorn took the lantern and walked with Drew back to the house to check on the women.

Early the next morning, Mac poured himself a fresh cup of coffee, then set the pot back on the stove. He would need plenty of it if he was going to make it through the day. The night had been long and tiring as he'd sat with Drew, who insisted on keeping watch in case the attacker returned.

He glanced at the younger man whose head rested on the wooden table. They had talked for hours after Rose took the children upstairs with her. Mac couldn't help but smile as memories of her dealing with the children played out in his thoughts. She was a good mother. And with all she had been through, she deserved a large family. Would she be willing to come home with him, help him with his girls? He let out a gust of disgust. No sense even thinking about that yet.

The knob on the outside door twisted. Mac dropped his cup and grabbed Drew's rifle.

The door opened. Judith walked in. When she saw the rifle, she screamed and dropped the basket she carried.

Drew's head jerked up from the table. "What in the—?"

Rose stepped into the kitchen with Emma in one arm and holding Carl's hand with her other hand. "Judith, stop that this instant. Thorn, put down that gun. Drew, take Carl."

Mac couldn't help but chuckle when everyone obeyed the little general.

"Is it safe to come out now?" Doc stuck his head out of Helen's room.

Carl shook loose of Drew's hand and raced to the old man. "How's my sister?"

"She's doing fine, but she's asleep right now. If you stay real quiet, you can go in and sit with her. But remember, stay real quiet unless she wakes up, then come and get me or Mrs. MacPherson."

Carl nodded so hard his hair flapped on his forehead, then he shot into the bedroom.

"What's going on here?" Judith bent and grabbed her basket.

Sarah stepped farther into the kitchen. "Helen was attacked last night. She'll be in bed for a few days. I need you to fill in for her here in the kitchen."

Judith's eyes widened as she raised a trembling hand and grasped the collar of her dress. "Is she...how is she?"

Sarah sucked in a breath and nodded. "Helen's resting in her room. The man cut her. The doctor will be checking on her during the next few days. Please assist him in anything he asks."

"Yes, ma'am." Judith glanced at Helen's bedroom door, then started breakfast.

"Drew, we need to talk." Sarah rested her hand on her brother's shoulder.

"In a minute." He patted her fingers but looked at the doctor. "Are you going to tell me who did this to Helen?"

Doc rubbed his hand over his white hair and headed toward the back door. "Sorry, son, but like I told you last night, the sheriff's handling it." He stopped for a moment and looked over his shoulder. "If she wakes up before I get back, give her some broth and tea."

He slipped outside before anyone could stop him.

Drew rubbed his hand over his face. "What do you want to talk about, sis?"

Sarah bit the inside of her cheek as she watched Judith stand by the dry sink with her back to them, not working but turned just a bit towards the table. Oh, how she hated eavesdroppers, always looking for information to trade or use. It reminded her so much of Stanley and the way her simplest words had been used against her and Drew.

"Let's go to the parlor."

"I can't leave Helen. Say what you need to."

Sarah glanced over at Thorn, who shrugged. She flicked her eyes over to Judith and back to Thorn.

He nodded and stood. "Let me help, Judith. I think we've about drained the pot." Their voices droned on as he talked with the woman.

Sarah pulled a chair as close to Drew as she could and sat. She kept her voice low. "I met with my lawyer in Denver. He told me that Grandfather had lost everything and then had a stroke."

Drew stood so fast that his chair fell over backwards. He clung to the table to keep from falling over as he balanced on his good leg. "How could he have lost everything?" The words came out low and guttural between his clenched teeth.

Thorn took a step toward them, but Sarah shook her head. He lifted Emma from her arms and turned back toward Judith who had turned to stare.

"Please sit down." Sarah pulled his chair upright. By his pale face and trembling hands, she knew this was hitting him hard. He'd just learned that everything he had worked for had been taken away. She understood what he was feeling, to have all choices taken away, to be left to another's mercy, to have no say in one's future. He had refused her offers of help in the past. Would he let her help him now?

She chanced a glance at Thorn. He gave her a quick smile and turned back to talk with Judith while Emma gummed a bread crust. "While this is still sinking in, let me say something. I've been thinking about this all night, and I have a solution, if you want to hear it."

He sat and dropped his head between his hands, his elbows resting on the table. "What choice do I have?"

Sarah twisted her fingers together. "It is just an idea, but I think it would work. We could…"

She stopped. Judith stood across the table, holding the coffee pot in her hands, but wasn't trying to refill any of the cups.

Sarah tightened her fists in her lap. "Judith, this is—"

Someone pounded on the front door. Setting the pot down, Judith scurried to answer it. A moment later, Stanley's voice bellowed down the hall and filled the kitchen. No one could make out the words as he and

Judith stayed in the hall. Hopefully Judith would turn him away, and they wouldn't have to deal with him until later in the day. She needed time with Drew to go over her plans.

No luck. Not that she'd ever thought Judith could stop the man. Stanley burst into the kitchen with Judith hurrying in behind him. "I just received word that a woman was attacked here last night, Sarah. I wanted to make sure you weren't hurt."

"I'm fine. Someone attacked Helen."

Stanley's eyebrows drew together as he frowned. "Helen?"

"My friend and housekeeper."

"Oh, the mousy brown-haired thing." He nodded while his face relaxed. "Good, everything is fine then." He cast a glance at Drew. "How much longer are you going to be lazing around? We have a lot to go over concerning the miners in Black Hawk and Nevadaville."

Drew stood but gripped the table with one hand. "Didn't you hear what Sarah said about Helen? I won't be in today."

"Come on, boy. This Helen woman is just a housekeeper. Business comes first. A lesson your grandfather should have taught you. I'd hate to write your grandfather and tell him you're slacking off." He tapped his cane on the floor. "Or what the outcome of that would be."

"Grandfather—" Drew looked down at Sarah's hand tightening on his wrist. He twisted his hand around and held her fingers in his fist. "I won't be in today. The miners can be dealt with tomorrow or the next day."

Stanley's eyes narrowed. His face grew redder and redder. "Be there tomorrow, or you will pay the consequences." He turned and stomped out, muttering as he left. Judith scurried after him.

Sarah waited for several moments for the front door to crash closed, then couldn't hold back a small cry of joy.

"Oh, Drew, I'm so proud of you for standing up to Stanley."

He let go of her hand and dropped onto the chair. "Helen comes first. I won't leave her unprotected."

"Good, now let's have breakfast, and later I'd like to talk in private." Sarah reached out her arms for Emma.

Sarah sat at the table, waiting for Drew. Between caring for the children and Helen, they hadn't had a chance to talk all day. But now Judith had gone home for the night, Carl and Emma had gone to bed, and Drew was waiting for Helen to go to sleep.

Thorn poured two cups of coffee, then sat at the table. He nudged one cup over to Sarah.

"Thank you." She fiddled with the handle of the cup, turning it one way then the other.

"Want me to leave?" Thorn glanced at her. "Give you privacy with Drew?"

"I'd like your opinion. You might have some different thoughts on the matter." Sarah wasn't sure if Thorn really would know much about what she planned, but she had gotten used to his presence. It soothed her somehow.

Thorn nodded and took a sip from his cup.

Drew hobbled into the kitchen, leaned his crutches against the table, then dropped onto one of the chairs. Thorn filled a cup for Drew and set it in front of him.

"Helen's asleep, but let's keep our voices down while we talk." Drew had dark smudges beneath his eyes, shadowing his unshaved face. His whole body slumped in the chair. "So tell me more of what happened to Grandfather, and what's this plan you have?"

"There's not much more. Like I said earlier, the lawyer in Denver reported that he'd made some bad investments and had a stroke. He's lost everything." Sarah didn't want to tell Drew what her instructions were concerning Grandfather. She wasn't sure herself why she'd provided for the old man.

Drew sipped his coffee in silence for a few moments, then gave her a half-smile. "All right, so what did you do to take care of the old goat? Don't tell me how you feel about him. I already know that, but I also know what your heart's like."

Sarah blinked back the tears that threatened to fall. She reached out and slipped her hand over her brother's. In as few words as she could, she told him her instructions concerning their grandfather.

Drew nodded. "That's more than he deserved."

"I'm having Grandmother's portrait, the family Bible, and a few other things shipped out here. Is there anything you want from the house?"

His hand tightened into a fist under hers. "There's nothing I want from there." Suddenly he pulled away. "Wait a minute. You're having them shipped here. Does that mean you're not going back to Boston? You're staying here?"

Sarah nodded. "There's nothing back there for me but bad memories. No friends, no ties, nothing. I can start fresh out here. I like Colorado. It's a place for a new start for Emma, for me, and I hope for you."

From the corner of her eye, Sarah noticed Thorn's shoulders easing down, and a smile came to his face. She turned her full attention back to her brother.

Drew's eyes shone. "To stay here. For good? I hadn't thought of staying here. I had, a little, but not really, more like a dream." He glanced at Helen's room. "I'd not allowed myself to consider it, knowing Grandfather would want me to return to Boston once things got up and going here. But if I can stay…"

Sarah nodded slowly. "You're no longer under his employ, or under Stanley's control for that matter." Sarah dropped her hands to her lap and twisted her fingers together. She had to tread carefully or Drew wouldn't listen. "I have a business deal to offer you. Please hear me out before you say anything."

Drew sat quietly for a several moments, then let out a deep sigh. He nodded. "All right, I'll listen."

"This town's growing. More than a hundred people a day are coming into the area, mostly men. And most of those don't cook or bake, since a lot of them have wives or mothers back home who did that for them. Added to that, Helen has already established a reputation for her baking and has customers already. We know she's a good cook and loves to do it. Also, before I hired her, I asked what her dreams were, and she said she wanted to own a bakery."

Drew slowly tapped his right index finger on the table as he listened. Sarah wasn't sure if he was truly listening or just waiting until she finished so he could return to Helen's side.

"It'd be a business deal," she said. "I'd have it drawn up legally, of course. I thought we could open a bakery and café. Helen could bake and, with a helper or two, could cook. You could manage it—you know enough about the business world, and what you don't know, you could learn. I would supply the beginning funds." She knew she was speaking too fast, but she had to get it all out before Drew said anything. "We'd set it up so you two could buy me out as the business grows, then you and Helen would own it together."

Sarah let out a big puff of air. She leaned back against her chair and waited for Drew's reaction.

Drew picked up his cup and took a long drink, set it down, twirled it around by the handle, then picked it up again and stared at the liquid as he swirled it around.

She turned to Thorn and raised her eyebrows. What did he think of the plan? Did he think Drew would accept it?

Thorn shrugged and tipped his head to the side.

Drew looked at her. "Sis, I've done a lot of thinking in the last…since Helen was attacked. I know I've been weak, not taking care of you, letting Grandfather use me against you."

He held up his hand when she started to interrupt him, then he swallowed a couple of times. "But I've seen how you've built a new life for yourself and Emma out here. You're getting stronger every day. I can see that. I want that for myself."

Sarah wanted to clasp his hand, to let her little brother know that she was there for him. But that was not what he needed. He wanted to stand up by himself. Drew was becoming a man who would have made their father proud. He made her proud. Her brother would have the life he should.

Drew set his cup down. "I've seen men come out here with nothing and work hard. Some made it. Some didn't. But they tried. They took control of their lives and tried. I'm ashamed admit that I haven't. I'm ashamed to admit I let too much of Grandfather influence me."

He smiled. "What you offer sounds like a good plan. I'll need to talk to Helen when she feels better."

Thorn cleared his throat. "About that. There's something you need to consider. What if after this business is up and running, Helen marries someone who doesn't want her working? Wants her to stay home and take care of her family? Could cause problems even if that husband let her work. A married woman and a single man working all day together might cause trouble."

"Thorn." Sarah gave him a look to quiet him. How could he even bring up something like that? What if Thorn's question made Drew decide not to take her up on her offer?

"No, Sarah." A deep red crept up Drew's face. "Mac's got a point. That's something else I thought about in the last few hours. Helen and I've spent a lot of time together lately, especially after I hurt my leg." He glanced at the closed door to Helen's room, then back to Sarah and grinned. "Like I said earlier, I need to talk to Helen."

Sarah wanted to shout for joy, but kept silent as she picked up the coffee cups the three of them had used. She hoped everything would work out like they planned.

Drew stood and set his crutches under his arms. "Thanks, sis. Think I'll check on Helen before I turn in. I'll leave the door open. You don't need to say anything."

Back in Boston it would be highly inappropriate, even scandalous, for Drew to be alone in Helen's bedroom. But Sara couldn't bring herself to say anything as she and Thorn turned to leave the kitchen. Helen was safe with Drew. He would honor her.

Drew balanced on his crutches and called to Sarah. "Just so you know, while you were gone, I saw Stanley talking to Pete Waller and a couple of other thugs around town." He nodded to Thorn. "Night, Mac. See you when you get back."

Drew knocked on Helen's door. He stood with his ear against the door, then grinned and slipped in.

Sarah turned toward Thorn. The joy of the last few moments was chased away as a sense of loneliness opened up somewhere in the darkest regions of her chest. The feeling grew with each step she took. "I forgot you had to leave on your route in the morning."

CHAPTER FIFTEEN

"Don't worry," Mac said. Not that it was worry he saw etched on her features. He wasn't quite sure what that was he saw there. "I talked to the sheriff. He's looked all over town and seems to think that the man who attacked Helen is long gone."

When he looked into Rose's upturned face, all he wanted to do was kiss her again. "I also asked a friend to watch the place while I'm gone. So don't be surprised if you see a man in buckskins walking around the house and barn, especially close to dark. His name's Adam Lone Eagle."

Her eyes grew wide at the name.

Thorn had seen enough people's reaction to Adam to understand her reaction. "He's not an Indian, just lived with them for a while. I've known him since before we moved to the territory. He's been a good friend."

Rose nodded slowly. "You trust him."

"With my life." He waited a moment to see if Rose would object to what he'd done, but she stayed silent. "With Helen hurt and Drew still unable to get around like he needs, I wanted to add an extra set of eyes while I'm gone."

And depending on how things went in the next few weeks, Mac might have to call in some of his cousins to help protect his family.

She worried her lower lip for a second or two. "But what about you? The lawyer said…"

Thorn placed his finger over her lips. "I'll be fine out on the road. I'm sure Stanley will be sticking around here. So don't worry about me."

Rose nodded silently. Either she agreed with his plan, or she was just too tired to argue.

"Let's get Emma from Carl's room so everyone can get some sleep. Tomorrow's going to be here before we know it."

A few moments later, after wishing Carl a good-night, Mac walked beside Rose as she carried her sleeping daughter. Contentment soaked through his bones when they climbed the stairs. His first real contentment in two years.

He opened the door to the nursery and lit the oil lamp, turning it down low. When Rose lay Emma down in her crib the little girl's eyes peeked open and a drooly grin lifted her chubby cheeks. "Momma. Dada."

Dada. The word rolled over him, capturing his heart and keeping his gaze solidly fixed on the child. It created an ache deep within him. He needed his whole family together—him, Rose, Emma, and his three girls, all on the ranch.

He snuck a peek at Rose and gripped the rails of the crib as his heart pounded. She was so lovely, so protective, so strong. He wanted to wrap this beautiful woman in his arms. Rose was the woman he wanted for his wife, to stay by his side, to help raise his girls, to love him forever. To sleep by his side. But he couldn't try to convince her to tear up those stupid papers he'd signed the day they married until he found the answers he needed.

Emma pulled herself up and jabbered, grinning the whole time.

"Looks like this little one wants to spend a few minutes with us." Sarah Rose picked up Emma and turned to him. "I know it's late, but would you like to stay with us until she falls back to sleep?"

Mac took the little girl in his arms. Sarah Rose smiled and sat on a comfortable sofa she'd put in the room. He joined her. "You did a good thing making that offer to your brother."

"Like I said, we have nothing back in Boston. This is our home now."

Emma grabbed Thorn's finger and gnawed on it. He chuckled "Looks like our little girl is teething again."

He glanced over at Sarah Rose to see if she agreed. But she was looking at him with a stunned expression, her hand against her chest right below her throat.

Something was wrong.

"Sarah Rose, are you all right?"

She gave a quick shake of her head and looked at him, but not quite in the eye. "I'm fine, just a little tired." She moved quickly off the sofa. "I, uh, I think we can put Emma down now. She'll probably go to sleep. I'll check on her before I go to bed."

"Rose, look at me." Mac stood, but she tensed when he got closer. "Please."

She still wouldn't meet his eye.

Thorn felt like he'd been gut-punched. "Rose, do you not want me to be around Emma? Are you afraid that I'll harm her some way? I won't. I'd die for this little girl."

At last, she looked him. "I know." Her voice was soft and low. "You're a good man. A man every little girl wants for her father."

"Then what is it?"

Rose wrapped one arm around her middle and held the other one out as if to stop him. "Let's just put Emma to bed."

Mac sighed. Something was going on in Rose's head, but he wasn't going to find out what it was tonight. If he pressed her, tired as she was, one of them might say something they both would regret. "All right."

Mac laid Emma in her bed. He stepped in front of Sarah who hadn't moved an inch. "I'll see you in the morning before I leave." He kissed her cheek but forced himself to take no more. Without another word, he walked out of the room and didn't stop until he was across the hall and in his own room.

He wanted to pound something, and pound it hard. All this had to end, or he was going to lose his mind.

Sarah moved slowly, like in a dream. She crossed the nursery floor and slipped into her room. Once on the bed, she gripped her hands together. She couldn't believe this was happening.

She was starting to fall in love with her husband. Her hands shook. That couldn't be right. Falling in love wasn't supposed to cause alarms to go off like someone pulling the bell to notify the community of a fire. But that's how she felt—scared, hot, and afraid. How could she love a man she didn't know, didn't trust because she didn't know him? Where had he come from? Why wasn't he with his daughters? Maybe most importantly, did she trust him to take care of her body and her heart?

She took a deep breath. It really didn't matter. She couldn't talk herself out of loving Mac by asking questions. All she could do was guard her heart until she knew more about him and how he really felt about her.

The day after Thorn left, Drew received a message from Stanley that he'd left town for an undetermined period. That gave time for Sarah, Drew, and Helen to consider the new business from every angle.

The days without Thorn dragged, but Sarah stayed busy, dealing with her lawyer about starting the business and arranging the money for it. And all during that week, Thorn and the realization that she was falling in love with him were not far from her mind. What was she going to do about it? She'd been so sure she would never…could never love a man. And there was still that voice asking if she could give control over her life to anyone, and willingly this time.

Sarah's lips still tingled when she thought about that night in Denver and the kiss in the nursery, one filled with sweet passion, the other gentleness. Thorn had a way of sliding under the barriers she had set around her heart.

A few days after Thorn left, they bought a lot to use for the bakery and cafe. It wasn't on the main street that ran through town, but one street back. Close enough for what they wanted. They returned to the house after they'd finalized the purchase. Sarah stood at the entrance to the parlor and shook her head just a bit as she watched Drew and Helen celebrate the beginning of the new business. No one had to tell her how her brother felt about Helen. Even though Helen's cheek was still bandaged, her eyes glowed with the attention Drew showed her.

Sarah entered the parlor and noticed Carl and Emma had fallen asleep on the rug. The two of them were getting as close as brother and sister. She turned her attention back to Drew and Helen. "One thing we must do is decide on a name for the business."

Drew, holding Helen's hand, grinned. "How about Helen's Bakery and Café?"

Helen giggled. "No, no, no. It has to be fancier that that."

"Well, sis, what do you think it should be?"

"Well, it could be Miller, Hollingsworth, and MacPherson Bakery and Café, but I think that's too long."

Drew grinned at Helen. "It could be Hollingsworth and MacPherson."

Sarah put her hands on her hips. "We can't leave Helen's name off."

"Wasn't planning to. Just thinking she might change her name sometime." He looked sideways at the housekeeper.

Helen playfully swatted him. "Don't joke about things like that."

He wrapped his fingers around her hand. "Who says I was joking?"

Sarah cleared her throat to hide her joy. "I thought Golden Nugget Bakery and Café would be a good name."

"Great idea, sis."

"Perfect."

"Well, I'm glad you both agree, but I think it's time that we all retire." Sarah picked up Emma and woke Carl, who sat up and let out a huge yawn.

Sarah handed Emma to Drew. "Please take her to her crib while I help Helen to her room." Even though Helen was doing better, she still needed help moving around.

"I don't mind helping her." Drew kept his fingers wrapped around Helen's hand.

"Brother, dearest, while you were allowed into Helen's room to check on her while she was confined to her bed, tonight I'll see to Helen, and you can take your niece up to her nursery."

He rolled his eyes. "Yes, little mama. Social rules must be followed at all times." He gave Helen a swift kiss on the lips, then hurried up the stairs, laughing.

Sarah wrapped her arm around Helen's waist as they walked to the back of the house. "You know he loves you?"

Helen touched her fingers to her bandaged cheek, and a little light left her eyes. "I know."

The next morning, Sarah found Helen crying at the kitchen table. What in the world? Sarah looked around. She'd heard Drew leave his room earlier, but he was nowhere in sight. "What's the matter?"

"Drew's angry with me." Helen raised her blotchy red face as she crumpled a damp hankie in her hand. "But I did it for him. He just doesn't understand." She went to the stove and grabbed the coffee pot. "He could get killed." She dropped the pot on the table with enough force to rattle the lid. "Why do men have to be so—so—?"

"So caring, so protective?" Sarah felt like she was in a poorly written play, and she was no more than a paper character asking questions.

"So male." Helen wiped her eyes, then slammed a fist on the table.

Sarah settled on a chair. "Tell me what this is all about."

"The sheriff came by earlier and told me that Jim Grayson's no longer in town. He'd heard that he'd been seen in Denver."

"Who's Jim Grayson?"

She sighed. "He's the man who attacked me. He's Widow Grayson's son, the pa of Carl's best friend, Mike."

Sarah sat. "Is Drew angry that you hadn't told him who hurt you?"

Helen shook her head. "He was upset when I told him that Jim had been bothering me for some time, and I'd kept quiet. Not telling Drew who attacked me only made it worse." She sniffled. "I was just afraid."

"I know. Drew could've been killed."

"And now he's angry."

"Don't worry. He'll get over it. Just give him time."

Later that afternoon, Sarah stepped into the kitchen as Judith pushed a roast into the oven. "Looks like we'll have a good supper tonight."

"I hope so. I'm not the cook Helen is." Judith wiped her moist face with a corner of her apron. "Doc left a few minutes ago. Said he took off Helen's bandages."

"Maybe I'd better check on her." Sarah started across the kitchen when a thud and a shattering of glass came from Helen's room. She raced the rest of the way and knocked on the door. "Helen, Helen, are you all right?"

"Go away." Helen's voice was muffled through the closed door, but the thickness of the door didn't shut out the crying.

Sarah had cried too many times by herself to leave her friend alone, bearing whatever pain that caused her crying. "It's Sarah. I'm coming in."

Silence.

Sarah took that for agreement. She stepped inside and closed the door behind her.

Helen sat on the side of her bed, her head bowed, weeping into her hands. Sun from the open curtains highlighted a book that lay on the floor, which was covered with glass from a broken mirror.

She moved a wooden chair near the bed and sat. "Helen, look at me."

After several moments, Helen raised her head. With the bandages gone, the damage to her face was clear. A long narrow scar ran down the side of her face from temple to chin. The skin around the cut was still swollen, the scar pink.

Helen covered the side of her face with her hand. "I'm ugly. Drew'll never want me now."

"Stuff and nonsense." Sarah leaned back in the chair. She hated to do this, but Helen didn't need sympathy now. She needed to see that there was so much more to her than a scar.

"Helen, you're a pretty woman who wears a badge of honor on your face. You fought back. You survived. Do you really believe that Drew's love for you is so shallow that a narrow line on your face will cause him to go screaming down the road away from you? My goodness, what do you think he'll do when both of you get older and have wrinkles across your foreheads and around your mouths?"

Helen sniffled. "You make me sound shallow and selfish."

"No. I know how it feels to have my face beaten and bruised, eyes swollen shut, lip split. To feel that I need to be thrown out with the garbage. But, Helen, I want you to know that the damage will heal. The scar will lighten. You'll be fine—different but fine. But you'll need time. Time to heal inside as well as out."

Silence settled around the room for several minutes. Sarah hoped that Helen was thinking about what she had said. Rather than staring at the poor girl as she sat on the bed, Sarah cleaned up the broken mirror.

At last, Helen wiped her nose on her hankie. "That's something else that has been on my mind. Since I started working for you, I've been seeing several women from church."

"Your friends are welcome to come here to visit."

"Sarah, the women I need to see can't come here. Most of them are too busy with their families or too sickly themselves. I've been taking them meals and running errands for them when I've had time off." Helen fiddled with her hankie. "They count on me."

Memories of her mother tending to those less fortunate in her father's congregation popped in Sarah's mind. She had pushed much of her early years into a hidden safe place in her mind after her parents' deaths. Such love and good memories couldn't live with the cruelty she had faced at the hands of her grandfather and husband.

She had Emma and Drew. And she had to admit it, if only to herself, she had Thorn. Still, there was more that she could do. She wanted to be like her parents. "Tell me how to get to them and what they need."

They formed a plan for what needed to be done, who needed to be seen, and what help could be extended. At last, Sarah stood. There was much to do.

Helen touched the scar on her face. "Could you ask Brother Joshua Pickman to come by and see me? He's the minister where I go to church. There's some things I need to talk to him about."

A chill ran down Sarah's spine. She hadn't been to a church building since her parents died. But for Helen, she would send a note. "I'll get word to him."

With trembling fingers, Helen grabbed Sarah's hand. "One more thing. Will you keep Emma and Carl in the nursery when Drew comes home? I'll wait for him the parlor, but I need to see him alone. So—so he can see me, my face. I don't want anyone watching us. I have to see how he'll be when it's just him and me."

The next day, Sarah sat in the parlor tatting while Emma played with a ball on the floor. She tried not to stare at her brother and Helen while they stood in the hall by the front door, whispering and giggling. Well, to be truthful, Drew whispered, and Helen giggled.

Sarah let out a small sigh. Last night's talk must have gone well. Drew kissed Helen and left to meet with the carpenter who was constructing the building for the bakery and café.

Blushing, Helen entered the parlor and sat on a nearby chair. "I need to ask you for a favor."

"What do you need?" Sarah, couldn't keep a smile from her face. She placed her tatting shuttle and thread on a small table, then lifted up Emma and cuddled her in her arms.

"I know you don't go to church, and I understand why. Well, some of it." One of Helen's hands balled in her lap while the other one hovered over the scar on her face.

"Tomorrow is Sunday, and I want to go to church. Will you come with me? Drew's agreed to come, but I need another woman with me. I'm not sure I can do it without you."

Sarah sucked in a quick breath, then let it out. "Why don't you wait a while longer, until the skin heals better, the scar lightens? Then you'll feel more like visiting."

Helen pulled both of her hands into her lap. Slowly, like a puddle filling from a gentle drizzle, her eyes filled. "I don't need to go so I can visit. I need to go so I can draw strength from those there. To start to forgive Jim Grayson."

"Forgive that criminal?" Sarah gripped Emma tighter and stood, then stared at Helen. "He needs to be hunted down and thrown in jail. He needs to be horsewhipped. He needs—"

"I know. Right now I hate him. And I know that's wrong, but it's how I feel." Helen pressed her fist to her chest. "I also know it'll take a long time and be a struggle to forgive him, but I already find my anger is pulling me from God. I don't sleep much at night, and if I do, Carl has to wake me up from my nightmares. I have to find peace. I don't want to be eaten up with anger. It may seem silly, but I think the heart is a strange thing. It's big enough to hold all the love in the world. Faith and forgiveness, too."

She took a deep breath and looked up at Sarah. "But it shrinks when hatred and unforgiveness live there. Those leave scars that keep the heart from growing, so it can hold only so much of the good things. So you see, I'm doing it for me. This is part of my healing. It may be selfish, but it's for me, not him."

Sarah couldn't speak for the tightness of her throat. Oh, to be like Helen. Even with all she had learned at her father's feet, she had never heard the need to forgive others put so simply or so heartfelt. She waited a moment for her heart to settle down, then took a deep breath. She couldn't forgive Grandfather or Alfred, but she could help her friend. "Yes, I'll go with you to church."

Sarah walked away. She wasn't sure she could ever forgive. Or even wanted to.

The next morning, Sarah was surprised when Helen directed them to a small church on the edge of town. Larger ones stood closer to their house. Drew pulled the buggy to a halt.

After he helped them down, they all stared at the structure that looked more like a barn than anything else. There were old folks and young ones talking in small groups, mostly women and children, but that was the way it was in so many congregations. They were dressed in their Sunday best, cleaned and pressed.

Helen chuckled. "I know this must seem so different from the pictures I've seen of the churches in Boston, but this is where I feel closest to God. And the people are the sweetest you'll ever find."

Using a cane now, Drew tucked Helen's hand into the crook of his elbow. "This looks more like the ones we grew up in than those in Boston."

"Really." Helen looked from Drew to Sarah and back to Drew.

"Why don't you go to church?" Carl looked at one then the other, just like his sister had.

"Carl, it isn't polite to ask questions like that." Helen tapped her gloved fingers on her brother's shoulder. "I'm sorry. He shouldn't have asked that. I'm sure you have your reasons."

The knot that had been in Sarah's chest ever since Helen had asked her to come to church grew tighter. She wanted to scream out that Grandfather had forbidden them to attend anything religious, and Alfred had beaten her the first time she had attended after they were married. She had prayed, oh, how she had prayed for so long after that, but nothing happened, nothing changed. At last, she just gave up.

She cast a glance at Drew. He tried to smile, but no joy, no gladness reached his eyes, only sorrow and pain. She took a deep breath. That was in the past. For now, she would just try and get through today.

Several women greeted them. Sarah recognized a few of them from when she and Drew had brought supplies to their cabins.

Carl led them inside and to a wooden bench. Drew followed him with Helen between him and Sarah. A simply dressed man in worn but clean trousers and shirt stood and announced the first hymn.

He had a good strong voice and led the group. "Guide me, O Thou great Jehovah. Pilgrim through this barren land; I am weak, but Thou art mighty; Hold me with Thy powerful hand." The people seemed to know the song even without songbooks.

Sarah hummed along. It was one of the songs she'd learned in the congregation where her father preached. But it had been so long since she had sung it, she'd forgotten the words.

Emma laughed, but no one seemed to hear it over the singing. Sarah looked down at her daughter to see what had caught her attention. The little girl was staring at Helen. Sarah peeked over at her friend and swallowed hard.

Helen sat tall and straight. The scar on her cheek was bright pink against her pale skin.

Earlier, Sarah had offered the use of a veil, but Helen refused, saying the scar was her badge of faith. She had called on God in her trouble, and He protected her. And now she sat here on a wooden bench, her eyes closed, her head tilted toward Heaven, with a smile bigger than Sarah had ever seen, singing praises to God.

Shame filled Sarah. She bowed her head. She couldn't even hum. Her heart felt too much, remembered too much. When was the last time she had radiated that kind of joy? Now her heart was filled with anger.

Emma continued to stare at Helen's smiling face.

Sarah wanted to be happy like her friend, but more than that, she wanted her daughter to live in happiness and joy.

The man had started a new song, one she wasn't familiar with. "When my love to Christ grows weak, when for deeper faith I seek, then in tho't I go to thee, Garden of Gethsemane! There I walk amid the shades, while the lingering twilight fades. See the suffering friendless One, weeping, praying there alone."

Sarah curled her fingers until her fingernails dug into the palms of her hands. The pain helped to shut out the song. It brought too many memories of years past, of the years of her suffering, of her loneliness. She just needed to get through the rest of the service, and then she could go home. Go home. Not come back. She had done what Helen asked.

A small voice she hadn't heard in a long, long time crept through her thoughts. *If you don't come back, how will Emma learn to be happy?*

When the singing stopped, a gray-haired man with a limp moved to the pulpit. Sarah shut him out too, planning instead what needed to be done to get the bakery and café ready.

When the last amen was said, Sarah loosened her balled-up fists. The congregation stood and milled about. Several women came over and greeted her, hugged Helen, and made sweet remarks about Emma. Drew was strangely quiet as he helped Helen out and into the buggy.

Back home, Judith, who didn't attend church anywhere, started putting the meal on the table. With Emma in her arms, Sarah climbed the stairs, needing a few minutes alone.

After setting Emma on the bed with the rag doll Thorn had given her, Sarah paced. Things were coming too fast—Albert's death, Emma's birth, moving to Central City, Grandfather's losses and stroke, Helen's attack, and Thorn. She just needed... something. She just wasn't sure what it was or how to get it.

Or maybe she knew, but wasn't ready to accept it yet.

CHAPTER SIXTEEN

A little while later, Sarah carried Emma down the hall. It was interesting how no one had made the decision, but after Helen's attack, everyone continued eating in the kitchen instead of using the dining room across from the parlor.

She entered the kitchen. Thorn sat at the table, talking to Drew and Helen.

Sarah's heart beat a little faster.

Emma clapped her hands. "Dada. Dada."

"I got in while you were gone." Thorn took the little girl and kissed her on the cheek. "Planned on being back last night, but had trouble with a wheel."

Sarah touched his shoulder. "I'm glad you made it in time to eat with us."

Everyone sat, and Judith placed roast, gravy, mashed potatoes, and green beans in the center of the table. Helen offered a prayer of thanksgiving, then Judith pulled the hot rolls from the oven. As they filled their plates, banging sounded at the front door.

Sarah set the gravy boat on its saucer. "Who could that be?"

Judith left the kitchen and headed down the hall. There was silence in the room as everyone waited to see who had interrupted Sunday dinner.

Moments later, Stanley, his face flushed and his eyes narrowed, pushed his way into the kitchen. "Sarah, I need to speak with you."

"Stanley, as you can see, we have just sat down to eat. If you wish, you may join us. When we're done, we can talk."

"I need to speak with you now." He stressed the last word and paused for a moment. "If we don't speak, you'll regret it."

Thorn stood, dropping his napkin on the table. He took a couple of steps closer to the red-faced man. "I'm sure you didn't mean for that to sound like a threat, right, Snodgrass?"

Stanley's lips twisted into a terrible sneer. "I'm not threatening anyone, but I will speak to Sarah."

Warmth filled Sarah's heart at Thorn's protective stance. She stood and placed her hand on Thorn's arm. He had no idea how treacherous it could be to cross Stanley unless one had prepared beforehand. "Let me get this unpleasantness over with so we can enjoy our meal."

Thorn clenched his jaw as he glared at her.

She patted his arm and smiled. "Thorn, would you please join us in the parlor?"

"What I have to say is to you. We don't need him interfering." Stanley stood like a puffy toad, his fists resting on his hips.

"This is my home, Stanley. You're welcome to leave whenever you wish. Feel free to set up an appointment at my lawyer's office for some time later this week." Sarah tightened her grip on Thorn's arm. She had to win this small battle, to let Stanley know he had no hold over her.

Stanley blustered for a moment or two, then agreed. "As you wish." He turned and stomped into the parlor.

While Sarah sat on the sofa, Stanley paced. Once she and Thorn were settled, he dropped onto the chair across from her.

"What have you heard from your grandfather?"

"Nothing, nor have I ever expected to. We both know he sent me out here to get rid of me. Since he couldn't control me or my inheritance, he had no use for me."

Stanley took out his handkerchief and wiped his brow. "Sarah, I'm sorry to tell you he had a stroke."

Sarah nodded and waited to see what else Stanley had to say.

He stood and paced. "It's even worse. Through some investments that went bad, he has had a reversal in fortunes. We need to discuss what we are going to do about things. With what you got from Alfred, you could help set things to rights and be in control of your grandfather's entire empire."

Thorn's fingers rested on her shoulder, massaging, reassuring her of his presence.

She drew in a deep breath. "I've no desire to have control of anything like that, so there's nothing to discuss. And before you try to use guilt to get me to do what you want, I've already taken care of Grandfather's needs."

"How?" Stanley stopped and stared at her. "When did you learn of this?"

"A couple of weeks back. It seems my lawyers and spies are better than yours."

"So what are you going to do about his banks, his other businesses in Boston and here?"

"Nothing. As far as I know there is nothing left of his business interests in Boston. And it is my understanding some kind of corporation took over his interest here in Central City."

Stanley's face grew redder. "I knew something was wrong when I didn't hear anything from your grandfather." His eyes narrowed. "But what of your brother?"

"You don't need to worry about me." Drew stepped into the parlor, an envelope in his hand. "I'd planned to leave this on your desk, just so you would be officially notified. But I can do it today."

Stanley stepped back and stared at the envelope. "What is it?"

"My resignation. I've a better offer." Drew smiled at his sister.

"You can't do this. We need to go back to Boston and work with the men there to re-establish your grandfather's empire."

Sarah shook her head. "No, that's all gone. You have the office here in Central City that you can work in, where you can take care of your sister. But let me warn you, I've been told that there are auditors coming in to examine the records. Don't even think you can disappear with the money people have invested in the businesses you and Grandfather planned. If you do, I'll personally put a reward on your head so large, everyone in the country will be hunting you down." Sarah stood. "After what you did to me in Boston, don't think I won't do it."

Stanley's face grew whiter than his shirt. "You will regret this." He turned on his heel and slammed out of the house, uttering curses all the way.

Sarah gave them her brightest smile. "Shall we return to dinner? Suddenly, I feel very hungry."

Mac was sure he enjoyed the meal, but his mind was on Rose and what had just happened. He loved the way she stood up to Snodgrass. He loved…no, he couldn't love her, but the feeling kept rolling through his chest.

All the time he ate apple pie with rich cream oozing down it, he kept seeing Rose on the ranch with his aunts and Granny doing whatever women did when they got together. He could see her dressed in a simpler style as she sat down for supper in his house with their family around the table—him, her, and the children.

Suddenly the pie turned to bitter ash. He struggled to get the last bite down. Something broke in his heart, and the blood seeped out, leaving a cold spot in his chest.

What if he never found Hank? How long could he keep looking? Could Sarah Rose be happy at the ranch? Would she welcome three more girls into her life?

Later that evening, Sarah swallowed down a laugh. Thorn held Emma's hand while she walked around the nursery, giggling, jabbering, and showing off. The little girl had wrapped the big man right around her thumb. They had come upstairs to put Emma to bed for the night. But she wouldn't stay down, and Thorn couldn't bear to hear her cry. She wondered what his girls were like. Were they with his grandparents or his wife's? Did he ever see them?

Thorn jiggled Emma's hand, and she laughed. "I'm not sure this little one is going to sleep tonight."

"Why don't you try rocking her? It might help." Sarah nodded to the rocking chair she had used quite often for that very purpose.

He lifted the girl and sat. The chair moved back and forth on the large rug. Sarah leaned against the back of the sofa. The soft creaking of the rocker, the gentle tapping of Thorn's boots as his knees moved up and down, and Emma's sleepy baby sounds filled the dimness the single lamp shed in the room.

Peace joined the other sounds. Peace and contentment. Contentment? Yes, Sarah let out a small sigh. Peace and contentment. That was what she felt. She was free of Grandfather and Stanley. Her daughter was growing and healthy. Drew and Helen were finding a new way of life.

"What put that look on your face?" Thorn's lowered voice floated to her while he laid the sleeping baby in her crib. Before Sarah could answer, he sat down beside her on the sofa.

"I was just thinking about Drew and Helen."

Thorn rubbed his hand down his pant leg, then looked at her through lowered eyelids. "I think they're good for each other. You aren't thinking about coming between them, are you?"

Stillness settled over Sarah, cold yet fiery. Why would he think something like that? She loved her brother. She loved the friend Helen had become. She wouldn't hurt either one of them. "Why are you trying to make problems where there aren't any?"

Thorn ran his fingers through his hair. "Not trying to make trouble, maybe trying to head it off."

"What do you mean?" she whispered as her fingers tapped on the sofa.

He dropped his hand over her fingers. "From what you've told me about what happened to you, I figured you didn't have a very high opinion of marriage. And I'm pretty sure that's where those two are headed."

Sarah stood and paced. "I'm pretty sure they are, too. And I'm happy for them, if that's what happens. Just because Grandfather forced me into a bad marriage doesn't mean that I hate the idea of marriage. My parents loved each other and had a good, strong marriage. Melody and her husband are the same. I'm not so blind I can't see that."

She stopped and looked at him. "How could you even think that of me, think I could be so cruel?" Her voice hissed out in a whisper, mindful of Emma even in her hurt.

He reached her before she could blink. His hands rested on her shoulders. "I don't think you are cruel or bad or anything like that. You're a woman who loves her brother and wants what you feel best for him. When I first met you, you seemed to want to control everything, but you've changed. I count your brother and Helen as close friends. And, like you, I want to see them happy."

Sarah couldn't stop the tears that filled her eyes. One leaked out and rolled down her cheek.

Thorn groaned and pulled her to this chest. He wrapped his arms around her, rubbing her back with his large hands. "Don't cry. I didn't mean to hurt you. I never would."

She lifted her head and gazed into his face. She believed him. More than that she trusted him. She had changed. When she had come here, she couldn't stand for anyone to touch her and now she wanted Thorn's arms around her. Suddenly she was staring at his lips. Lips that had brought her such wonderful feelings.

His arms tightened around her and his lips came closer. She closed her eyes as those lips covered hers. The feelings were back. The sweet, wonderful feelings.

How long they stood there in each other's arms, she wasn't sure. Time didn't matter. But when he pulled back, they both gulped in deep breaths.

He stroked her face with his fingertips, gave her a short, gentle kiss, then pulled farther away. "Think it would be a good idea if we sat for a bit. There's something I want to talk to you about before I leave in the morning."

Did he want to talk about them getting closer, about not ending the marriage? After the last few minutes, it was something she would like to talk about. She loved being with him, sharing these moments of excitement. She didn't have to live in a cold world of fear. She was moving past that. And she had him to thank for it.

They settled on the sofa, and Thorn took her hand in his, rubbing his thumb over the back of it. Sweet tingling spread up Sarah's arm.

"Sarah, while I'm gone, I don't want you to go out by yourself. You'll need to always take someone with you. Not just Helen or Judith, but someone who can protect you if Snodgrass tries something." He smiled at her. "I know a couple of young men that I trust. They can help out around here and go with you whenever you need to leave."

Coldness replaced the tingling. Memories of Alfred's control rolled over the trust she had felt for Thorn just minutes before like a broken dam flooding a town below, choking, drowning, wiping out all that got in its way. Oh, Alfred was willing for her to go out in public, be seen, have her little trips, but only if she was shackled to a man of his choice. She tried to push the flood back, tried to build back the dam, but she couldn't.

She jerked her hand away and stood.

Thorn let a deep, harsh sigh. "Clearly I'm not saying this right."

"What part of having your men watch my every move, only going out when I'm permitted if they decide, of being held prisoner in my own house, don't I understand?"

When he stood, she turned toward her room. She had to get away. The dreams that had been so beautiful just a few moments before lay shattered on the rug.

Thorn encircled her wrist with his hand. With a slight tug, he turned her toward him. "I only meant to warn you about Stanley and offer some protection for you. You are nobody's prisoner. I believe the man is dangerous. You see him defeated, powerless without your grandfather's backing. But he's like a cornered snake with nothing to lose. He's lost what he held most dear. What do you think he will do? How far do you think he will go? What happens to Emma if Snodgrass comes after you?"

She tried to focus on his words, to believe he had her best interest at heart. But all she could see was Alfred's face. All she could hear was Alfred's threatening voice. She couldn't think. She had to get away from Thorn. "Let go of my arm. You're hurting me."

"My hand's loose on your wrist. I'd never harm you. You should know that by now. You don't have to lump me with your cur of a husband." He dropped her hand and walked to the door, then looked over his shoulder at her. "All you had to do was say no and tell me how you planned to protect yourself. I would have listened. Stay safe. I'll be back in a week or so."

CHAPTER SEVENTEEN

Early the next morning, Mac stepped into the nursery and stared down at the sleeping baby. This little girl held his heart in her tiny hands and didn't even know it.

He glanced at the door to Rose's room. Was she sleeping or just waiting for him to leave? How could she still not trust him? And how could she not understand the effect she had on him?

He closed his eyes and gripped the edge of the crib. He wanted to go into that room and make their marriage real, be a true husband to his wife. To offer her the love that filled his heart. But he couldn't, not yet, maybe never.

A lot depended on completing his mission, for that was what his search for Hank had become—a mission. But making his marriage real depended even more on Rose trusting—truly trusting—herself and him. Maybe her scars went too deep, or maybe they had just scabbed over and kept the poison in, slowly killing her heart.

He just didn't know. With a last look at Emma, he turned toward the hall, but paused at the door to Rose's room. He raised his fist to knock, but he stopped just short of the wood. Placing his palm against the door, he rested his head on his outstretched arm. He had to give her time, however much she needed. He would give her whatever was in his power to give.

Dropping his hand, he turned to the door that opened to the hall and found it blocked.

Drew stood in the doorway, his lips twisted in a sad smile. "Come on, let's have breakfast before you head out."

⚮

The sun streamed through the curtains when Sarah woke. The birds sang, but she could barely hear them over Emma's howling.

Sarah's head pounded from the lack of sleep. She pulled herself out of bed and opened the door between their rooms.

Emma stood in her crib, tears trailing down her flushed chubby cheeks. Her nose was running and her usual golden curls stuck out in spikes all over her head. "Dada…Dada!"

Sarah picked up the little girl and wiped her face with a nearby cloth. Emma fought her and cried louder.

"I know, precious, but he's not here. He's gone away." Sarah's stomach clenched at the words. Thorn was gone. She had sent him away in anger. Now it would be at least a week before she could talk to him again. In the long hours the night before as she'd lain in bed, wide awake, she'd realized that she'd reacted badly to what he said. He wasn't trying to control her. He had her best interest at heart. But his words had pulled up old memories, things she thought she had gotten past.

Sarah cleaned and dressed Emma. Holding her daughter close, she carried her to the kitchen.

Emma clapped her hands. "Dada. Dada."

"I'm sorry, Daddy's not here. He left because your Momma's an old shrew."

Emma tried to lift her leg. "Sho. Sho."

Sarah dropped a kiss onto her daughter's combed hair. "No darling—not shoe, oh well you don't need to know that word right now." Pushing open the door, she almost bumped into Helen on the other side.

"Now who's a shrew?" Helen brushed a hand against Emma's curls. "Surely not this angel." Helen's head tilted, her eyebrows raised above red-rimmed eyes. But with a wobbly smile on her face, she looked at Sarah. "Who does that leave?"

Sarah set Emma in a raised chair and tied a long piece of fabric around her middle and through the spokes at the back of the chair. "Do I really come off as a shrew?"

Helen turned to the counter and filled a cup with coffee. She set it on the table along with a piece of toast she had cut into small bites earlier. Sarah took the coffee while Emma grabbed a bite of toast and shoved it into her mouth like she hadn't eaten in a week. She took two more and did the same thing.

Sarah's whole body tightened at Helen's lack of response. "Sit and talk to me, please. I need to know."

"All right." Helen sat. "You've never been less than a friend to me, a loving sister to your brother, and a loving mother to Emma." She rolled her eyes. "And I think you treat Stanley Snodgrass better than he deserves."

"But?"

Helen ran her finger over the scar on her face. "I think I'm beginning to understand your feelings a little better. There's something precious taken when you're attacked. I thought when I forgave Jim, I'd get it back. Don't get me wrong. I needed to forgive him for me." Helen rested her hand over her heart. "I don't even know what it is I've lost, but I do know that it has changed me, changed the way I see people, even the way I see Drew. Like I said, I don't know what it is, but I want it back."

"It's trust you've lost, and it's trust you're trying to find." Sarah reached over and covered Helen's hand with hers. "Drew probably understands because of what I've been through. Let him help you. He loves you, and together you might just find what you're looking for."

At the mention of Drew's name, a tear overflowed from Helen's eye. She pulled back her hand and grabbed for the drop of moisture before it hit her cheek, then wiped her fingers on her apron.

Pain shot through Sarah's heart. "Is there a problem with Drew?" Please, no, not with Helen and Drew.

She shook her head. "Drew said something Mac and—" She tapped her finger against her lips, then let out a sigh. "It's really silly, but it made me angry."

Sarah waited for a moment or two when the thought struck her. "Is this about Thorn and me?"

Helen sat still for several seconds, then nodded. "Don't you trust Mac? He won't hurt you, you know."

Was her relationship with Thorn causing problems with two of the people she loved so much? She couldn't let that happen. "Maybe."

She shrugged.

Helen smiled. "I'll make a deal with you. I'll try to trust more, if you will too." She picked up her cup. "And Sarah, try to forgive those who hurt you deeply."

Sarah's head snapped up. But before she could argue, Helen held up her hand, palm outward. "Forgive your grandfather and your first husband for your sake, not theirs. You won't ever see them again this side of the Judgment Day." She touched the scar on her cheek. "I understand more now than before. Do this for yourself, for your healing."

The back door opened. Judith and Sally walked in.

Sarah stood and held herself together with her arms wrapped around her middle. She had to get out of the kitchen before she said something she would regret. "Please, look after Emma for a little bit."

She rushed out of the room, but Helen's words followed her.

By mid-morning, Mac had reached his second stop as he pulled his wagon next to a wooden building. He'd just started the longest of his routes, and already he was chafing to get back to Sarah Rose. The way they had parted rubbed him the wrong way. And Drew hadn't been any help at breakfast, staying silent and shoving food into his mouth.

"Afternoon, Mac. Glad to see you." The potbellied store owner came out in the hot sun, his bald head shining in the sunlight. "Already run out of flour and salt. Be glad to get re-stocked."

Mac nodded. He pulled out two bags of salt and handed them to the man while he grabbed a couple bags of flour. After several more trips, he had the man's order filled. And as he always did at each of his stops, he asked the storeowner if he'd seen anyone fitting Hank's description.

The man scratched his head for a moment, then his eyes lit up. "Now you mention it, my boy said something 'bout a man who came by a couple, maybe three days ago. Said the man had a birthmark on his face like you described, covering his ear. Don't know which way he went though."

Excitement raced through Mac. So close. "Can I talk to your boy?"

"Sorry, he left yesterday. Gonna visit his grandparents in Kansas for a bit." The storeowner handed Mac the cash for his supplies. "Good luck on finding that feller."

After the man returned to his store, Mac smashed his gloved fist into the side of his wagon. Two days, maybe three. Where was Hank? Why couldn't he find him? He had to find him soon. Everything depended on it.

The words—shrew, trust, forgiveness—continued with her the rest of the week. By the time Mac returned, she knew they had to work out some things.

After much thought, Sarah figured out a plan. The morning after Thorn arrived home, she put it into action.

Sarah dressed with great care in a simple cotton dress and serviceable leather boots. After peeking into the nursery and finding Emma gone, she hurried down to the kitchen.

She opened the door and was greeted with the sight she expected. Thorn sat at the table drinking coffee, Emma sat tied to her chair munching on toast. Drew stood near the stove with his arm around Helen. They all greeted her.

Helen poured a cup of coffee and handed it to Sarah.

"Thank you." Sarah sat, then turned toward Thorn. "I'm glad you're back. Did everything go well?"

Thorn stared at her.

For a moment, she worried he wouldn't respond.

Finally, he said in an even voice, "No problems. Delivered everything."

She was struck again about how harsh she'd been the last time they'd seen each other. Taking a deep breath, then letting it out, she knew she had to make the first move. "If you don't have anything planned for today, I was wondering if you'd like to go on a picnic."

Emma sneezed and wiped slimy stuff all over her face.

Helen cleaned the little girl's cheeks, mouth, and chin. "I think a picnic for the two of you is a wonderful idea, but I think I should keep Emma here with me today. I can have a basket ready in no time."

Sarah nodded. This wasn't quite what she had planned. Emma would have been a good buffer between her and Thorn, but she couldn't control everything. "That sounds good."

She glanced over at Thorn. "If you didn't have anything else planned."

Mac looked at everyone in the room. Something was going on here, and he seemed to be the only one who was in the dark.

Drew stood by the stove, his cup covering half his face. Helen held on to the baby like she was holding the answer to the world's mysteries, and Rose sat there straight as a board looking calm and in control.

He caught some movement in the corner of his eye. Rose's fingers were tapping on her skirt, not a light-hearted tapping. No, this was a heavy, nervous movement, almost a pounding. Time to find out what was going on. "I've got a few things to see about. It'll take me about an hour. And a picnic sounds good. Any place in particular you want to go?"

"Good. I mean, I didn't have any place in mind. Maybe you know a good spot?"

"I do." Thorn stood. Suddenly, he didn't feel hungry. Right now he just needed to get out of this house. The undercurrents here were getting a mite strong. If a man wasn't careful, he might just drown. He looked at his pocket watch. "I'll be back by nine. It'll take a little while to get to the place I'm thinking about."

Before anyone could say anything, he made his escape.

By the time Thorn pulled the buggy off the road onto a small trail, the butterflies in Sarah's middle had all been eaten up by the huge grasshoppers that now hopped around in there. It had not been an easy trip so far. Neither one of them had said much.

After another half hour, Thorn directed the horse through a narrow grouping of rocks. He stopped the buggy. They were in a circle of boulders. A carpet of green grass spread out before them.

She gripped his hand when he helped her from the buggy. She could hardly believe they were in the same state. The land around them looked untouched, from the little waterfall that formed a pool to the shade trees that surrounded it.

"Where are we?"

He grinned. "Place belongs to one of my cousins. We found it when we were hunting one day shortly after we staked out our land further south of here. He decided to build here. If we'd followed the main road back there, we would've come to his homestead."

"It's beautiful, and so peaceful."

Thorn tipped his hat back on his head. "And a good place if you want to spend some time uninterrupted."

Sarah grabbed her middle. The grasshoppers had come back with a vengeance. Did Thorn know what she wanted to talk about?

He handed her a quilt and took the basket Helen had packed, along with a couple fishing poles and a can of dirt. "Drew tells me that you used to be pretty good at fishing when you were younger."

She wanted to tap her foot and demand to know what else Drew had said about her, but on second thought maybe she would just wait and see what Thorn had to say. She followed him under the trees and spread out the quilt while he took care of the horse.

Slowly, the grasshoppers settled down. She was here to come to a better understanding with Thorn. It wouldn't help if she stayed all worked up.

Recalling the enjoyment shared with her family as a child, she grabbed the poles and the can, then stepped to the water's edge. By the time he joined her, she had worms on both hooks, and hers in the water.

Thorn grinned and took his pole. "Is this a fishing contest? 'Cause if it is, you've already cheated by starting early."

"No, just a little memory of the past and a little peace for the day." Childhood giddiness filled her. She tilted her head and glanced up at him. "But if you want to make it a contest…"

Thorn flipped the hook out over the water and sat on the bank next to her, his legs outstretched. He wore a bigger grin than before. "Didn't know a Bostonian lady knew how to fish."

"I was a country preacher's daughter before I ever lived in Boston."

"Tell me about that."

Sarah rubbed the pole with her thumbs and let her mind drift back to the happiest time she had ever known. "Until I was six, I was the apple of my parents' eyes. And just after my sixth birthday, I got the most wonderful present ever—my own baby."

Thorn scooted up against the trunk of a large tree. "Your own baby?"

"That's what Mama called Drew. She let me pick out his clothes and dress him. When he was older, I got to feed him with the little spoon Mama had used when I was a baby. I didn't even care when the older girls teased me and said Mama was just calling him that so I wouldn't complain when I took care of him." She shook her head. "It didn't matter. I knew he was mine to take care of and to love. He was so smart. I taught him his ABCs and how to climb trees. We would go fishing together. Oh, how he loved to dig for worms."

Thorn chuckled. "Did you teach him how to do that?"

"I told him what to do, and he did it." Sarah jiggled her pole. "I guess boys are born knowing how to do things like that, kind of like girls know how to be mamas and make mud pies."

"Sounds like you had a happy childhood."

"We did, full of love and happiness. Our parents saw to that." She sighed. "Until the day they died, then it was just Drew and me."

Her fingers tightened on the pole until her knuckles turned white. "We could have survived together. The owner of the general store had agreed that I could work in his store. There was a room in the back where Drew and I could stay. But Grandfather demanded we go to Boston. A week later, he made me marry Albert."

Mac's hands tightened on the fishing pole. He wasn't a crying man, but he had to blink hard while he listened to what happened to his Rose. If her grandfather were standing here right now, well, he wouldn't be standing. The old man would be lying on the ground, bloody and hurting. "Did you get to see him when he was growing up, talk to him?"

"Even Grandfather couldn't keep Drew and me completely apart." Sarah Rose relaxed a bit, with a small smile flirting across her lips. "Mrs. Dowdy, Grandfather's housekeeper, had been with the family since before my father was born. She'd helped Grandmother raise my father and loved him almost as much as she would have loved her own child.

Sarah Rose gave her fishing pole a little jiggle, then settled back on the quilt. "The thing Grandfather didn't know was that Mrs. Dowdy's sister was the head cook at the academy where Grandfather sent Drew. They worked out a system that allowed Drew and me to exchange letters." She let out a deep shuddering sigh. "I don't know what I would have done if I hadn't had that connection. There were many, many days when I didn't want to go on, wasn't sure I could go on." She brushed a finger beneath her eye. "But I knew I had to keep living for him."

Mac dropped his pole. Her pain, her tears, her courage called to him.

Before he could wrap his arms around her, she cried out. "Thorn, your pole! Grab your pole! You've got a fish!"

He turned to the pond. His pole was wiggling its way down to the water. With a quick jump, he grabbed it, flicked his wrist, and pulled a big, shiny catfish out. It flew through the air and landed on the grass behind him.

Before he could congratulate himself on such a good catch, Sarah Rose let out a scream. "Thorn, Thorn, I got one!"

It must have been a huge one, for she was struggling something fierce. Her hands gripped the pole, which was bending so much Thorn feared it would break. He raced over, then stood behind her and wrapped his hands over hers. Together they jerked, and a second catfish flew through the air, only this one was much bigger than the first.

They laughed together for a minute or two. Then all at once the hairs on the back of Mac's neck prickled. Why had he left his rifle in the buggy? He tightened his left arm around his Rose. With a deep breath, he turned a little to the right, pushing her behind his body. She pushed his arm away and stood beside him.

In front of him sat four filthy cowboys, all grinning ear to ear. The dirtiest of them all looked at Sarah Rose from head to foot, then nodded to the fish. "Think you might have enough to share?"

"Don't cotton much to sharing today." Mac stared the cowboy in the eye.

"You never did like sharing." The dirty man flipped his leg over his saddle and slid down. "Granny should've whupped your backside a lot more than she ever did."

Mac felt it when the fear drained out of his Rose. She glared at him.

She nodded to the dirty cowboy. "Is he one of the eighty-one?"

Mac couldn't help but chuckle. "Yup, along with four more of them, but he's late in coming and kinda the runt."

The cowboy puffed up and placed his fists on his hips. "Them could be taken for fighting words." He dropped his hands and turned to Rose. "But who wants to fight when there's a pretty girl around?"

He removed his hat and bowed just a tad. "Since this heathen has failed to do so, let me introduce myself. I am

Adair MacPherson, owner of this land and a single man who is looking for a wife to share it with." He grinned. "Would you be of a mind to marry me and share all I have? A woman who can fish like that is a rare treasure to be sure."

Mac was the one resting his hands on his hips now. The kid had gone too far. "She's my wife. Find your own girl."

His cousins' eyes widened. Their mouths dropped open.

Rose pushed past him. "Thorn, I asked you on this picnic so we could find out more about each other. I've told you all about me. I think I have just figured out how to find out about you." She glanced up at the cowboys. "We have plenty, more than enough food to share. Why don't you all join us for a picnic?"

Mac's stomach gripped so tight he thought he might have been shot. With all these cousins trying to impress her and talking about him, how was he going to keep her from finding out what she didn't need to know, at least not until he found truth?

CHAPTER EIGHTEEN

Mac's sides and shoulders ached from the tension that had gripped him over the last couple of hours. He might as well have been in a Saturday night brawl. Rose waved to his cousins as the cowboys left. No one said a word about Lizzie and what happened two years before. Oh, the boys had gone on and on, bringing up every embarrassing thing that had happened to him growing up. They'd entertained Rose, making her laugh until she grabbed her sides and begged them to stop.

Rose relaxed against the back of the buggy seat. "I like your cousins, and I think I learned a great deal about you today."

Thorn snapped the reins, and they started back toward Central City. "You said something about that earlier. So that's what this day was about?"

Rose blushed redder than the roses outside her house. "I need to know more about you. We're married. But until today, I knew precious little about you."

Mac's heart pounded a little harder. "Is it important to know all about me?"

Rose dropped her head and fiddled with her fingers. "Yes." The word came out as a whisper and was carried away by the warm breeze.

"Why?" Mac's question was just as low.

Seconds passed, each one slower than the one before.

At last, Rose raised her head. "Because I have feelings for you. Feelings I've never had before." Her hands trembled as she twisted them together. "I hate the fight we had the other night. I know you were trying to protect me from Stanley. But I thought...it felt like you were trying to control me like Alfred used to do. Trust is a precious thing, and I need to trust you, but I don't know how. Maybe if I know more about you...."

Mac felt gut-punched. Rose had feelings for him. He should be thrilled. Isn't this what he wanted? But he couldn't accept those feelings, not until he learned more about what happened to Lizzie. Then, and only then, would he be free, able to accept and return those feelings. Assuming he wasn't the reason she ended her life.

Sarah Rose stared at him with eyes questioning and waiting.

So many things to respond to from her little speech. What a cad his next words revealed him to be. "Well, just as long as you understand Stanley's a threat to you."

She turned her head and no longer looked at him as she shifted away from him. "Oh, I understand all about Stanley Snodgrass." Her voice had turned to ice. "Stanley was always sent for after Alfred beat me, killed my babies, nearly killed me. I overheard that black-hearted miscreant ordering the doctor to keep me alive because Grandfather needed me to control Drew. Believe me, I know just how evil he is." She wiggled her reticule where it lay on her lap. "Which is why I always carry a gun with me."

Mac pulled on the reins. The horse stopped. He looked from her bag to her face. "You've got a gun in there? Do you know how to use it?"

"Of course. It wouldn't do me any good if I didn't."

He wasn't sure if he should worry more or less about Rose's safety. He sucked in a deep breath and snapped the reins over the horse. "Hope you don't get angry with me."

"Oh, you've made me plenty angry with you, just not too angry." She paused and let a tiny smile play on her lips. "Yet."

Mac couldn't keep back a burst of laughter. Life was getting more interesting every day.

With all the stories she'd heard the day before from Thorn's cousins still rolling around in her head, Sarah slipped her corset over her chemise and pulled to tighten the laces. In the last few weeks, she had gotten more lax in dressing in all the layers of undergarments as she worked with Helen and Drew on the bakery and café, but today was Sunday. And like her mother always taught her, she would wear her Sunday best for church. Still to go were the petticoats and her new dress.

A few minutes later she ran her hand down the royal blue fabric as she finished sliding the last of the mother-of-pearl buttons through their holes. The color matched that of her eyes. At least that's what the seamstress said the week before at the final fitting. Hopefully, Thorn would find her attractive in it.

Sarah finished her hair just before Emma let everyone listening know that she was awake.

While she moved quickly across the woven rug on her bedroom floor, Sarah reached up and touched the locket around her neck—Poppa's last gift to Grandmother. Only she had died before he could give it to her. A smile tugged at her lips. Her father had named her after his mother and had given the necklace to Sarah on her twelfth birthday. After opening the adjoining door, she smiled at Emma. The little girl grinned back.

"I promised Helen we would go to church with her this morning, so let's get you cleaned up." Sarah quickly changed Emma's diaper and washed her face. She would wait until after breakfast to dress her. No sense in putting clean clothes on her until after the little girl ate.

When they entered the bacon- and coffee-scented kitchen, Thorn sat at the table drinking coffee.

"Dada. Dada." Emma reached for him. Sarah almost lost her hold on Emma when the little girl reached for Thorn.

He took Emma and eyed Sarah from head to shoe, then grinned and winked.

Heat filled Sarah's cheeks, and she turned away. She grabbed a cup. With her back to him, she filled it and took a sip. Maybe they would think her cheeks were red because she burned her tongue. "Oh, that's hot."

She patted her cheeks and turned around. Drew and Helen tried to smother their laughter. That ploy hadn't fooled anyone. She gave up and joined them at the table.

Helen headed for the oven. "I think the biscuits are about done, so we'll have plenty of time to eat before church."

Sarah glanced at Thorn. She had gone to church with Helen several times and had asked him each time if he would go with them. He'd never accepted her invitation. She hoped today would be different. "We're all going to church this morning. Will you go with us?"

Thorn turned his attention to Emma and tickled her under one of her chins. "Not today. Maybe some other time."

Sarah bit the inside of her lip. True to the promise she had made to herself during the first time she had attended the church service with Helen, Sarah had continued to go for Emma's sake. She'd been reading her Bible again for the same reason. Even though she had lost her joy in God, she wanted it for her daughter.

The thing was, as she did those things for Emma, her own heart was changing. But just because she was coming back to God, albeit little by little, didn't mean Thorn was ready to return. Another thought struck her. Maybe he had never come to God in the first place.

Church, religion, God, Jesus were all things they had
never discussed.

The starch started oozing out her spine again. No. If
she had gone so far from God and yet was coming back,
Thorn could, too. It would just take time. Besides, right
now she didn't have the strength to bring him along. Her
life was still in too much of an upheaval.

"All right, maybe next time." She gave him a smile,
hoping he knew she understood.

He turned towards her and nodded, lifted his lips into a
smile and winked again.

Sarah raised her cup to her mouth. His
acknowledgement of her acceptance of his denial had to
be the cause of the heat rising in her cheeks, and not the
wink from those green MacPherson eyes. Right?

The wooden benches were filling up fast by the time
Sarah and the others arrived at the small building. They
had just gotten settled on the last bench when Toby Barr
stood and welcomed the group. Helen had told her that
Mr. Barr had become the song leader mainly because he
had a strong voice, was willing to serve, and had the only
songbook. After flipping through his book, he cleared his
throat and led them in several songs, then a prayer.

With a nod to the man who gave a talk each Sunday,
Toby flipped to another page in his songbook. "The song
before the lesson has always been one of my favorites
and when Brother Joshua told me he planned to talk
about Joseph today, I thought it would fit in just fine.
Would you all stand and join me in singing 'How Firm a
Foundation?'"

Sarah knew the hymn. It had been one of her father's
favorites, too. He'd always had it sung before he
preached about Job. During the first verse of the song,
she thought of the trials the young boy Joseph faced—
taken from the only home he had ever known, sold into

slavery, abused and lied about, imprisoned. She considered how he'd gone on to build a new life. She had never thought how she had so much in common with Joseph before now.

When they started another verse, she thought of how that young boy reacted to things that had happened to him and how it differed from the way she had. "When through the deep waters I call thee to go, The rivers of sorrow shall not overflow, For I will be with thee thy trails to bless, And sanctify to thee thy deepest distress."

Blood pounded in Sarah's chest. God hadn't been with her when Alfred beat her, had He? Oh, Satan was there. She had felt him standing in the room and laughing every time. She could still remember the stench of his evil breath over Alfred's whiskey-soaked one.

The next verse started. "When through fiery trials thy pathway shall lie, My grace, all-sufficient shall be thy supply; The flame shall not hurt thee: I only design thy dross to consume, and thy gold to refine."

But the flame did hurt. The flame of Alfred's beatings hurt so badly and took so much. How could the loss of three babies not hurt?

Sarah looked sideways as Helen touched her arm. Brown eyes looked at her, then at Emma. Sarah hadn't realized her arms were shaking, and the baby was about to cry. With a nod, she handed Emma to Helen, then wrapped her arms around her middle. The song was nearly over. "The soul that on Jesus hath leaned for repose, I will not—I will not desert to his foes; that soul, though all hell should endeavor to shake, I'll never—no, never—no, never forsake."

With a smothered cry, Sarah forced herself to remain seated. She still had to get through the sermon. She blotted out whatever Brother Joshua said. The only way she could sit quietly was to count the number of threads in the lacy shawl of the woman in front of her, one hundred twenty-four little white stitches from side to side.

She had just finished counting the stitches from top to bottom when Helen touched her arm again.

"Let's go."

Sarah looked around. People were standing, visiting, leaving. That's right. She had to leave, go home, get to her room. Without a word, she hurried out of the building and into their buggy. All the way home, she could feel Helen watching her. While her mind fought the memories of the past, a separate part of her was grateful that someone was taking care of her daughter. Thankful because she knew right then she couldn't do it.

When Drew pulled the horse to a halt, Sarah jumped down. She hit the ground and glanced up at Helen. "Take care of Emma, please." Her voice was no more than a whisper, but at least she got that much out. She turned on her heel and raced to the house, not sure what she was running to or running from.

The kitchen door burst open, and Mac stood so fast his chair crashed backwards. Sarah, pale-faced and wide-eyed, ran past him without a word. He set the cup down and hurried across the kitchen. If Snodgrass was out there, he'd beat him to within an inch of his life. He stopped mid-stride when Drew and Helen, carrying Emma, walked through the doorway.

"What happened? Rose just came through here looking like a ghost was chasing her—a ghost or Snodgrass."

Drew ran his hand through his hair and took a deep breath. "I don't know. I've never seen her so upset."

Helen bit her lip and told him that she'd gotten upset during the service. Lot of help that was.

"Did someone say something?"

"We arrived late and didn't have a chance to speak to anyone before the service began."

Mac wasn't sure he could help his Rose, but he wanted to try. He headed for the hallway. "Why don't you all eat? I'm sure Emma's hungry. I'll check on Rose."

"Wait." Drew followed him across the room. "Maybe I should be the one to check on her."

"Thanks, Drew." Mac rested his hand on the younger man's shoulder. He admired his willingness to look after his sister, but it wasn't his job anymore. "She's my wife. I'll go to her."

CHAPTER NINETEEN

Mac stood outside Rose's bedroom door, his hand raised to knock. The sounds inside made him wait. He had no idea what to do. But at the sound of her sharp, low scream and the tearing of fabric, he opened the door without knocking, stepped inside, and closed it.

Rose stood by the bed, tears running down her face, her dress ripped from neck to waist. "I can't get out of this."

He stepped beside her slowly and carefully undid the buttons that were still attached. He eased the dress off her body. He thought she'd fight. Instead, she stood like a doll, not helping, not hindering. Tears rolled down her cheeks as her chest heaved with her jagged breaths. He needed to help her calm down before he could find out what was wrong. Remembering how Lizzie hadn't been able to relax all trussed up like a turkey, he knew he would have to help Rose get out of her undergarments, or at least most of them. He would leave on the short dress-like thing and her long bloomers.

As he did that, he spied a wrapper on a hook by her washstand. Using his hand, he directed her to sit on the bed, and he unlaced her shoes and took them off. While she sat there, he grabbed her wrapper. He got her to stand. She let him slide it over her shoulders and help her get her arms through the sleeves.

Once he had the sash around her waist tied, he thought about removing the locket from around her neck. But he was afraid of how she might react with his hands so close to her neck, so it stayed hanging there.

He stood in front of her, wondering what to do next. Should he try to talk to her? To get her to talk to him?

She collapsed on the bed. "Sing your song."

"MacPherson's Lament?"

She nodded.

"All right, but first let's get you more comfortable."

She didn't object when he shifted her higher on the bed and laid her head on one of the pillows. With nothing in the room sturdy enough to hold him, he sat beside her on the bed and started humming. When she relaxed a bit, he sang, keeping his voice low.

As he ended the song, her eyes fluttered closed. He stood. She needed to sleep. Later if she wanted to talk, they would.

Before he took a step, her eyes opened. "Don't leave. I don't want to be alone." Her hands crept around her middle. "I've been alone for so long. Please stay. Talk to me. Sing to me again."

She turned on her side and faced him with dry, empty eyes. He had never seen any woman so broken, so fragile.

She wasn't asking him to stay as a wife wants a husband, but he'd stay and help her with whatever was crushing her spirit.

He pulled off his boots and lay next to her on the bed.

She gripped the front of his shirt.

He slid his arm around her shoulders and sang the song again, and again, and again.

As the room heated up with the afternoon sun, she loosened her grip on his shirt. "I don't know what happened. We were singing. I knew the words, but the words weren't true. God wasn't there when Alfred beat me, when he forced himself on me, when I begged for Him to let me die, to release me from the hell I was

living. But He wasn't there. He never helped me. He
didn't let me die. He just kept me there in that torment.
Why? Why did God do that?"

Mac cradled her closer as her tears fell again. He
hadn't realized she had so much pain inside her small
body. He had no idea how she survived those years,
especially with no one to lean on. Well, she did have
Someone, but in her pain, she wasn't able to see Him.

Maybe this was what God wanted him to understand.
God had been there with Rose. He had been there with
Lizzie. He had been there and He hated the things that
were done to His children. But what good came out of it?
What was the use of all the suffering?

Every time he shifted, she cried out and held onto him.
So he held her as the sun continued its journey across the
sky. Finally, little by little, she relaxed. At last, she fell
into a deep sleep.

When he was sure she would not wake, he stood and
looked down at the face of the woman he loved. One day,
he would be the husband she deserved. He bent down and
sealed his promise with a kiss on her cheek, then left her
room.

Sarah sat at the table, a pot of tea cooling in front of
her. It had been difficult to see Thorn before he left on his
route just after dawn. He'd been so kind, and she'd felt
foolish for the way she acted the day before, but she had
slept better than she had in a long time. No nightmares.
Just restful sleep.

"Good morning." Helen stepped into the kitchen.
"How are you today?"

Sarah picked up the teapot to make a fresh pot.
"Rested and ready to work on the bakery."

Helen placed her hand on Sarah's arm. "Truly?"

"Truly." Sarah had an idea and couldn't wait to share
it. "What if—?"

The door from the hall opened. Drew walked in. "Morning, ladies. Did you both sleep well last night?"

Sarah turned toward the stove while Drew kissed Helen. "Let me know when you two are through. There's something I'd like to talk to you both about."

"In a minute, sis."

"Drew, stop that. Let's hear what your sister has to say."

An exaggerated sigh filled the air. "All right. We're done, for now."

Helen giggled, and chairs scraped the wooden floor.

Sarah turned around and found Drew and Helen sitting next to each other, his arm around her shoulders. "Good. Since you're both here, I'll only have to say this once."

She rested her hands on the table. "Since the bottom part of the building is all cleaned and painted, and we have the kitchen things that Thorn brought on his last freighting trip, why don't we open the bakery now? That way we could start building a customer base while we finish the other things for the café and the upstairs."

Drew and Helen turned to each other and burst out laughing.

Sarah looked from one to the other. "What's so funny?"

Drew wiped his eyes. "We talked about the same thing last night. Thought it was a good idea, too. That way we can start making money."

Sarah bit her tongue. She wanted to tell Drew that he didn't have to worry about making money, but she knew that would only start an argument, and she didn't need that today. "Good. When do you think we can open? Tomorrow? The next day?"

Helen pulled a paper from her pocket and grinned. "I need to get supplies from the general store and try out the kitchen there first. Let's try for the day after tomorrow."

Stanley leaned back in his chair while Sarah's maid Judith fidgeted in the chair in front of his desk. The foolish biddy had provided precious little information about the happenings at Sarah's house. "What have you to report?"

Judith twisted the cords of her reticule around her fingers. "They plan to open their bakery in two days."

"Anything else?"

She shook her head.

"When is MacPherson scheduled back?"

"In about a week, give or take a day or two." The woman's voice was starting to quiver. Her knuckles grew whiter as she gripped the cords tighter.

Stanley watched the fear grow in the old hen's face. This was the way he liked those under his thumb, scared enough to obey him, whatever his orders were.

He leaned back in his chair while he thought about what the woman said. A week. Enough time to have Waller and Grayson to do a job for him, then he wouldn't have to worry about MacPherson any more. He pulled a small bag from his desk drawer and tossed it to her.

She caught it and shoved the bag with its chinking contents into her reticule.

"Get out, and don't let anyone see you leaving."

The maid jumped up and scurried to the door that opened into the alley.

When the door closed, Stanley took out a cigar. Time for a little celebration. Soon Sarah would be a widow again. Only this time, he would make sure the next wedding ring on her finger was his. Then, all her fortune would be his, too.

At last, things were ready, well, ready enough. Well before sunrise, Sarah and Drew joined Helen in the kitchen. She asked if they could meet and have a prayer together, asking God to bless their efforts. With excitement racing through her, Sarah watched Drew leave with Helen in order to make sure the cinnamon rolls and doughnuts would be ready by the time they opened. Sarah had Emma up and dressed by the time Judith and Sally arrived. Drew returned to escort Sarah. They headed down the hill to the main part of town and their new business.

Once in front of their new business, Drew helped Sarah down. They stood outside while a carpenter finished hanging the new sign. Helen came outside, trembling with excitement. "I can hardly believe the day has come." Wrapped in a long white apron, a dusting of flour across her cheek, she stared up at the sign. "The Golden Nugget Bakery and Café."

Sarah nudged Helen. "It's a beautiful sign, but we better get inside. There's miners headed this way, and they look hungry."

Helen giggled. "They're some of my old customers. Carl helped spread the word that we're opening today."

"Let me take care of this while you ladies take care of our customers." Drew climbed back on the buggy and headed for the livery.

Helen turned to the miners and waved. "Come on boys, we're ready for you."

Sarah grabbed Helen's hand and hurried her inside as the men stepped up their pace. She entered the building and gasped. She had seen the room the day before with its clean, pale yellow walls and yellow gingham-checked curtains. But now, the display cases and shelves were filled with Helen's pies and cakes and the whole area smelled of cinnamon and apples and other spices. It was everything they had dreamed it would be. Homey and delicious and real. Three pots of coffee bubbled on the small stove on the side wall next to a table stacked with mugs, making it easy for those who wanted coffee to get it themselves.

No sooner had Sarah and Helen gotten behind the counter than the bell over the door tinkled, and the room filled with loud, hungry miners, all waving coins or small pouches of gold dust and shouting their orders.

Drew came up from the back, puffing a bit from his race back from the livery. "Men, we have enough for everyone. Please form lines in front of one of the two ladies or myself, and we'll fill your orders as quickly as we can. Just know we have enough for everyone. Miss Helen has been baking for days, and many of you know how good her cooking is. For our opening today, the coffee is on the house."

With much laughing, shoving, and shouting, the mad rush finally ended. Many of the men left with one or more pies, several dozen cookies, a few with cakes, and most with loaves of bread. And they all left with grins on their faces.

The ones who remained sat at tables and chairs, dunking their doughnuts in their coffee or *aahing* over their fresh-baked cinnamon rolls.

Sarah surveyed the room. She was glad they had opted for natural wood for the tables and chairs instead of painting them white. The tables, chairs, and floor would need a good cleaning every day, an even harder scrubbing on the days they were closed.

She turned back to the cases and shelves. They were almost empty, but Helen had already started restocking them. The poor woman must be exhausted from all the baking that she had done in the last two days, but she glowed with excitement, so she must think all the effort had been worth it. Sarah had to agree.

By late-morning, Sarah was thankful the crowd had eased for now. She placed the money for two donuts into the till.

Drew came up beside her, his face glowing. "We're doing even better than I'd expected."

Before she could agree, the door opened. A tall, thin woman, the hotel owner, walked in. Sarah wondered if she had heard that her niece was part owner of the bakery. "May I help you?"

The woman tilted her head to one side and pursed her lips. She looked around for a moment, then back at Sarah and Drew behind the display case with a puzzled look on her face.

Sarah understood the woman's confusion. When Sarah had stayed at the hotel, she had worn the latest fashions from the East. Her hair had been arranged in the style popular in Boston, and she had been trussed up like a turkey in a corset and crinoline in order to look the proper lady. Now she had her hair at the back of her neck in a tidy bun. She wore a comfortable skirt and shirtwaist without the hated corset. And all of that was covered by a huge white apron.

With a slight shake of her head, the woman stepped up to the counter. "I saw several, uh, men going past the hotel with baked goods. I hadn't realized anyone was putting in a bakery, although we needed one desperately. Since my ungrateful niece deserted me, I've had a terrible time finding a decent baker, to say nothing of anyone who could make cinnamon rolls as tasty as hers. As a matter of fact, I just got back from visiting my sister in Denver yesterday, hoping I could bring a baker back with me, but I couldn't find a decent one that wanted to come here. So when I saw your sign this morning, I decided to check out your goods and see if they met my standards."

Sarah pressed the fingers of one hand against those of the other hand, trying not to let on that the niece she was defaming was the baker here.

"I'd like to try a sampling of your goods, enough for my family. That way we can decide which ones we want for our restaurant on a regular basis. If I find them acceptable, I'll place a regular order each week. But mind you, they must be of truly good quality." She straightened a bit. "After all, I do run one of the best hotels and restaurants in Central City."

Sarah took a cinnamon roll from the pan in the display case, placed it on a small plate, and handed it to the woman. "Why don't you enjoy this and a cup of coffee, while I talk to the baker? She's also part owner. I'll be back in just a minute."

The woman grabbed the sweet roll and hurried over to the side of the room, where she poured herself a cup of coffee, then sat at one of the tables.

Sarah slipped into the kitchen. She tried to stop grinning. "We have a special request from a businesswoman."

Helen lifted her rolling pin from the pie crust she was working on. "And what kind of request would that be?"

"A certain woman who owns a hotel and restaurant wants to sample our goods, a woman I believe you are quite familiar with."

Helen touched the back of her neck where her hair had barely grown long enough to twist up into a small bun. "Aunt Caroline?"

"Oh, she wants a sampling of all we do, sufficient for her whole family, so they can decide if what we offer is good enough for her hotel and restaurant." Sarah peeked around the open door between the kitchen and the dining room. The woman sat in a recently vacated chair, sipping free coffee and devouring the roll. "You're part owner, and she's your aunt. How do you want to handle this?"

"I want to stomp out there and kick her out of the bakery, demanding she never step in here again." She let out a deep sigh. "But as a business woman, I can't do that. So I guess I'll have to handle her as honestly as I can. My aunt is a great manipulator, always trying to get things to her advantage, either by her haughtiness or her threats. " Helen sent a smile to Sarah. "There's been a verse I've always tried to use when dealing with my aunt. 'A soft answer turns away wrath: but grievous words stir up anger.'"

"You're afraid of her anger?"

Helen shook her head as she turned toward the dining room. "Not hers, mine. I don't like to be angry. It pits my soul and tarnishes the life I want to live."

Sarah started to follow, but Helen held up her hand. "Please, let me handle this by myself." Not waiting for an answer, she passed through the doorway and to the table where her aunt was still eating her cinnamon roll.

Sarah stayed in the kitchen, but Helen hadn't said anything about not watching. She leaned on the doorjamb to see what would happen.

The woman's eyes grew wide when Helen stopped at her table. She glanced down at the roll, then back at Helen. Words were exchanged, more from the older lady along with finger-pointing and pouty lips. Several of the miners stopped eating and watched the two women, then went back to their treats.

At last, Helen's aunt stopped talking and stomped out of the building.

Sarah hurried over while Helen cleaned up the mess her aunt had left.

"Aunt Caroline doesn't like the idea of paying for me to furnish baked goods for her restaurant. Poor lady would rather nurse a grudge than make a good business transaction. Be that as it may. Besides, I think we'll be too busy making things for our café. We won't have time or energy to supply other places."

"I think you're right." Something twisted in Sarah's chest. She wondered if she would ever be as forgiving as Helen. The idea of forgiving Grandfather had always made anger swell up in her heart, but now it might be different. After all, he was far away and would never have any power over her again. She could almost pretend he didn't even exist. If she didn't think about him, didn't let her anger dwell on him, wouldn't that be the same as forgiveness? Maybe that was the answer.

CHAPTER TWENTY

Mac pulled up behind Sarah's house and gripped the side of the wagon seat with one fist while he wrapped his other arm around his chest. This was going to hurt. He took a couple deep breaths, as deep as he could manage without too much pain. With a shifting and a painful twist, he lowered himself to the ground, then rested his head against the wagon side. His strength was oozing out just like his blood had earlier. But he had to take care of the mules.

Inch by inch, he crept up to the front of the mules. With hands scraped and bruised, he removed the harnesses from the animals. He led them into the barn and made sure they had feed and water. His breathing came in jagged puffs. He only had to get to the house and up those back stairs.

Tair shuffled alongside him, whimpering as he went. With every step, it seemed like the distance to the house grew by two feet. At long last, his hand cupped the newel post at the bottom of the back stairs. He grunted as he pulled himself up the first step. With the next step, dizziness attacked him. Only two more to go.

He held onto the post at the top of the stairs as fire flared in his leg. A few more steps and he would be inside. Rose would be there. Sweet Rose. What seemed like a century later, he finally made it across the porch and opened the door into the kitchen.

Judith stood by the stove, stirring something that smelled better than his cooking on the trail, but not near as good as Helen's. She looked him up and down, then shrugged. "Expected you back last night."

Not the welcome Mac expected, but then Judith had never really taken to him. She didn't seem to notice that his clothes were torn and bloody. Today, that was just fine. He was bone-weary, and his head hurt something fierce. His chest made it hard to breathe. All he wanted to do was get to bed and sleep until morning. "Good to see you, too. Where's everybody?"

"They're all out. They probably won't be back 'til late. At least they haven't been on time for the last three days." Judith gave a disgruntled snort. "How can a body serve a meal if no one gets here on time?"

He knew it was a mistake to ask and cause the woman to keep talking, but his interest was stirred. "And where have they been that makes them so late for meals?"

"The bakery, of course. With its opening on Wednesday, all they do is bake, sell, and clean. The missus hasn't even taken time to tend to the baby properly. I've had to do it all around here since Sally's ma got sick this morning."

Mac looked around the kitchen and his heart beat a little faster. "If you're taking care of Emma, where is she?"

Judith poured herself a cup of coffee and sat at the table. "In the parlor. Carl's watching after her so I can get the cooking done."

Without another word, Mac shuffled out of the kitchen and down the hall. No sounds came from the parlor. He peeked around the open door. Carl and Emma lay sleeping on the rug near the sofa, his arm wrapped around her shoulders. The ball of fluff Rose called a dog was curled up at their feet.

Mac wanted to go in the room and pick up his little girl, but dizziness changed his mind. Blinking a couple times, he headed for the stairs and once again pulled himself up one step at a time. He pushed open the door to his bedroom. Pain in all parts of his body roared to life. It was hard to breathe. The room spun. He stumbled to the bed and fell. After that he remembered nothing, except pain and burning, heat and ice and nightmare after nightmare, and blackness.

Sarah couldn't hold back a grin as she sat next to Helen while Drew set the brake on the buggy behind the house. Thorn was home. She had worried about him all day, but now he was home and safe.

Drew got out of the buggy and walked over to the freight wagon. "It's not like Mac to leave his wagon out like this, and his stuff's still in it."

His whole body grew still, very still. "Sarah, there're bloody quilts back here."

Not waiting for her brother's help, Sarah jumped down from the buggy, grabbed her skirt in her fists, and raced into the house. She burst into the kitchen and struggled to get her breath. Judith sat at the table with a mug in her hand. "Where's Thorn?"

"He came in a bit ago." Judith pointed to the door which led to the hall.

Sarah ran down the hall to the parlor. The children were asleep in the floor. She raced up the stairs. The door to Thorn's room was open. Her hand trembled as she pushed the door farther open. Her heart nearly stopped beating.

Thorn lay half off the bed. She crept over and touched his shoulder. Even through the fabric of his shirt, heat poured off of him. Memories of the fevers that took her parents flooded her mind.

Breathing hard, Drew and Helen followed Sarah through the door.

"I don't know what's wrong, but help me get him on the bed." She tried to keep her voice low. Fear and panic would not control her.

Drew came alongside. "You and Helen take his legs while I handle his shoulders. I'll twist and move him farther on the bed while you two bring his legs up on it."

In the dimness of the room, they worked together and repositioned Thorn on his bed. Drew lit the lamp by the bed. Sarah covered her mouth to hold the scream inside. The leg she had been holding was blood-soaked. White bandages, streaked with red, peeked through the gash in the denim.

Her gaze traveled up his body. His shirt was dirty and torn. Several missing buttons revealed even more bandages wrapped around his chest. His face was bruised. Small cuts covered his face.

Sarah's legs threatened to give out. Drew carried a chair from across the room and set it behind her. She dropped onto the seat and picked up Thorn's hand. Broken skin and scraped knuckles joined the calluses he had earned from hard work.

"What happened to him?" Sarah pulled his damaged hand to her cheek. "Drew, help him."

"Helen, will you get some hot water to clean him? I'll get the doctor." Drew rushed out of the room. In a moment or two, the front door slammed.

Sarah couldn't bear to leave Thorn's side. What happened to him? Stanley's face danced in her mind as it did every time something bad happened. Surely he hadn't done this to Thorn. No, not on his own, but the man would stoop to hiring thugs to do it.

Faster than Sarah thought possible, Helen returned with a pitcher of hot water. She poured some into the bowl from the washstand and brought it to the bed. She placed it on a small table, then grabbed the towel and soap from the washstand.

Sarah took the towel, dipped a corner of it into the water, and wiped it across Thorn's knuckles as gently as she could.

Helen stood at the bedroom door. "I need to see to the children. Emma's awake and crying."

Sarah nodded. Other things would be taken care of. She cleaned Thorn gently and methodically, watching all the while for his eyes to open or flicker. By the time her brother returned, the worst of the blood was washed away, and Thorn hadn't stirred.

She turned to Drew. "Where's the doctor?"

Drew crouched down beside her. "He's not coming, at least not right now. He's already seen Mac." He took in a deep breath. "Seems Mac got hurt helping a miner named Nelson and his family. Two men came to their place, beat the father, ra—uh, hurt the older sister. He got in a fight with one of the men, and got cut when the man pulled out a knife. The other one saw his chance and slung a large piece of wood at Mac, hitting him in the ribs."

She tightened her grip on Thorn's hand. "He could've been killed."

"Probably would've been, if the girl hadn't gotten her father's rifle. But she was shaking so bad, she missed them when she fired. Apparently it was enough to scare the men, because they took off. Between her and Mac, they got the father into Mac's wagon and made it to Doc's place. They're still there, but the father doesn't look like he'll make it."

Sarah nodded and turned back to her husband. He took care of everyone, especially her. Now was her time to care for him. "Could you bring me some cool water? I need to get his fever down."

Drew brought her the water along with a supper tray, which she left untouched.

Sarah replaced the cool compresses as they warmed from the heat coming off Thorn's body. About midnight, he started thrashing about the bed.

He mumbled about barns and ropes. "Keep the girls away." His hands formed fists and pounded against the bed. "Take them to the main house. Don't...don't let them see."

Sarah rested her hands on his shoulder to hold him down and keep him from hurting himself.

He grabbed her arms. "Let me go. Let me go. I gotta get her down."

"Shush, Thorn." She shook one of his hands off her arm. "Everything's going to be all right. Just relax. Take it easy."

Her voice seemed to soothe him. He settled back against the pillow. But then his head twisted from side to side, and he let out a deep, pain-filled moan. "Lizzie, why? Why did you do it?"

At last, he dropped his other hand from Sarah's arm. When she sat, he reached out and grabbed her hand. "Don't leave me. I need you. I love you." His body relaxed, and he kept mumbling something about faith, grace, and mercy, over and over.

Sarah replaced the cloth on his forehead with a cooler one and settled back to rest a moment. His words had surprised her. With Thorn refusing to go to church, she'd wondered if he believed in God. But here in his tortured thoughts, he seemed to be calling out for Him.

Sarah sipped the coffee Drew had brought her a few moments before. The clock in the parlor chimed the two o'clock hour. Thorn thrashed again. "Gavenia, don't cry. Have to go. Love you. Love you."

Sarah took his hand with one of hers and rubbed her other hand along his forearm. "They love you, too. Just rest, Thorn. Rest so you can go to them."

Once again, her words seemed to settle him. His breathing got deeper and slower. His last words were slow and slurred. "Can't go back. Can't stay. Hurt them."

Thorn finally fell into a deep sleep.

Sarah slumped back on the chair by the bed. Who were Lizzie and Gavenia? On the trip to Denver, he'd said that he had been married before, but his wife was gone. Was one of those two women his wife? Had he been married to both of them at different times?

After a short rest, she stood and paced across the room. He started mumbling about Lizzie again. How far in Thorn's past was this Lizzie? The more she thought about the day of the picnic, the more she realized the look on the MacPherson cousins' faces was shock when Thorn introduced her as his wife.

She had to find out more of Thorn's past. Her future depended on it.

The next morning dawned. Still, Sarah sat in the chair next to Thorn. Her arms ached from fatigue, from wringing out the cool cloths and trying to hold him down while he thrashed about. But each moan he made, each time he cried out in pain hurt Sarah in a way she couldn't ease. She knew the pain a fist or booted foot could cause and the agonizingly long time it took to recover from those injuries.

The shuffle of a boot across the rug sounded behind Sarah as it had several times during the night. "I think he's sleeping a little better, but I'd feel better if the doctor could check him again."

"He's here." Drew came up beside her. "But there's something we need to discuss."

"All right." She moved from Thorn's bed. "He's running a fever."

The doctor took her place. "I was afraid that might happen, but I had to take care of the other man." His shoulders slumped. "But you can't save them all."

Sarah's head jerked up. "The father died?"

The doctor set his black bag on the table by the bed. "Yup. His children don't know yet. My wife's watching over them. They're still sleeping. It's gonna hit 'em hard." He shook his head. "Don't know what them young'uns are going to do now." He sat in the chair. "Why don't you go down and have something to eat? Wouldn't mind some coffee in a little while."

Drew touched Sarah's elbow. They left the room. Neither said anything until they got to the kitchen. Helen already had coffee going. While they dropped onto the chairs, she poured three cups and joined them at the table, sitting next to Drew. "Emma slept in my room last night."

Sarah nodded. "Drew told me you had taken her. Thank you." She took a sip from her cup and let the warm liquid drain down her throat, then turned to her brother. "What was it you wanted to talk about?"

"Same thing Doc talked about. That girl and her brother and sister need help. Their mother died several years ago, and now their father's gone."

Helen gasped. "I didn't know that."

"Doc just told us." Drew shrugged and circled the top of his cup with his index finger, round and round. "Helen and I talked about them last night, about how they need someone even more, now they are all alone. Like we were all those years ago. She's only sixteen, and her brother's younger."

Sarah saw the similarities, children who had lost their parents, the girl taken against her will. She had thought of them during the night, too, and had come up with a plan. "We've got to help them. There was no one for us, but we can help them. I wish we had more room here in the house."

"Thought that's what you'd say." Drew reached over and covered Helen's hand with his. "We've been talking about marriage." He sat up a little taller. "Actually, before the bakery opened, I asked her to marry me, and she agreed."

"Oh, Drew, Helen, I'm thrilled for you both. I think you'll be so happy together."

Drew held up his hand. "We were going to wait and see how the business was going before we made plans for the wedding."

Helen squeezed his hand and explained. "Last night, we decided to get married immediately and move into the space above the bakery. The children can live here, if that's all right with you." She rushed on, as if she feared someone would stop her. "When the older girl feels like it, she can help out in the bakery. Her younger sister and brother, too, if they want. That way, they won't feel like they're at anybody's mercy. They'll be making their own money."

It was a good plan, but Sarah didn't want the two of them rushing into marriage because of these orphans. "What about letting them stay in the rooms above the bakery until you have time to plan your wedding? They could still work there, if they wanted."

Helen moved off her chair. She stood behind Drew and rested her hands on his shoulders.

He reached up and patted one of her hands. "Whether the children stay here or over the bakery doesn't matter. Helen and I have decided to get married next Sunday afternoon." He reached out and touched Sarah's hand. "We love each other. Be happy for us."

"I'm so happy for you. I just wanted to give you all the things a young couple should have when they marry—a beautiful wedding, a honeymoon trip, a wonderful home in which to start your life together." All the things she had dreamed when she was a child, things she'd never had as a bride. Sarah smiled at her brother and his future wife. "I just want you to be happy."

"All I want is Drew for my husband and the rooms above the bakery where we can start our mornings together, go down and work side by side, then go upstairs to our home and spend the night together."

Sarah hugged her soon-to-be sister-in-law and giggled, either from happiness or exhaustion. "Are you sure you don't want to get married today instead of waiting a whole week?"

Drew chuckled and wrapped his arms around Helen and Sarah. "Now that would be rushing it a mite. We still have to furnish those rooms. Much as I love this woman, I don't relish the idea of sleeping on hard wooden floors."

Sarah nodded. "Next Sunday then. But don't be surprised at what I do between now and then. After all, I only have one brother."

CHAPTER TWENTY-ONE

"Your room's ready for the two girls." Helen entered Thorn's room. "How's he doing?"

Sarah sat beside the bed. "He seems a little better, not as hot. Doc changed the bandages on his leg and said that it was healing fine."

Helen rubbed the scar on her cheek. "I know lots of men carry knives. But you don't think it was Jim Grayson who attacked Mac, do you?"

Sarah hadn't thought of that. "I don't know. But like you said, there are a lot of men with knives."

Carl ran up the steps and stopped outside the door to Thorn's room. "Drew's back, and he's got those people with him."

"Helen, could you sit with Thorn a few minutes?" Sarah waited until Helen took her place, then went down the stairs, followed by Carl.

Sarah stood in the shadows just outside the parlor and looked into the room. Three young people sat on the sofa. The older girl, who looked to be about sixteen, was in the middle with her brother and sister on either side of her. She thought the boy was about twelve years old and the girl couldn't have been more than ten.

From her spot in the hall, Sarah watched the oldest one for a few moments and wondered if she had looked that young and sad, that hurt and scared, when she'd gone to Grandfather's house the first time. One of her mother's

favorite verses, one she had often recited when there was
a decision to be made, floated through Sarah's thoughts.
*Who knoweth whether thou art come to the kingdom for
such a time as this?* She understood much of what these
children were going through, but could she truly help
them by giving them more than a place to live and work?

The next morning, Sarah shook her head on the way
out of Thorn's room. Men out here amazed her. Not two
days before, Thorn had been on the brink of death. At
least, she'd thought so, although the doctor disagreed
with her diagnosis. And now here he was arguing that he
was well enough to go back to freighting.

She moved across the hall and opened the door to the
nursery. The sofa, which was good to sit on while playing
with Emma, wasn't the most comfortable for sleeping.
Thankfully, she would only have to sleep on it a few
more days. After Drew and Helen married and moved to
the rooms over the bakery, the three Nelson children
would move into Helen and Carl's old rooms.

Sarah carried an oil lamp. She opened the door to the
nursery as quietly as she could. Hopefully, Emma would
stay asleep. She closed the door and stopped.

Linda, the oldest of the Nelson children, stood at the
crib. Her hands trembled as they grasped the crib railing.

She looked over her shoulder at Sarah. "What if he left
me in the family way?" Her voice was barely a whisper,
but the pain echoed around the room. "What then?"

Sarah set the lamp on the small table near the door and
came over in small, slow steps. When she reached the
crib, she placed her hand over Linda's. "Will you sit with
me a bit?"

Linda jerked her hand back. Sarah didn't say anything.
She knew what it felt like to be trapped, to have no
control over who touched you. Even in the darkly lit
room, a small glow filled her heart. She had overcome

that desire not to be touched by another person. Maybe she could help Linda. At the very least, she knew one thing she could do that would bring relief to the girl.

She held out her hand toward the sofa. "Will you join me?"

With a quick nod, Linda followed Sarah and sat.

"I'll be blunt. If you're with child from your attack, I'll stand by you and help you in any way you need. If you want to keep the child, I'll help you, either here in Central City or in Denver. If you don't want the child, I'll care for it and adopt it."

Linda pressed her fist over her middle. "Why? Why would you do that? Help me? Want a baby made that way?"

Sarah stood and walked to the crib. Her daughter slept in peaceful slumber, her thumb between her lips, her little bottom stuck up in the air. She kissed the tips of her fingers and touched them to the golden hair of her daughter's head.

Sarah turned back toward Linda. "Because I know how you feel, the pain, the fear, the revulsion."

Linda stared at the crib with its lacy covering and then at Sarah. She shook her head. Her eyes narrowed and her hands drew into fists. "You can't know how it feels to have a man hold you down, rip off your clothes, and steal what should have been given freely and in love. With all this." She swung her arm around, pointing to the furnishings in the room. "With all this, there's no way you could know the hurt and the pain…and the hopelessness of losing what I can never get back."

A low, keening cry passed the girl's lips. "Of knowing no decent man will ever want me now, at least not for a wife."

Sarah sat on the sofa but far enough away that she wouldn't crowd Linda. "You're wrong." She kept her voice low, not wanting her baby to hear this, even knowing Emma wouldn't understand. "When I was sixteen, I lost my parents to influenza. My grandfather took me and my brother to Boston, but he didn't want me. So he traded me to a business partner who married me." She scoffed at the word. "He beat and raped me for the next thirteen years."

"Mac did that to you?"

"No, my first husband, Alfred. Thorn would never treat a woman that way."

Linda gasped. "How did you live through it?"

"One day at a time. Just like you will. And I'll be here to help you." Sarah reached out and touched the girl's hand. This time Linda didn't pull away. "Any time you need to talk, I'm here."

Tears started down Linda's cheeks, tears of pain, tears of release, tears of hope.

Sarah opened her arms and wrapped them around Linda, who scooted across the sofa. Sarah hummed Thorn's song, the one that had soothed her. And that Bible verse popped into her head again. Maybe it was true. Maybe she had endured all those things for just such as time as this. For the first time in many years, Sarah opened her heart and sent a prayer to God. *Thank you for letting me know what to say and do for Linda. Please hold her in Your comfort. Please heal her pain.*

Sometime later and exhausted beyond all thought, Sarah walked Linda to the door between the nursery and the bedroom. She gave the girl a smile and a nod. "It will get better."

She turned to leave.

Linda grabbed hold of her hand. "That man...there were two of them. One was named Grayson. He had some kind of scar across his cheek. And—and the one who—the other one was called Waller." She drew a deep breath. "He had yellow hair and stunk like old whiskey."

Sarah's stomach tumbled. Jim Grayson and Petey Waller. How did those two get together? "Thank you for letting me know."

"Before they left, they said they would find us and kill Jack, then sell me and Nancy to a brothel."

Sarah patted the hand that gripped her own like a claw. "Don't worry about that. I'll have someone watching out for them. They'll never get to you or your brother and sister again."

"Thank you." Linda nodded and went into the bedroom.

Sarah looked into Emma's crib and brushed the yellow locks back from the small, relaxed face. What a precious jewel she had been given. A shudder ran through her. If she hadn't been there for the baby, would Emma have ended up with her uncle? Would he have sold her off for whatever he could get for her? She dropped her head to her chest. *Please, God, help me protect those You've put in my care.*

"You fools!" Stanley gripped the arms of his chair as he considered the worthless men slouching across from him. At least they had waited until dark so no one could see them sneak down the alley to his office. "I sent you out to get rid of MacPherson, not mess around with some dirty miner's daughter."

Grayson twisted the brim of his dirty hat with even dirtier fingers. "We got ahead of him on his route just like you said."

Waller had an even nastier hat. "We were there a couple days early even. We just needed something to do until he got there."

"It was his idea to mess with that miner and his family." Grayson looked at the other thug. "After he got a belly full of liquor."

"Enough!" Stanley slammed his hand on his desk. Without taking his eyes off the men, he pulled a gun from a side drawer. He held it in one hand and stroked the barrel with the palm of the other. "If it wouldn't make a mess on the floor, I'd shoot you both right now." He stared at both men until they squirmed. "Get out now. I'll send word when I need you."

After the two left, Stanley replaced his gun in the drawer and leaned back in his chair. He had to come up with another plan. A plan that didn't rely on stupid idiots to pull off. No, this time, he would need to be involved to make sure it worked since he was running out of money.

He chuckled as he realized how to bait the trap. Now he needed to plot out each angle so as not to be caught.

Sarah rose very early the next morning. She told herself it was because she had so much to do. But as she rubbed her sore back, she knew that it had to do more with the sofa in the nursery than the list of things to do.

She hummed a tune while she dressed herself and Emma, thinking of what needed to be done.

A soft knock sounded on the door that connected the nursery and Sarah's bedroom, where Linda and Nancy had spent the night.

"Come in." Sarah set down the small brush she had used on Emma's hair.

The door opened. Linda and her sister moved into the room. Both were dressed in the threadbare clothes they'd worn the day before.

Linda held her sister's hand. Both of them had pale faces and dark smudges beneath their eyes. "We're wondering what you want us to do."

Sarah picked up Emma and headed for the door to the hall. "Let's go down and have breakfast. We can talk then."

With a nod, the girls walked behind Sarah like ducklings following their mother.

Judith hadn't arrived, but Helen had left a pot of coffee and one of hot cocoa still warm on the stove before she and Drew went to the bakery. On the counter near the stove rested a covered plate of warm cinnamon rolls. Sarah couldn't help but smile. Drew must have brought them from the bakery, knowing Judith would be upset with all the extra work the Nelson children would cause.

It only took a few minutes to serve everyone. After they all sat, Carl offered to ask the blessing for the food. Sarah nodded. When he finished, the children munched on the warm, sweet rolls. It wasn't long before Jack and Nancy, the two younger Nelson children, along with Carl, all wore brown mustaches above their grinning lips. Sarah and Linda smiled at each other while they sipped their coffee.

When the younger children finished eating, they cleaned their faces. Sarah took Emma from her chair. "Carl, would you take Emma and the others into the parlor, please? Linda and I are going to have a little more coffee."

Linda stood and started clearing the table.

"Leave those for a few minutes. We need to talk." Sarah got the coffee pot and refilled their cups.

After she sat back down, Linda clasped her hands in front of her on the table. "When do you want us to leave?"

"No, you've got it wrong. When I asked you, Jack, and Nancy to come here yesterday, I was offering you all a place to live. And if you're wondering why, just remember what I said last night about knowing how it feels like to lose everything."

Tears filled Linda's eyes. "Thank you, ma'am. We'd like to stay." And then as another thought popped into her head, her mouth opened, then closed. "But we can't stay in your room now."

"Just until Sunday. My brother and Helen are getting married then. They, along with Helen's brother, will be moving to the rooms above the bakery we just opened." Sarah pointed to the rooms Helen and Carl were using, just off the kitchen. "Those will be your rooms. That way you three will still be together and have some privacy."

"Thank you, ma'am. We'd like that just fine."

"Good. Now there're a few more things I'd like to talk about. First, I hope it's all right with you that I arranged for your father's burial. It will take place tomorrow at ten o'clock."

"Thank you, ma'am. I—I didn't know what to do about him."

"Well, it's all taken care of." Sarah swallowed to clear her throat. "And please stop calling me 'ma'am.' Call me Sarah." She smiled as she stood. "There's a lot to do this week, and I could really use your help. We have a wedding to plan, a home to set up, Mac to tend to, and the children to care for."

By the end of the day, fatigue weighed Sarah and Linda like heavy winter robes. They had hired carpenters and painters, shopped at several stores getting new clothes for the Nelsons, dishes, linens, rugs, and furniture for Drew and Helen's new home, and made preparations for the wedding, including the purchase of a dress for Helen. During all of it Linda showed a surprising ability to coordinate the needs of a new home. With lots of luck, everything should be ready by Sunday.

On Friday, Mac struggled to get down the stairs. When Sarah had told him she'd be out most of the day, he made plans to be up and about before she got back. The woman was a tyrant when she got control of someone. She'd barely let him out of the bed since he'd dragged himself up the stairs several days ago.

He had planned to be downstairs earlier, but after he had cleaned himself up and put on fresh clothes, he had to rest for a bit. As he hobbled down the stairs, the clock in the parlor chimed noon.

Mac pushed open the kitchen door open to find the table surrounded by children and steaming bowls of food ready to be eaten.

Carl grinned. "Mac! Yah! Mac's gonna eat with us!"

"Hi, Mac." The boy next to Carl smiled.

But the sweetest sound came from his gap-toothed girl when she clapped her pudgy hands together. "Dada, Dada!"

Knowing he wasn't strong enough to pick her up, he dropped onto a chair next to her, leaned over, and gave her a big kiss on her cheek. She giggled, then grabbed his face and kissed him back. "Dada, Dada."

Judith stood at the stove, tapping her foot with a tray in her hands. The same tray he had seen three times a day. The same tray that held nothing but weak coffee and broth. A man needed more than that to build back his strength.

Unlike the children, there was no smile of welcome on Judith's face. "I was about to bring up your dinner."

"Well, I'm down here, saving you the trouble of climbing the stairs." When she set the items from the tray in front of him, he gave her a long, hard stare. "If it wouldn't be too much trouble, could I have what you made the others?"

"But Mrs. MacPherson said—"

"I am Mr. MacPherson. Please do as I ask." The words sounded clearly in the quiet of the kitchen, but with enough force behind them that Judith scurried and pulled a plate and fork from the cabinet, then placed them before him. He bit his lip to keep from smiling. Every once in a while, his Scottish laird great-grandfather's blood came out in him. And it felt good not to be trapped up in that bedroom.

Something made a sound at the back door. Mac stayed in his seat. He didn't have the strength to stand and check it out. Judith snuck a peek at him, then grabbed a bowl of scraps.

"I'll be back in minute. I'll take these out while you're eating." She hurried to the door and opened it just enough to slip out, then closed it hard behind her.

Mac thought he heard voices, but they sounded more like muted mumblings. He pulled himself up and shuffled across the room to the window. He glanced at the table and put his finger to his lips. The children nodded. He looked back out the window.

Judith stood there talking to the boy from the hotel, the one who had tried to beat his dog. Balancing the bowl in one arm, she pulled a paper from her apron pocket with her other hand. She glanced at the back door, then handed the boy the paper. He tucked it into his pocket and handed her a small bag. They walked down the steps together. Then the boy took off toward the street, and Judith headed for the garbage.

Mac shuffled back to the table and sat. What was she doing with that boy? What had he given her, and more importantly, what had she given him?

What he saw could have been some innocent transaction, but he was almost certain that it wasn't. He just wasn't sure if it had to do with Snodgrass, Waller, or Grayson, or all three. The one thing he did know was that he had to get some help to look after his family. And that couldn't wait.

CHAPTER TWENTY-TWO

Late Saturday night, Sarah sat at the kitchen table with a pot of tea steeping before her. Time to relax. Everyone else had gone to bed. She couldn't believe how quickly the week had passed, but then she hadn't had a moment to stop and think about it either. The planning, the details were all done. Everything for the wedding was in place. Added to that, Thorn was feeling better.

As if thinking about him brought him down the stairs and into the kitchen, he stepped into the room, more steady on his feet than he had been since the fight.

He carefully slipped onto one of the chairs at the table and let out a small moan. Sarah lowered her eyes and held her tongue, refusing to say anything about how hard he was pushing himself. The man knew what he was feeling, so no reason to state the obvious.

She stood and crossed the kitchen to get a cup. "Would you like some tea?"

"Thank you, that sounds good."

She felt him watching her while she moved around the kitchen. She returned to the table and poured them each a cup.

He took a slow sip of the tea and smiled. "You make a good pot of tea."

"Thank you." Ignoring her cup, she pulled a package from her pocket and slid it over to him. It was addressed to Thorn and came from a jewelry store in Denver. "This came today."

Thorn grinned even wider. "I was wondering when this would arrive." He ripped the paper off the box and opened it. In it lay two metal circles, one larger than the other. "I wanted you to wear something of mine. And since you're a MacPherson bride, this only seemed appropriate."

He held out the larger one to her.

She took it and ran her finger around the edge. It looked like a belt formed into a circle with a cat sitting in the middle, one paw raised. There were words engraved on the top part of the circle. "Touch not the cat but a glove." Interesting, but what did it mean? The wording and the brooch or whatever it was.

Sarah raised her face to Thorn.

Thorn smiled. "It's the MacPherson clan shield." He raised his index finger and touched her between her left shoulder and her heart. "On a man, it's worn about here. Of course, it's usually worn to hold the plaid that hangs down the back and around to his kilt. Women wear it in the same place, but usually they have their family tartan as a sash, across one shoulder and tied on the opposite hip. Even though you don't have a sash yet, I thought you might like to have it." He flushed as he handed her the smaller one. "I had one made for Emma, too."

The word kilt stood out in her mind. She knew what it was, that little skirt Scottish men wore in their home country, but... She wondered if Thorn ever had—

"No."

She tried not to smile. "No, what?"

"No, I've never worn the kilt." He tapped her nose with his finger. "That's what you were thinking, wasn't it?"

Visions of Thorn in a plaid skirt, his legs exposed, flashed in Sarah's head. She felt heat rise in her cheeks. She nodded and lowered her eyes.

Suddenly another question burned in her mind. Had he gotten one of these things for Lizzie? For Gavenia? No, she wouldn't question him about them now. Maybe when the time was right, when things settled down after the wedding, when the Nelson children found their place in the household, when Thorn healed a little more, then she would ask about the two women who haunted her dreams.

"What does this mean?" She pointed to the words on the top of the shield.

"It's our clan motto. 'Touch not the cat bot a glove.' It means don't touch the cat when it's without a glove."

She ran her finger over the cat several times, then grinned up at him. "I don't understand. Either you're playing dress-up with a cat and have some tiny gloves hidden away somewhere, in which case this whole thing is pretty silly, or it has some other meaning."

"Woman, never tease a Scotsman concerning his clan shield." He reached out and took her hand that held the pin. With his other hand, he touched the cat on the shield. "The glove of the wildcat is this part here, the soft underpart of its paw. When the cat is ready to attack or takes a war-like attitude, its paw is ungloved or spread, showing its very dangerous and sharp claws. While the motto sounds simple enough, it is a warning to those who would be foolish or hasty as to engage in battle when the claw of the wildcat is ungloved."

She ran her finger around the shield again. "Like if Stanley did something foolish or hasty."

Thorn's lips thinned to a hard, narrow line. He nodded. "To you or any of those under the MacPherson protection. And the cat can be deadly with its claws out."

She slipped her hand from his. "Do you give these out to all those you protect?"

"Nay, only those born to the clan MacPherson and to the MacPherson brides."

"What about Emma? She's neither born a MacPherson nor married to one."

"I'm hoping one day you'll let me adopt her. On that day, she'll be a MacPherson and have every right to wear the clan shield." He wrapped his fingers around the smaller circle. "On that day, I'll give her this."

Sarah nodded and wrapped her fingers around the larger shield. Warmth spread through her when Thorn talked about the future. If he adopted Emma that would mean they would still be together. Was he trying to tell her that he wanted her? Maybe loved her?

That still didn't answer what kept running through her mind. Had Thorn given one of these to the mysterious Lizzie or Gavenia? Had either one been his MacPherson bride?

Suddenly, she had to know. She drew in a breath, then blew out the question with the breath, "Did Gavenia or Lizzie have a clan shield?"

He blinked. Shocked, but it was more than that. Sorrow and pain filled his eyes. "How did you know about them?"

"When you were feverish, you mumbled something about them. Called out their names."

He nodded. "Aye, they both did."

Sarah pushed her toes against the bottoms of her shoes, trying to keep calm. Maybe she would get some answers now. "Who are—?"

The door from the hall burst open. Helen glided in, almost as if she were floating, her eyes shining and her lips spread in a huge smile. She clasped her hand to her chest. "Tomorrow I'm getting married. Can you believe it?"

Thorn chuckled and stood. "I'm happy for you. Sleep well. I'll see you both in the morning."

Sarah watched as he left the room. Soon, she would get the answers she needed.

Sarah wore one of her finer gowns. This one was of medium blue silk and lace, with the MacPherson clan shield pinned on it. And even though her dress was lovely, she had no fear she'd outshine the bride.

The dress she'd had the seamstress create for her new sister-in-law was beautiful. It had been a battle to get Helen to agree to the snow-white creation. Nothing gaudy, but not plain either. With its triple tiers, it showed off Helen's small waist. Although how the woman could keep such a small waist with all the baking and tasting she did was beyond Sarah.

The midday meal after church services had been light. The ceremony was scheduled for two in the afternoon. Sarah stepped into the kitchen and tapped on Helen's bedroom door.

The door creaked open just a bit. Helen reached out and grabbed Sarah's hand. "Come in and shut the door."

Sarah couldn't help but laugh. "Oh, dear. What's the problem?"

"My hair. I can't do anything with my hair." Helen wiped an embroidered hankie across her eyes. "I always dreamed of walking down the aisle to my groom with my hair flowing to my waist." She flipped the short hair that just brushed her shoulders.

"Your hair will be covered by your veil. Besides, Drew's not going to be thinking about how long your hair is. He's going to be too busy trying to not fall down from nerves."

"And I'll be there to hold him up." Helen giggled and picked up her hairbrush. "You know just what to say, but then you've been married twice."

And not in love either time. Sarah took the brush and motioned Helen onto a chair. A few minutes later, she had pinned up Helen's hair and concealed it under a beaded ornament. Curly ringlets framed her face. Next came the veil. Once that was in place, Helen was ready to meet her groom.

Sarah stood at the door and peeked into the kitchen. No Drew. Carl came out of his room in a new suit, his hair plastered down and looking solemn. Tears filled his eyes.

He stuck out his elbow. "I'm ready to give you away. Drew said it's my d-duty to do that, since I'm family."

Helen bent down, heedless of the wrinkles to her dress. "Oh, sweetie, that's just a saying. All it means is that you are going to walk with me, like best friends. Remember how we talked about moving into the rooms over the bakery? Your room is all ready for you. We hadn't taken you there before because Sarah wanted you to be surprised."

"Truly?"

"Truly."

Carl swiped the back of his hand across his eyes. "Let's get you married then, so we can have some cake."

Together they walked down the hall to the parlor. Sarah hadn't let Helen see it earlier for she wanted that to be a surprise, too. Sarah stepped into the room and the fragrance of roses greeted her. She glanced at Helen to see her reaction, but all the bride looked at was her groom. Joy filled Sarah's heart. That was the way it should be.

Sarah started to the end of the room where Drew and the preacher stood. She smiled and nodded to the guests. Helen's aunt and uncle had been invited, but they had refused to attend. Several elderly ladies from church, women Helen helped with food and chores, sat on the sofa, giggling and whispering among themselves.

Sarah looked to where the preacher stood and almost stumbled when she saw Thorn standing next to her brother. She knew he was going to stand up with Drew, but she had never seen him look so...so good. Not even the day they married. Their wedding day brought memories of the kiss they shared at the end of the ceremony, and then much later at Duncan's house in Denver. Heat rose up her neck and into her cheeks. She chanced a glance at Thorn. His eyes stared straight at her. Small flutters ran through her.

She stepped to the left and waited for Helen, but she couldn't take her eyes off Thorn. When Helen joined them, they all stepped closer to the preacher. The words the preacher spoke—of love, of commitment, of unity, even the words from the book of Ruth—they all seemed new as she looked at Thorn. She had heard them many times before while growing up. Of course, they were in her own weddings, first to Alfred, then to Thorn, but this time it was different.

The words touched her heart. While the vows were spoken, she repeated them in her mind as she looked at Thorn. This time she was agreeing to them of her own will because she wanted to. It seemed the same for Thorn. After Drew spoke his vows, Thorn looked at her and nodded slightly. When Helen said hers, Sarah did the same. She had to force herself to stand still when the preacher said the groom could kiss his bride.

Grinning, Drew led Helen to the dining room for the reception.

Sarah slipped her hand into the bend of Thorn's elbow and walked beside him. He pressed her hand close to his side. She stared up at him. A soft smile lifted his lips as his green eyes held onto hers. Her hand trembled and he pressed it closer. Joy filled her heart.

A few minutes later, they cut the cake Helen had baked and decorated, and the Nelson children passed the refreshments out to all the guests. Sarah slipped back into the kitchen to heat more water for tea. The elderly ladies seemed to enjoy that the most, that and repeating everything that happened during the wedding—as if anybody had forgotten the events of just a few minutes before.

Sarah was filling the teapot when the back door opened. She didn't want to burn herself, so she didn't look, but she figured it was Thorn. Had he slipped out the front and sneaked around back to steal a kiss? The thought warmed her cheeks, but at least she could blame that on the steaming water. Bouncing in her shoes and wetting her suddenly dry lips, she took a sudden breath and froze. The smell that drifted to her was not Thorn's. It was the stench that Stanley always wore. Some women might think it wonderful and masculine, but to Sarah, it carried the smell of death and pain.

Sarah turned to the back door and faced Stanley. "What are you doing here?"

"We need to talk."

She set the teapot on the table, but kept her hand on the handle. Never hurt to have a weapon handy. "I can't think of anything we have to talk about."

"The business, of course."

"What business?"

"Your grandfather's business here in Central City. The corporation will not advance the money to complete everything that needs to be done to get them all up and running. You need to invest some money."

Sarah tightened her grip on the teapot. "Stanley, whatever business matters you had with my grandfather don't affect me in the least. I have no interest in them, either monetarily or emotionally. Deal with the corporation that has control over the businesses. Whatever you do here, I want no part in it."

"You can't put me off like this. Your grandfather and I had an arrangement." He took a couple of steps into the kitchen. "Under his authority, I have made certain deals. Deals that need to be completed."

Sarah picked up the teapot. "I think our discussion is completed. Please excuse me. I have guests waiting."

When she moved around the table, he stepped forward and grabbed her arm.

She bit back a cry of pain.

He held her firm. "You have obligations."

"She owes you nothing." Thorn closed the door to the hall with one hand and held a pistol in the other. "And if you don't get your hand off my wife this instant, you'll be missing it."

Stanley let go but leaned closer to her. He kept his voice low so that only Sarah could hear him. "Your husband isn't always here. I can be an extremely patient man." He spun away and pushed through the back door, leaving his stink behind.

Thorn stepped to her side and lifted her arm with great care. She knew the moment he saw the red marks. A deep growl sounded in his chest. "What did he say?"

"The same thing he's said for as long as I've known him." She gently tugged her arm. Thorn released it and stepped back a pace. "He's been my grandfather's lackey for so long, I'm not sure he knows how to think for himself."

Thorn reached up and cupped her cheek with his hand. "He's more dangerous than you think. Don't trust him."

"You don't have to worry on that count."

"Just be careful. I don't want anything to happen to you." He took a step closer. His head dropped as his fingers slid up her arms.

Her feet had a mind of their own. Her toes pressed down into her shoes. Her heels raised. Her lips came closer to his.

Their breath mingled.

Judith burst into the kitchen. "Oh, excuse me."

Sarah stepped away.

Thorn let out a growl.

"Some of the ladies asked for more tea." With her eyes lowered, Judith moved further into the room and grabbed the teapot. "I'll get this to them."

The door had barely closed before it opened again. This time, it was Linda. "Some of the guests are getting ready to leave."

"I'll be right out." Sarah started for the door.

"Rose, when this is all over"—Thorn waved his arm toward the wedding reception—"We need to talk."

She nodded. With all that had been going on for the last week or so, she wasn't sure exactly what it was he wanted to discuss. All she knew was that butterflies filled her stomach, and she didn't know if they were angry, worried, or scared.

CHAPTER TWENTY-THREE

After the newly married couple and the guests had departed, Thorn sat on the swing by the kitchen door. The last rays of light were fading and the night breeze had picked up. He had asked Rose to join him after she put Emma to bed. He grunted as he stretched his arm along the back of the swing. Some muscles still weren't like they should be, and by tomorrow night, they would probably be screaming for rest.

But his time was getting short, and he didn't like leaving Rose here with Drew moving to the rooms above the bakery. Not that he faulted the man one bit. If Rose were his wife in more than name only, he'd want to take her to the ranch and keep her for himself.

He couldn't stop the sound that burst through his lips, not a laugh exactly, but not a grunt either. There was no way he would have Rose just for himself. There were four girls, his three and Emma, that would be around, at least for the next twenty years or so. Besides any children he and his Rose might have.

He pounded his fist on his good leg. He had to stop thinking like that. First he had to find Hank while keeping Rose safe. With Stanley's visit, worry sat upon him even heavier.

The door opened and Rose stepped out. "Sorry it took so long but Emma's finally asleep. I think all the people and excitement got to her today."

Thorn stood and held out his hand. "Join me?"

The chains rattled and the wooden swing creaked as they sat. Thorn used the heel of his boot to set the swing to moving. "Rose, would you be agreeable to having a couple men around your place? Cousins—part of the eighty-one?"

"Why?"

"Protection."

"You could stay and that would be protection enough."

"Ah, Rose. I can't stop freighting right now. Maybe soon, I hope. But not right now."

"If you gave it up, you could start another business in Central City. The town's growing so fast. And that way you could stay at home."

How could he explain? Maybe he could give her something, a little bit for her to hold onto. But not the full story. With the way her grandfather and husband treated her, if she ever found out that his first wife was found hanging in his barn, he would lose the little trust he'd built. "Rose, there's a man I have to find. That's why I haul freight to the different mining areas. That way I can build trust and ask questions. I can't settle down anywhere until I find him."

"Is he an outlaw? Can't someone else go after him?"

Mac shook his head. "No, nothing like that. He has answers I need." Mac shook his head. "I'm probably the only man he'll talk to, if only I could find him."

A still, uncomfortable silence filled the air.

Mac wanted to ask Rose what she was thinking but knew better. He felt rather than saw Rose shift and turn toward him.

She looked boldly at his face. "What do you want out of this marriage?"

He wanted to love her, take her to his family ranch, live with her the rest of their days, but until he knew the role he'd played in Lizzie's death, he could say none of that.

After a moment, she asked, "Do you want to end our marriage?"

That was one answer he did have. "No."

She stood. "You don't want to end it, but you don't know what you want out of it?"

His gut twisted, but he still couldn't give her the answers she wanted.

"You have a good heart. I've seen you with Emma and the Nelson children, and even Drew. I know you aren't cruel. When you discover the answers to my questions, please share them with me." She stood and walked away. Each snap of her heels against the wooden porch shouted out her anger. She entered the house and closed the door with a hard shove.

Early the next morning, Thorn brought his wagon out of the barn. It had been a little over a week since he'd returned home bloody and beaten. But it was time to get back to his mission. And that meant leaving those he loved. If he couldn't admit it to Rose, he could be honest and admit it to himself. Somehow he had to work harder, dig deeper. Somehow he had to find Hank. His life and his family, here and at the ranch, depended on it.

He waved to cousins, Kerr and Dougal, as they walked to the barn. Each carried a rifle. The nice thing about his family, and one thing he missed most—besides his girls—was the way they stood by each other, no questions asked.

"Be off with you, cousin. We'll look after your lady and the wee babe." Kerr grasped Mac forearm to forearm.

Mac returned the pressure. He liked the feeling better than a handshake. He greeted Dougal the same way.

"Thank you for coming on such short notice."

"Ah, 'tis what family's for." Kerr looked around the back of the house. "Nice place."

"Rose hasn't exactly agreed to your staying here. If she kicks you out, stay nearby so you can keep an eye on her, especially if Snodgrass shows his face." Mac glanced back at the house, hoping to see a glimpse of Rose.

"Be gone with you, so we can begin looking after the fair maiden." Kerr swatted Mac on the shoulder and grinned.

Mac took one more look at the house. Did the curtain in the kitchen move? Was she watching him leave? He stared at it a moment, then shook his head, climbed up on the wagon, and snapped the reins, leaving the woman he loved behind.

Sarah had watched Thorn stop by the barn and talk to two young men, each carrying a rifle. She recognized them as two of the cowboys who'd been with Adair at the picnic.

She gripped the curtain. Why had she run away in anger last night? Mac wasn't like Alfred or Grandfather, or even Stanley. Too many years of not trusting men, of hating them, had poisoned her. Now she wasn't sure how to trust the man she loved. Somehow, she and Thorn had to come to an understanding about what they wanted, where they stood with each other, what kind of future they would have. But she didn't know how.

Mac was long out of sight. She dropped the curtain. At least she could welcome the men he'd left to protect her. She set a pot of coffee to boil, then laid some bacon in a skillet. Judith didn't come in this early, but Sarah could prepare breakfast for those two young men. Maybe they would tell her more than childhood stories about Thorn like they had at the picnic, now that he wasn't here to glare at them.

Two hours after the men had eaten, Judith arrived. While Dougal took the Nelson children to the bakery, Sarah sat at the desk in the parlor, planning to deal with the household accounts.

Someone knocked at the front door, a slow steady knocking. A chill ran down Sarah's spine. She moved to see who was calling so early in the day. It wasn't Stanley. His knock was sharp, rapid, as if he were too busy to wait for someone to answer his summons.

She opened the door. Mr. Carlyle stood on the other side.

"Please come in." She stepped aside and closed the door behind him. She had not seen the lawyer since she'd summoned him after Petey Waller made his demands about Emma. She took his hat and set it on the small table in the foyer, then directed him to the parlor.

Judith barreled down the hall.

Sarah turned to the woman. "Would you bring us some coffee, please?"

The housekeeper nodded and hurried to the kitchen.

Mr. Carlyle waited until Sarah seated herself on the sofa before he sat on a nearby chair. They exchanged a few pleasantries. He looked somber as he settled his leather case on his lap, then folded his hands on top of it.

Puffing slightly, Judith rushed back into the room carrying a tray with the coffee. She set it on the table in front of Sarah, then stood nearby.

"Thank you, Judith. Would you see if Kerr and Dougal need anything?" Sarah lifted the coffee pot and filled the cups. Judith moved slowly out of the room—slowly compared to the way she had rushed to get the coffee. Sarah waited to hear the tapping of her shoes on the wood floor, but never heard it.

Sarah shrugged. She wasn't going to worry about a nosy cook. "If you had let me know, I could have come to your office and saved you this trip."

"Considering the situation, I didn't want to wait for that." He pulled an envelope from his coat pocket and withdrew a sheet of paper. "I have some sad and potentially disturbing news. Just this morning, I received word from my partner in Denver, Mr. Williams." He paused for a moment.

She braced herself for whatever was to come, then waved him to continue.

He cleared his throat. "I hate to be this abrupt, but there is no other way. Mr. Williams asked me to inform you that your grandfather has passed away."

Sarah's hands trembled. She set her cup down and wrapped her arms around her middle. Grandfather's death was a shock. She had thought he was so full of meanness he would live for many more years just to spite everyone. "What happened to him?"

"Apparently, he'd been declining, which was why, when the brother of one of the maids you retained to look after him asked to visit him, your grandfather agreed. The brother was a minister at a small congregation, one your family had not attended."

"My family didn't attend any congregation in Boston." Hurt and anger built in Sarah's chest as memories of the past flooded her mind. "Grandfather hated anything to do with religion."

"Be that as it may, the young man visited with your grandfather on several occasions." He looked down at one of the pieces of paper he held. "After one such visit, according to the minister, your grandfather repented of the cruel and sinful life he had lived and asked God to forgive him and accept him back into his fold."

Sarah choked as she swallowed a sob. "Accept him back? Grandfather never was in the fold."

"Your lawyer in Boston believed the same thing, so he did some checking for you. It seems your grandfather had been very active in the church while growing up, and had, in fact, married the daughter of a small village preacher.

But as he started to rise in the financial world, he turned his back on his earlier faith, and money became his master."

"I don't believe this." Sarah shook her head. "It's impossible."

"According to this report, the morning after that final visit with the minister, the maid found your grandfather dead. He was holding a small portrait of your grandmother. Your Boston lawyer passed on the information that your grandfather wished to be buried next to his wife. He carried out that request." Mr. Carlyle drew another envelope from his pocket. "I have one more thing for you." He held out the envelope. Her name was written in jagged letters, like a child's early scrawl. Or a sick man's trembling hand.

She didn't want to take it. It was too much like taking poison into her hands, poison that could seep out of the envelope and soak into her skin.

"Please take it." Mr. Carlyle moved it a little closer. "The minister said it couldn't hurt you."

She took the envelope and shoved it into her pocket, then stood. "Thank you for delivering the news. Will that be all?"

Sarah hoped so. She wasn't sure how much more she could take before she fell apart. A few minutes. That's all she needed. A few minutes to absorb the news about Grandfather, and then a few minutes holding Emma to remember all the goodness in the world.

Mr. Carlyle rose and cleared his throat. "Everything except a warning. Be extra careful of Stanley Snodgrass. He has nothing to lose now."

"All support to Stanley stopped with Grandfather's stroke. His death won't change anything."

"Mr. Snodgrass has been using your grandfather's name and former reputation to try and gain support with businessmen in Boston." The lawyer shook his head. "But with Mr. Hollingsworth's passing, Mr. Snodgrass will have to rely completely on himself. And he has built a reputation here in Central City as a bit of an unsavory character, especially with some of his associates."

After he left, she leaned against the wall. Why did Thorn have to leave this morning? She needed him. His arms. His words. Gripping her hands tightly together, she walked up the stairs, the letter rustling in her pocket.

With Kerr guarding the house and Sally taking care of Emma, Sarah had Dougal take her to the bakery, the unopened letter still in her pocket. As usual, Monday at the bakery was a very busy day. Linda and Nancy were restocking the shelves while Jack and Carl cleaned the tables and took the dirty cups and plates to the kitchen.

When Sarah entered the kitchen, Helen pulled herself from Drew's arms and blushed, then shrugged. Drew laughed but let his wife go.

Helen rushed to Sarah's side and gave her a hug. "And how are you doing today, sister of mine?"

"Did you know you have a streak of flour on your cheek and nose?" Sarah handed Helen a tea towel.

Helen wiped her face with the fabric. "Of course, I knew. Your brother just dusted me with it and proclaimed me the queen of the flour fairies." She giggled. Drew turned red and shrugged.

Sarah tried to laugh. It sounded false.

Drew stepped closer to her. "What's the matter, sis?"

"I don't want to spoil your honeymoon." Sarah gripped her hands together.

"Oh, don't worry about that. We plan for our honeymoon to last us the rest of our lives, don't we, husband of mine?" Helen flashed a smile at Drew, then tugged on Sarah's hands. "I think it's time for a break. Linda and Nancy can handle the bakery for a few minutes. Let's grab us some coffee and go upstairs."

Drew motioned for Linda and Nancy to help with the customers.

As she and Helen started for the stairs, Sarah looked over her shoulder. "Drew, please come too."

Once they were upstairs, Helen led them to the small dining table, and they all sat. "Now tell us what put that look in your eye."

"I hate to bring bad news the day after your wedding." Sarah wrapped her fingers around the cup filled from the pot Drew had brought upstairs, welcoming the warmth to her cold hands.

"Unless you are going to tell me Drew already has a wife, we can handle it."

Drew shook his head and rolled his eyes. He turned his attention to Sarah. "What's wrong?"

Sarah took a deep breath, then let it out in big puff. "Mr. Carlyle came by this morning to tell me that Grandfather passed away. He was buried next to Grandmother." She went on to tell them everything else the lawyer said, except the part about the envelope in her pocket.

"It's over then." Drew took a large swallow of his coffee. "I hope he's at peace now."

Sarah's fingers gripped the cup so tightly she was afraid it would shatter in her hands. How could Drew talk like that? He had suffered at the hands of that man like she had. Grandfather had tried to take the joy and happiness from Drew's life, had tried to make her sweet brother into a monster, like the great Andrew Elijah Hollingsworth.

Drew touched her hand. "Sis, you've got to let it go."

Nancy stood by the door they had left open. "Drew, Mrs. Thompson from the hotel insists she must speak to you right now."

"I'll be right there." He stood and touched Sarah's shoulder. "If you don't let it go, it'll destroy you."

He walked out the door.

Sarah felt like the walls were caving in on her. And Drew acted as if nothing had changed. "It doesn't bother him, Grandfather's dying."

Helen leaned a little closer to Sarah. "No, it doesn't. He's made peace with his grandfather."

"How? When? He never told me he had communicated with Grandfather."

"He didn't. He talked to God." Helen smiled a glorious smile. "He turned it over, and now he's at peace."

Sarah's heart felt leaden, cold and hard. She stretched out her hands, palms up, wishing the answers, the path to that peace, would fall into them. "How did he do that?"

"It wasn't easy. Forgiveness doesn't happen in an instant."

"Or ever."

Helen ran her finger over her scar, then took one of Sarah's hands and held it with both of hers. "No, it's not easy, and it's not only for the person who did the wrong. Forgiveness is also for the person who forgives. Drew forgave, but his grandfather never knew. Drew's free from the burden of anger and hatred."

She took a deep breath. "After I was attacked, I had a hard time forgiving Jim Grayson. My heart was hard, becoming as ugly as my face." Sarah started to say Helen never was ugly, even with the scar, but Helen held up her hand. "Let me finish. The anger in my heart kept sucking the forgiveness from my mind and kicking it away. Finally, I understood. Forgiveness is a commitment you make in your mind, you bind in your heart, and you live out in your life."

Sarah tapped her fingers on the table as she tried to follow what Helen was saying. Some of what Helen said made sense, but she was still having a hard time seeing how she could forgive Grandfather and Alfred. But because Helen had forgiven her attacker, and through Helen, Drew had forgiven Grandfather, Sarah knew she needed to understand. "I'm not sure I can follow your example."

"Once I committed—truly committed, to forgiving Jim Grayson, I had to forgive him every day in my mind until my heart took over the job. During that time, I hurt a lot and cried many tears. It wasn't his heart I was trying to change. It was mine. And now I don't carry that load of anger."

Sarah pulled the envelope out of her pocket and handed it to Helen. "Mr. Carlyle brought this. I can't open it. You do it."

When Helen unsealed the envelope, a broken silver chain with a silver cross fell out. She looked up at Sarah.

Sarah studied the jewelry as it lay on the table between them. She hadn't seen it in so many years. She couldn't believe Grandfather had kept it.

Helen nodded and withdrew a single sheet of paper. It didn't take long to read. Like Sarah's name on the envelope, the words on the letter were scrawled and there were only two of them written there. "Sorry. Forgive."

Sarah balled her hands into fists. "I can't do it. I can't forgive him just like that. Like nothing ever happened."

Helen rested a hand on Sarah's fist. "If nothing ever happened, you wouldn't need to forgive him. But please, think about it. Think of the joy of not carrying that anger in your heart. Think of how you can teach Emma what forgiveness is when she does something wrong or a wrong is done to her."

Sarah grabbed the paper, the necklace, and the envelope. She shoved them in her pocket. "I'll think about it."

She stood and left, the two words pounding in her head. *Sorry. Forgive.*

CHAPTER TWENTY-FOUR

Mac snapped the reins over the backs of his mules. He'd made a quick trip to Denver and then on to several of the mining camps. In the three weeks he had been on this route, he was no closer to finding Hank than he had been a year ago. Frustration and anger grew stronger inside him as he tightened his grip on the leather straps in his gloved hands.

He still had several more stops before he would be back in Central City, but how could he face Rose without the answers she needed?

As the sun set, Mac stopped at one of his usual camping spots and settled in for the night. With the scent of the campfire and coffee filling the air, he leaned against a wagon wheel and ruffled the hair on Tair's neck while the dog rested his head on his crossed paws.

Something changed, in the air, in the feeling of not being alone. Mac set down his coffee cup and inched his hand over the smooth stock of his rifle lying on the ground next to his leg.

Tair lifted his head and growled. A twig snapped outside the campfire's light. Tair stood, his growls growing deeper and louder. The grass to the side of the trail rustled. Another dog bounded out of the darkness. The dog looked familiar. Lizzy had found a dog just like it. The mutt had been more dead than alive that day, but she had nursed it back to life, then named it Moibel. He'd been her protector from then on.

Tair bared his teeth. The little dog stopped yapping and stared at them both.

Mac blinked and shook his head. No one had seen Moibel since the day he found Lizzie hang...since his brother-in-law disappeared.

Another twig snapped.

"Hank?"

Mac released his hold on the gun. Either the man already had a bead on him with a rifle, or he was coming to talk. Either way, tonight everything would end—his life or his quest to find the truth.

"I'm coming in, Thorn, don't shoot." A thin man with shaggy brown hair and a drawn face entered the ring of light. Moibel moved to his side and snuffled his hand.

Mac rested his hand on Tair's head. The dog settled down. "Looks like you made friends with your sister's dog."

"He's all I got left—of her, of my family, of what was before." Hank rubbed his hand along his leg. "Heard you've been hunt...uh, asking after me."

"Aye, for some time. Seems everywhere I look, you've just left." Mac stared at his brother-in-law. Not yet eighteen, but he had the worn look of a man three times his age. His eyes were haunted. His hands trembled.

"Sit before you fall. Are you sick?" Mac picked up his cup and sipped. Hank had been as close as any of his own brothers back on the family ranch. Closer, since he had lived in the house with him, Lizzie, and the girls. They had shared work, faith, dreams, and family.

Hank dropped to the ground, his shoulders slumped. "Not sick, just empty." He wrapped his long skinny arm around Moibel and rested his head against the fur.

"Aye, I know the feeling. Have had it since I found Lizzie hanging in the barn."

Hank raised his head and swallowed hard. "I didn't know about that for a long time." Moisture coated his eyes. "If I'd…if I'd known that would've happened, I'd have stayed until you got back. Or I'd have taken her with me." He shook his head. "I just didn't know."

Moibel made little crying sounds, as if to comfort him.

Mac's chest tightened. His breath drew harsher. When the truth finally came out, would he be at peace?

Tair shifted closer to him. A soft whine rose in his throat.

Mac grabbed another cup from his supplies, filled it with coffee and handed it to Hank, then settled back against his bedroll. "You know I've been tracking you for several months?"

Hank nodded. "At first, all I heard was someone was asking after me. Wasn't sure who. So I moved around a bit."

"Would've helped if you'd stayed put."

Hank shook his head. "Couldn't. Too…too scared."

What did the boy have to be scared of? He had the whole MacPherson clan to look after him. All he had to do was go home, and he would've had their protection. "Too scared of what?"

Hank fisted his hand into the fur of Lizzie's dog. He raised his head. His eyes were deep pools of pain. Haunted, as if a ghostly haint lived there, feeding on the young man's agony. "You weren't there that day. You don't know what it was like. Lizzie begged me to go." A cry as haunted as his eyes filled the night air. "If only I had stayed. If only…"

Chills ran down Mac's back. What had happened that day? It couldn't have been worse than he had imagined, could it? What more didn't he know? "Tell me everything."

Hank's throat jerked as he swallowed. He licked his lips. "First, tell me, did they bury my sister with the other MacPhersons?"

Pain shot through Mac. The kid knew. He knew. How could he have left his sister hanging there? Why hadn't he stopped her? "Of course. She was a MacPherson bride. Why would you think she wouldn't have been buried with the family?"

Mac's hand inched toward his rifle. He wasn't sure what he was going to do. A lot depended on the next words out of the kid's mouth. Had he watched his sister hang herself? Had he helped? Had he done it to her himself?

Hank closed his eyes for a long moment. When he opened them, tears flowed down his dirty cheeks. "Because of what those men did to her."

A powerful force hit Mac in the chest. He couldn't breathe. "Go on." The words came out harsh and clipped, like ice slamming against a window pane in mid-winter.

Hank rubbed the back of his hand over his face, smearing the moisture off. He drew a deep breath, then let it out in a rush. "Lizzie had me take your girls over to the main house just after breakfast so she could get ready for your homecoming. Thorn, she was so excited about you returning home. She couldn't wait for you to get back."

The kid rubbed his face again. "That's how I remember her, with that smile on her face and her eyes shining."

"What happened?" Mac wanted to grab Hank by the shoulders and shake the rest of the story out of him.

Hank shrank into himself. "I'd taken the girls in the wagon, 'cause I was also taking the food Lizzie had made for the homecoming celebration." His hands tightened into fists. "As I neared your place on the way back, I saw three horses in the front of the house, then I heard Lizzie screaming." He rubbed his hands over his ears. "I'll never forget the terror of those screams."

He shook his head and looked straight at Mac. "I jumped out of the wagon with my rifle. They had her in the barn. She was lying in the hay, sobbing, her clothes ripped. Those men all stood around her, laughing, saying it would be fine and dandy if they had put a Baxter baby in her MacPherson belly. I shot the one who said that right in the heart, then threw my knife into the chest of the next one."

Memories of the Baxter gang flashed through Mac's head, how his granny had been called on to help the father's young wife in childbirth. The man's anger when she died. His brothers' threats against the MacPhersons. How cattle had disappeared after that. How fires started for no reason. But eventually everything had quieted down, and the Macphersons thought the Baxters had moved on.

Guilt rolled over Mac in waves. How wrong they had all been.

Hank groaned, low and painful. "Lizzie—Lizzie grabbed the pitchfork and stabbed the last one in the neck."

Mac swallowed the bitter bile that rose in his throat. His mind filled in the pictures. The pain, the agony, the fear his Lizzie had gone through. His stone heart came to life and bled before it ripped in pieces. His hand gripped his rifle. One last question had to be asked. "Did you know she was going to hang herself?"

Hank's head shot up. "Lizzie didn't do that. She loved you and her girls too much. She loved God too much to ever do that."

A log in the fire snapped, sending sparks heavenward.

"I found her note." Mac eased his hand off the rifle. Truth rang in the boy's voice.

"What did it say?"

Mac didn't have to think about the words. They were seared into his mind, but he pulled the pouch from under his shirt, ripped the cord that held it around his neck and tossed it to Hank.

Mac recited the words that had haunted his life for two years, "I'm sorry about what I have to do. Please forgive me. I'll always love you. Lizzie."

Hank caught the bag and cradled it in his hands. He pulled out the paper and rubbed his finger over it. "She didn't mean what you think. As that last man lay dying, he said we wouldn't live to see the next morning 'cause the rest of his gang was coming any time, and they'd kill us."

He brushed a hand over his eyes. "Lizzie didn't want any harm to come to the MacPhersons. She loved you all so much." He drew in a deep breath. "So she helped me load the dead men on the wagon and told me to take them to one of the old caves in the mountains and cause a cave-in with some dynamite. That way their deaths couldn't be tied to the MacPhersons."

The kid shoved the paper back into the pouch. "She was going to leave. Just until she knew if the man was right...about leaving her with a Baxter baby. She said she had to know that before she could face you. I saddled her horse while she went to change. She told me she left you a note." He held up the pouch. "We left at the same time—me to the hills and her to your folks' place to tell the girls she had to go on a trip. She'd planned to stay in Denver."

Things weren't adding up right. "How could she have ridden anywhere with the way she'd been beaten up?"

Hank narrowed his eyes. "They hadn't beat her. Didn't have to—there were three of them. They just—" Hank's face lost all its color and grew white as a dead miner caught in the winter's snow. "The rest of the Baxters must have caught up with her and brought her back to the house." He dropped Mac's pouch on the dirt, then dug his hands into his hair. "What they must have done to her."

Hank jumped up and ran into the darkness. The sounds of retching filled the air, followed by howls of pain.

Mac wished he could rid himself of the images so easily. Lizzie hadn't killed herself, but what horrors had she faced in her last moments of life? He took in deep breaths, then blew them out, trying to focus on anything else. His girls—he had to focus on his girls. They needed him.

Hank crawled back to the campfire and collapsed. Moibel nudged against him. "What happens now?"

"You go back to the ranch, if you want. There'll always be a home for you there." Mac nodded to Hank. "The girls have missed their favorite uncle."

"I'd like that, but what about you?"

Drained as he was, Mac couldn't keep Sarah's face out of his thoughts. He had to see her, talk things over with her. He was free now, free from the worry of harming another woman like he feared he had hurt Lizzie. But there was one thing he had to do first.

Sarah stood by the crib and watched her precious girl sleep. She touched her fingers and leaned forward to place a kiss on Emma's cheek. The last words from her grandfather flashed through her thoughts, just as they had for the last three weeks. She jerked back, her hand resting in mid-air.

Those two words haunted her. Trying not to think about Grandfather had not worked. Deep down she'd known it wouldn't. Not thinking about abuse was not the same as forgiving the person who caused the abuse. And even if Helen hadn't said as much, Sarah had to acknowledge that she wasn't strong enough by herself to do it.

Oh, she could decide to forgive him. How easy would that be, now that he was dead and she wouldn't have to deal with him ever again? But had she ever truly committed in her mind to forgive Grandfather? Make a pact with her heart that no matter what, she would forgive? But then, was her mind ready to help her heart forgive?

Sarah rested her hand on her chest. Her heart beat sure and strong to feed the rest of her body with what it needed to survive. But what about the other heart, the one that couldn't be seen by any but God, the one that would feed her mind? Had it grown hard and scarred with her hatred of those who had hurt her, who were dead and could no longer do anything to her?

It did no good to keep the memories and hatred alive. The only one it served...

Her hand trembled.

Her father had preached enough about the devil for her to recognize him now. How could she have turned from God who loved her enough to send Jesus to die for her, the Savior she had given her life to before Grandfather snatched her away? Even in her pain, how could she have pushed God out of her heart and let hate live there?

She wouldn't let Satan live in her heart anymore.

She fell to the floor as the words of a hymn she learned just before her parents died filled her head. *I heard the voice of Jesus say, "Come unto Me and rest; Lay down, thou weary one, lay down Thy head upon My breast." I came to Jesus as I was, weary and worn and sad; I found in Him a resting place, and He has made me glad.*

She was weary and worn and sad. She needed the peace, strength, and joy she had known when she had first committed her whole being—her mind, her heart, and her body—to God through Jesus. When had she taken her eyes off Him? When had she turned inward instead of looking upward?

The song started again in her mind. *I heard the voice of Jesus say, "I am this dark world's Light; Look unto Me, thy morn shall rise, And all thy day be bright." I looked to Jesus, and I found in Him my Star, my Sun; And in that light of life I'll walk, Till traveling days are done.*

Grandfather wasn't the only one who needed to be forgiven. She did, too—by God. Oh, how ashamed He must be of her! The tears rolled down her cheeks. Ashamed but still loved. Just like God loved Grandfather and forgave him. What right had she to withhold forgiveness from someone God had already forgiven? Both of them were His children, both had gone astray and returned.

She wiped her eyes on her sleeve, then clasped her hands together. Raising her head to heaven, she went before God in the presence of His Son and with the help of His Spirit. "Dear God and Father, I come to You in the name of your Son and my Savior. You are so loving and forgiving, patient, wanting and waiting for Your children to come to you. Father, I have strayed so far away. Thank you for letting me come home. Thank you for Your welcoming arms. Please help me to walk close to you each day. Please strengthen me and guide me. And Father, I pray that You will help me forgive Grandfather, Alfred, and Stanley for all the hurts they have caused me. So soften my heart so I can truly forgive each of them. Amen."

She sat there for a few minutes, feeling the love of God surround her. Then softly singing the hymn, she went to bed and slept better than she had for more than thirteen years.

Mac packed up camp after breakfast. "I decided to make a detour and go by the ranch. Want to travel with me?"

Hank's head bobbed up and down faster than a cork on a fishing line. "Yes!"

Two days later, with the sun setting over the Rockies to the west, Mac pulled up to the family ranch house. Grandda and Granny hobbled out to greet him, followed by the rest of the clan living there.

Granny clung to his arm and pulled him down for a kiss. Grandda embraced him, forearm to forearm. Both had tears in their eyes.

"Ye're early. We hadn't expected ye for a few weeks yet." Granny wiped her eyes with the corner of her white apron.

Mac looked Granny straight in the eye, something he hadn't been able to do since he found Lizzie's note. "I have to pull out in the morn. There's something back in Central City I need to take care of. But I'll be back real soon."

"Something or someone?" She patted his arm.

Grandda harrumphed. "Mary MacPherson, leave the boy alone."

Granny giggled. "After all these years, he still likes to call me that. Glad I broke with Scottish tradition and took his name instead of keeping me own."

"Aye, but your sister'll never let you hear the end of it." Grandda harrumphed again. "And now the old bid—"

"Angus MacPherson, ye'll not call me sister such names." Granny tapped the toe of her boot on the ground.

Mac held back a chuckle when his brawny grandda buckled to his wee wife's order. As far as he knew, she was the only one who'd ever had that control over the chief of this branch of the American MacPhersons. Would he and Sarah be like that in fifty years? He hoped so.

"As I was saying, me wife's sister and her husband're coming here ta live, them and their Campbell band."

Granny slipped her work-roughened hand into Mac's. "I wished we had known ye were coming."

Thorn looked around for his girls.

Grandda rested his hand on Granny's shoulder. "Nia took the lasses over to Jason's spread. Yer aunt Quennie wanted to see them since yer cousin hasn't settled down and given her any grandchildren."

Thorn dropped his head to his chest. He had needed to see them now, not only to hug them, but to let them know that he would be home to stay soon. But maybe it was better this way. When he left in the morning, he wouldn't have to see the tears in their eyes.

He sucked in a breath and raised his head.

Granny's face lost its grin as she looked past him. "Hank? Is that really you?"

Everyone stopped and looked at the young man who stood by the wagon. Shuffling his feet, he waved. "Hello."

Everyone glanced from the young man to Mac and back. He knew they waited for a sign about how to welcome the young man.

Mac stepped over and rested his hand on Hank's shoulder. "Look who I brought home."

As he knew they would, the family swamped the young man with greetings, hugs, and kisses.

After supper, Mac went outside. He didn't really need the lantern he'd lit to find his way. But he wanted it to read the words, words that he had not let himself read before.

He settled on the ground before Lizzie's headstone, then bowed his head. For the first time in two years, he let happy memories flow over him. The first time he saw Lizzie with her pigtails half-undone from climbing the tree outside her house. The day they married, the love in her eyes when she said, "I do," and then that first kiss as man and wife. The day their daughter was born, then the second, and the third. All times filled with love and devotion.

How could he have thought she would have hanged herself? She was too strong for that. He let loose tears of shame at the thoughts he'd held against her for two years. She had survived not one but two attacks that day, had killed a man to protect her brother and herself, and had prepared to give up home and family until she knew what her future held.

It wouldn't have mattered if she had decided to wait for him at home. The curs who killed her would have found her either way.

Mac lifted his head and brought the lantern closer to the headstone. It wasn't grief that had prevented Mac from ordering it himself. It was anger and shame and guilt. Anger that she had left him. Shame that she had taken her own life. Guilt that he had not been the husband she needed.

The light shone on the words Grandda had chosen. Words that he hadn't been able to let himself read before.

ELIZABETH ANN MACPHERSON
Born September 15, 1832
Died May 12, 1859
LOVING WIFE TO THORN
BELOVED MOTHER TO FAITH, GRACE, AND
MERCY
FAITHFUL CHRISTIAN TO
HER SAVIOR AND KING

Tears ran down his weathered cheeks for the first time since he'd found the note in the house and her body hanging in the barn. Cries and jumbled words mingled with the tears until at last, the pain washed away.

Mac leaned his head against the tree that shaded the grave in summer and stared at the headstone. "Lizzie Ann, I know you aren't in the grave, at least not the part of you that matters, but I need to say some things, and I don't know where else to go."

He took in a deep breath and let it out bit by bit. "If you were here, I'd ask your forgiveness for what I've held against you." He made a choked noise in his throat. "'Course, if you were here I wouldn't have to ask your forgiveness, at least not for what I thought you did. I know you'd have forgiven me, no matter what. That was just the kind of woman you were, the kind of women I hope our girls will grow up to be."

He picked up a small branch and rubbed it back and forth in the grass. "Lizzie Ann, I have to admit that I've found someone new. Her name's Sarah Rose. She's got the same kind of strength you did. I used to think she was a bit snooty, but I've come to realize she was just trying to cover up her hurt. You'd have understood her, and she you. And I've learned from both of you how strong a woman can be, must be, to live with men. But you never let that strength be what controlled you. It was your love—love for those around you, for your family, and for me."

His hand tightened on the stick. "As I loved you, I have come to love her. Funny, I married you because I loved you, and I married Sarah Rose before I realized I loved her. Given time, I think we've a good chance of making a true marriage together. I hope to bring her back here and add her to the clan. Together we'll raise the girls, but we'll never let them forget you. And you'll always have a special place in my heart. Good-bye, my Lizzie Ann."

Mac dropped the stick and blew out the flame in the lantern. In his mind and heart and soul, he entered the throne room of God and came home. And for the first time since he saw Lizzie Ann hanging in the barn, he felt at peace.

When the first pinks lightened the darkness of night, Mac stood and headed to the house. It would take another two weeks, but he needed to finish taking the freight to the men who were waiting for it, and then get back to Central City and his wife. It might take time, but he was sure that he and Sarah Rose had a future together.

Stanley sat in his chair and tapped his finger on the wood desk. Cigar smoke filled the room. Time was short. He had to act soon. There were men…

Someone tapped on the back door.

He unlocked it. Waller and Grayson entered.

"Sit." Stanley paced behind his chair. "I've waited long enough. It's time to take action. Grayson, get that Indian—Three Toes you said his name was? Well, get him here by the day after tomorrow." He pulled out a small bag of money from his pocket. "Give him this and tell him there's more when he completes his job.'

Stanley stopped pacing, sat, and outlined his plan.

"Now that's settled, get out of here." Stanley moved over to the door and opened it. "Let me know when the Indian is here."

The two men scurried into the dark alley, like the vermin they were.

Stanley sat behind his desk and savored the moment. Soon he'd have everything he wanted—power, wealth, and a wife whose family name would get him into Boston's upper society. As memories of being thrown out of her kitchen slipped into his thoughts, he pulled out a cigar and lit it. Sarah could have partnered with him, and they could have built an empire to rival Elijah Hollingsworth's, but she refused. Now she would pay for that rejection. She would learn the cost of crossing Stanley Snodgrass. And if she didn't like the price, that would be too bad. Just as long as he got her name on a marriage license and her fortune under his control.

CHAPTER TWENTY-FIVE

Sarah couldn't take her eyes off the white curtains that billowed in the early morning breeze, like clouds on a spring day. That was how her heart felt—floating, light, and free. Hatred, which had burdened her for so long, had fled. Now love filled her, love for God and Thorn.

She loved Thornton MacPherson. At last, she had found a man she could trust. Somehow, she'd help him find a way to solve whatever it was that kept him from her, and she'd trust God to help him accept the fact she couldn't give him a son. Love casts out fear. She'd trust.

God was good. With arms wrapped around her middle, she danced around the carpet that covered the wooden floors, humming one of the songs her mother used to sing.

At last, winded from all her flitting about, she pounced on the bed. Never, never, never would she have thought that this would happen. Sarah Rose Hollingsworth Greer MacPherson loved...no! The past was the past. Today starts her new life. The old has passed away, the new begins. *Rose Macpherson loves Thornton MacPherson. Rose and Thorn. Miss Rose loves Mr. Thorn.*

She giggled, then stopped. When was the last time she actually giggled? She waved her hand. That didn't matter. It was in the past, too. Another giggle burst out of her. She couldn't wait until Thorn got home. She wanted to make the marriage real. Thorn and Rose, a true husband and wife.

She flung herself back on the bed. Warmth rushed through her as the feel of Thorn's lips on hers filled her thoughts, the look in his eyes the other night, the touch of his fingers on her neck. They'd make their marriage into the beautiful thing it should be.

She rested her hand on the small table beside the bed as she sat up. Her fingers brushed the Bible Helen had loaned her. She picked it up and crushed it to her chest. Dropping to her knees beside the bed, she bowed her head.

For several long moments, she knelt there on the floor as memories of the past flowed around her. The joyful look on her parents' faces when they held each other under the apple tree in the twilight. The tender glances they exchanged. The little winks they gave each other when they thought no one else was watching them, even though Mama told her it wasn't polite for a woman to wink.

Raising her head and with eyes closed, she came before God. "Dear Father, please bless our marriage. Help me to be a good wife to him, a loving and true wife. Help him to understand my fears. But more than that, dear God, help me to understand him, to truly accept him with love and faithfulness. I ask this prayer in Jesus' name. Amen."

She started to stand, but dropped back down and grabbed the Bible even closer. "And Father, please help me to forgive Grandfather and Albert." She paused for a moment, then continued. "And Stanley, too. Help me to look forward and not backward. Please God, help me continue to fill my heart with Your love and forgiveness, and not let back in the anger and hatred that has controlled me for so long. This too I ask in Jesus' name. Amen."

Sarah smiled as Emma's babbling floated in the air. "Commitment made. Now to live it out."

She set the Bible on the table and hurried to check on her daughter.

"Good morning, Emma. How is Momma's girl doing today?" She tickled her daughter under to her chin.

"Momma, Momma!"

"That's right, Emma sweetie, and Daddy should be home today."

"Dada, dada, dada."

Sarah's laughter caused Emma to laugh. She picked up her daughter and swung around, which caused them both to laugh even more.

"All right, sweetie, let's get you cleaned up and ready for the day. We have lots to do before your daddy gets home." Sarah changed Emma's clothes.

Before they went downstairs, Sarah remembered her locket. She had worn it the day before, and Emma had pulled on the chain and broken it. Maybe the jeweler could fix it. She took it from the top of the dresser and slipped it into her pocket, then headed to the kitchen with Emma in her arms.

By the time breakfast was over, Judith and Sally arrived. With Sally taking care of Emma, Sarah and the Nelson children crowded into the buggy while Dougal rode alongside.

Sarah and Linda left the children at the home of a widow who had agreed to teach the children and continued to the bakery. They walked in the back in time to spy the newlyweds pull apart, giggling. Sarah shook her head. Well, wasn't this what she wanted for her brother—happiness, love, and a good life?

Once most of the customers left in the early afternoon, Helen picked up her shopping basket, gave Drew a peck on the cheek, and turned to Sarah. "I think I need a few things from the mercantile. Would you like to come with me?"

Sarah didn't need a second invitation, although she caught the lopsided grin Drew gave them.

She grabbed her reticule and motioned to Dougal, who sat at a table watching everything going on. He stood and followed them out, but stayed a few feet behind while they walked to the mercantile.

Helen was glowing. Sarah wondered if she would look like that after she and Thorn made their marriage real.

A little while later, they stepped out of the mercantile. Sarah looked for Dougal, but he wasn't in sight.

Joy oozed out on the breeze while the stink Sarah hated surrounded her. Stanley slipped in between them and grabbed Helen's arm. He shifted his hand. Sarah looked down.

He pushed a gun against Helen's side. "Let's step around the corner, ladies."

Sarah bit back a scream as Helen's eyes grew huge in her pale face.

In the narrow space between the buildings, Sarah almost stumbled when she saw Petey Waller kick Dougal, bloody and groaning, as he lay on the ground. Another man leaned over Dougal and stuck a piece of paper in the pocket of his shirt.

"Now, MacPherson'll know where to come looking for you." Stanley grinned as he glanced at Sarah. "Too bad he won't make it there."

Stanley's sister, Cynthia, pranced up on her horse. The young woman smirked. "You probably thought you'd never see me again."

She pulled a blanket from the bundle in her arms.

Emma blinked three or four times in the bright sunshine, then cried out when she spotted her mother.

Sarah gasped at the sight of her daughter. She moved toward Emma.

"If you take another step, Cynthia will ride out of here, and you'll never see the child again." Stanley nodded when Sarah stopped.

Suddenly she realized these people had been in her house. Sarah looked at Stanley. "Judith? Kerr? Sally?"

Stanley nodded toward the corner, where two men dragged Kerr from behind the horses. They dumped him beside Dougal.

Stanley snickered. "You are too trusting. Judith has been in my employ from the time she started working for you. As far as that cowboy, two or three men can easily overpower one, as you just witnessed. The other girl—we just left at your house."

He tightened his hold on Helen. "Now before you get any idea and your dear sister-in-law gets hurt, take that gun from your bag and put it on the ground."

Sarah tightened her fingers on the ties of her reticule as she looked at Cynthia.

Stanley chuckled. "It was so good of you to tell my sister about your little toy. Too bad you discovered who she was before you could have shared more of your secrets with her."

Very slowly, Sarah opened her bag and wrapped her hand around the gun, her finger on the trigger.

The click of Stanley cocking his pistol sounded in the alley.

Sarah slipped her finger from the trigger and did what she was told.

Stanley nodded to the men. "Let's get out of here."

A man stepped over and took hold of Helen's arm. Her face grew even paler than before, making the scar on her cheek stand out. Her lips trembled. "Jim?"

He touched Helen's scar which ran from temple to chin. "Didn't mean to hurt you, but you shouldn't have fought me." He set her on a horse, then tied her hands to the saddle horn. "Ready, boss."

Stanley led Sarah to another horse. "Here, let me help you up."

A shudder ran through Sarah at the thought of Stanley wrapping his hands around her waist, but then she looked at Emma in Cynthia's arms. She'd do whatever it took to protect her daughter.

She allowed Stanley, whom she had asked God to help her forgive just that morning, to assist her onto the horse.

A few minutes later, Sarah rode out of town with her baby, her brother's wife, and the outlaws who were stealing her dreams.

※

Thorn, not Mac.

Mac was a freighter who hunted a man from mining camp to mining camp. Mac had turned away from God in anger. Mac had left the family he loved on a quest that was now finished.

He was Thorn MacPherson. He rolled his shoulders, liking the feel of the skin he lived in, much like a butterfly breaking out of its cocoon and stretching its wings, ready to live a new life. He chuckled at the comparison. It sounded like something his sister, Gavenia, would have said.

After taking care of his wagon and team, Thorn climbed the steps to the back porch of the house in Central City. Rose's house, for now. Once he convinced her he loved her, and hopefully won her love in return, he would take her and Emma back to the ranch to live with the rest of his family.

He stepped inside and listened. Nothing was on the stove. No sounds. No voices. Strange. Judith wasn't in the kitchen or anywhere else downstairs.

Uneasiness filled him as he checked the parlor, then upstairs. The feeling grew stronger as he went to the nursery. The rocking chair was overturned. Emma's crib was empty.

His heart pounded as he searched for any clues to what had happened.

Something thudded in the small room off the nursery. He shoved the door open. The sound grew louder.

He raced to the large wardrobe and jerked open the door.

Sally lay in the bottom, bound and gagged.

With his knife, he cut the ropes around her wrists. "What happened? Where's Emma? Who did this?"

Once Sally's hands were freed, she pulled the cloth from her mouth while Thorn severed the ropes binding her legs. She rubbed her hand over her lips. "A man pointed a gun at me while Miss Snodgrass tied me up. Then…then they took Emma and left." She grabbed Thorn's arm. "Did they hurt Judith? She never came up here."

Black thoughts filled Thorn's head as he remembered how secretive Judith had been as he was recovering from his beating, the way she had snuck out the back and given a note to the hotel owner's boy. Now the house had been attacked and Judith couldn't be found, and there wasn't any sign of a scuffle downstairs. With the Snodgrass girl involved, was Judith in the pay of Stanley? Had she let the men steal Emma?

His heart squeezed so tightly he couldn't breathe. He shot down the stairs. He had to find Sarah and rescue Emma. He had to find his family.

He rushed to the barn, saddled his horse, and raced away. Outside the bakery, he leaped off his horse and slapped the reins over the hitching post.

With a big grin, Drew stepped out. "Good to see you back." He glanced sideways for a moment. "Did you see Helen and Sarah? They went to the mercantile a while ago."

Thorn gripped his brother-in-law's arm. "We have to find them. My cousins have disappeared, and Snodgrass kidnapped Emma."

Drew's face lost its color. "No!"

A rider barreled down the dusty street. "Fire! There's a fire at the other end of town. It's starting to spread."

The people on the street yelled as they ran to where the smoke was rising.

Drew yanked the bakery door open. "Linda, stay in here. I've got to find Helen and Sarah."

Something caught in Thorn's gut. Something didn't feel right. He headed for the mercantile, while Drew raced to catch up with him.

Before they arrived, his friend, Adam Lone Eagle, stepped out of the narrow alley between the mercantile and the next building. A deep frown marked his face. "Thorn, come."

Thorn didn't have to ask what Adam was worried about. Halfway down the alley, his cousins lay in the dirt. Dougal had blood smeared across his face. His lip was bleeding. His arms were wrapped around his middle. When Thorn knelt beside him, Dougal opened his swollen eyelids.

"Snodgrass…got…your Rose…Helen…"

Dougal's eyelids fluttered and closed.

For just a moment, Thorn watched to make sure Dougal's chest continued to rise and fall. Next, he moved over to Kerr. Someone had tied him up. He had a knot on the back of his head.

"Kerr was at the house." Drew's face paled. "With Emma."

"Judith's gone. They tied up Sally." Thorn pounded his fist against his leg. He thought he'd provided enough protection for his family, but he was wrong. Rose, Helen, and Emma would not pay the price for that failure. He'd get Snodgrass and that cur would never hurt his family again.

The store owner joined beside them. "Adam told me what happened. I sent my oldest boy to get the doc. We'll take care of these men. Go get the men who did this."

"Thanks." Thorn started to turn away when the store owner called him back.

"There's something stuck in the man's shirt." The man held out a piece of paper.

Thorn bit hard on his lip. He had just come to peace with the last note that had been left for him. He unfolded the paper. *I've got them. Bring Drew. Go to the bend between old McGruder's cabin and Jacobson's mining site. You'll be met and brought to me. Bring five thousand dollars.*

That location was a pretty broad area to the east, with several places for ambushes between there and Central City.

Thorn looked at Drew and Adam. "They're baiting a trap, and with that fire, we're on our own." He ripped his hat off and rammed his fingers through his hair, then shoved the hat back on his head. "I'm going after the cur that has them."

Adam nodded. "I'm with you."

"Good. I'll need a tracker and another gun." Thorn turned to Drew.

"Of course." Drew nodded. "Let me tell Linda and the others, then gather what supplies we need."

"I'll get the horses." Adam headed for the livery.

"I'll get some guns and ammunition." Thorn started for the mercantile. "Meet back here in fifteen minutes."

In less than twelve, they headed out of town.

After they'd traveled several miles on the road to Denver, they veered onto an overgrown path. Adam dismounted. Drew started to get down, too.

"Stay on your horse. Let Adam read the signs. He's the best tracker in these parts. He'll find their trail." Thorn stayed mounted, but never took his eyes off Adam.

After a few minutes, Adam turned. "Looks to be seven riders. Three of the horses are carrying light. Must be the women."

Thorn nodded. "So it looks like we have four men to deal with."

Adam led the way. Way too soon the sun dipped behind the mountains.

The farther they went, the drier Thorn's throat got, the tighter his hands gripped his reins. With the darkness, they wouldn't be able to follow the trail. Even Adam wasn't that good. Keeping his eyes on the trail, Thorn prayed. *God, please help us. Protect Sarah and Emma and Helen. If we can't get to them tonight, please stand their guard.*

They kept on for a while longer until Adam called a halt. "We'll stop here, rest the horses. If there's going to be an ambush tonight, this'll probably be where they do it."

Drew started to object, but Thorn shook his head. "They're gonna be coming for us. Let's fight it on our terms."

The men unsaddled the horses and gave them some feed. Drew brought out the sack Linda had filled at the bakery. He pulled out sandwiches, then something bulky in a towel. He unwrapped it.

Even in the dimness, Thorn could see Adam's grinning white teeth.

"You two can have the sandwiches. Just let me have that pie." Adam pulled a large knife from the sheath at his side and cut a large chunk out of it. "Your wife make this?"

"Yeah." Drew stared at the pie.

"Good thing you married her first, or I would've." Adam chuckled, then took another bite. "When we get her back to Central City, I'll expect another one of these."

"When we get Helen back, you can have a dozen."

"I'll hold you to that."

Thorn wasn't sure he was going to be able to swallow a bite.. He couldn't lose Rose now. Or Emma. Both of them were so deep in his heart, he wasn't sure he could survive the loss.

Adam stood and gathered wood. "We need to make a fire."

"Won't we make a good target for Snodgrass and his men around the fire?" Drew shoved the remains of their meal back into the sack.

"Yep, if we're around the fire." Adam dumped his armload of sticks. "Me, I plan to be far enough back, I'll be able to shoot any varmint that gets too close."

By the time the full moon lightened the darkness, the men had bedrolls spread out and stuffed with dry brush around the raging campfire.

Darkness shrouded the abandoned barn. Highlighted in the tiny shafts of moonlight slipping between the rotting wall boards, dust motes danced in the dusty air, teasing Sarah with their freedom. Helen, with Emma by her side, slept on a ratty blanket nearby.

Sarah glanced around the barn for what felt like the thousandth time. Had Thorn returned to Central City? Did he know they were kidnapped? Was he coming for them? What about Dougal and Kerr? Were they all right?

She swallowed back hot tears and dropped her head into her hands. *Oh, God, please take care of Thorn and Drew, Dougal and Kerr. Protect them and guide them to us. Please, God.*

As the minutes passed, Sarah stared through the dimness and tried to figure out a way of escape. If only they could push out the rotten boards and escape through the back. Sarah jiggled the hand shackles Stanley had clamped on her wrist. He had attached a chain to them, then wrapped and locked the chain to a post that held up the barn roof. He had done the same thing to Helen. Oh, poor Helen. Sarah's heart ached for her sister-in-law and her brother. Their family was being torn apart.

Sarah had tried a couple times to loosen the pole. But every time she did, dirt and parts of the roof fell down on them. What was the good of getting the chains off the pole if the roof collapsed and trapped them? What would happen to Emma? What if Helen were hurt? That couldn't happen. Drew deserved his future with Helen. And no matter what, she would see that they got it.

Voices filtered in from outside the barn. Sarah strained to hear but couldn't make out what the men were saying. Then, the voices stopped, replaced by the sound of a horse's hooves pounding, coming nearer.

Grasping her chain so it wouldn't rattle, Sarah stepped over the litter-filled barn floor and leaned against the wall. In the faint light from the outlaws' campfire, she saw four men standing. The men kept their voices low, then two of them mounted their horses. As they left, Stanley said something to Waller about somebody being dead before sunrise.

All at once, the muscles in her legs gave out. She dropped to the ground and bowed her head. *Oh, God, help us. Please save us. You are our only hope. Please wrap your arms of protection around us. Please protect Thorn and Drew.*

She rubbed the fingers of her right hand over her left, which had once been wonderfully bare, but now was surrounded by the ring of the man she loved. She closed her eyes. Maybe with morning, salvation would come.

CHAPTER TWENTY-SIX

An owl hooted. Thorn rested under a pile of brush with his rifle by his side. If anyone snuck up on him, they would stumble over him before they saw him, even with the light of the full moon. Drew hunkered down a ways to Thorn's right under another pile of brush. Adam, with his quiet, sure-footed tread, weaved his way around the camp.

Thorn's leg threatened to cramp from staying in the same position for so long as minutes dragged into hours. He wished he had Tair by his side, then swallowed the chuckle that threatened to burst out at the memories of Tair rolling around with that fluffball of a dog Rose kept. When they were all out at the ranch, he would have to keep a special eye on the little fella so a coyote didn't get him.

Thoughts of Rose on his ranch filled a vast empty spot in his heart, one that had been black for so long. He had to rescue her. He couldn't lose another wife. He had loved Lizzie as they'd grown up together. Their families had always known they would marry. It had been a good life filled with the hard work of farming, then ranching, and the birth of three daughters. They had their bumps along the way, but the clan had always been there to cushion the problems and keep everything on an even keel.

Lizzie's murder had changed all that. Just as he couldn't share his fears that he'd caused her death, his family hadn't been able to comfort him in his pain. But maybe that was a part of God's plan for him. Maybe God had allowed him to understand such a depth of pain so he could be what Rose needed. Maybe—

A breath of air brushed against his ear. Adam crouched down beside him. "Sighted two men about a hundred feet up the trail. They're coming in slow with rifles ready. Already told Drew. Gonna circle back and get behind them."

Thorn nodded. Adam disappeared into the night without a rustle of leaves or the snap of a twig.

Sure enough, a few minutes later, two shadows crept into the camp. Silently, one threw his knife into the nearest bedroll, then aimed his rifle and shot into a second one. The other shadow shot into the one nearest Thorn's hiding place. Petey Waller's voice cackled. "You stupid bumpkins! You got what you deserved, didn't you? Now I'll get what I deserve."

Thorn stood, revealing his hiding place. "That's for sure."

Waller took a step backward when Drew stood. An evil grin crossed Waller's face while he pointed his pistol at Rose's brother. "At least, Snodgrass'll get part of what he paid for."

Thorn raised his rifle. Two guns exploded. Drew cried out and grabbed his arm. Waller fell to the ground, blood coming from his chest.

Drew cried out and grabbed his arm.

The second man pulled another knife from his belt and aimed it at Thorn.

Before Thorn got him in his sights, the man fell forward, facedown into the dirt. A knife stuck out of his back, right where his heart no longer pumped.

Adam walked into the circle of light thrown by the campfire, pulled the knife from the man, and nudged him with his foot. "Three Crows." He pointed over to the other man on the ground. "Know that man?"

Thorn nodded. "Petey Waller. Rose's adopted daughter's uncle."

Drew gripped his arm as blood ran down his sleeve.

Thorn moved over to check out Drew's wound.

Squatting, Adam wiped his knife on the dead man's clothes, then slipped it back into its sheath. "Odds're better in our favor now."

Thorn shook his head. "Yeah, but Snodgrass's got nothing to lose. That makes him doubly dangerous."

The early morning's palest light crept silently through the cracks in the barn, but it pulled roaring hunger pangs through Sarah's stomach along with it. Emma was still sleeping or she would be crying for her breakfast. Sarah was thankful for that one small favor, anyway. There was no telling what Stanley would do when irritated with a baby's crying.

Sarah paced the hard-packed dirt floor, sending dust into the air, unable to calm her restlessness. There had to be some way out of this mess.

She looked at the horses. Two were still missing. That meant only Stanley, Cynthia, and Grayson remained.

The barn door creaked. Someone pulled it open just enough to slide through. Lamplight, along with that smell, distinctive and distasteful, entered the barn. How often in the early weeks after she had been brought to her grandfather's house had she smelled that scent in her room, then discovered her things had been rifled through? Or worse, the times she had fought through the barriers of pain after one of her husband's beatings and found herself surrounded by that scent while Stanley's voice mingled with the doctor's.

Stanley's aftershave performed a function he was ignorant of. It gave her time to prepare for battle. She threw back her slumped shoulders and straightened her spine. She would not cower. Not ever again.

"Aren't you tired of this game yet? You know you'll lose." Sarah crossed her arms in front of her and kept from tapping her foot. Let him see her anger. How dare he hold her here like some animal waiting for slaughter?

Stanley dropped a bag at her feet, then saddled three of the horses. His eyes narrowed when he turned to her. "You had better watch your mouth. I sent Waller and Three Crows back to ambush Drew and MacPherson. Your brother and husband are dead by now. That makes you a widow, but not for long."

Sarah couldn't keep the gasp from slipping out. No, it couldn't be true. She'd known Stanley long enough to not trust anything he said. And right now, all she had was his blustering words.

His thin lips shifted into a leering grin. "But you needn't worry. I'll protect you."

Sarah swatted the air, as if batting away a tiresome gnat. "Protection from you would be like a rattlesnake wrapped around my neck waiting to strike."

Stanley's jaws tightened. He raised his hand as if to strike her.

Rage flowed through her veins—rage against the hopelessness she had endured in the past, rage at the injustice that this man was trying to force on her, rage at what Grandfather had done to her and the ways this man had helped. "Do you really think I am afraid of a slap across my face?"

She laughed and even to her own ears, it wasn't a pretty sound. "I've endured much worse than that."

She dug her nails into the palms of her balled-up hands. She had to keep some control. If she didn't, she would tear out the man's eyes.

Stanley dropped his hand, but his lips kept their hard straight line. "And you'll *endure* more. You're in my control, and all that money you've got will be mine."

He grabbed the reins of the saddled horses and led them out of the barn.

A cold chill rolled through Sarah's body as she remembered Stanley's words about Thorn and Drew. She ran her hands up and down her arms. They couldn't be dead. She had to keep fighting until they came.

Helen and Emma woke. Sarah changed Emma's diaper, then snuggled her daughter against her chest. The weight of the little body strengthened Sarah's determination. Somehow she would figure out how to get out of this situation.

Helen opened the bag Stanley left and pulled out some bread and a jar of water. She tore off a piece and handed it to Sarah. Emma grabbed a bite and shoved it into her mouth.

Sarah kissed the top of her daughter's head, then closed her eyes. *Dear God, help us, please. I know that Helen and I can't get out of this without you. You are our hope and our rock.*

Angry shouts filled the air outside, and she tightened her hold on Emma. The voices grew closer. Someone jerked open the sagging barn door.

Stanley strode in, then called over his shoulder, "You can leave if you want, but you're leaving with nothing."

Jim Grayson, carrying a rifle, followed him in.

Stanley stalked across the barn, wrenched Emma from her arms, and shoved Sarah to the ground.

Helen screamed and rushed forward. Stanley swung around and hit her with enough force to sling her backward. She hit her head on the post she was tied to, then crumpled to the ground.

Grayson stared at Helen, then raised his rifle to his shoulder. "You shouldn't have done that. Now you'll lose your woman."

Stanley drew his pistol and fired at Grayson before the man could pull the trigger.

Sarah screamed. A red stain spread across Grayson's chest.

"Shut up and hold up your hands." Stanley kept a tight grip on Emma while he used a key to open the handcuffs around Sarah's wrist. The chain and cuff fell to the ground with a clanking sound. "Get out of the barn and get on that horse."

Fear for Helen and Emma battled with anger at the man before her. Sarah started for Helen, praying her sister-in-law was all right. "I'm not going anywhere with you."

"Fine. Cyn can take care of the kid." Stanley moved toward the barn door.

Sarah froze. She turned slowly.

Cynthia stood at the door, holding the reins of her horse. A smirk spread across her face. "Oh, I'm going to love having a baby. All the fun of motherhood, without ruining my figure."

Panic replaced anger. Sarah felt the blood drain from her head. "No! You can't take Emma."

Stanley shrugged. "Then do as I say."

Sarah didn't have a choice. While she mounted her horse, Stanley fashioned a sling around his neck and shoulder, then slipped Emma into it.

"We got to get out of here." Stanley held the reins in his fists.

Sarah looked back at the barn. *God, please be with Helen. Help her. Send someone to care for her.* With a last backward look at her dearest friend and sister-in-law, Sarah followed Stanley.

Cynthia sat on her horse beside her brother. She held out her arms. "Let me carry Emma. We get along so well."

"No. I need the brat to control her." Stanley glanced over at Sarah. "You are going to do just what you're told, aren't you?" He pinched Emma and laughed when the little girl cried out.

Sarah mumbled something. She wasn't even sure what she said, but it seemed to satisfy Stanley.

"Good. Just so you know, my little sister has a gun in her bag. In case you get any ideas of trying to escape when I'm not looking. Now let's get to Denver." He laughed as he snapped the reins and kicked the horse with his heels.

Sarah swallowed the bile that rose in her throat and nudged her horse. She had to stay with him until she could get Emma away from the monster and his sister.

Thorn wiped the sweat off his face with the sleeve of his shirt. It wasn't that the early morning was hot. It was what they might find in the dilapidated barn that put the fear into him. Adam had tracked Three Crows and Waller here. The smell of a recent campfire filled the air with old smoke, but it was the open barn door that worried him. That and the other smell, the faint smell of something dead.

Like the night before, he and Drew hid at the edge of the open area around the barn while Adam snuck closer to have a look. Adam stepped in his sure-footed way until he slid along the side of the barn. In a blink of an eye, he slipped inside.

"Thorn! Drew!" Adam's voice boomed out of the barn. "Get in here quick."

Thorn almost ran into Drew as they raced inside. Adam knelt beside Helen, crumpled on the hard ground. He touched the back of her head. His fingers came away smeared red.

Drew dropped down beside her, took her hand and squeezed it. "Helen, can you hear me? Helen, wake up."

Her eyelids fluttered for a moment, then stilled.

"Helen, come on, darling. Wake up."

Thorn nudged the body of the dead man.

Adam came up beside him. "Know him?"

"Jim Grayson. He put that scar on Helen's face."
Thorn searched the rest of the barn, looking for signs of
Sarah and Emma. He found a soiled diaper on a ratty
quilt. No signs of struggle. No other blood. No other
bodies.

His temper flared when he spied Helen tethered to the
post and saw the other set of shackles in the dirt. He
closed his eyes and sucked in a deep breath while he
imagined Rose chained to the post and held captive. He
opened his eyes to dispel the vision.

Adam moved out of the barn.

"Thorn, Helen's coming around." Drew wrapped his
arm around his wife's shoulders and helped her sit.

She moaned, then cried out in pain and grabbed her
head.

Drew struggled with his wounded arm but pulled her
to his chest. "Take it easy. Just rest a bit."

Adam returned with a canteen and uncapped it. He
handed it to Drew, who raised it to Helen's lips.

She took a sip, then pushed the canteen away. A
trickle of water ran down her chin.

"Help…Sarah…Emma…" Her eyes closed, and she
passed out again.

"I have to stay with Helen." Drew glanced at Thorn,
then Adam. "Go, get Sarah and Emma. If Stanley's got
them, they'll never be safe."

Thorn gripped Drew's shoulder and nodded.

Adam pulled a pouch from his belt and handed it to
Drew. "Make her some tea with the herbs. Use the salve
on the back of her head and wrap the bandages around.
She will sleep."

Without another word they left the barn, mounted their
horses, and took out after Rose, Emma, and their
kidnappers.

Thorn let the tracker take the lead, but he kept a
watchful eye along the trail. And he did one more thing.

God in Heaven. Please protect Sarah and Emma. Let us find them safe and bring them home. Please, dear God.

For an hour, Sarah bounced along the rough, overgrown path. She peeked at Stanley several times to keep an eye on Emma, who had cried and screamed nearly the whole hour. After the third time she shifted to get a peek and almost caused her horse to stumble, Stanley ordered her to keep her eyes on the trail, or neither she nor the baby would get anything to eat. For Emma's sake, she had to obey. Poor Emma had finally cried herself into an exhausted sleep.

Finally, the trail merged with the mail stage route that went to Denver. Sarah thanked God when they left the brush and thorny plants that had grabbed at her legs and torn the tender skin on her calves.

She'd been surprised that Cynthia had not cried out and complained. But the girl rode alongside her brother quiet as a wooden stick.

Suddenly, Stanley cursed and reined in his horse, then dismounted.

Cynthia looked at her brother. "What's the matter?"

"Horse lost its shoe and pulled up lame. We'll have to stop and get another mount. There's a family of homesteaders up the road a bit." He narrowed his eyes and stared up at Sarah. "Get down here and walk with me."

"Well, don't expect me to walk." Cynthia stayed mounted.

Stanley shook his head. "Little sister, I don't expect anything from you."

The girl frowned, then kicked her horse in the sides and left them in a cloud of dust. She stopped several yards up the trail and looked over her shoulder. "All right, Stanley. Let's get moving. I want to get to Denver and have a hot bath."

Sarah struggled to keep up with Stanley while she tried to think of a way of escape, but all she could think about was Emma, and how hot and hungry the baby had to be.

"Well, now that we have a few minutes to talk, would you like to know your future?" Stanley glanced at her as if savoring his victory like a cat playing with its captured mouse.

Sarah didn't answer, instead keeping her head raised and her eyes straight ahead. No way would she give him the satisfaction of bowing before him. She'd had enough of that with Grandfather and Alfred.

Stanley chuckled. "Ah, it does my heart good to see that feistiness in you. It will make it all the more interesting and rewarding as I bend you to my will." He chuckled again when she ignored him. "First, we will marry."

That stopped Sarah in the middle of the road. "Don't be foolish. You know that I'm already married. You have no proof of anything different."

Stanley removed his hat and wiped his forehead with his handkerchief. A smirk settled on his face. "You, my lady, are a widow for the second time, and, as such, are eligible for marriage. Take my word for it. The judge will." He placed his hat back on his head and walked while he whistled a lively tune.

The huge gripping hand that had been her companion for so long wrapped its fingers around her insides and squeezed. She hurried to catch up with Stanley. "What judge?"

"The one who has a death certificate all ready to be signed. All he's waiting on is my signature as witness to the death of Thornton MacPherson." The last word came out with such disgust. "By the way, the only thing saving you right now is the fact that you never let that creature into your bed."

Sarah stopped and tried to catch her breath. "How—why—I love my husband. Why would you even think that…that we…we didn't share the same room?"

"It's so much fun to shock you." He flicked her chin with his index finger. "Judith reported to me everything that happened in your household. Amazing what a good maid sees. How else do you think Cynthia knew to take this brat?"

He chuckled again. "But the idea of setting the fire to draw the town's attention away from any kidnapping was Cynthia's idea. As a matter of fact, she started the fire. Marvelous sister I have, don't you agree?" When Sarah made a choking sound, Stanley went on. "Oh, but you must, since she will be your sister-in-law. Just think how close the two of you would already have been, if you hadn't barred her from your house."

Sarah clenched her fists by her side. Betrayed. Oh, she knew she couldn't trust Cynthia too far, but apparently the girl hadn't deserved any trust at all. She was just as evil as her brother. But Judith, that was a true betrayal. The woman had worked in her house, cooked their food, watched over Emma. What else had she done to betray the trust she'd been given?

Stanley strolled on, seemingly content that his plan was working out so well. "Once the judge marries us and you have signed over all your affairs and accounts to me, we shall start to work on creating a son for me, maybe three or four sons. It all depends on how agreeable you are. Or how much you want to keep your daughter safe."

He licked his lips as he looked her up and down.

She crossed her arms and tried not to be sick.

"The one thing your grandfather had right was the need to leave a dynasty behind. He failed, but rest assured, I won't. My son, bearing the name of Elijah Hollingsworth Snodgrass, will be welcomed into any mansion in Boston." He chuckled. "And just think of all the fun we will have conceiving that son."

Sarah shuddered at the thought of what it would take to give Stanley that dynasty, but then she couldn't help but laugh. "You know as well as I do that there'll never be a son. You were there when the doctor told Alfred that I couldn't have any more children."

"Oh, my dear wife-to-be, I hadn't realized you heard that. It was my plan to protect you. Even back then, I was looking after you."

"What do you mean?"

"Simple. I told the doctor to inform Alfred that he had done too much damage to you. If he wanted to have another son to hold over his wayward one, he would need to leave you alone for at least a year. See how I protected you?"

Bile moved up her throat like a volcano ready to erupt. Because of Stanley's trick, she had been saved from Alfred, but Emma's poor mother had taken the brunt of Alfred's abuse. Now Alfred was dead, as well as Emma's mother and grandmother.

Sarah spread her fingers over her middle. She couldn't face such cruelty again. *God, help me. You are all I have. Please show me the way out of this. Please.*

CHAPTER TWENTY-SEVEN

Sarah bit her lip to keep from crying out. Her shoes had not been designed for walking. The rough road added to the discomfort. She knew she had at least one blister on the back of her heel, and the bottom of both feet felt bruised.

Cynthia still rode her horse a little ways ahead of them, although the horse was slowing down a bit. Stanley called out and motioned for his sister to take the turnoff.

She trotted back. "Isn't the stage station just ahead? Why can't we stop there and rest for a little while, maybe take the stage to Denver?"

"Stop your whining." Stanley glared at his sister. "The stage won't be there for hours. By that time, I plan to be in Denver and married. You can rest after that."

Cynthia pouted but followed his instructions.

With a quick look at the direction Cynthia went, a rocky mound caught Sarah's eye. Behind it stood two trees that had grown entangled and now grew tall and straight together. She bit her lips to keep a cry of joy from escaping. She knew where she was. Melody's place must be the one he was talking about. Just as fast as the thrill of joy raced through her, the gnarled hand of fear reached out and shoved it out of the way. After what he did to Helen and Grayson in the barn, how would Stanley deal with Melody's family?

Questions and fears and memories twisted together while the seconds ticked by. Were Thorn and Drew all right? Had Emma's uncle shot them? Or had God let them live? She could feel her heart pounding at the thought of losing either of the men she loved most in the world. She struggled to swallow. Surely, God wouldn't...He couldn't...

Sarah shoved those doubts away. She would trust God to work out everything. With each clip-clop of the horse's hooves on the dirt road, a plan formed in her mind. Like an angel holding back Abraham's hand and the ram in the bushes, was God working out His plan for her?

She had to believe that Thorn was alive and searching for her. She needed to leave a clue to where she was. Her grandmother's necklace—would he remember it? She prayed he would.

Stanley jerked on his limping horse's reins. Sarah slipped the locket with its broken chain out of her pocket. When the horse balked at turning off the smoother mail route and distracted Stanley, she flicked the necklace onto a bush beside the road. It caught on the branches and hung like an ornament on a Christmas tree.

They were close to the farmhouse when another thought popped into Sarah's mind. "Stanley, if a woman comes out, let me talk to her. I don't want anyone hurt."

He stared at her for a moment or two, then nodded. "Good idea. Nice to know you're with me."

When they neared the house, Melody stepped outside, raising a rifle over her flat middle. Her oldest son stood by her side. "Who are you, and what do you want?"

Sarah shifted so Melody could see her. *Please, God, don't let her say the wrong thing.*

Melody's eyes widened.

Sarah's stomach fluttered. "Name's Prudence Hill." She nodded to the man in front of her. "This is Stanley and his sister, and in front of him is my baby girl, Emma.

We wondered if you have any horses for sale. Ours went lame, and we need to get to Denver."

Melody gave the slightest nod. "Think we might be able to help you. Son, run out and wait for your pa. Tell him a woman named Prudence Hill and her husband."— She looked at Sarah—"Stanley you said?" She turned back to the boy. "Tell him they want to buy one of his horses."

The boy looked from Sarah to his mother, then took off running down the road. Melody lowered her rifle. "Might as well come in. My man had to deliver a horse to the stage station down the road, but he should be getting back pretty soon. You're welcome to sit a spell and have something to eat and drink. Don't get company out this way much. Sure would like to visit."

"Thank you." Sarah clenched her hands at her side and walked beside the man who held her captive—captive with the love she had for her daughter, and now her friend, even though he didn't know he held that card.

Thorn forced his jaw to relax. If he didn't, his teeth would be ground to nothing by the time they found Rose. But it was so hard following Adam's lead while he tracked the three horses.

Adam halted and dismounted. He walked around in a circle, then came up next to Thorn's horse. "We're in luck. Looks like the big horse has come up lame. A man and woman are walking now."

Thank you, God. Thorn nodded. "They'll be traveling slower until they find another horse or two."

"Probably stop at the stage station." Adam mounted his horse.

"Unless they try a place closer. There's one between here and the stage station."

Adam glanced at Thorn, then the sky. Thick, dark clouds were gathering, and the air picked up, sending dust in all directions. "The Dunn place. Hopefully, the rain holds off so we don't lose the trail."

Thorn's jaw tightened again. Maybe Rose wouldn't mind if he didn't have any jaw teeth left by the time he found her, as long as he got to her. That thought went up as the first drop of rain splashed down on his pants leg.

"Let's check out as much of the trail as we can before the rain washes it away." Adam nudged his horse. Thorn did the same.

A short while later, they stared at the mud-soaked trail where the path to the Dunns' place branched off. All traces of Rose's trail had been washed away by the rain. Pain started in Thorn's chest and spread down to his gut. They were losing valuable time, but they needed to make the right choice. Thorn took a deep breath. *God, please help me to know which way to take.*

Thorn looked down the path that led to the Dunn's place. Something glittering caught his eye. He rode to the bushes and snatched a locket from a broken branch. He turned it over in his gloved hand. It was Rose's, the one she had worn that Sunday when she had gotten so upset at church and he had helped her change clothes. She had left her own trail. He shoved it into his shirt pocket. "They went this way."

The pounding of hooves made him turn around.

Jase Dunn and his oldest boy barreled down the road,

"Sarah's at my place." Jase struggled to get his breath.

Thorn pulled out the locket and held it up. "We know. How do we want to handle this?"

"Seems this Snodgrass wants to buy a horse." Dunn wiped his forehead. "Why don't you two circle around and come in the back side of the barn? I'll just bring him out to see which horse he wants. Toby can go in the house and help his ma with that other woman."

They all agreed and set out for the farm. Thorn had already figured out where to cut off the road in order to get to the barn unseen. Just before the last bend came into view, he signaled Adam to follow him. By the time Dunn and his son entered the house, Thorn and Adam were in the barn.

Holding Emma, who was now full of bread and butter and drifting off to sleep, Sarah kept an eye on Stanley.

Melody sat in her rocking chair with her newborn daughter in her arms. When she had served pie and coffee to the visitors earlier, she had sent her boys out with orders to bring back enough fish for supper.

Stanley seemed to relax a bit once the children left the house with shouts of joy. He'd been quiet for a while, but in the last few minutes he'd started scowling as he fiddled with the cuffs of his shirt. "How much longer do you think it will take for your husband to arrive?"

Shifting her baby to one arm, Melody stood and brought over the coffee pot. She refilled his cup, then did the same for Cynthia's. "Oh, it shouldn't be long now. I know he'll be eager to make a sale. He plans to go to Denver next week and sure could use the extra money."

Stanley rolled his eyes and tapped his fingers on the table.

The door banged open, and Toby burst into the house. "Pa's coming."

Sarah tightened her hold on Emma while Stanley slid his half-drawn pistol back into his coat. *Oh, God, please protect this family. Hold them in your hand. Don't let any of them get hurt because of me.*

A moment later, Jase Dunn entered the house. "Toby, if I've told you once, I've told you a thousand times. Don't burst into the house like that. Your ma don't like it none." He turned to Stanley and smiled, his hand outstretched. "Son tells me you folks want to buy a horse or two. Glad to hear it."

Stanley frowned as he shook the man's hand, then put his own hand behind him and wiped it against his pants.

"That's correct. Your wife's assured me you have some to sell."

Jase waved him to the door. "Well, let's go out to the barn, and I'll show you what I've got. Wish you would've been here yesterday. I could've sold you a couple of those I took to the stage station earlier. Would've had a better selection."

Sarah's heart sped up. With Stanley and Cynthia separated, here was her chance. If they could get control of Cynthia, they could stop Stanley.

"Whatever you have will be fine." Stanley looked over his shoulder at Cynthia. "You've got everything you need?"

Cynthia slipped her hand in her reticule and smiled. "Oh, yes. Everything."

With a nod, Stanley followed Jase outside.

Sarah watched the door close behind Stanley. Glancing around the room, she tried to find something she could use as a weapon if she got the opportunity. Before any ideas had formed, Melody headed for the bedroom.

Cynthia's eyes narrowed. Her hand inched out of her reticule, pulling the gun with it. "Where are you going?"

Melody looked over her shoulder. "Time to put the baby down. Now she's asleep, I can get some work done."

Sarah wanted to call her friend back, fearing that Cynthia might do something foolish and Melody would be hurt.

Cynthia's hand was almost out of the bag when Melody came back into the room. "Prudence, why don't you put your daughter on the bed? She can sleep in there until you're ready to leave, unless her aunt wants to hold her for a while. Don't you just love to look at the sleeping face of a child?"

Sarah glanced over at Cynthia, who frowned and nodded toward the bedroom.

"Oh, good, now I think I'll bake a pie for supper. Which would you and your brother prefer, apple or berry?" She set a bowl of flour on the table, then turned back to the shelves over the wooden counter along the wall.

When Sarah came back to the table, Melody glanced at her, then down to the bowl of flour, then back to Sarah.

With a nod, Sarah stood at the table.

Melody picked up a wooden rolling pin.

"Don't bother making any pies for us. We won't be here that long." Cynthia kept glancing over at the door.

Stanley fingered the pistol in his pocket. He had wasted too much time already, especially since he had no money to pay for a horse. If he had known for sure they could have escaped with the horses before the man returned, Stanley wouldn't have waited. But the chances of meeting the farmer on the road while riding his horses were too great.

As soon as he got the farmer in the barn, he would get rid of him. Then he wouldn't have to worry about being followed.

The man kept jabbering as they walked to the barn. "Yep, I got a couple of horses I think you might like, a bay and a sorrel. Both are well broke."

The door creaked open. Stanley walked into the building and started to pull out his gun. Another few minutes and he would be one step closer to having enough money to get his life back, the life he had grown accustomed to, the life he deserved.

Stanley tightened his fingers around his pistol.

Thorn adjusted his grip on his rifle and watched Snodgrass and Jase walk deeper into the barn.

Snodgrass had his hand resting on the pistol at his side. "Sounds good. Will you take my horse in trade?"

Snodgrass stopped a few paces inside the barn while Jase walked a little bit further.

Jase turned around. Snodgrass gripped his pistol and lifted it from his holster.

"Stop right there, you worthless cur." Thorn stepped into the light from the open barn door.

Snodgrass whipped around and aimed at Thorn.

Sarah's heart pounded as she waited for the best opportunity to attack Cynthia.

Suddenly a shot rang out, maybe two. She grabbed the bowl and threw the flour in Cynthia's face while Melody slammed the rolling pin against Cynthia's arm. A crack, followed by a pain-filled scream, filled the room.

Dropping her reticule on the floor, Cynthia jumped up, still screaming and holding her right arm with her left. Flour fell from her face and hair. "You both are going to die for this! Just wait until Stanley gets back in."

Sarah grabbed the reticule and drew out the pistol. She aimed it at Cynthia.

The door opened. Thorn walked in with a gun in his hand and red streaks across his shirt. "Your brother's not coming in."

Sarah shoved the pistol into Melody's hand and ran to Thorn. She searched for the cause of the blood.

"You killed Stanley!" Cynthia's voice grew louder. "You killed my brother!"

Melody pushed Cynthia down on a chair.

Thorn shook his head. "He's not dead, even though he deserves to be for what he's done." He wrapped his free arm around Sarah's shoulders. "Let's just say he's not going to be walking for a while."

CHAPTER TWENTY-EIGHT

Thorn looked at Adam sitting on an overturned bucket in the barn with a rifle between his knees, but tipped his head toward the man lying on a pile of hay. "How's he doing?"

"Bandaged him up. He'll make it." Adam stood. "With you and Jase here, I think I'll head back to that barn and see if Drew needs me. I can make a travois if his woman can't ride." He mounted his horse. "See you in Central City."

Thorn couldn't help but laugh. Sarah and Emma were safe. They could be a family now. They *would* be a family. He pulled his hat off and ran his hand through his hair. All he had to do now was explain everything to Rose. He should have done that a long time ago.

The next day, Stanley and Cynthia were brought to Central City and then put in separate cells.

Sarah felt peace flow through her as she and Melody stepped out onto the boardwalk in front of the sheriff's office, followed by Thorn and Jase.

Adam Lone Eagle walked up and stopped in front of Sarah. "Drew and his wife are at their place. Doc said they're doing fine." He grinned. "Don't understand the message, but Doc said for you not to go over there before nine tomorrow morning. Not seven. Not eight. Not before nine." He tilted his head and looked at Thorn. "He said for you to make sure she doesn't."

Thorn laughed. "I'm not sure anybody can keep her from doing anything she wants. She's one strong woman."

"I know. Need to find me one like that." Adam waved his hand as he walked off.

Thorn called out for Adam and waited for the man to look over his shoulder. "I know one just like that."

"I do too. That's why I'm staying away from your place for a while. I like to do the hunting." He turned the corner and disappeared.

Sarah caught Thorn's eye. "What was that about?"

Thorn grinned. "My little sister, Gavenia, has had her eye on him since they met."

Ah, so that was who Gavenia was. Sarah thought she might like this sister of Thorn's once she got to know her.

Darkness settled. The lightning bugs floated around. Thorn sat on the porch swing at the back of the house. Sarah was getting everyone settled and had promised to meet him out here.

The meal they had eaten at the hotel restaurant sat heavy in his gut. Not that it wasn't good. Helen's aunt had finally gotten a good cook. No, the problem was how Rose was going to handle the truth about Lizzie and the violence of her death.

He leaned back in the swing and shoved it with the heel of his boot. She had told him she had feelings for him a while back, but she had never said she loved him. Of course, he had never told her he loved her either.

The door opened and Sarah came out. She walked over to the swing, even though it was too dark for her to see him.

He held out his hand and took hold of hers. She slipped onto the seat beside him, and he wrapped his arm around her shoulders. There'd been a time that even that would have made her flinch, but no more.

They rocked for a few minutes. Thorn debated different ways to tell Sarah about his wife and daughters. There was no easy way.

"Rose, I need to tell you about me and my life before I met you."

Sarah squeezed his hand. "All right."

"You know I was married before. I didn't tell you everything." Thorn went on to explain about Lizzie's death, and why he had to find his brother-in-law to find out what had happened. "I was so afraid that I'd done something wrong. I feared I'd do the same with Faith, Grace, and Mercy."

Her shoe stuck to the porch, causing the swing to stop. "Those are your daughters' names—Faith Grace, and Mercy?"

"Yeah. You like them?"

She pushed her foot against the wooden planks and started the swing moving again. "When you came home so badly hurt, you mumbled something about faith, grace, and mercy. I figured you must have believed in God to talk like that. That was when I started thinking about trusting you." She gave his hand another gentle squeeze. "Are you ready to be with your girls?"

"I am." He tried to see her face in the dark.

She laid her head against his shoulder.

"Rose, I'm sorry I didn't trust you enough to tell you all about it. It was just too close, too hurtful."

"I understand."

"My sweet Rose, do you think we can start over?"

Sarah giggled.

Thorn couldn't keep from smiling. That was the prettiest sound he had ever heard. "Ah, darling Rose, I love you."

"Well, Mr. Thorn, Miss Rose loves you right back." She reached up and gave him a quick kiss, then shifted backward. "Start over? You mean we need to get married again?"

Thorn was silent a moment. His heart pounded. She loved him. "Would you like to get married again? We could do it at the ranch. You'll live at the ranch with me and my girls, won't you? My grandda and granny live there along with aunts and uncles and some of the eighty-one."

"I would like nothing better." She tucked her head closer to his chest. "And maybe someday, we'll have a son."

Thorn lowered his head and brushed his lips across his wife's. Soon he had her in his lap and the kisses got better. "Rose, why don't we go upstairs?"

"I put Melody and Jase in your room and the boys in Drew's old room. You'll have to sleep in my room."

"I think that sounds more than fine to me, Mrs. MacPherson." Thorn took her hand, and they went inside together.

EPILOGUE

Sarah kept her arms around Emma while the little girl bounced on her lap. At last, Thorn drove up to the main house of the MacPherson ranch. Would his family like her? Thorn had tried to assure her they would, but she knew almost nothing of their customs and traditions. What kind of mother would she be to his three daughters?

Thorn pulled the reins and set the brake on the freight wagon. No longer filled with supplies for the miners, it was filled with her things, along with their two dogs.

"Don't worry so. They'll love you, just as I do." Thorn clasped her hand while people rushed out of the house, the barn, and the other outbuildings. Letting go of her hand, he jumped down, then reached up for Emma.

"Dada. Dada." Emma laughed when she dropped into his waiting arms.

A small, white-haired woman took Emma while Thorn helped Sarah from the wagon. He wrapped his arm around her. Together they faced the old woman. "Granny, this is my wife, Sarah Rose."

Granny flicked a toil-worn finger over the small clan shield on Emma's dress.

"Is this one a MacPherson?"

Even though Thorn said his family would love her, Sarah clung to her husband. She smiled at the comfort he gave with his arm around her.

Thorn's face lit up. "Aye, that she is. Duncan saw to the recording of her adoption personally."

"Good enough." She stepped back when a man nearly as tall as Thorn stepped up. Well, he would be as tall if he weren't stooped over and leaning on a cane.

"Are ye a MacPherson bride?" The old man eyed her hand where she wore the band Thorn had given her when they married.

Before she could answer, Thorn cleared his throat. "We were married legally in Central City, but we wish to repeat our vows here with the family."

"Good enough." The old man nodded and turned to the people gathering. "Tonight we'll be having a wedding and welcoming the newest MacPherson bride."

With nods and shouts of welcome, the people scattered, leaving a woman and three young girls hopping up and down before Sarah and Thorn.

"Poppa, you're home!"

"Hold me, Poppa."

"Poppa, don't go away again."

He bent down and wrapped all the girls in his arms while the woman stared at Sarah. "This fierce-looking woman is my sister, Gavenia."

Sarah couldn't keep from smiling. "Ah, the one Adam—"

Thorn stood up quickly and wrapped his arm around his sister's shoulder, then gave a small hug. "Gavenia, will you help Rose get settled and prepared for the wedding?"

Thorn's sister eyed them both for a moment. "Do you love each other?"

Thorn and Sarah looked at each other and said, "Aye" at the same time. Sarah giggled. She'd been doing that a lot lately.

"Good enough. Come, sister of mine. Let's get you ready because I know my brother and he can be a most impatient man."

Sarah laughed as she was pulled into the house.

After the family meal that night, an elderly man in full Scottish dress, kilt and all, pulled his bagpipes into his arms and played.

Sarah stood in a bedroom off the main room where everyone was gathered. Gavenia placed a sash of MacPherson plaid over Sarah's left shoulder and across her chest. She grabbed the end of the sash from around Sarah's back and tied them together, so they rested near her left hip.

Sarah pinned her clan shield on her dress between her left shoulder and her heart. Gavenia, as well as all the other women in the room, had the same plaid sash and pin.

Thorn's grandmother hobbled in front of Sarah and unfolded a lace wedding veil. "This was me mother's and her mother's before her. I wore it when I married me husband on a ship to America. All me girls wore it when they married, as well as many of me son's brides. Many of me granddaughters have worn it, as well. I'd be honored if ye wore it."

Sarah couldn't keep a tear from falling. She remembered the story Thorn had told her of how his grandmother left Scotland to follow the man she loved, and how she brought her mother's wedding veil. And now she was being offered the privilege of sharing in the tradition. "I would be honored, as I hope all Thorn's daughters will wear it when they become MacPherson brides."

"Aye, and any of yer sons' wives, too." With tears in her eyes, Granny smiled and set the veil on Sarah's head. "Good enough. Ye'll do."

The bagpiper started a new melody outside the bedroom door. The women hurried out to the great room.

Holding a red rose surrounded by white heather that Granny had prepared for her, Sarah followed the man and his bagpipes through the crowd of people. She could see Thorn standing beside an elderly man holding a book. The bagpiper stepped to the side.

Sarah Rose MacPherson moved to stand beside her husband, ready to start her life as a MacPherson bride.

THE END

OTHER BOOKS

The Scar and The Star
The Hawk and The Eagle

AUTHORS BIO

Mischelle Creager writes inspirational historical romances set in the mid-1800s. She's not sure which she loves more—researching or writing. When she's not doing one of those two things, she can probably be found reading or baking.

She is a wife whose wonderful husband told her, when he retired several years ago, that he wanted to support her in her writing and took over all the household chores, including sweeping, dusting, and laundry. He even cleans up for her after she bakes! Her son and daughter are always available to help with social media questions.

Mischelle loves to share her historical research and has a website, Under the Attic Eaves, filled with tidbits she's found in books written in the 19th Century. She also "reprints" a historical magazine, Worbly's Family Monthly Magazine, filled with items from books and magazines published in the middle of the 1800s. You can visit these two sites at http://undertheatticeaves.com/ and http://worblysmagazine.com/

If you would like to know more about Mischelle and her family, please visit her blog, Families Across the Generations at

http://familiesacrossthegenerations.blogspot.com/

You can contact her at http://mischellecreager.com/